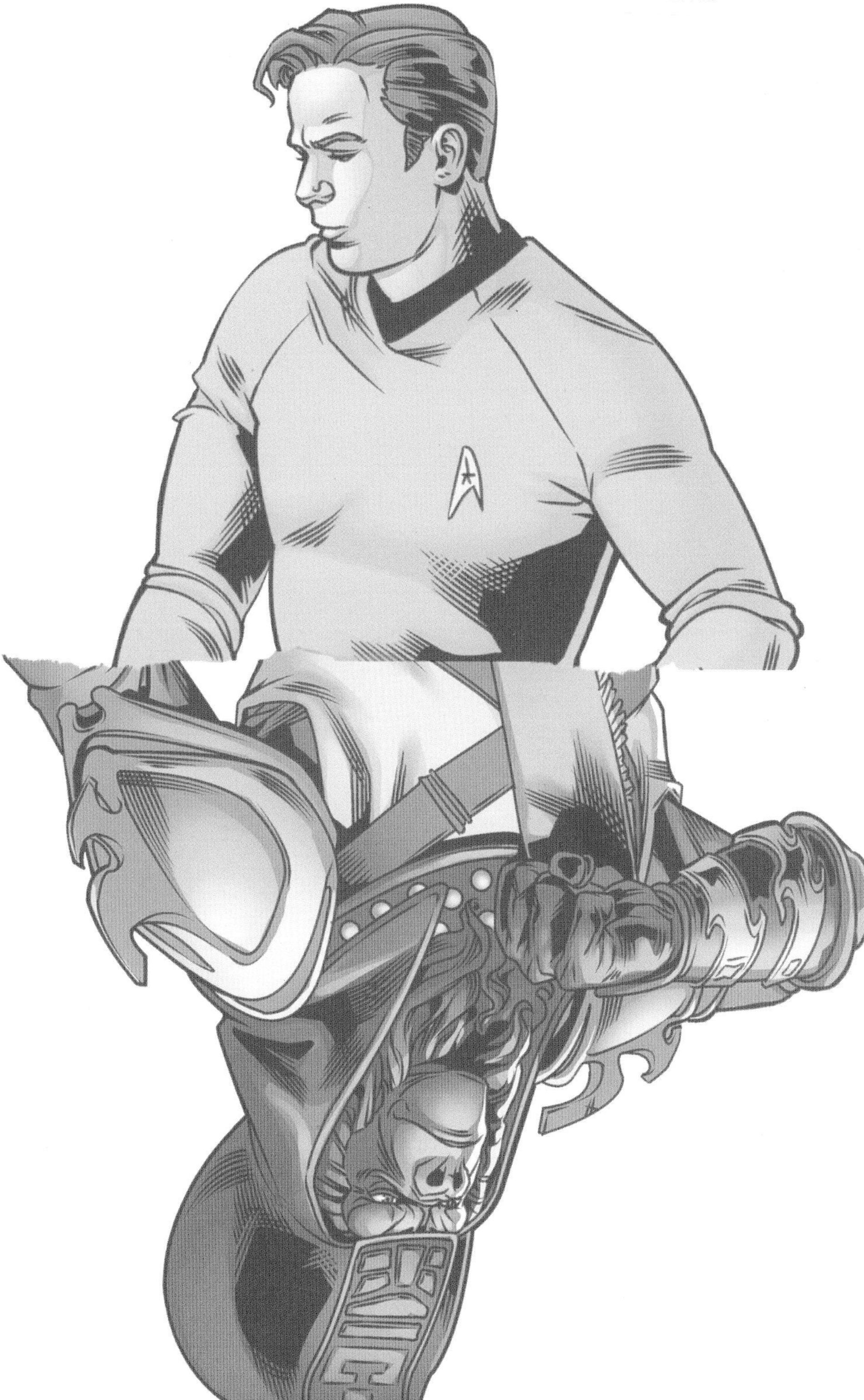

MW01036711

COLLECTION EDITS BY **JUSTIN EISINGER** AND **ALONZO SIMON**
COLLECTION DESIGN BY **JEFF POWELL**

ROSS RICHIE CEO & Founder • **MARK SMYLIE** Founder of Archaia • **MATT GAGNON** Editor-in-Chief • **FILIP SABLIK** President of Publishing & Marketing • **STEPHEN CHRISTY** President of Development
LANCE KREITER VP of Licensing & Merchandising • **PHIL BARBARO** VP of Finance • **BRYCE CARLSON** Managing Editor • **MEL CAYLO** Marketing Manager • **SCOTT NEWMAN** Production Design Manager
IRENE BRADISH Operations Manager • **CHRISTINE DINH** Brand Communications Manager • **DAFNA PLEBAN** Editor • **SHANNON WATTERS** Editor • **ERIC HARBURN** Editor • **IAN BRILL** Editor • **WHITNEY LEOPARD** Associate Editor
JASMINE AMIRI Associate Editor • **CHRIS ROSA** Assistant Editor • **ALEX GALER** Assistant Editor • **CAMERON CHITTOCK** Assistant Editor • **MARY GUMPORT** Assistant Editor • **KELSEY DIETERICH** Production Designer
JILLIAN CRAB Production Designer • **KARA LEOPARD** Production Designer • **MICHELLE ANKLEY** Production Design Assistant • **DEVIN FUNCHES** E-Commerce & Inventory Coordinator • **AARON FERRARA** Operations Coordinator
JOSÉ MEZA Sales Assistant • **ELIZABETH LOUGHRIDGE** Accounting Assistant • **STEPHANIE HOCUTT** Marketing Assistant • **HILLARY LEVI** Executive Assistant • **KATE ALBIN** Administrative Assistant • **JAMES ARRIOLA** Mailroom Assistant

Special thanks to Risa Kessler and John Van Citters of CBS Consumer Products, Joshua Izzo and Lauren Winarski of Fox, Jeff Briggs, and the Heston Estate for their invaluable assistance.

ISBN: 978-1-63140-362-0   18 17 16 15   1 2 3

Ted Adams, CEO & Publisher
Greg Goldstein, President & COO
Robbie Robbins, EVP/Sr. Graphic Artist
Chris Ryall, Chief Creative Officer/Editor-in-Chief
Matthew Ruzicka, CPA, Chief Financial Officer
Alan Payne, VP of Sales
Dirk Wood, VP of Marketing
Lorelei Bunjes, VP of Digital Services
Jeff Webber, VP of Digital Publishing & Business Development

www.IDWPUBLISHING.com
IDW founded by Ted Adams, Alex Garner, Kris Oprisko, and Robbie Robbins

Facebook: **facebook.com/idwpublishing**
Twitter: **@idwpublishing**
YouTube: **youtube.com/idwpublishing**
Instagram: **instagram.com/idwpublishing**
deviantART: **idwpublishing.deviantart.com**
Pinterest: **pinterest.com/idwpublishing/idw-staff-faves**

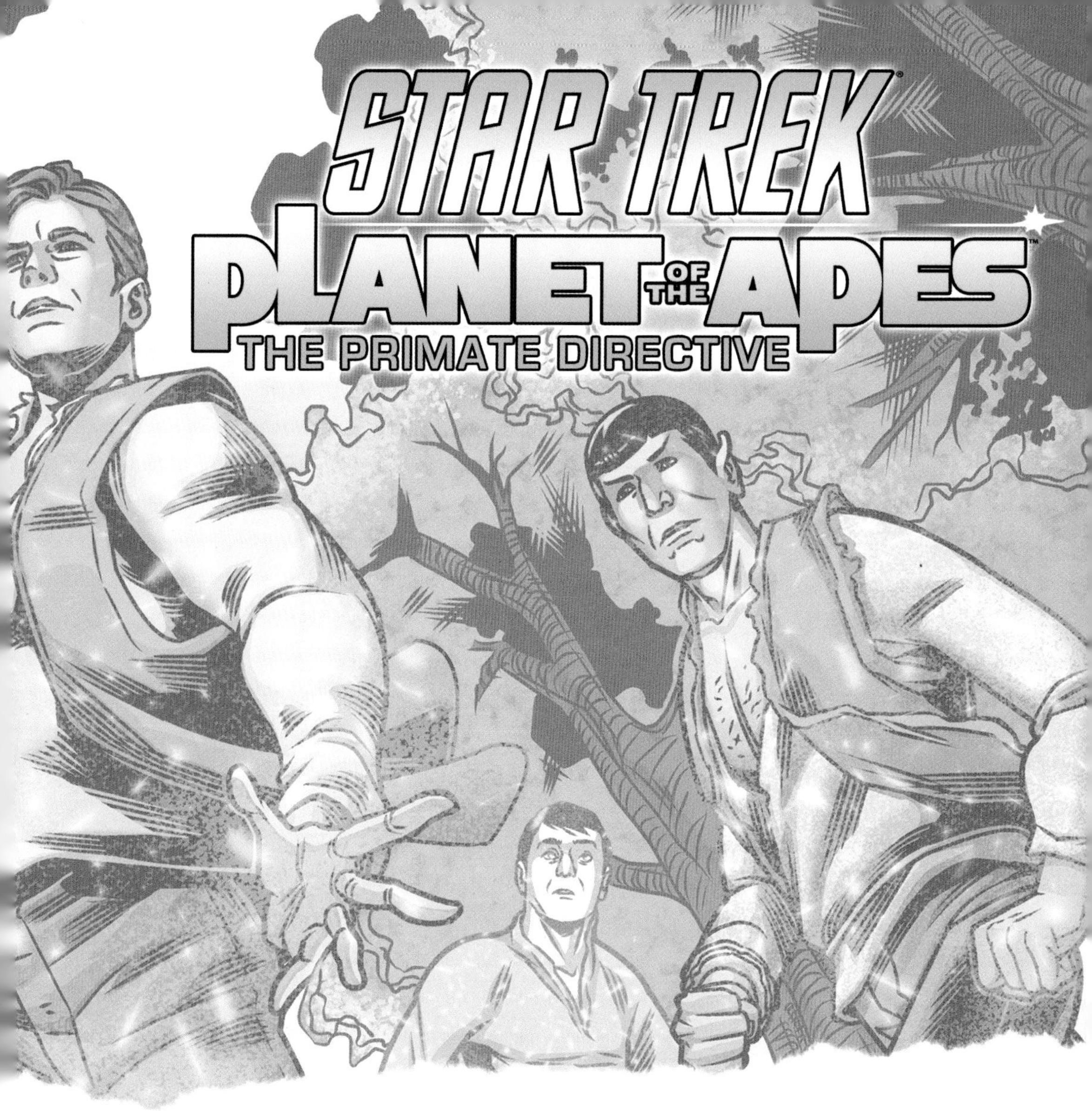
STAR TREK
PLANET OF THE APES
THE PRIMATE DIRECTIVE

WRITTEN BY
SCOTT TIPTON AND **DAVID TIPTON**

ART BY
RACHAEL STOTT

COLORS BY
CHARLIE KIRCHOFF

LETTERS BY
TOM B. LONG

SERIES EDITS BY
IDW'S **SARAH GAYDOS** AND BOOM! STUDIOS' **DAFNA PLEBAN**

ESSAYS BY
DANA GOULD

COVER BY **RACHAEL STOTT** AND **CHARLIE KIRCHOFF**

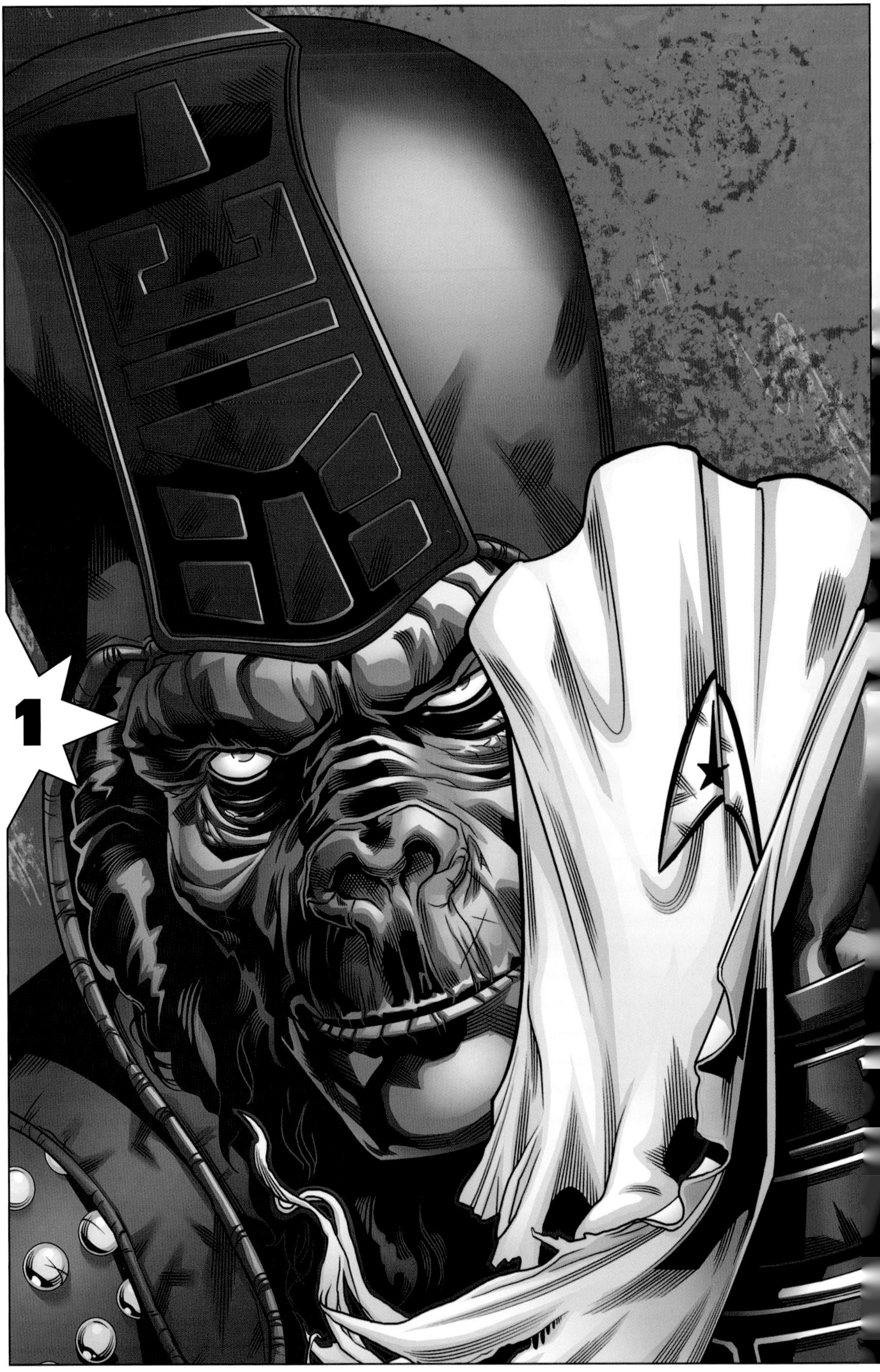
1

BY **RACHAEL STOTT** COLORS BY **CHARLIE KIRCHOFF**

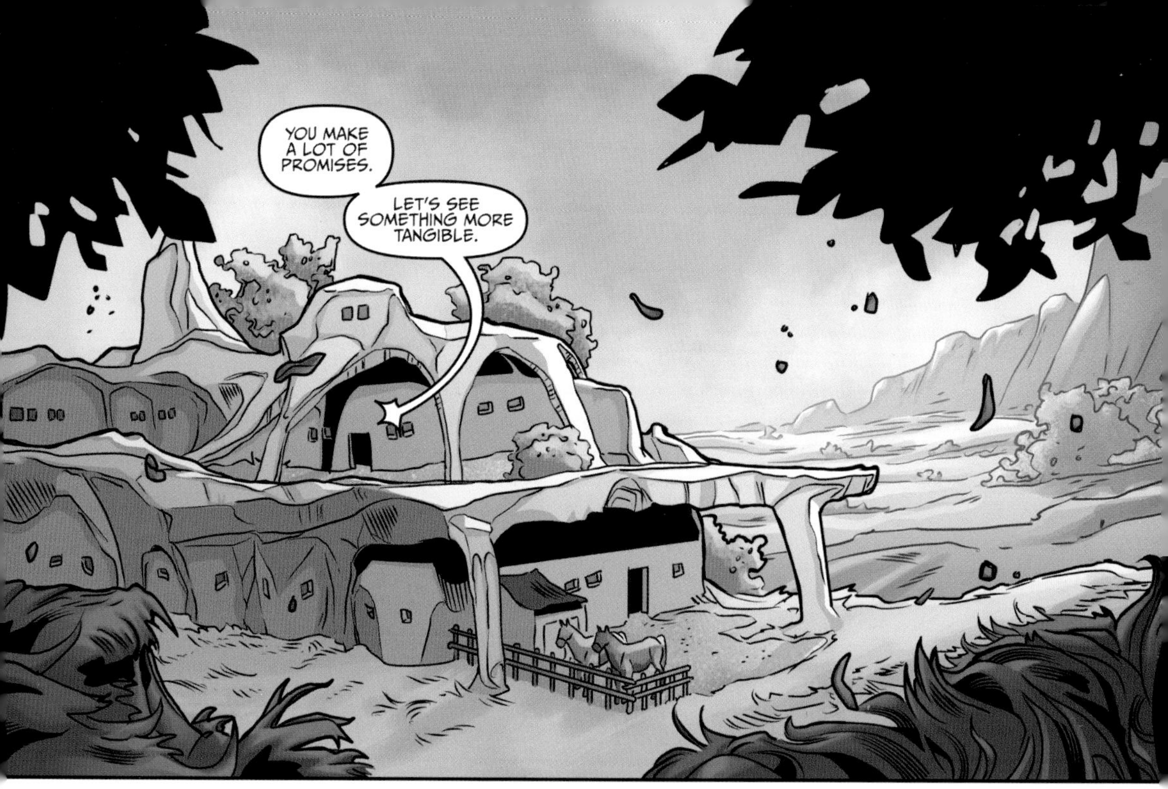
YOU MAKE A LOT OF PROMISES.
LET'S SEE SOMETHING MORE TANGIBLE.

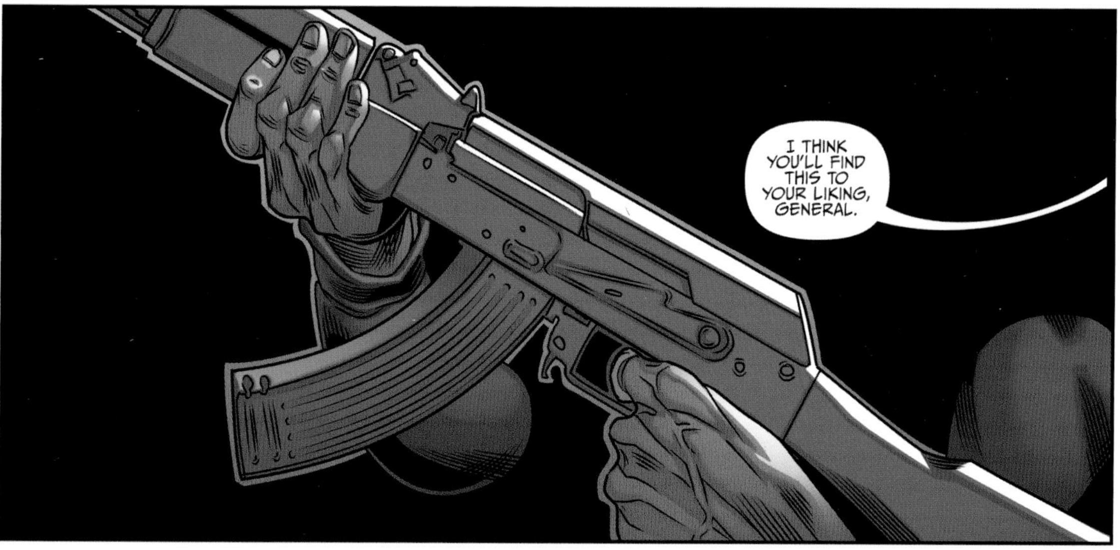
I THINK YOU'LL FIND THIS TO YOUR LIKING, GENERAL.

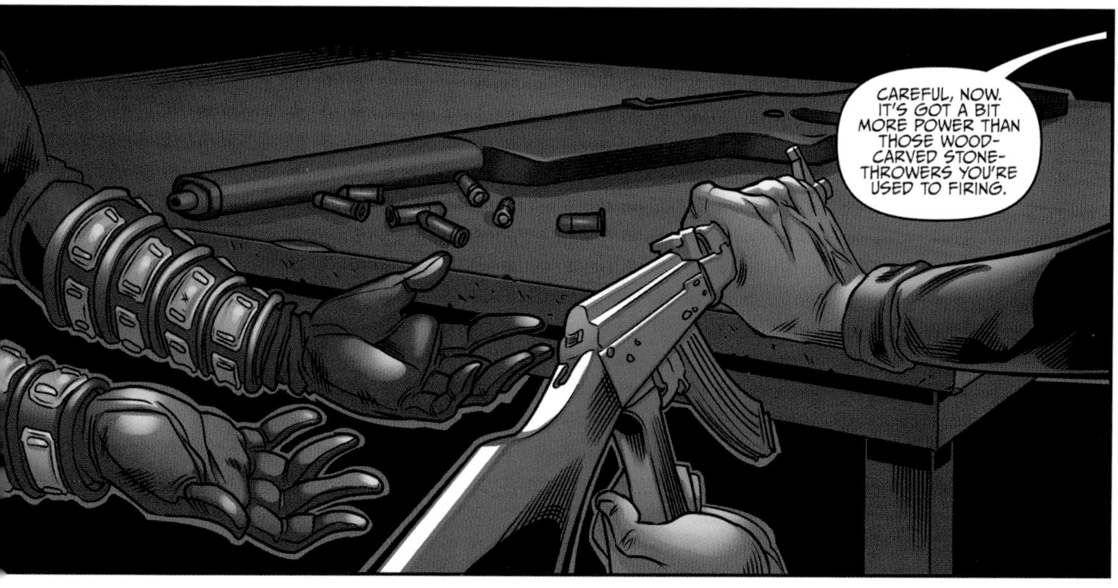
CAREFUL, NOW. IT'S GOT A BIT MORE POWER THAN THOSE WOOD-CARVED STONE-THROWERS YOU'RE USED TO FIRING.

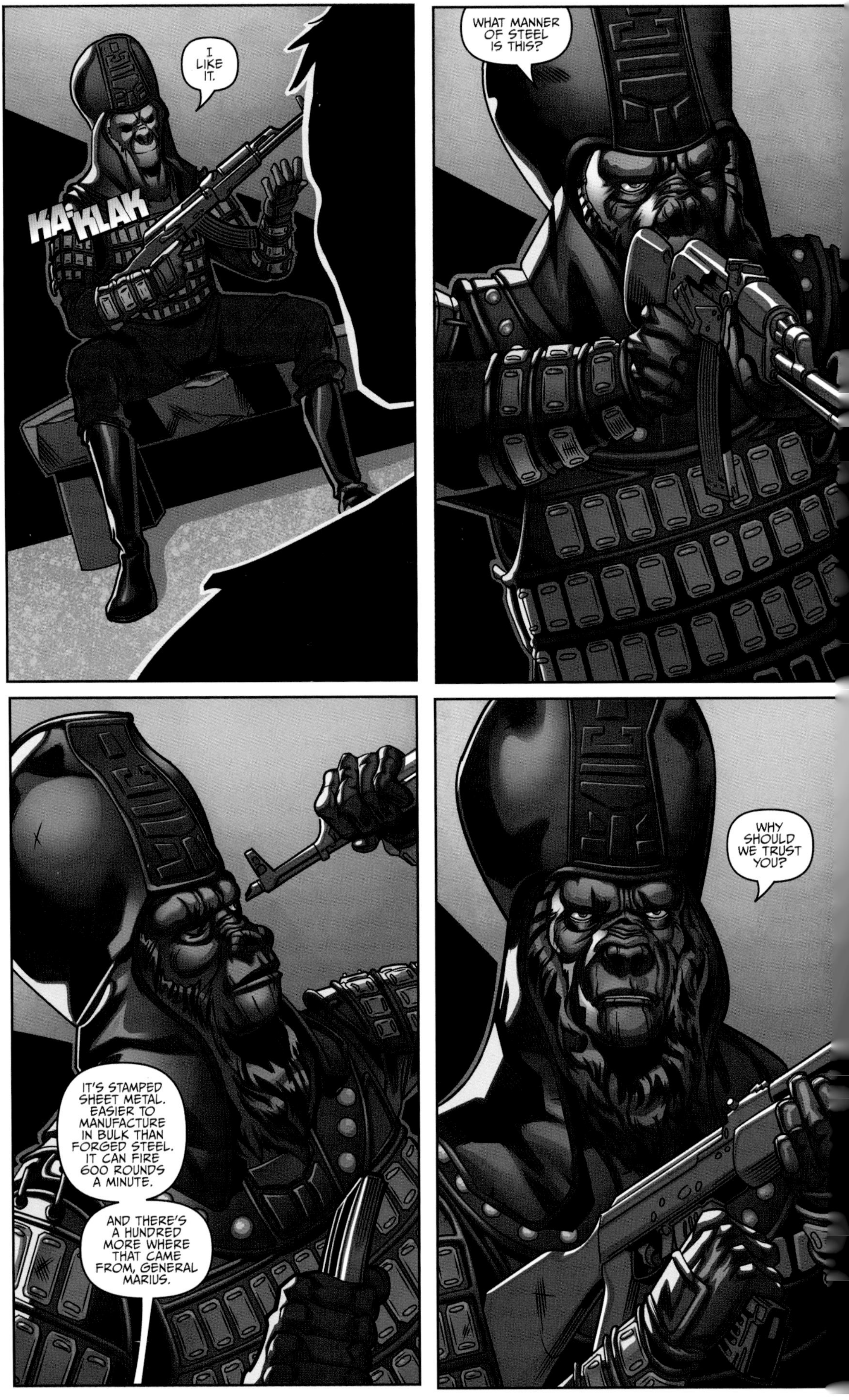
I LIKE IT.
KA-KLAK
WHAT MANNER OF STEEL IS THIS?
IT'S STAMPED SHEET METAL. EASIER TO MANUFACTURE IN BULK THAN FORGED STEEL. IT CAN FIRE 600 ROUNDS A MINUTE.
AND THERE'S A HUNDRED MORE WHERE THAT CAME FROM, GENERAL MARIUS.
WHY SHOULD WE TRUST YOU?

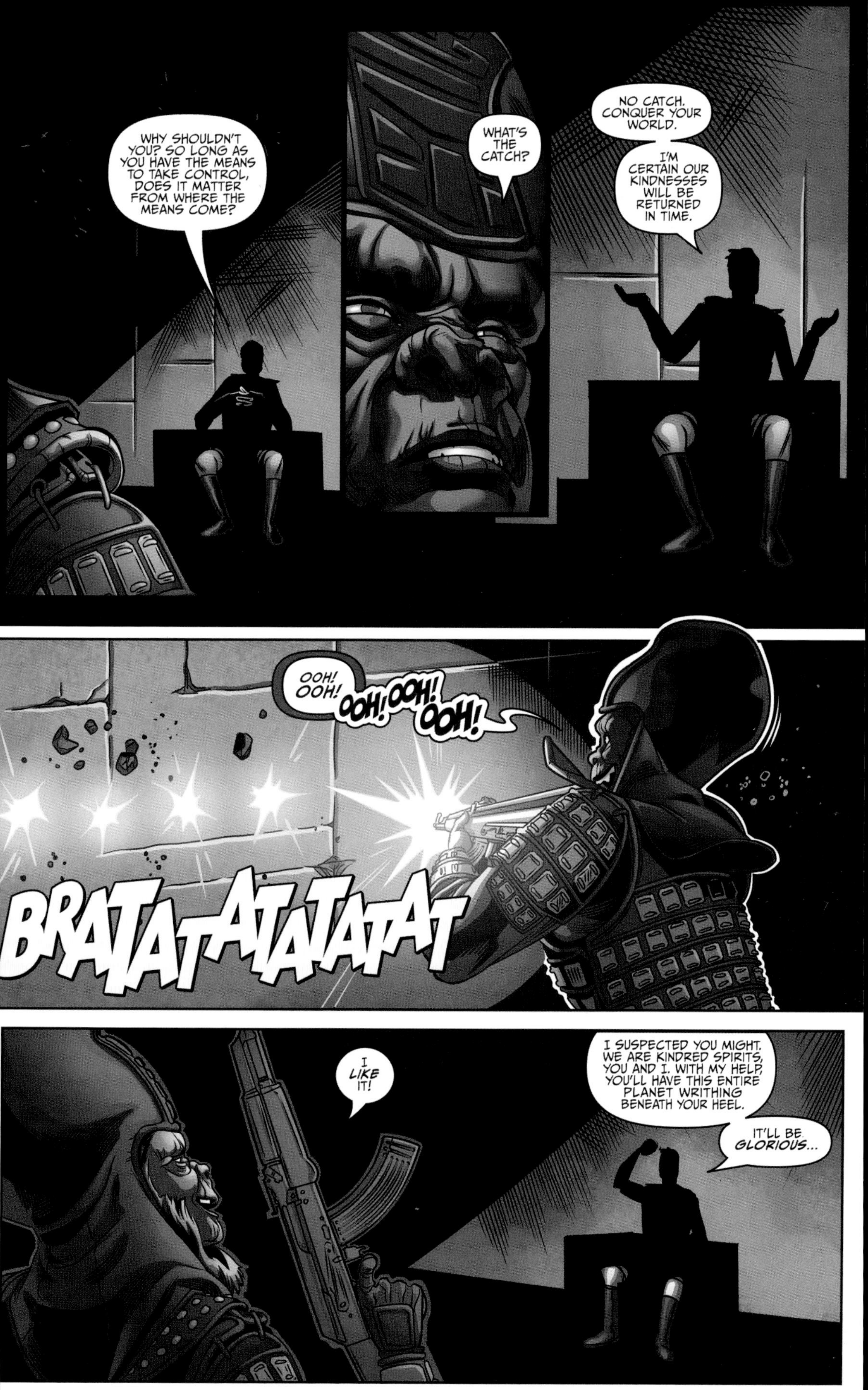
WHY SHOULDN'T YOU? SO LONG AS YOU HAVE THE MEANS TO TAKE CONTROL, DOES IT MATTER FROM WHERE THE MEANS COME?
WHAT'S THE CATCH?
NO CATCH. CONQUER YOUR WORLD.
I'M CERTAIN OUR KINDNESSES WILL BE RETURNED IN TIME.
OOH! OOH! OOH! OOH! OOH!
BRATATATATATAT
I LIKE IT!
I SUSPECTED YOU MIGHT. WE ARE KINDRED SPIRITS, YOU AND I. WITH MY HELP, YOU'LL HAVE THIS ENTIRE PLANET WRITHING BENEATH YOUR HEEL.
IT'LL BE GLORIOUS...

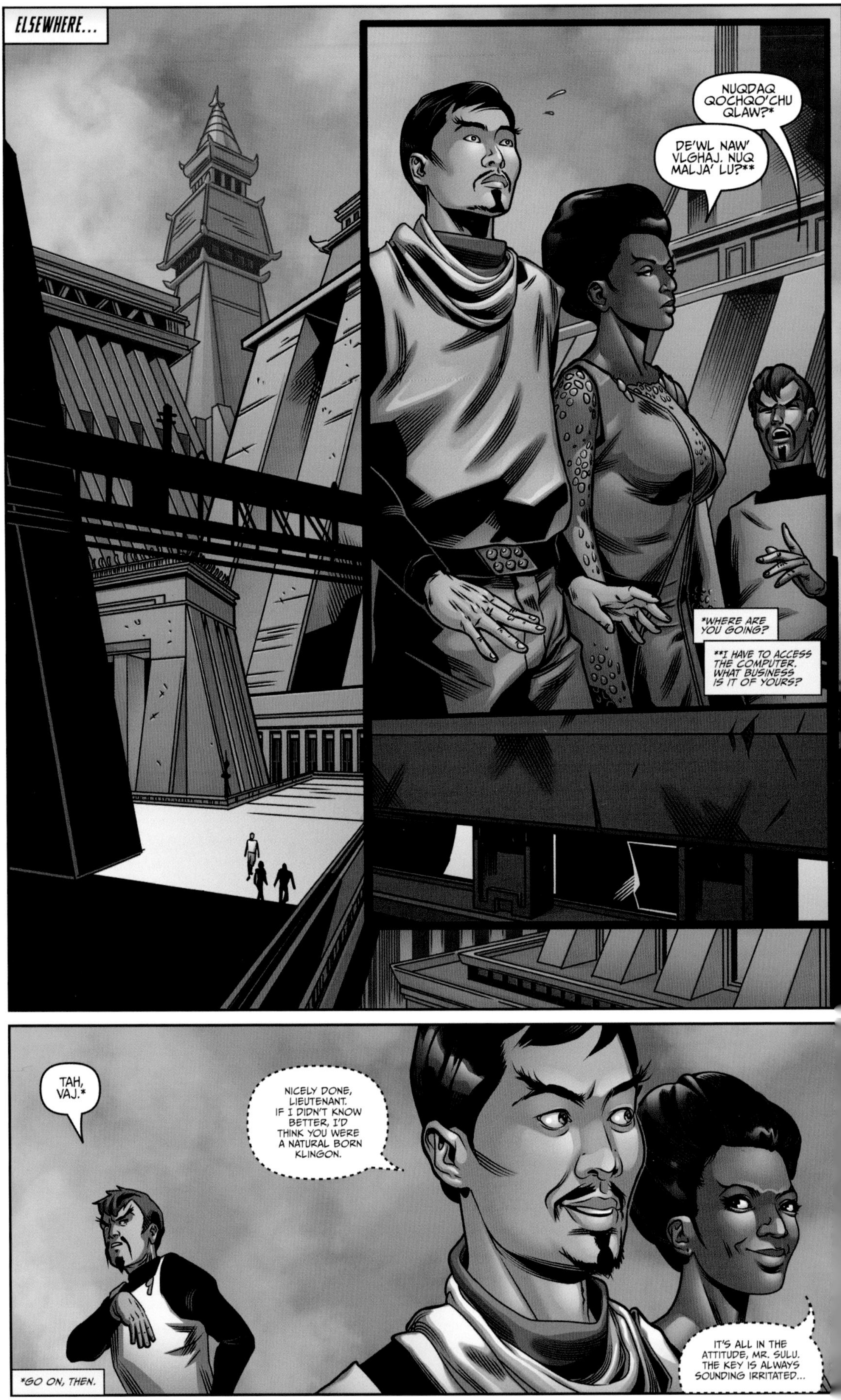
ELSEWHERE...
NUQDAQ QOCHQO'CHU QLAW?*
DE'WL NAW' VLGHAJ. NUQ MALJA' LU?**
*WHERE ARE YOU GOING?
**I HAVE TO ACCESS THE COMPUTER. WHAT BUSINESS IS IT OF YOURS?
TAH, VAJ.*
NICELY DONE, LIEUTENANT. IF I DIDN'T KNOW BETTER, I'D THINK YOU WERE A NATURAL BORN KLINGON.
IT'S ALL IN THE ATTITUDE, MR. SULU. THE KEY IS ALWAYS SOUNDING IRRITATED...
*GO ON, THEN.

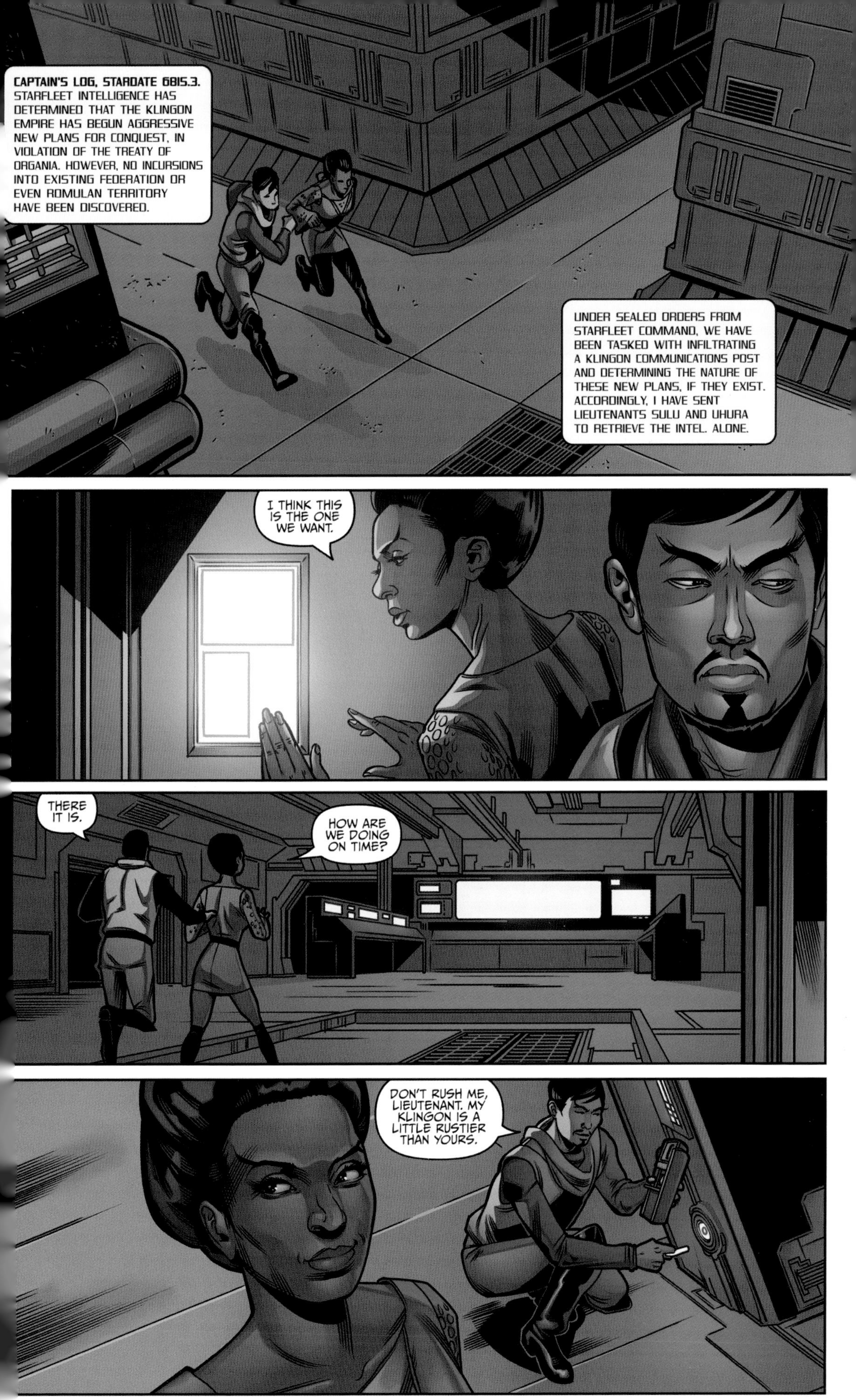
CAPTAIN'S LOG, STARDATE 6815.3. STARFLEET INTELLIGENCE HAS DETERMINED THAT THE KLINGON EMPIRE HAS BEGUN AGGRESSIVE NEW PLANS FOR CONQUEST, IN VIOLATION OF THE TREATY OF ORGANIA. HOWEVER, NO INCURSIONS INTO EXISTING FEDERATION OR EVEN ROMULAN TERRITORY HAVE BEEN DISCOVERED.
UNDER SEALED ORDERS FROM STARFLEET COMMAND, WE HAVE BEEN TASKED WITH INFILTRATING A KLINGON COMMUNICATIONS POST AND DETERMINING THE NATURE OF THESE NEW PLANS, IF THEY EXIST. ACCORDINGLY, I HAVE SENT LIEUTENANTS SULU AND UHURA TO RETRIEVE THE INTEL. ALONE.
I THINK THIS IS THE ONE WE WANT.
THERE IT IS.
HOW ARE WE DOING ON TIME?
DON'T RUSH ME, LIEUTENANT. MY KLINGON IS A LITTLE RUSTIER THAN YOURS.

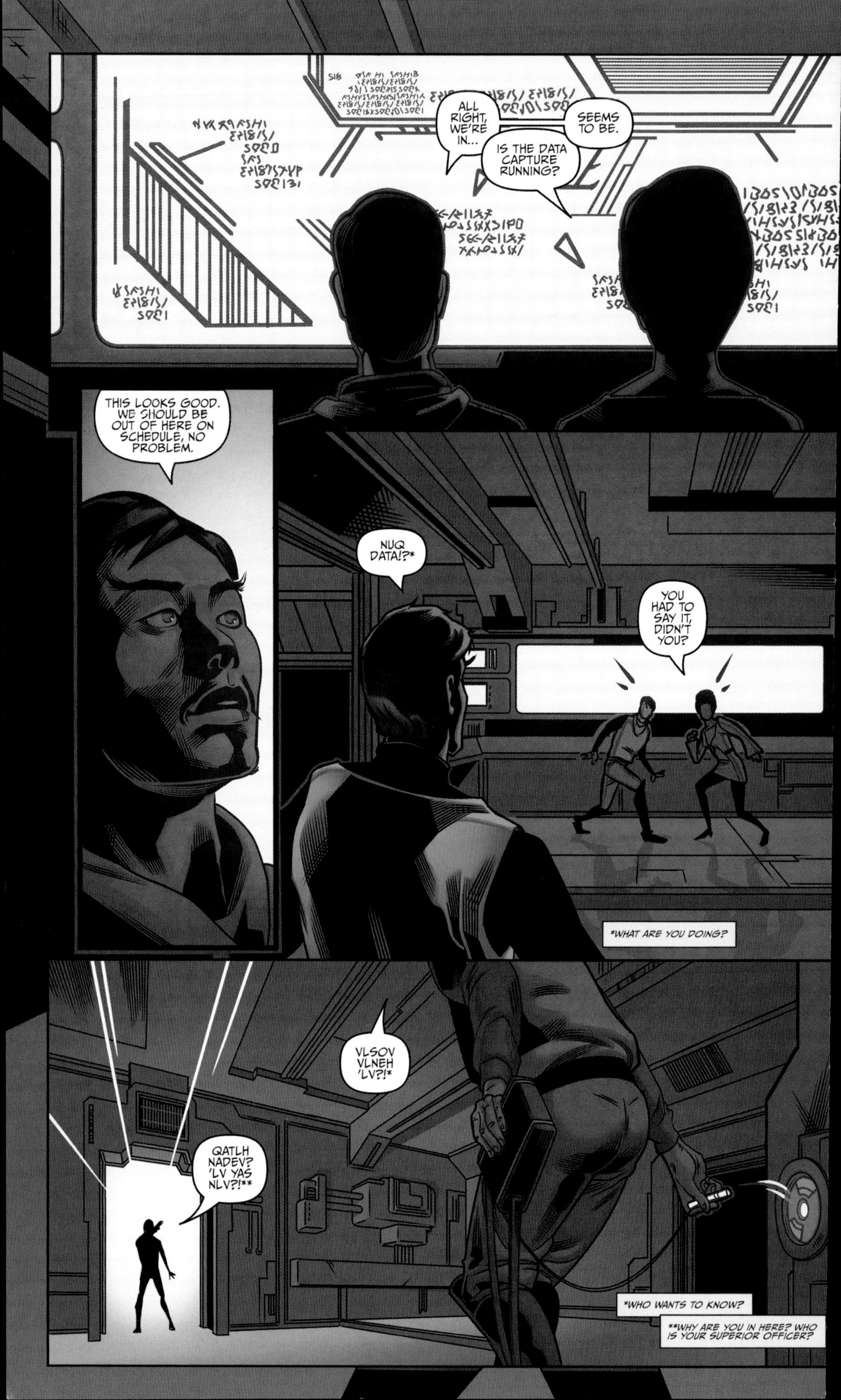
ALL RIGHT, WE'RE IN...
SEEMS TO BE.
IS THE DATA CAPTURE RUNNING?
THIS LOOKS GOOD. WE SHOULD BE OUT OF HERE ON SCHEDULE, NO PROBLEM.
NUQ DATA!?*
YOU HAD TO SAY IT, DIDN'T YOU?
*WHAT ARE YOU DOING?
VLSOV VLNEH 'LV?!*
QATLH NADEV? 'LV YAS NLV?!**
*WHO WANTS TO KNOW?
**WHY ARE YOU IN HERE? WHO IS YOUR SUPERIOR OFFICER?

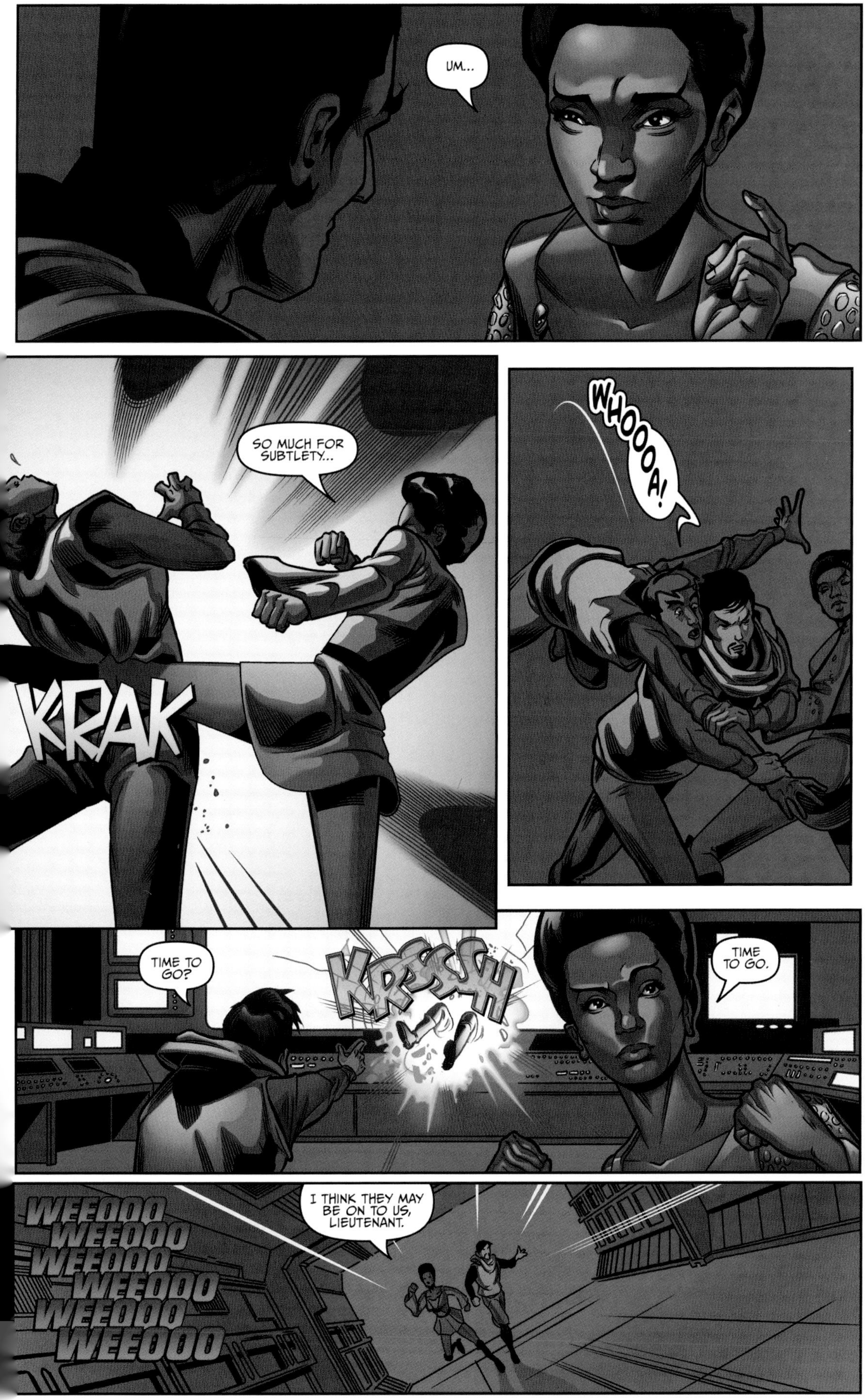

UM...
SO MUCH FOR SUBTLETY...
KRAK
WHOOOOA!
TIME TO GO?
KRSSSH
TIME TO GO.
WEEOOO WEEOOO WEEOOO WEEOOO WEEOOO WEEOOO
I THINK THEY MAY BE ON TO US, LIEUTENANT.

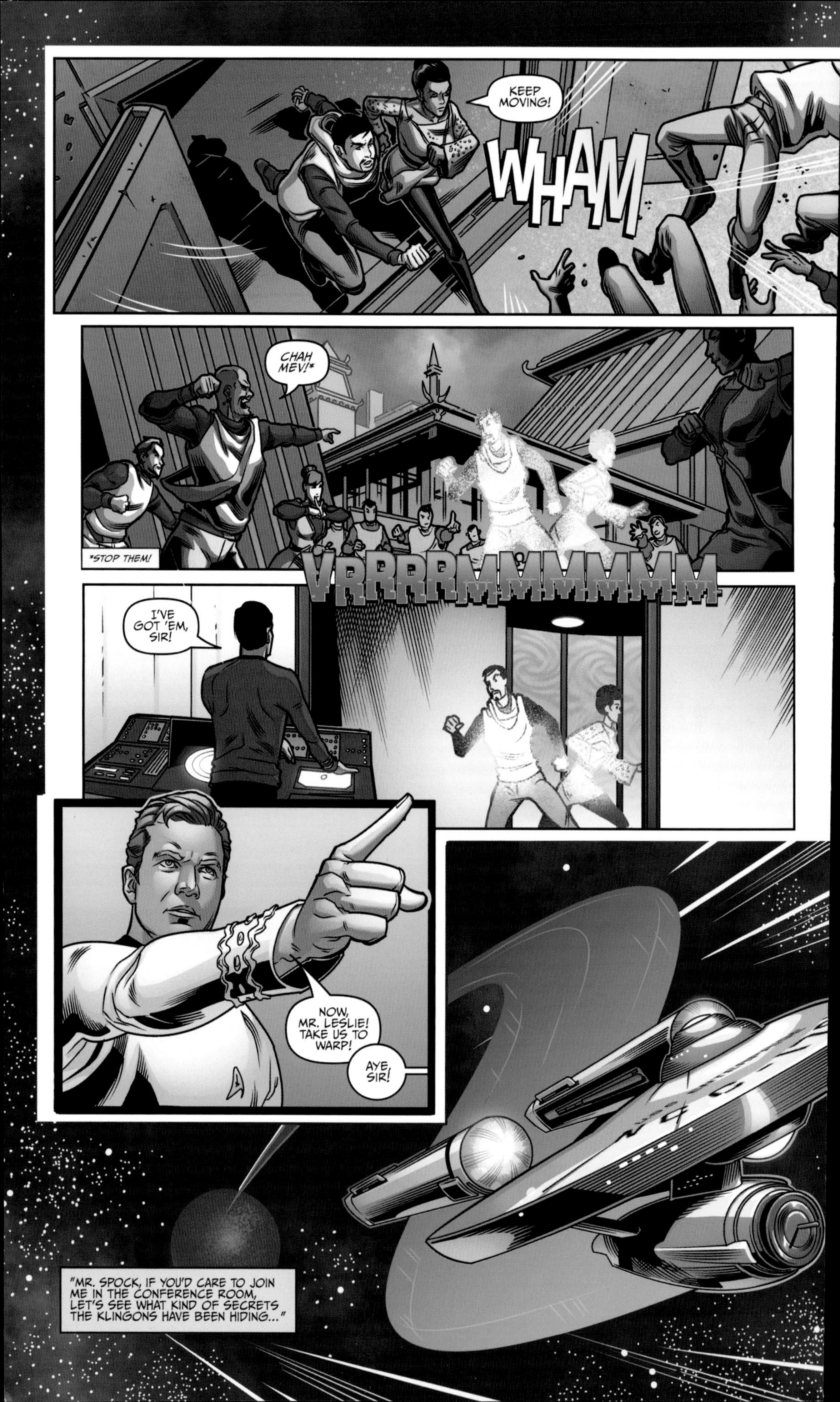
KEEP MOVING!
WHAM
CHAH MEV!*
*STOP THEM!
VRRRRMMMMMMM
I'VE GOT 'EM, SIR!
NOW, MR. LESLIE! TAKE US TO WARP!
AYE, SIR!
"MR. SPOCK, IF YOU'D CARE TO JOIN ME IN THE CONFERENCE ROOM, LET'S SEE WHAT KIND OF SECRETS THE KLINGONS HAVE BEEN HIDING..."

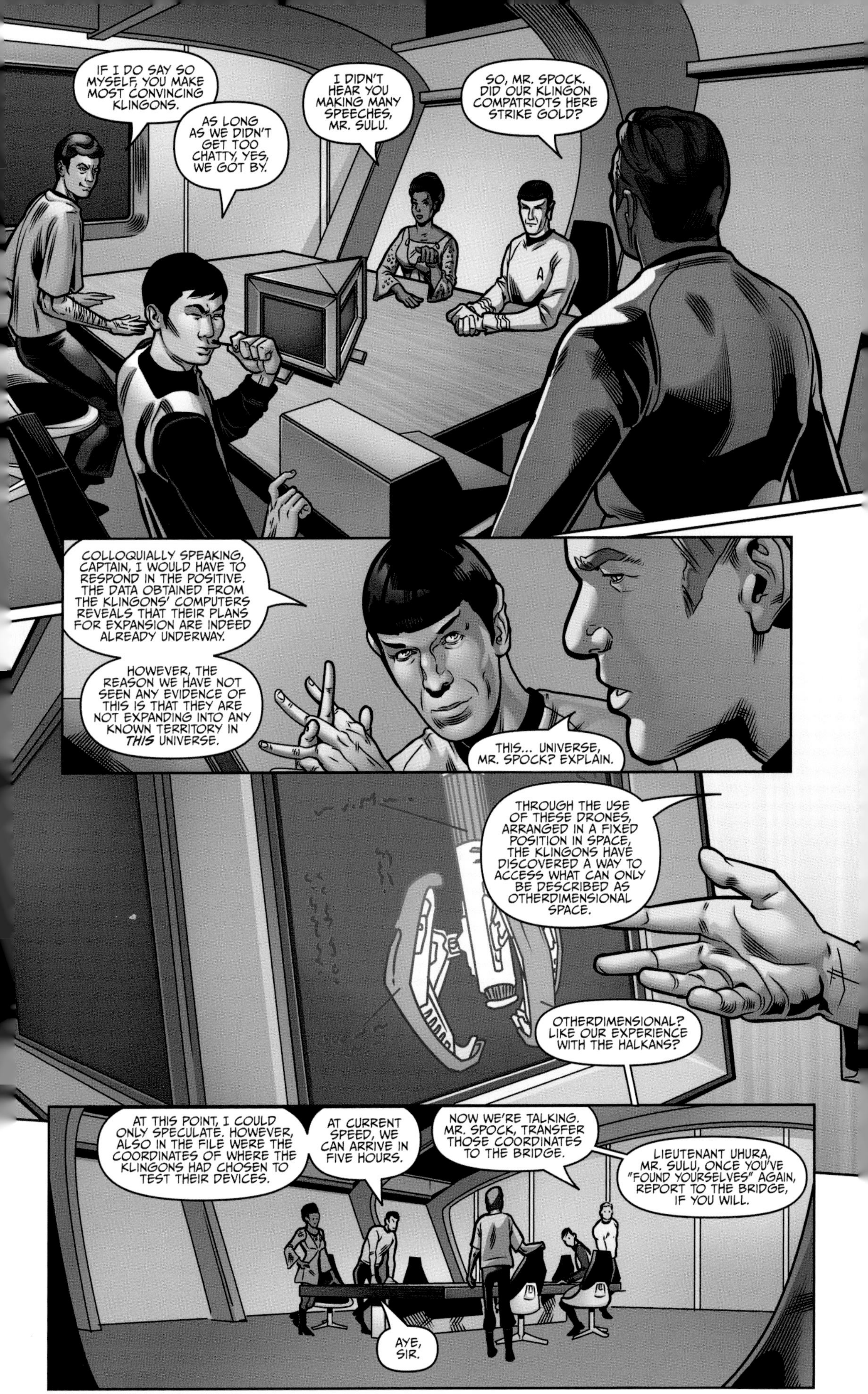

IF I DO SAY SO MYSELF, YOU MAKE MOST CONVINCING KLINGONS.
AS LONG AS WE DIDN'T GET TOO CHATTY, YES, WE GOT BY.
I DIDN'T HEAR YOU MAKING MANY SPEECHES, MR. SULU.
SO, MR. SPOCK. DID OUR KLINGON COMPATRIOTS HERE STRIKE GOLD?
COLLOQUIALLY SPEAKING, CAPTAIN, I WOULD HAVE TO RESPOND IN THE POSITIVE. THE DATA OBTAINED FROM THE KLINGONS' COMPUTERS REVEALS THAT THEIR PLANS FOR EXPANSION ARE INDEED ALREADY UNDERWAY.
HOWEVER, THE REASON WE HAVE NOT SEEN ANY EVIDENCE OF THIS IS THAT THEY ARE NOT EXPANDING INTO ANY KNOWN TERRITORY IN *THIS* UNIVERSE.
THIS... UNIVERSE, MR. SPOCK? EXPLAIN.
THROUGH THE USE OF THESE DRONES, ARRANGED IN A FIXED POSITION IN SPACE, THE KLINGONS HAVE DISCOVERED A WAY TO ACCESS WHAT CAN ONLY BE DESCRIBED AS OTHERDIMENSIONAL SPACE.
OTHERDIMENSIONAL? LIKE OUR EXPERIENCE WITH THE HALKANS?
AT THIS POINT, I COULD ONLY SPECULATE. HOWEVER, ALSO IN THE FILE WERE THE COORDINATES OF WHERE THE KLINGONS HAD CHOSEN TO TEST THEIR DEVICES.
AT CURRENT SPEED, WE CAN ARRIVE IN FIVE HOURS.
NOW WE'RE TALKING. MR. SPOCK, TRANSFER THOSE COORDINATES TO THE BRIDGE.
LIEUTENANT UHURA, MR. SULU, ONCE YOU'VE "FOUND YOURSELVES" AGAIN, REPORT TO THE BRIDGE, IF YOU WILL.
AYE, SIR.

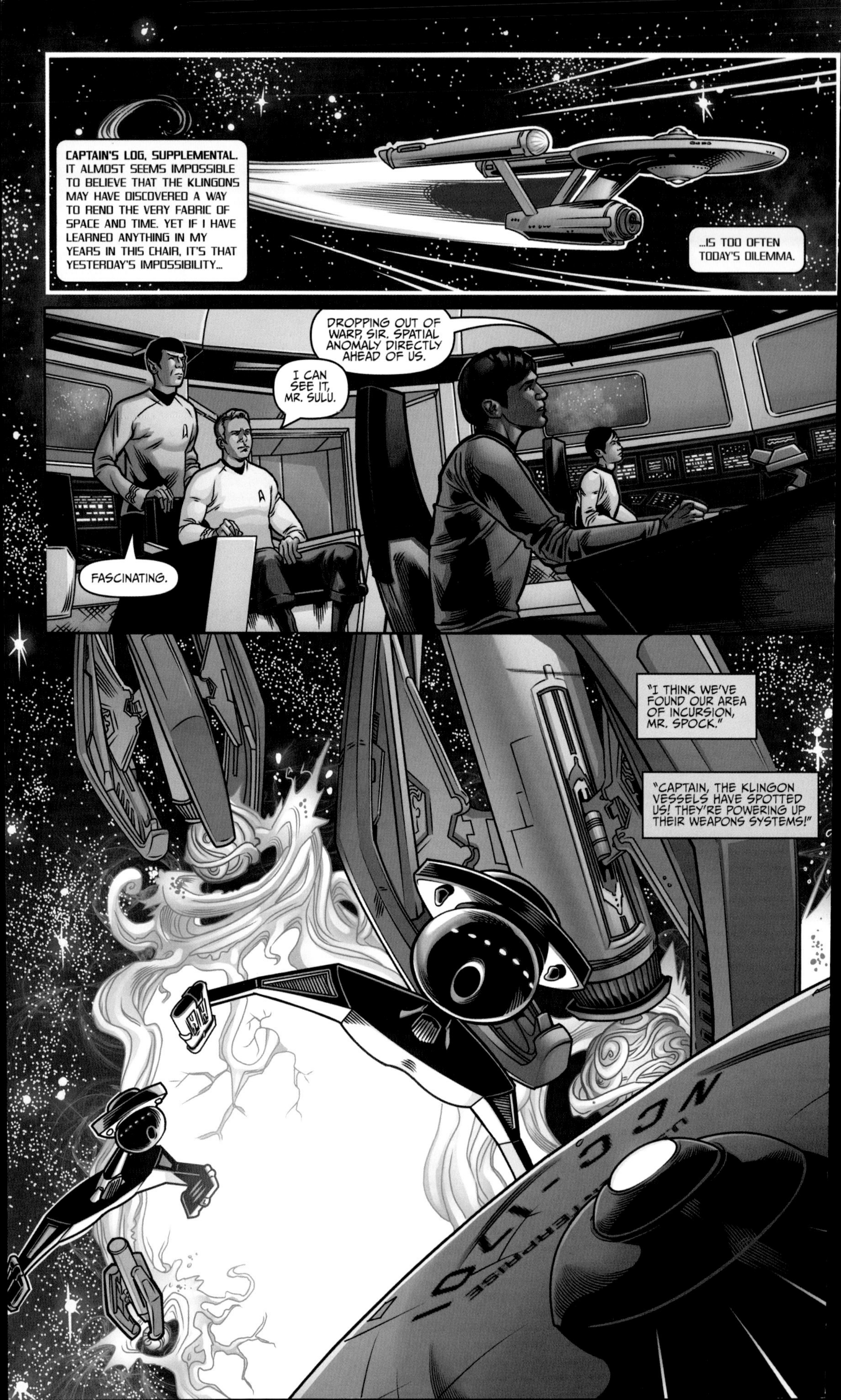

CAPTAIN'S LOG, SUPPLEMENTAL. IT ALMOST SEEMS IMPOSSIBLE TO BELIEVE THAT THE KLINGONS MAY HAVE DISCOVERED A WAY TO REND THE VERY FABRIC OF SPACE AND TIME. YET IF I HAVE LEARNED ANYTHING IN MY YEARS IN THIS CHAIR, IT'S THAT YESTERDAY'S IMPOSSIBILITY...
...IS TOO OFTEN TODAY'S DILEMMA.
DROPPING OUT OF WARP, SIR. SPATIAL ANOMALY DIRECTLY AHEAD OF US.
I CAN SEE IT, MR. SULU.
FASCINATING.
"I THINK WE'VE FOUND OUR AREA OF INCURSION, MR. SPOCK."
"CAPTAIN, THE KLINGON VESSELS HAVE SPOTTED US! THEY'RE POWERING UP THEIR WEAPONS SYSTEMS!"
NCC-1701

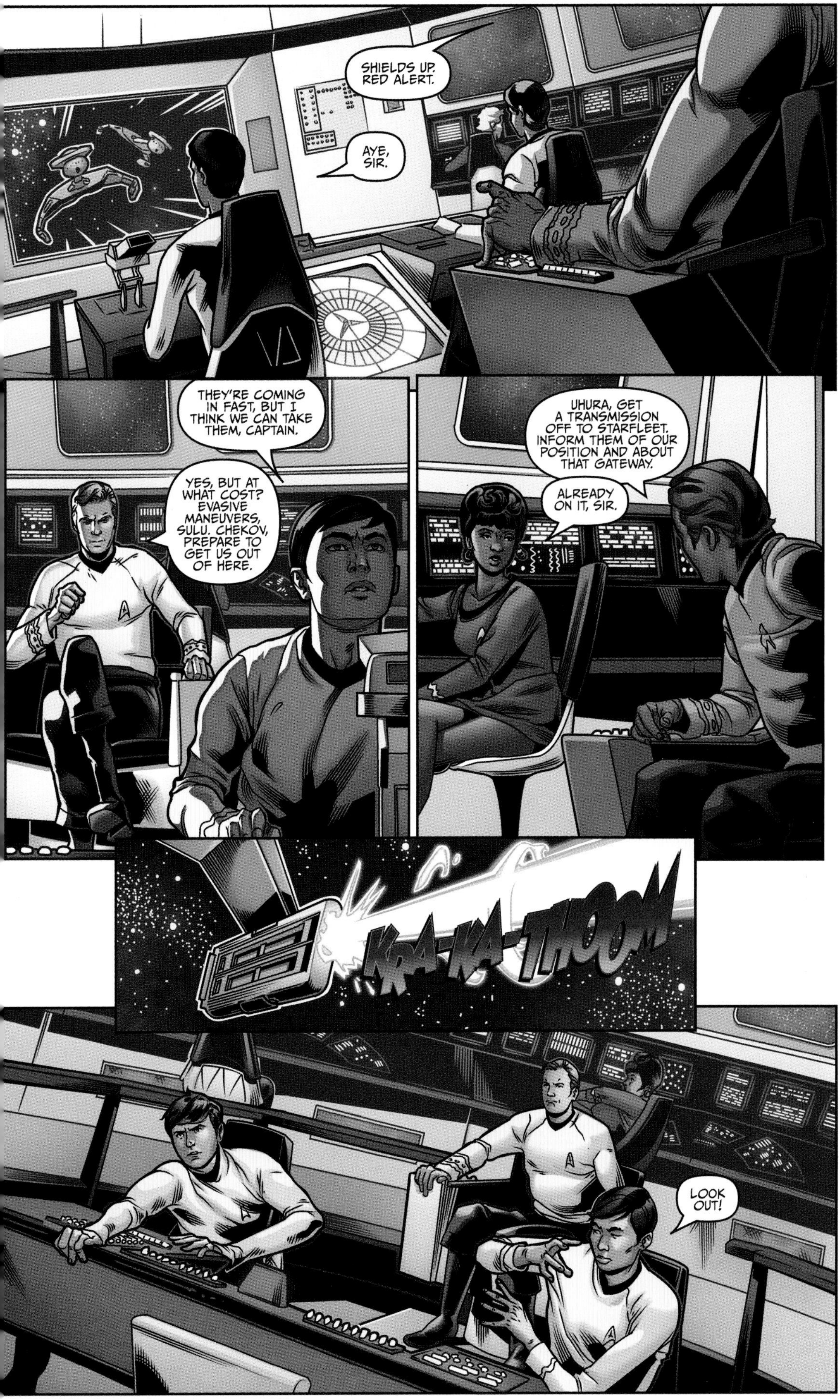
SHIELDS UP. RED ALERT.
AYE, SIR.
THEY'RE COMING IN FAST, BUT I THINK WE CAN TAKE THEM, CAPTAIN.
YES, BUT AT WHAT COST? EVASIVE MANEUVERS, SULU. CHEKOV, PREPARE TO GET US OUT OF HERE.
UHURA, GET A TRANSMISSION OFF TO STARFLEET. INFORM THEM OF OUR POSITION AND ABOUT THAT GATEWAY.
ALREADY ON IT, SIR.
KRA-KA-THOOM
LOOK OUT!

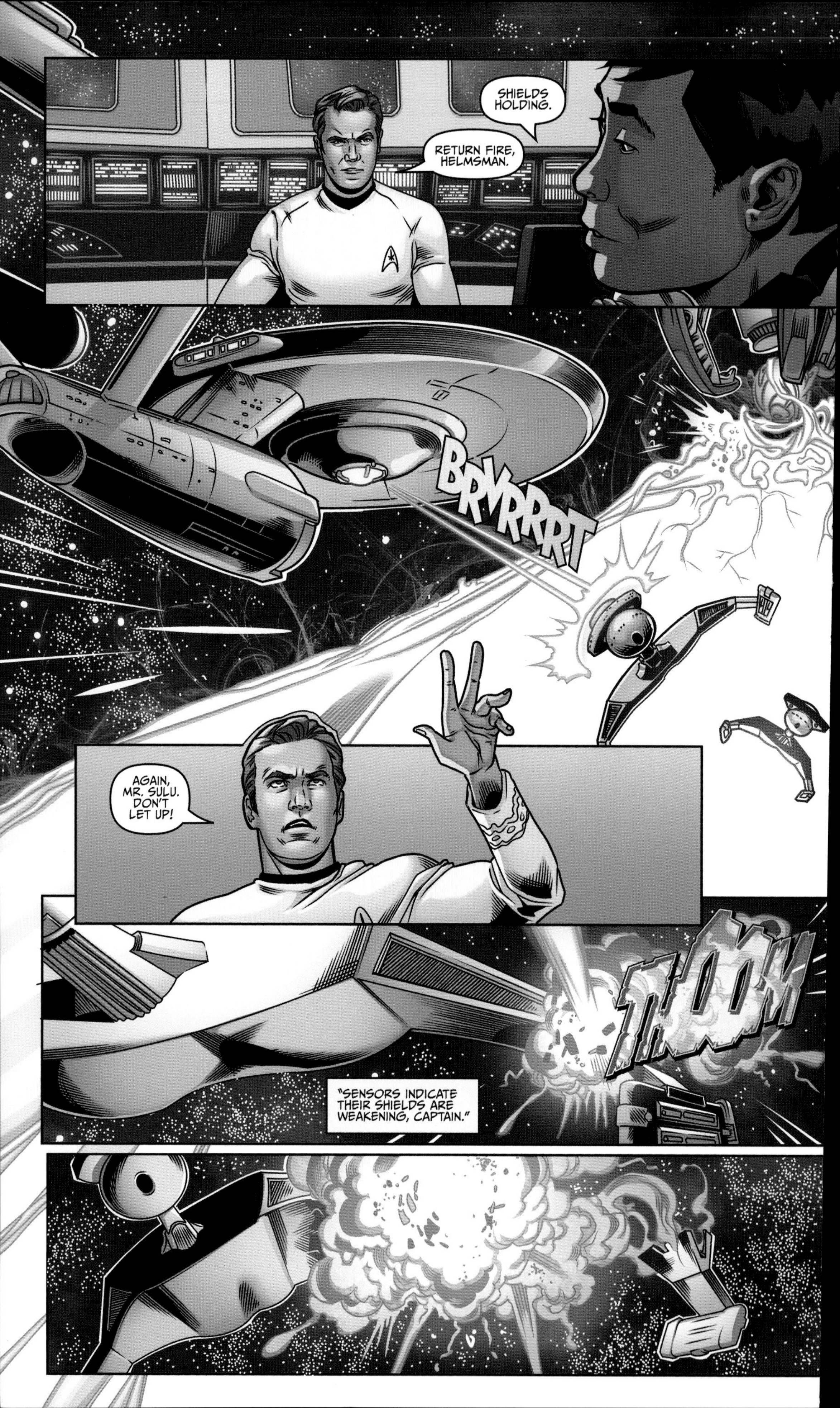
SHIELDS HOLDING.
RETURN FIRE, HELMSMAN.
BRVRRRT
AGAIN, MR. SULU. DON'T LET UP!
THOOM
"SENSORS INDICATE THEIR SHIELDS ARE WEAKENING, CAPTAIN."

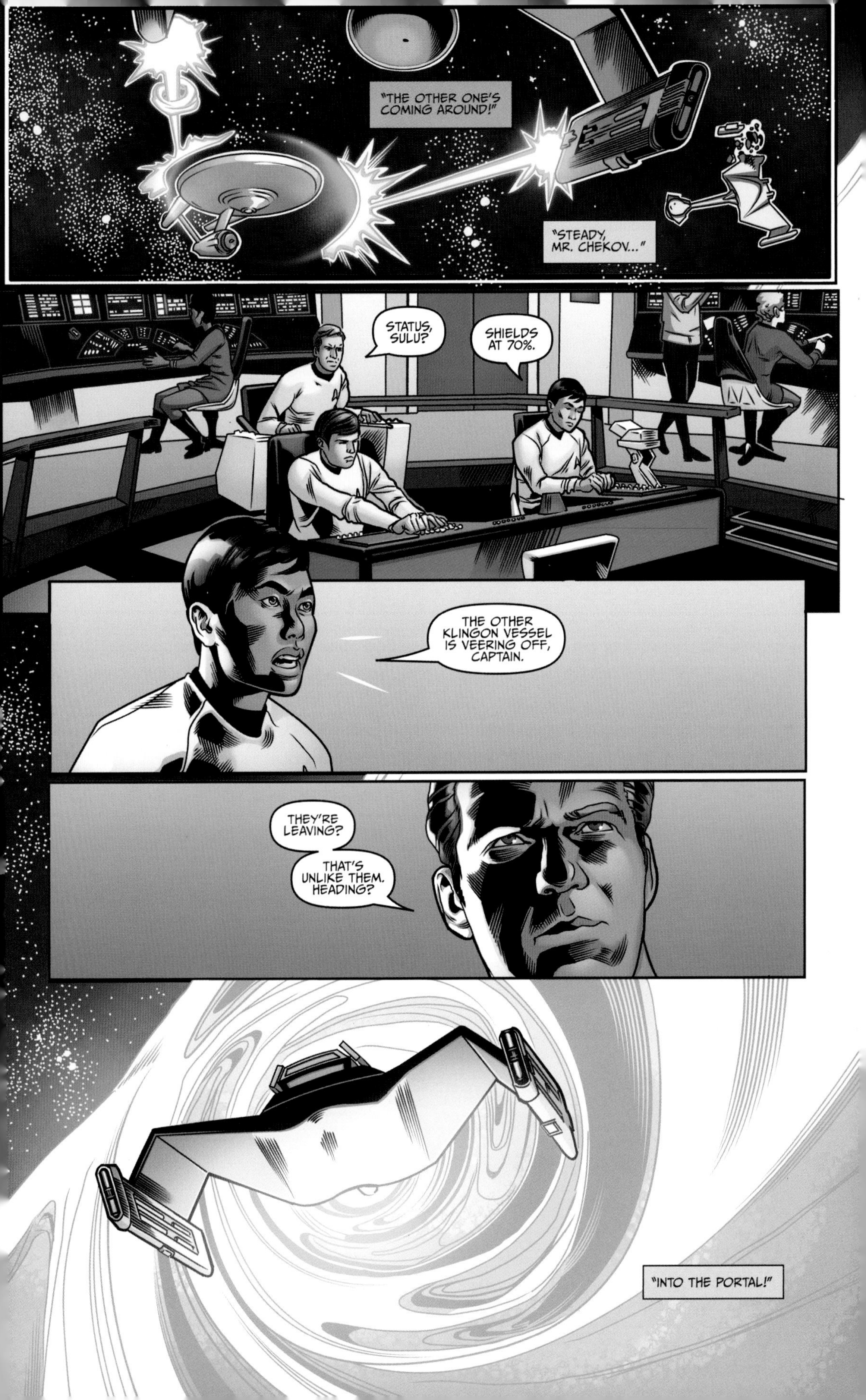
"THE OTHER ONE'S COMING AROUND!"
"STEADY, MR. CHEKOV..."
STATUS, SULU?
SHIELDS AT 70%.
THE OTHER KLINGON VESSEL IS VEERING OFF, CAPTAIN.
THEY'RE LEAVING?
THAT'S UNLIKE THEM. HEADING?
"INTO THE PORTAL!"

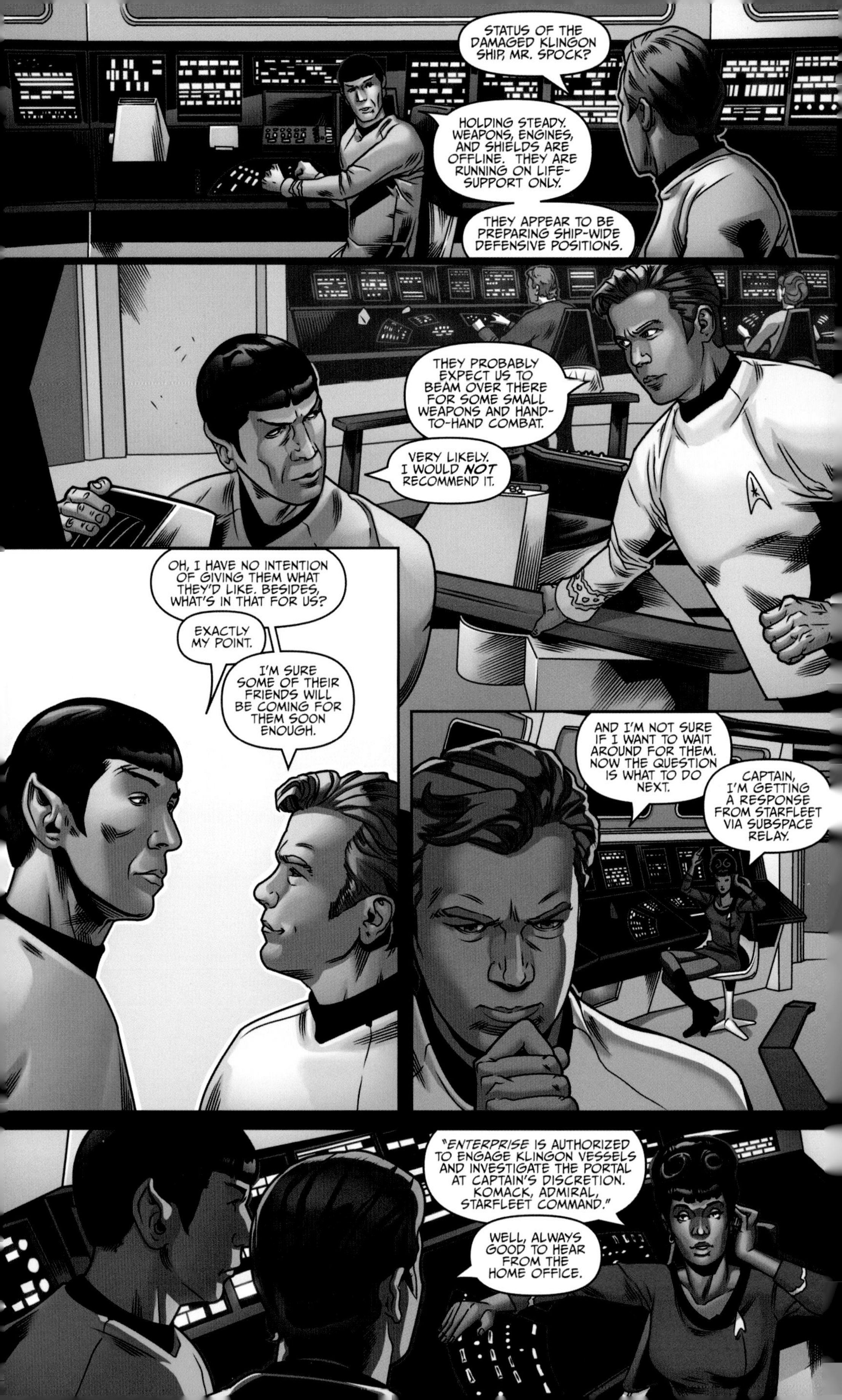
STATUS OF THE DAMAGED KLINGON SHIP, MR. SPOCK?
HOLDING STEADY. WEAPONS, ENGINES, AND SHIELDS ARE OFFLINE. THEY ARE RUNNING ON LIFE-SUPPORT ONLY.
THEY APPEAR TO BE PREPARING SHIP-WIDE DEFENSIVE POSITIONS.
THEY PROBABLY EXPECT US TO BEAM OVER THERE FOR SOME SMALL WEAPONS AND HAND-TO-HAND COMBAT.
VERY LIKELY. I WOULD ***NOT*** RECOMMEND IT.
OH, I HAVE NO INTENTION OF GIVING THEM WHAT THEY'D LIKE. BESIDES, WHAT'S IN THAT FOR US?
EXACTLY MY POINT.
I'M SURE SOME OF THEIR FRIENDS WILL BE COMING FOR THEM SOON ENOUGH.
AND I'M NOT SURE IF I WANT TO WAIT AROUND FOR THEM. NOW THE QUESTION IS WHAT TO DO NEXT.
CAPTAIN, I'M GETTING A RESPONSE FROM STARFLEET VIA SUBSPACE RELAY.
"*ENTERPRISE* IS AUTHORIZED TO ENGAGE KLINGON VESSELS AND INVESTIGATE THE PORTAL AT CAPTAIN'S DISCRETION. KOMACK, ADMIRAL, STARFLEET COMMAND."
WELL, ALWAYS GOOD TO HEAR FROM THE HOME OFFICE.

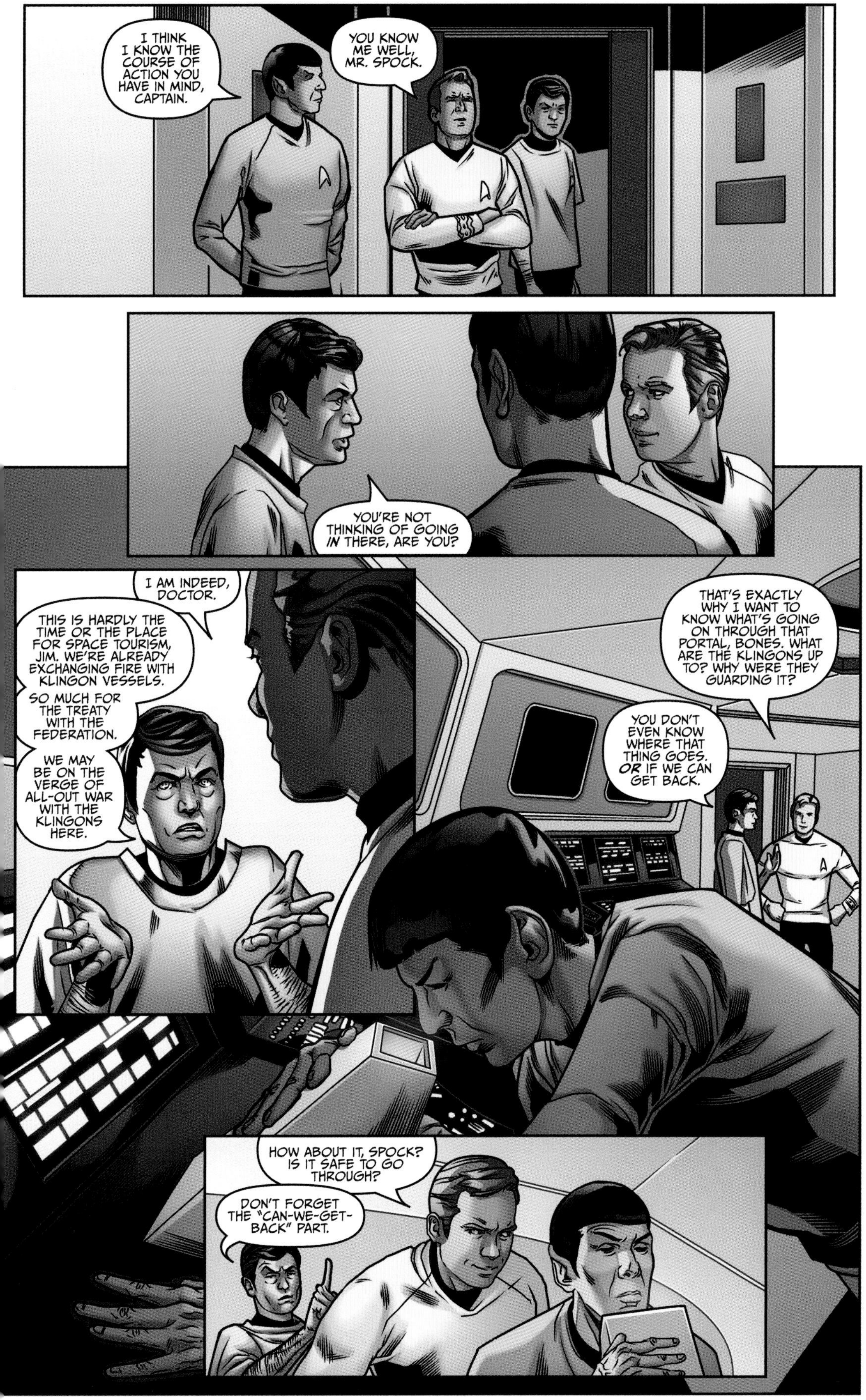
I THINK I KNOW THE COURSE OF ACTION YOU HAVE IN MIND, CAPTAIN.
YOU KNOW ME WELL, MR. SPOCK.
YOU'RE NOT THINKING OF GOING *IN* THERE, ARE YOU?
I AM INDEED, DOCTOR.
THIS IS HARDLY THE TIME OR THE PLACE FOR SPACE TOURISM, JIM. WE'RE ALREADY EXCHANGING FIRE WITH KLINGON VESSELS.
SO MUCH FOR THE TREATY WITH THE FEDERATION.
WE MAY BE ON THE VERGE OF ALL-OUT WAR WITH THE KLINGONS HERE.
THAT'S EXACTLY WHY I WANT TO KNOW WHAT'S GOING ON THROUGH THAT PORTAL, BONES. WHAT ARE THE KLINGONS UP TO? WHY WERE THEY GUARDING IT?
YOU DON'T EVEN KNOW WHERE THAT THING GOES. **OR** IF WE CAN GET BACK.
HOW ABOUT IT, SPOCK? IS IT SAFE TO GO THROUGH?
DON'T FORGET THE "CAN-WE-GET-BACK" PART.

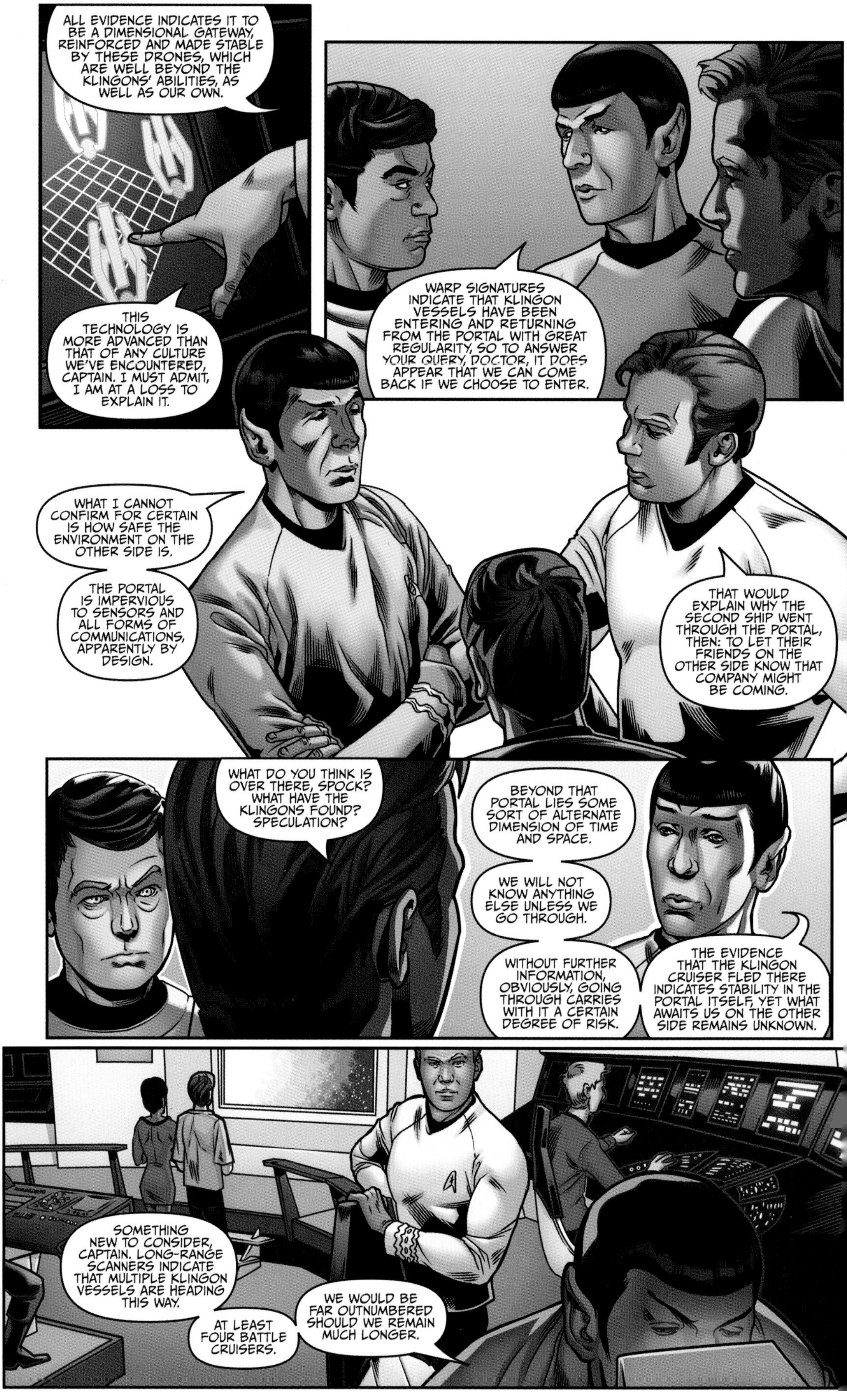
ALL EVIDENCE INDICATES IT TO BE A DIMENSIONAL GATEWAY, REINFORCED AND MADE STABLE BY THESE DRONES, WHICH ARE WELL BEYOND THE KLINGONS' ABILITIES, AS WELL AS OUR OWN.
THIS TECHNOLOGY IS MORE ADVANCED THAN THAT OF ANY CULTURE WE'VE ENCOUNTERED, CAPTAIN. I MUST ADMIT, I AM AT A LOSS TO EXPLAIN IT.
WARP SIGNATURES INDICATE THAT KLINGON VESSELS HAVE BEEN ENTERING AND RETURNING FROM THE PORTAL WITH GREAT REGULARITY, SO TO ANSWER YOUR QUERY, DOCTOR, IT DOES APPEAR THAT WE CAN COME BACK IF WE CHOOSE TO ENTER.
WHAT I CANNOT CONFIRM FOR CERTAIN IS HOW SAFE THE ENVIRONMENT ON THE OTHER SIDE IS.
THE PORTAL IS IMPERVIOUS TO SENSORS AND ALL FORMS OF COMMUNICATIONS, APPARENTLY BY DESIGN.
THAT WOULD EXPLAIN WHY THE SECOND SHIP WENT THROUGH THE PORTAL, THEN: TO LET THEIR FRIENDS ON THE OTHER SIDE KNOW THAT COMPANY MIGHT BE COMING.
WHAT DO YOU THINK IS OVER THERE, SPOCK? WHAT HAVE THE KLINGONS FOUND? SPECULATION?
BEYOND THAT PORTAL LIES SOME SORT OF ALTERNATE DIMENSION OF TIME AND SPACE.
WE WILL NOT KNOW ANYTHING ELSE UNLESS WE GO THROUGH.
WITHOUT FURTHER INFORMATION, OBVIOUSLY, GOING THROUGH CARRIES WITH IT A CERTAIN DEGREE OF RISK.
THE EVIDENCE THAT THE KLINGON CRUISER FLED THERE INDICATES STABILITY IN THE PORTAL ITSELF, YET WHAT AWAITS US ON THE OTHER SIDE REMAINS UNKNOWN.
SOMETHING NEW TO CONSIDER, CAPTAIN. LONG-RANGE SCANNERS INDICATE THAT MULTIPLE KLINGON VESSELS ARE HEADING THIS WAY.
AT LEAST FOUR BATTLE CRUISERS.
WE WOULD BE FAR OUTNUMBERED SHOULD WE REMAIN MUCH LONGER.

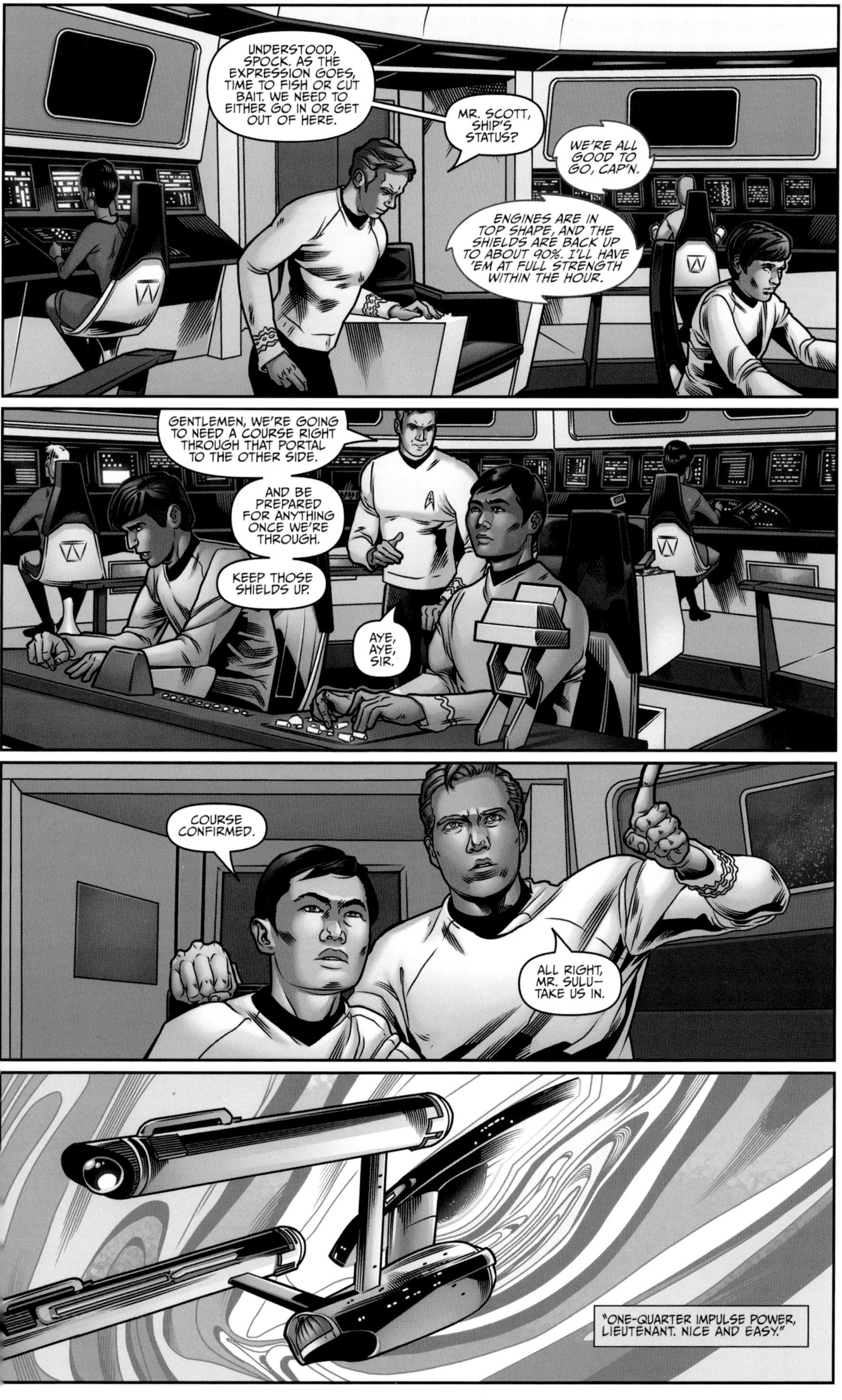
UNDERSTOOD, SPOCK. AS THE EXPRESSION GOES, TIME TO FISH OR CUT BAIT. WE NEED TO EITHER GO IN OR GET OUT OF HERE.
MR. SCOTT, SHIP'S STATUS?
WE'RE ALL GOOD TO GO, CAP'N.
ENGINES ARE IN TOP SHAPE, AND THE SHIELDS ARE BACK UP TO ABOUT 90%. I'LL HAVE 'EM AT FULL STRENGTH WITHIN THE HOUR.
GENTLEMEN, WE'RE GOING TO NEED A COURSE RIGHT THROUGH THAT PORTAL TO THE OTHER SIDE.
AND BE PREPARED FOR ANYTHING ONCE WE'RE THROUGH.
KEEP THOSE SHIELDS UP.
AYE, AYE, SIR.
COURSE CONFIRMED.
ALL RIGHT, MR. SULU– TAKE US IN.
"ONE-QUARTER IMPULSE POWER, LIEUTENANT. NICE AND EASY."

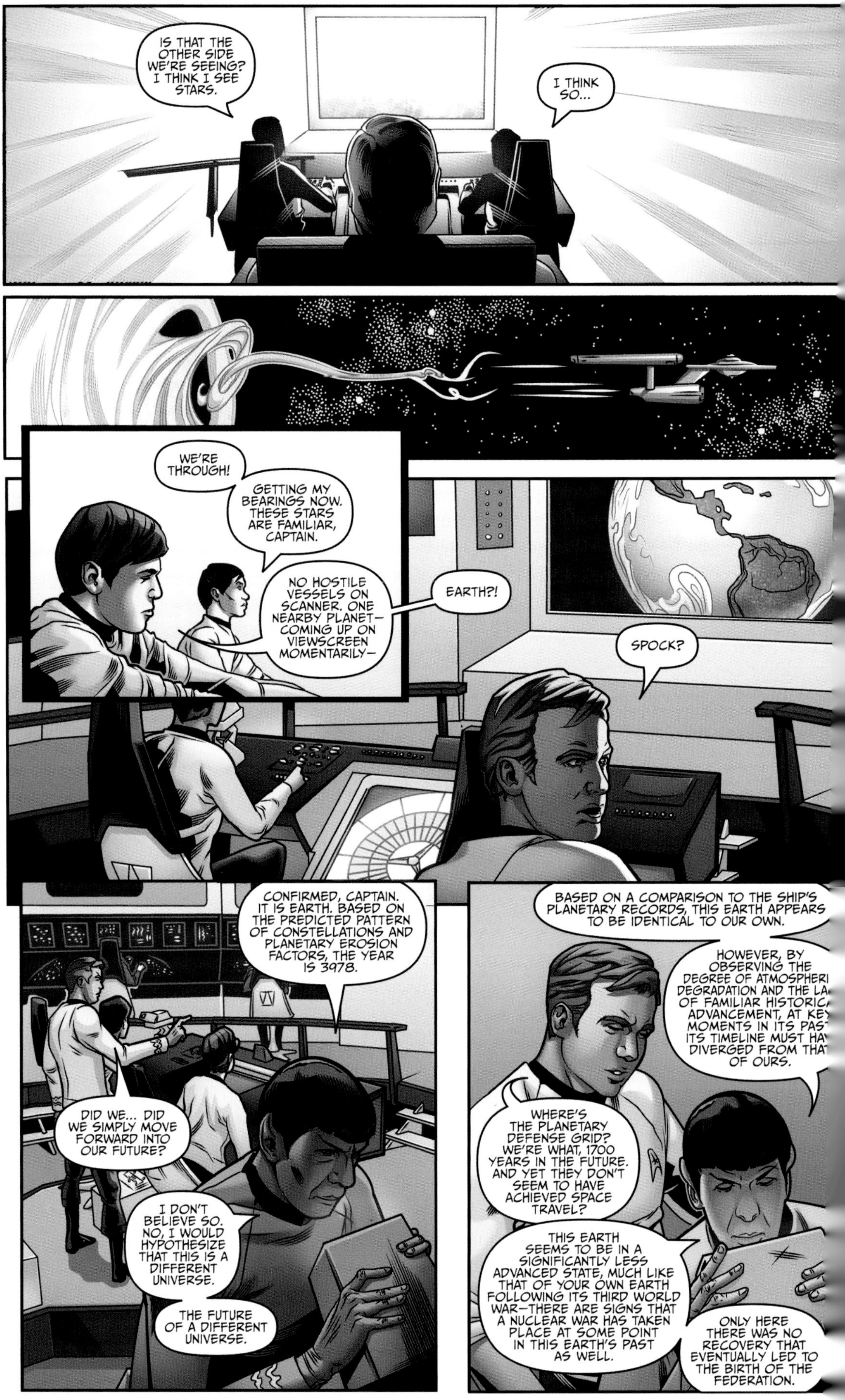
IS THAT THE OTHER SIDE WE'RE SEEING? I THINK I SEE STARS.
I THINK SO...
WE'RE THROUGH!
GETTING MY BEARINGS NOW. THESE STARS ARE FAMILIAR, CAPTAIN.
NO HOSTILE VESSELS ON SCANNER. ONE NEARBY PLANET-- COMING UP ON VIEWSCREEN MOMENTARILY--
EARTH?!
SPOCK?
CONFIRMED, CAPTAIN. IT IS EARTH. BASED ON THE PREDICTED PATTERN OF CONSTELLATIONS AND PLANETARY EROSION FACTORS, THE YEAR IS 3978.
DID WE... DID WE SIMPLY MOVE FORWARD INTO OUR FUTURE?
I DON'T BELIEVE SO. NO, I WOULD HYPOTHESIZE THAT THIS IS A DIFFERENT UNIVERSE.
THE FUTURE OF A DIFFERENT UNIVERSE.
BASED ON A COMPARISON TO THE SHIP'S PLANETARY RECORDS, THIS EARTH APPEARS TO BE IDENTICAL TO OUR OWN.
WHERE'S THE PLANETARY DEFENSE GRID? WE'RE WHAT, 1700 YEARS IN THE FUTURE. AND YET THEY DON'T SEEM TO HAVE ACHIEVED SPACE TRAVEL?
THIS EARTH SEEMS TO BE IN A SIGNIFICANTLY LESS ADVANCED STATE, MUCH LIKE THAT OF YOUR OWN EARTH FOLLOWING ITS THIRD WORLD WAR--THERE ARE SIGNS THAT A NUCLEAR WAR HAS TAKEN PLACE AT SOME POINT IN THIS EARTH'S PAST AS WELL.
ONLY HERE THERE WAS NO RECOVERY THAT EVENTUALLY LED TO THE BIRTH OF THE FEDERATION.

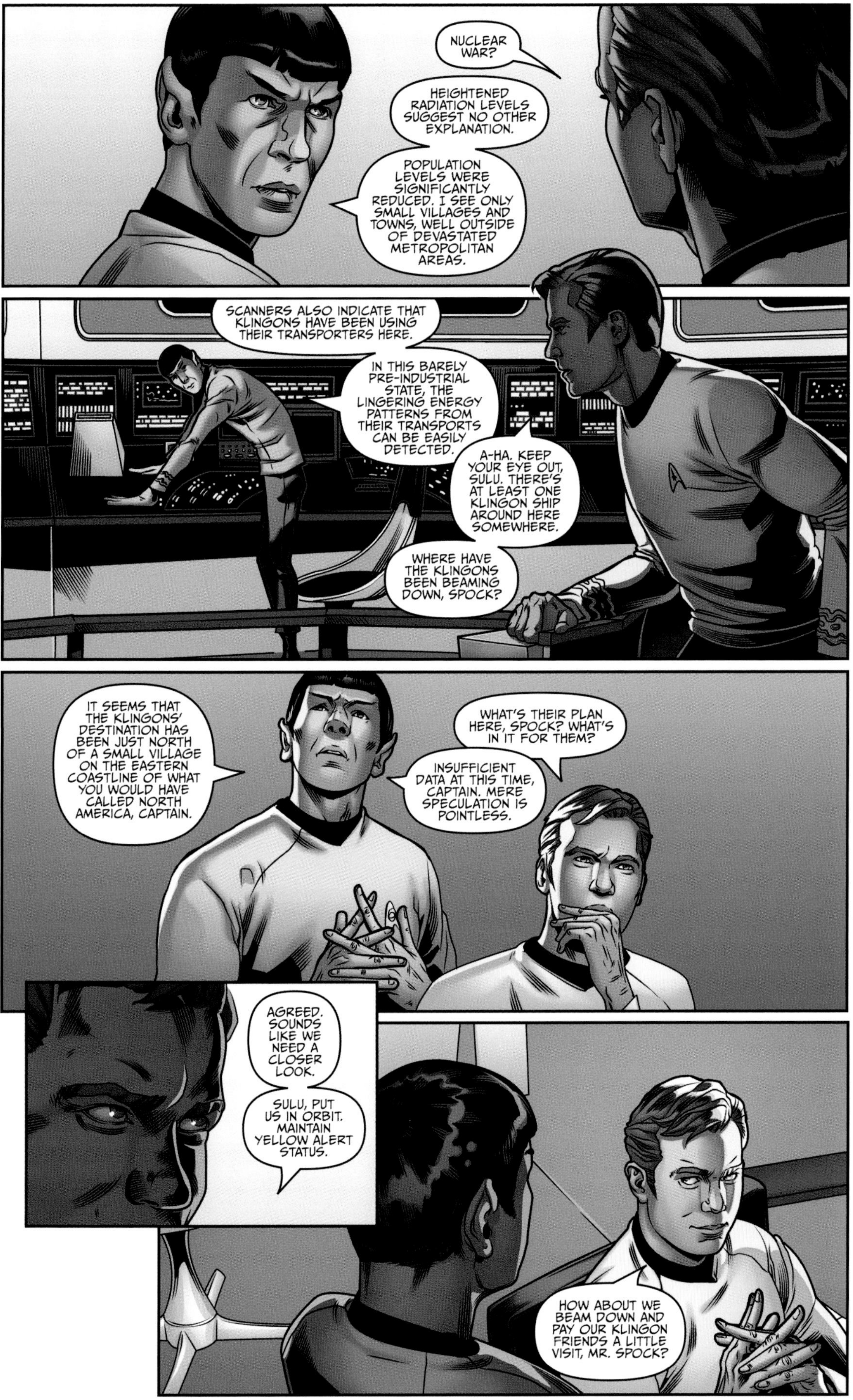
NUCLEAR WAR?
HEIGHTENED RADIATION LEVELS SUGGEST NO OTHER EXPLANATION.
POPULATION LEVELS WERE SIGNIFICANTLY REDUCED. I SEE ONLY SMALL VILLAGES AND TOWNS, WELL OUTSIDE OF DEVASTATED METROPOLITAN AREAS.
SCANNERS ALSO INDICATE THAT KLINGONS HAVE BEEN USING THEIR TRANSPORTERS HERE.
IN THIS BARELY PRE-INDUSTRIAL STATE, THE LINGERING ENERGY PATTERNS FROM THEIR TRANSPORTS CAN BE EASILY DETECTED.
A-HA. KEEP YOUR EYE OUT, SULU. THERE'S AT LEAST ONE KLINGON SHIP AROUND HERE SOMEWHERE.
WHERE HAVE THE KLINGONS BEEN BEAMING DOWN, SPOCK?
IT SEEMS THAT THE KLINGONS' DESTINATION HAS BEEN JUST NORTH OF A SMALL VILLAGE ON THE EASTERN COASTLINE OF WHAT YOU WOULD HAVE CALLED NORTH AMERICA, CAPTAIN.
WHAT'S THEIR PLAN HERE, SPOCK? WHAT'S IN IT FOR THEM?
INSUFFICIENT DATA AT THIS TIME, CAPTAIN. MERE SPECULATION IS POINTLESS.
AGREED. SOUNDS LIKE WE NEED A CLOSER LOOK.
SULU, PUT US IN ORBIT. MAINTAIN YELLOW ALERT STATUS.
HOW ABOUT WE BEAM DOWN AND PAY OUR KLINGON FRIENDS A LITTLE VISIT, MR. SPOCK?

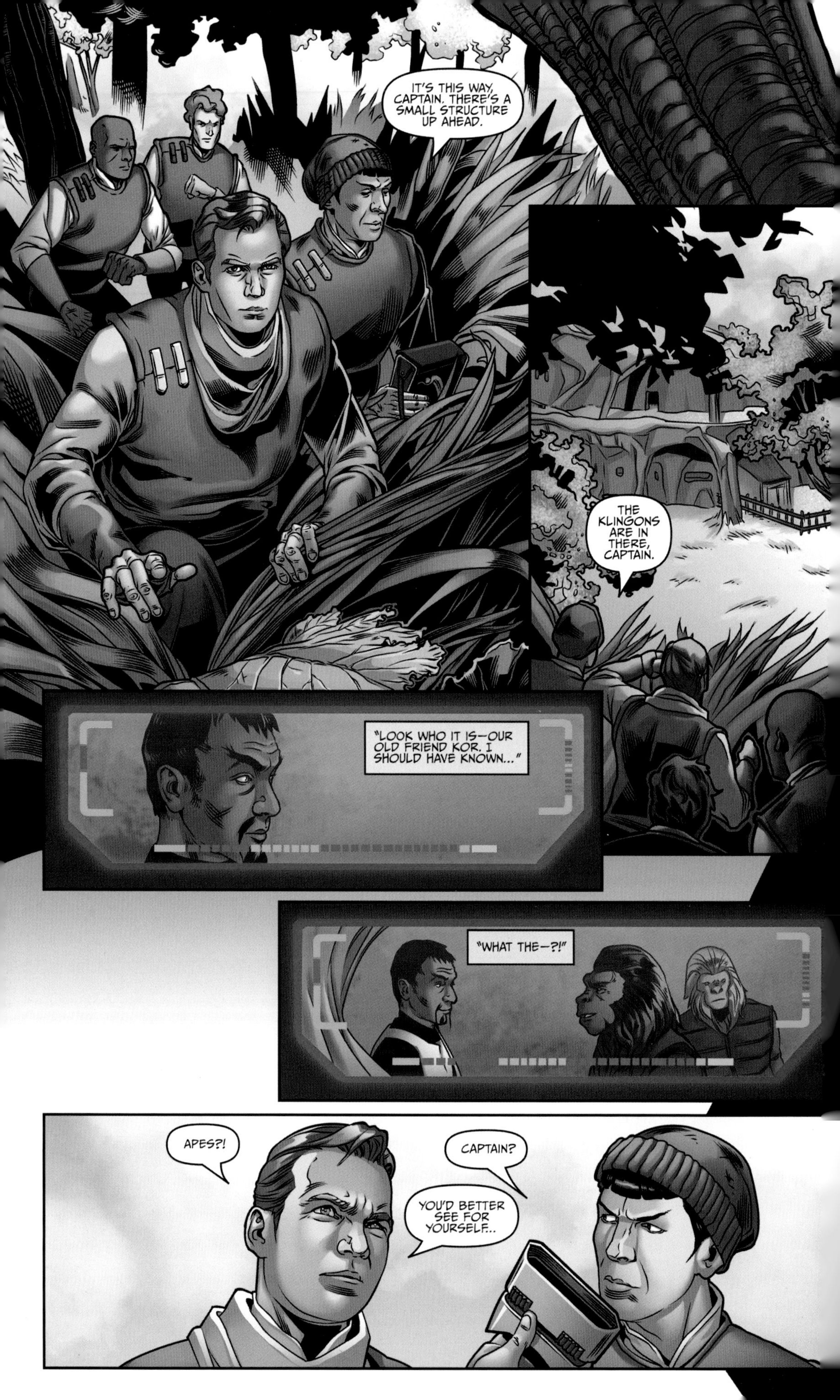

IT'S THIS WAY, CAPTAIN. THERE'S A SMALL STRUCTURE UP AHEAD.
THE KLINGONS ARE IN THERE, CAPTAIN.
"LOOK WHO IT IS—OUR OLD FRIEND KOR. I SHOULD HAVE KNOWN..."
"WHAT THE—?!"
APES?!
CAPTAIN?
YOU'D BETTER SEE FOR YOURSELF...

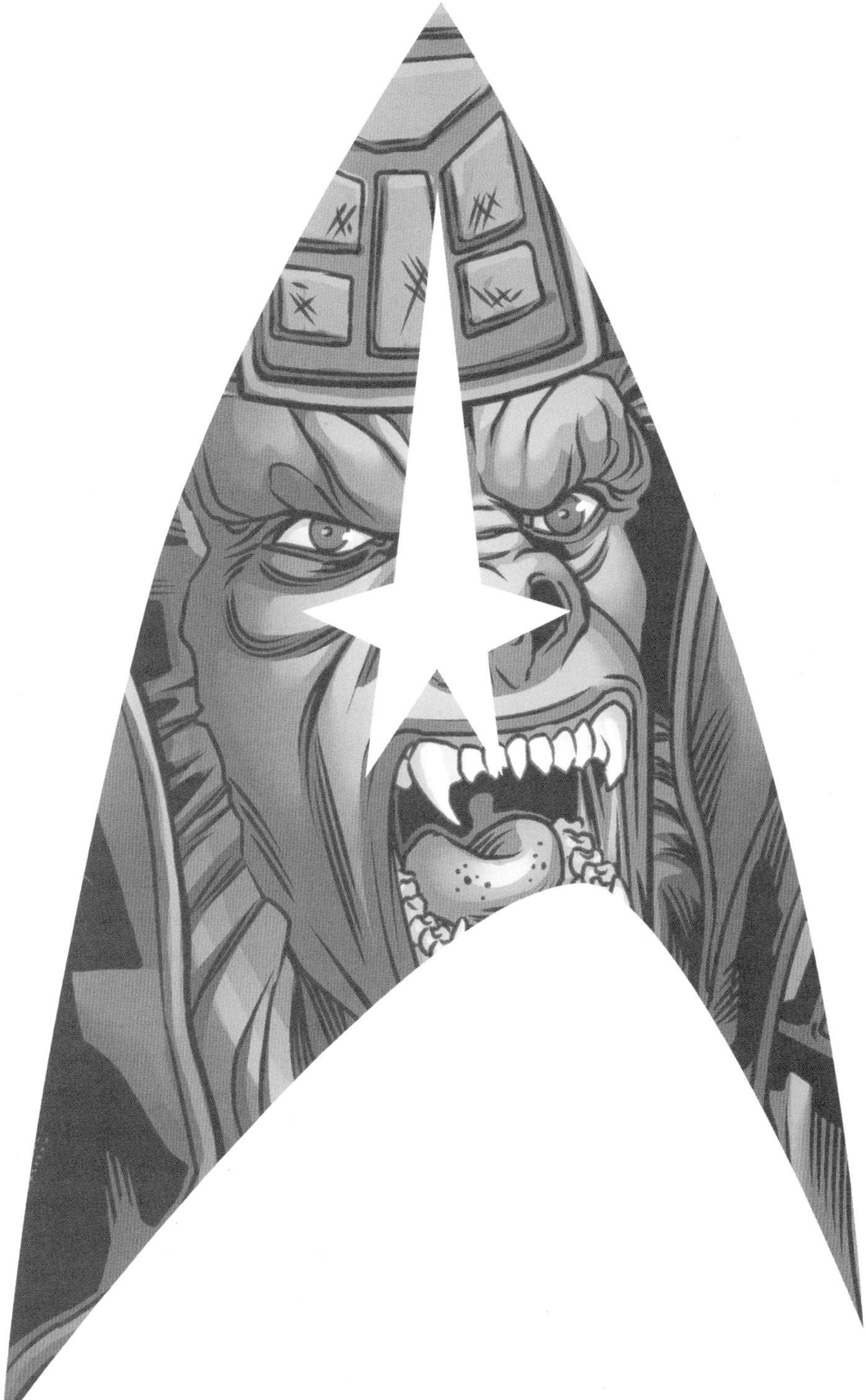

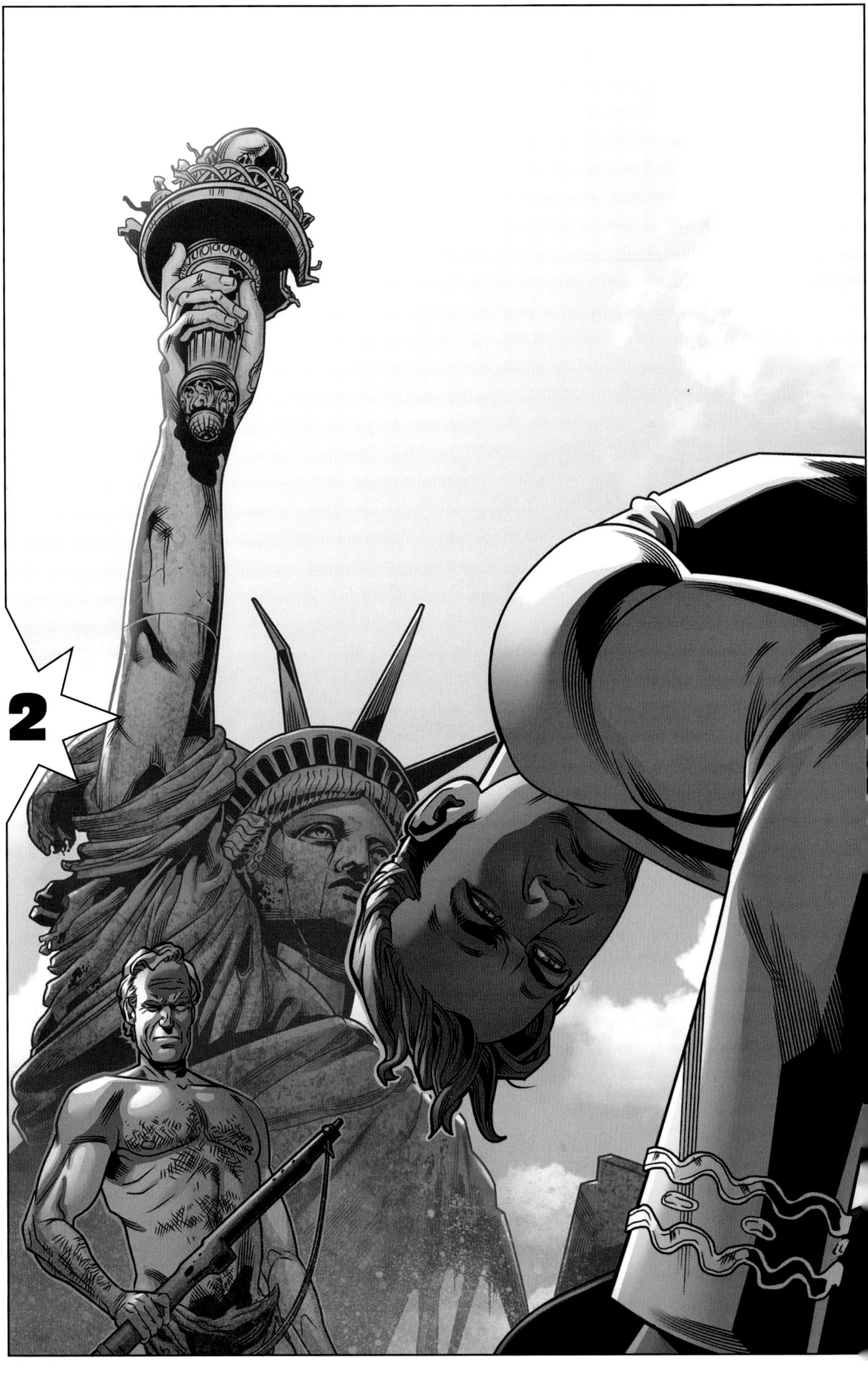
2

BY **RACHAEL STOTT** COLORS BY **CHARLIE KIRCHOFF**

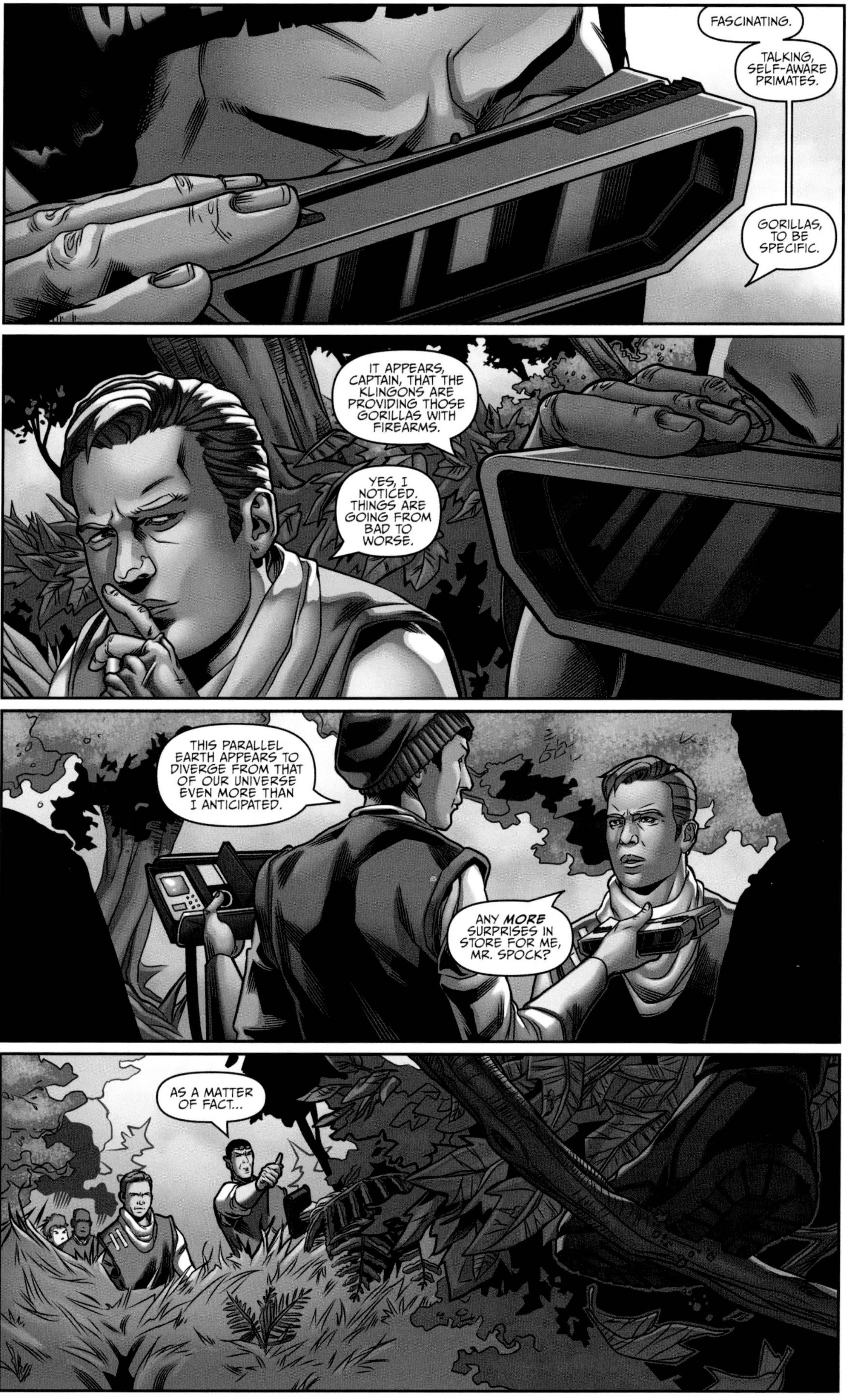

FASCINATING.
TALKING, SELF-AWARE PRIMATES.
GORILLAS, TO BE SPECIFIC.
IT APPEARS, CAPTAIN, THAT THE KLINGONS ARE PROVIDING THOSE GORILLAS WITH FIREARMS.
YES, I NOTICED. THINGS ARE GOING FROM BAD TO WORSE.
THIS PARALLEL EARTH APPEARS TO DIVERGE FROM THAT OF OUR UNIVERSE EVEN MORE THAN I ANTICIPATED.
ANY *MORE* SURPRISES IN STORE FOR ME, MR. SPOCK?
AS A MATTER OF FACT...

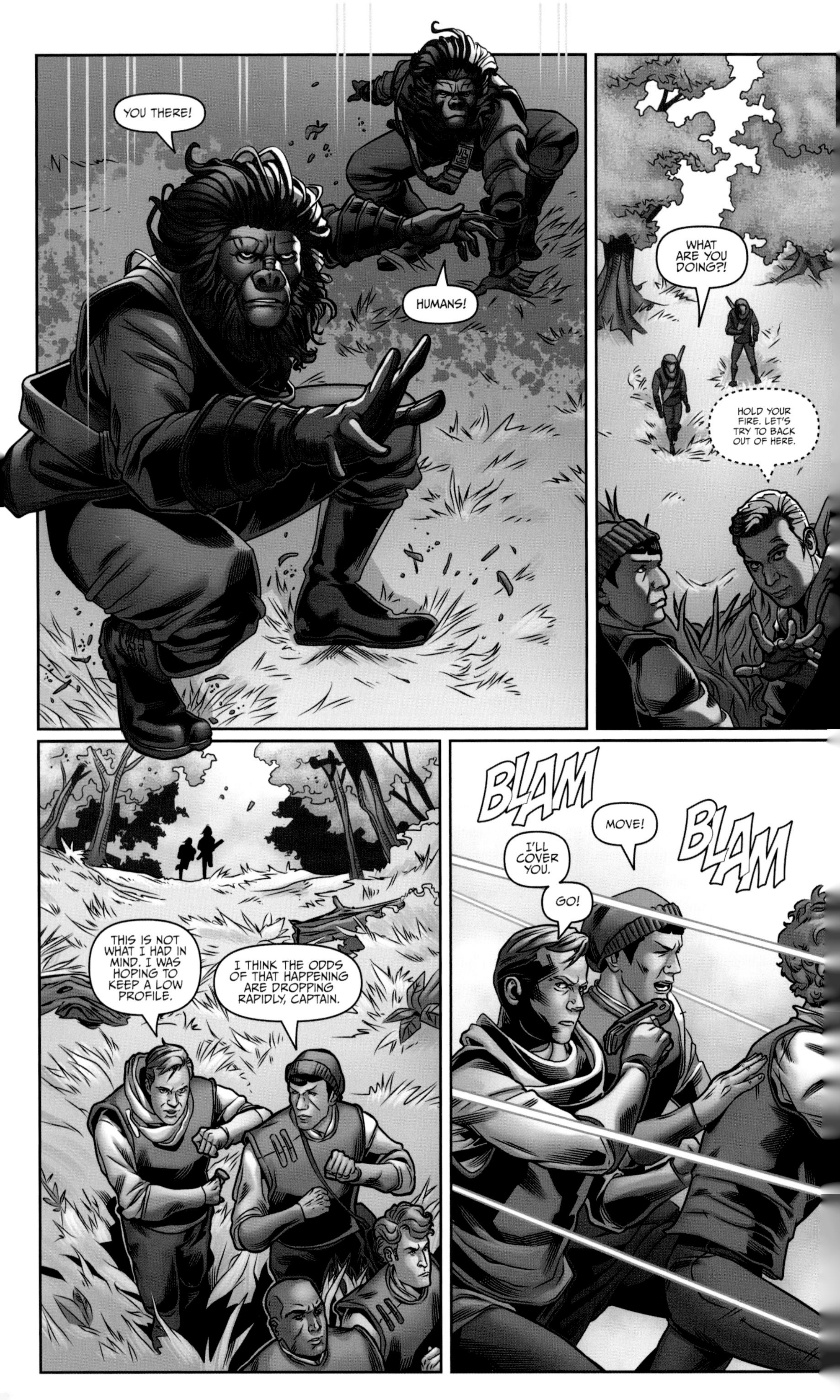
YOU THERE!
HUMANS!
WHAT ARE YOU DOING?!
HOLD YOUR FIRE. LET'S TRY TO BACK OUT OF HERE.
THIS IS NOT WHAT I HAD IN MIND. I WAS HOPING TO KEEP A LOW PROFILE.
I THINK THE ODDS OF THAT HAPPENING ARE DROPPING RAPIDLY, CAPTAIN.
BLAM
MOVE!
BLAM
I'LL COVER YOU.
GO!

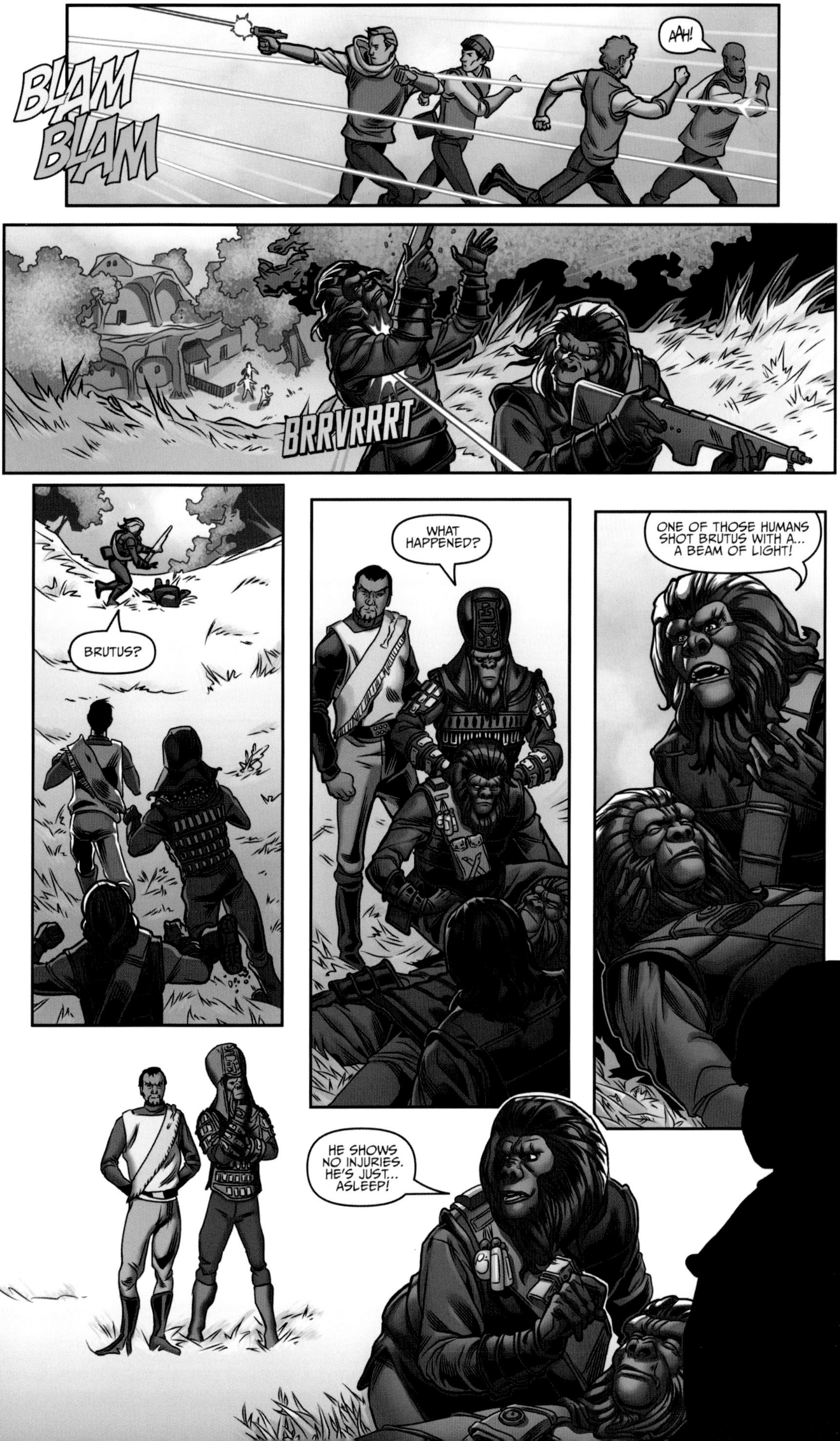
BLAM
BLAM
AAH!
BRRVRRRT
BRUTUS?
WHAT HAPPENED?
ONE OF THOSE HUMANS SHOT BRUTUS WITH A... A BEAM OF LIGHT!
HE SHOWS NO INJURIES. HE'S JUST... ASLEEP!

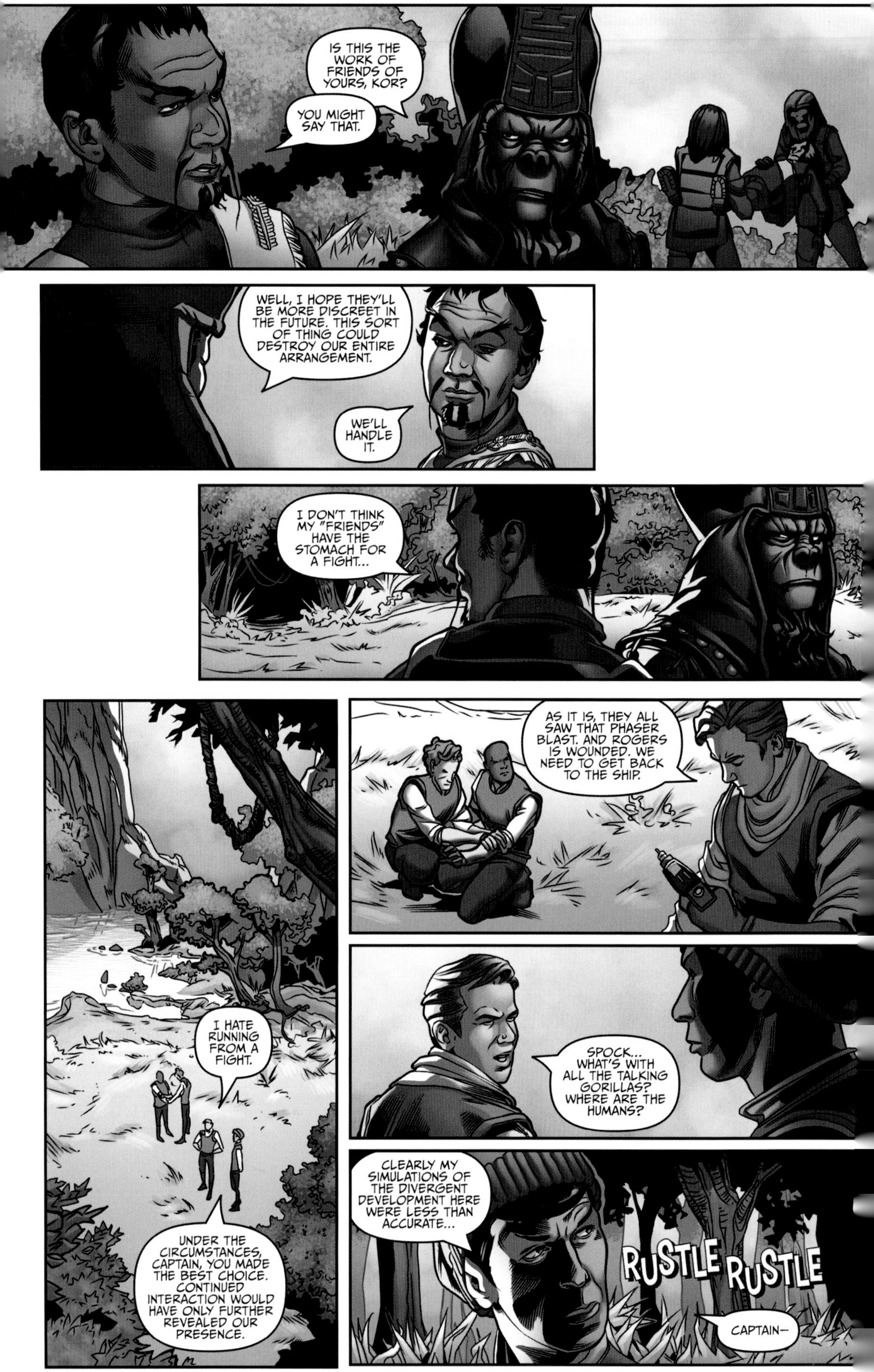
IS THIS THE WORK OF FRIENDS OF YOURS, KOR?
YOU MIGHT SAY THAT.
WELL, I HOPE THEY'LL BE MORE DISCREET IN THE FUTURE. THIS SORT OF THING COULD DESTROY OUR ENTIRE ARRANGEMENT.
WE'LL HANDLE IT.
I DON'T THINK MY "FRIENDS" HAVE THE STOMACH FOR A FIGHT...
I HATE RUNNING FROM A FIGHT.
UNDER THE CIRCUMSTANCES, CAPTAIN, YOU MADE THE BEST CHOICE. CONTINUED INTERACTION WOULD HAVE ONLY FURTHER REVEALED OUR PRESENCE.
AS IT IS, THEY ALL SAW THAT PHASER BLAST. AND ROGERS IS WOUNDED. WE NEED TO GET BACK TO THE SHIP.
SPOCK... WHAT'S WITH ALL THE TALKING GORILLAS? WHERE ARE THE HUMANS?
CLEARLY MY SIMULATIONS OF THE DIVERGENT DEVELOPMENT HERE WERE LESS THAN ACCURATE...
RUSTLE RUSTLE
CAPTAIN—

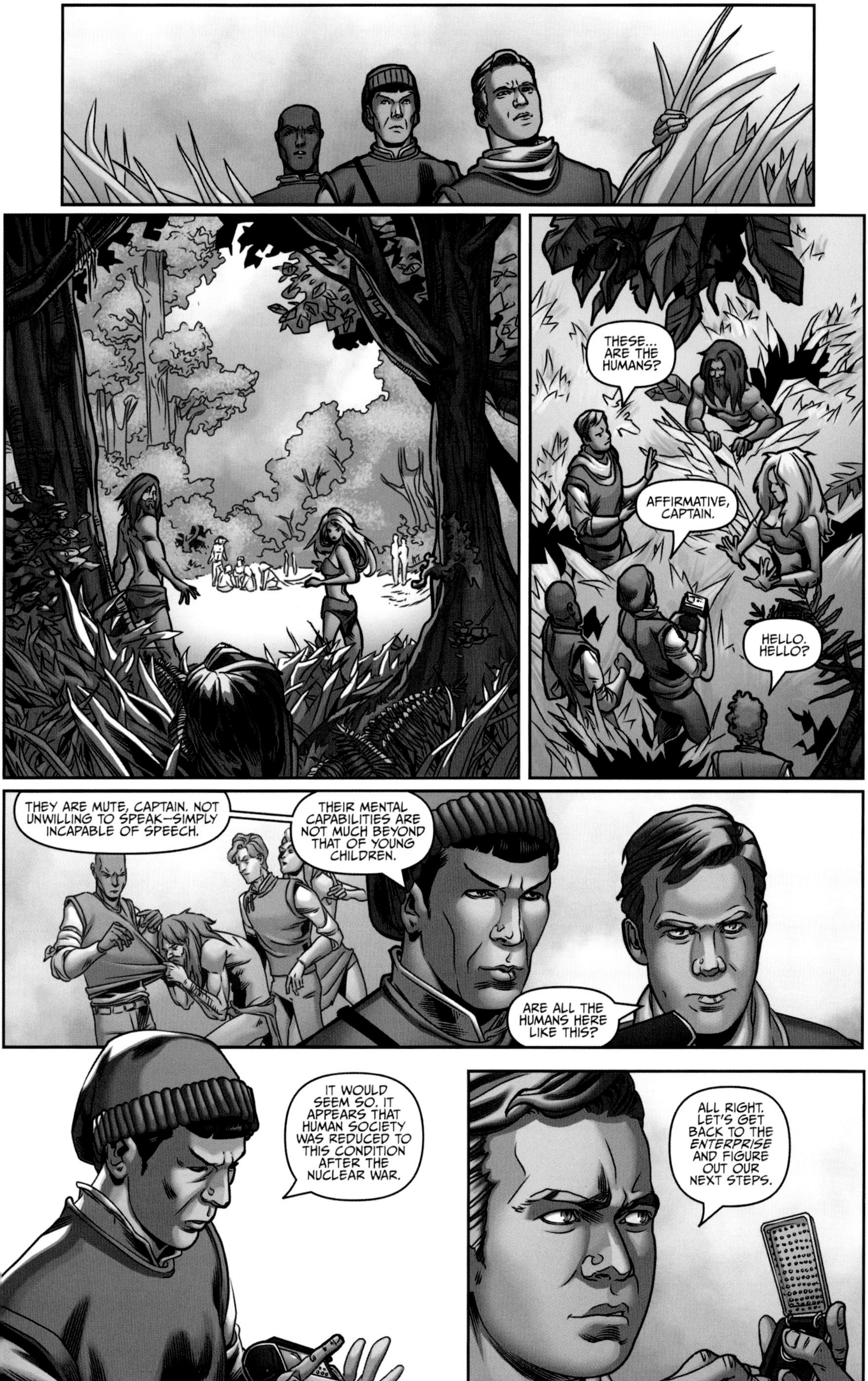
THESE... ARE THE HUMANS?
AFFIRMATIVE, CAPTAIN.
HELLO. HELLO?
THEY ARE MUTE, CAPTAIN. NOT UNWILLING TO SPEAK—SIMPLY INCAPABLE OF SPEECH.
THEIR MENTAL CAPABILITIES ARE NOT MUCH BEYOND THAT OF YOUNG CHILDREN.
ARE ALL THE HUMANS HERE LIKE THIS?
IT WOULD SEEM SO. IT APPEARS THAT HUMAN SOCIETY WAS REDUCED TO THIS CONDITION AFTER THE NUCLEAR WAR.
ALL RIGHT. LET'S GET BACK TO THE *ENTERPRISE* AND FIGURE OUT OUR NEXT STEPS.

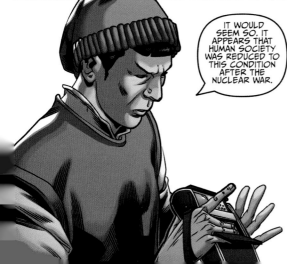

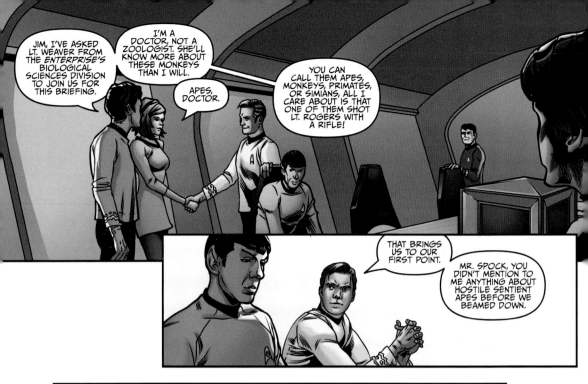

JIM, I'VE ASKED LT. WEAVER FROM THE *ENTERPRISE'S* BIOLOGICAL SCIENCES DIVISION TO JOIN US FOR THIS BRIEFING.

I'M A DOCTOR, NOT A ZOOLOGIST. SHE'LL KNOW MORE ABOUT THESE MONKEYS THAN I WILL.

APES, DOCTOR.

YOU CAN CALL THEM APES, MONKEYS, PRIMATES, OR SIMIANS, ALL I CARE ABOUT IS THAT ONE OF THEM SHOT LT. ROGERS WITH A RIFLE!

THAT BRINGS US TO OUR FIRST POINT.

MR. SPOCK, YOU DIDN'T MENTION TO ME ANYTHING ABOUT HOSTILE SENTIENT APES BEFORE WE BEAMED DOWN.

I ADMIT, CAPTAIN, THAT I WAS TAKEN BY SURPRISE MYSELF. USING HODGKIN'S LAW OF PARALLEL PLANETARY DEVELOPMENT, I RAN SEVERAL SIMULATIONS THROUGH THE *ENTERPRISE'S* COMPUTER FOR SCENARIOS OF WHAT THIS ALTERNATIVE EARTH MIGHT BE LIKE.

WHAT I DID NOT FULLY APPRECIATE, HOWEVER, IS THAT THE NUCLEAR WAR THAT DEVASTATED THIS EARTH HAS INTRODUCED SO MANY VARIABLES INTO THE EQUATION THAT IT'S NEARLY IMPOSSIBLE TO MAKE ACCURATE PREDICTIONS OF PLANETARY DEVELOPMENT.

PLANETARY SCANS IDENTIFIED BIPEDAL PRIMATES, AND BOTH THE COMPUTER AND I MADE THE UNDERSTANDABLE BUT INACCURATE ASSUMPTION THAT THEY WERE ALL HUMANS.

THE APES ON THE PLANET BELOW SHOW ADVANCED THOUGHT PROCESSES AND LANGUAGE SKILLS. THEY ARE, I WOULD SAY, ROUGHLY COMPARABLE TO THE HUMANS OF OUR OWN UNIVERSE.

THEIR SOCIETAL STRUCTURE IS YOUNG, HOWEVER, AND STILL VERY MUCH IN THE PROCESS OF DEVELOPMENT.

FURTHER SIMULATIONS USING THE NEW DATA WE ACQUIRED SUGGEST THAT IN THE AFTERMATH OF NUCLEAR WAR, THE GORILLAS, CHIMPANZEES, AND ORANGUTANS THAT WERE ONCE HELD AS PETS ON THIS EARTH EMERGED AFTER THE HOLOCAUST AS THE DOMINANT SOCIETY.

HUMAN SOCIETY, IN CONTRAST, DEVASTATED BY WAR AND RADIOACTIVE CONTAMINATION, COMPLETELY COLLAPSED.

CAPTAIN, THIS IS A ONCE-IN-A-LIFETIME CHANCE TO STUDY PARALLEL AND DIVERGENT DEVELOPMENT.

THERE'S NEVER BEEN QUITE SUCH AN OPPORTUNITY TO OBSERVE THE PRINCIPLES OF HODGKIN'S LAW!

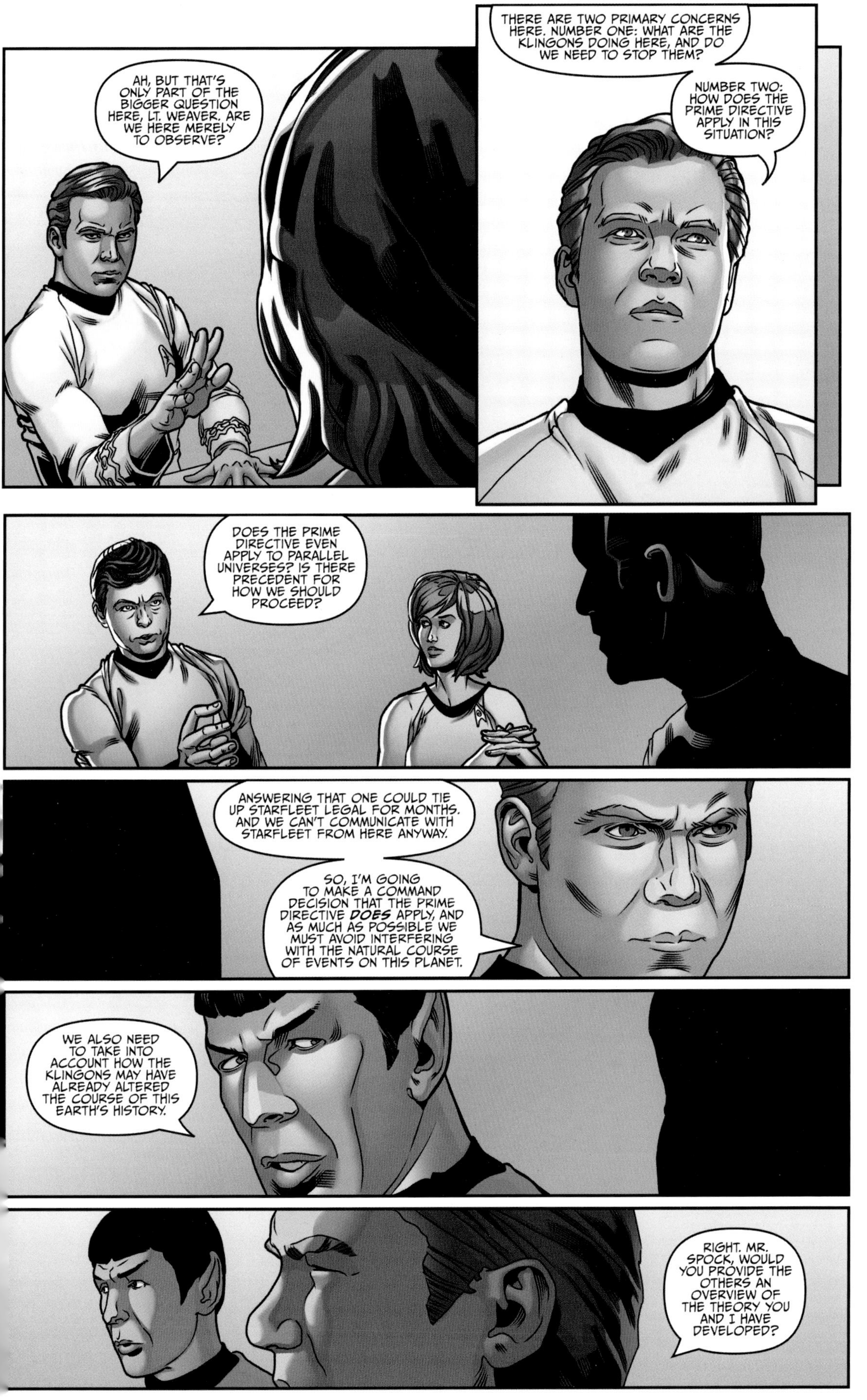
AH, BUT THAT'S ONLY PART OF THE BIGGER QUESTION HERE, LT. WEAVER. ARE WE HERE MERELY TO OBSERVE?
THERE ARE TWO PRIMARY CONCERNS HERE. NUMBER ONE: WHAT ARE THE KLINGONS DOING HERE, AND DO WE NEED TO STOP THEM?
NUMBER TWO: HOW DOES THE PRIME DIRECTIVE APPLY IN THIS SITUATION?
DOES THE PRIME DIRECTIVE EVEN APPLY TO PARALLEL UNIVERSES? IS THERE PRECEDENT FOR HOW WE SHOULD PROCEED?
ANSWERING THAT ONE COULD TIE UP STARFLEET LEGAL FOR MONTHS. AND WE CAN'T COMMUNICATE WITH STARFLEET FROM HERE ANYWAY.
SO, I'M GOING TO MAKE A COMMAND DECISION THAT THE PRIME DIRECTIVE DOES APPLY, AND AS MUCH AS POSSIBLE WE MUST AVOID INTERFERING WITH THE NATURAL COURSE OF EVENTS ON THIS PLANET.
WE ALSO NEED TO TAKE INTO ACCOUNT HOW THE KLINGONS MAY HAVE ALREADY ALTERED THE COURSE OF THIS EARTH'S HISTORY.
RIGHT. MR. SPOCK, WOULD YOU PROVIDE THE OTHERS AN OVERVIEW OF THE THEORY YOU AND I HAVE DEVELOPED?

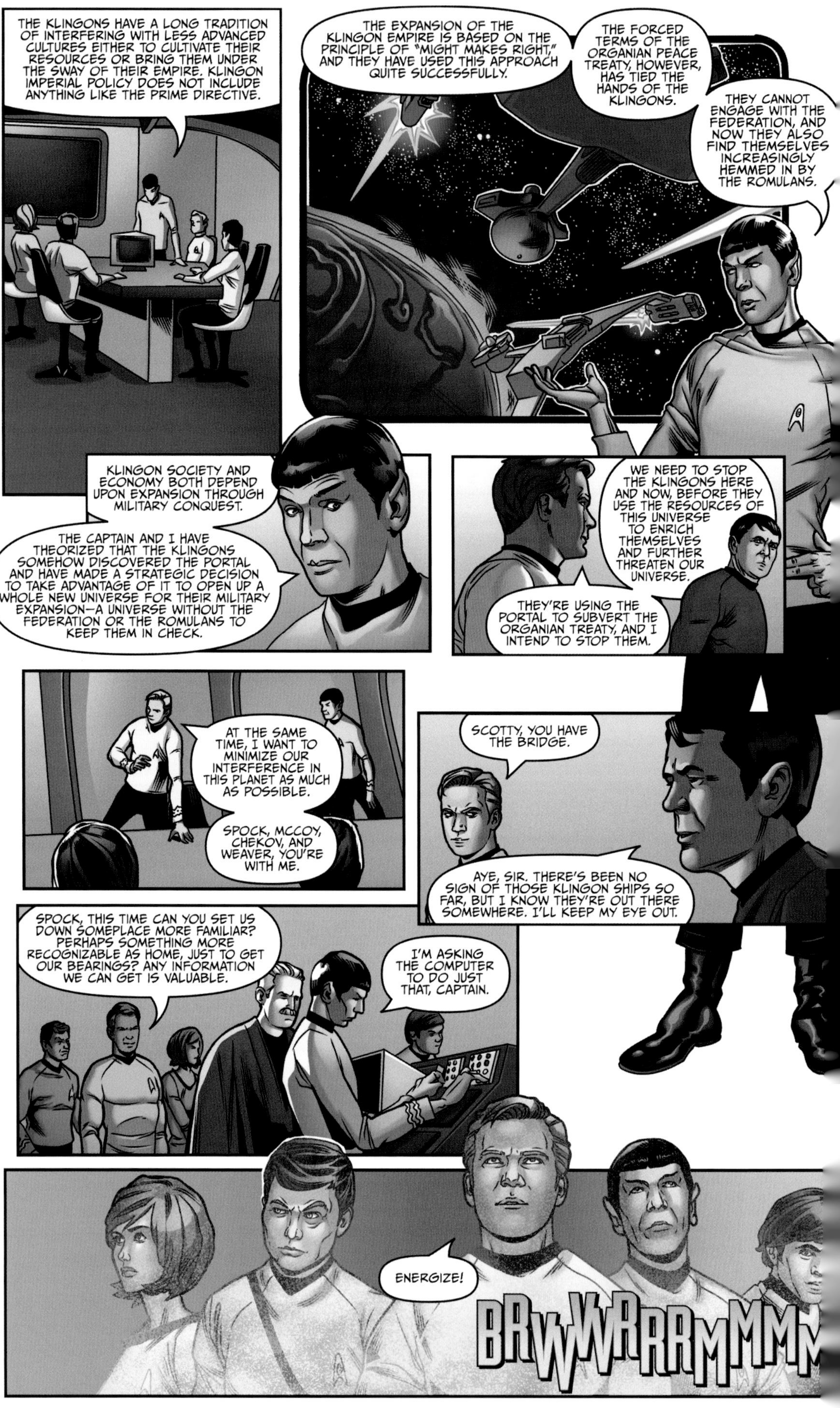
THE KLINGONS HAVE A LONG TRADITION OF INTERFERING WITH LESS ADVANCED CULTURES EITHER TO CULTIVATE THEIR RESOURCES OR BRING THEM UNDER THE SWAY OF THEIR EMPIRE. KLINGON IMPERIAL POLICY DOES NOT INCLUDE ANYTHING LIKE THE PRIME DIRECTIVE.
THE EXPANSION OF THE KLINGON EMPIRE IS BASED ON THE PRINCIPLE OF "MIGHT MAKES RIGHT," AND THEY HAVE USED THIS APPROACH QUITE SUCCESSFULLY.
THE FORCED TERMS OF THE ORGANIAN PEACE TREATY, HOWEVER, HAS TIED THE HANDS OF THE KLINGONS.
THEY CANNOT ENGAGE WITH THE FEDERATION, AND NOW THEY ALSO FIND THEMSELVES INCREASINGLY HEMMED IN BY THE ROMULANS.
KLINGON SOCIETY AND ECONOMY BOTH DEPEND UPON EXPANSION THROUGH MILITARY CONQUEST.
THE CAPTAIN AND I HAVE THEORIZED THAT THE KLINGONS SOMEHOW DISCOVERED THE PORTAL AND HAVE MADE A STRATEGIC DECISION TO TAKE ADVANTAGE OF IT TO OPEN UP A WHOLE NEW UNIVERSE FOR THEIR MILITARY EXPANSION—A UNIVERSE WITHOUT THE FEDERATION OR THE ROMULANS TO KEEP THEM IN CHECK.
WE NEED TO STOP THE KLINGONS HERE AND NOW, BEFORE THEY USE THE RESOURCES OF THIS UNIVERSE TO ENRICH THEMSELVES AND FURTHER THREATEN OUR UNIVERSE.
THEY'RE USING THE PORTAL TO SUBVERT THE ORGANIAN TREATY, AND I INTEND TO STOP THEM.
AT THE SAME TIME, I WANT TO MINIMIZE OUR INTERFERENCE IN THIS PLANET AS MUCH AS POSSIBLE.
SPOCK, MCCOY, CHEKOV, AND WEAVER, YOU'RE WITH ME.
SCOTTY, YOU HAVE THE BRIDGE.
AYE, SIR. THERE'S BEEN NO SIGN OF THOSE KLINGON SHIPS SO FAR, BUT I KNOW THEY'RE OUT THERE SOMEWHERE. I'LL KEEP MY EYE OUT.
SPOCK, THIS TIME CAN YOU SET US DOWN SOMEPLACE MORE FAMILIAR? PERHAPS SOMETHING MORE RECOGNIZABLE AS HOME, JUST TO GET OUR BEARINGS? ANY INFORMATION WE CAN GET IS VALUABLE.
I'M ASKING THE COMPUTER TO DO JUST THAT, CAPTAIN.
ENERGIZE!
BRWWVRRRMMMM

BRWWRRMMMM

GOOD LORD.

THIS IS NOT EXACTLY WHAT I HAD IN MIND, MR. SPOCK.

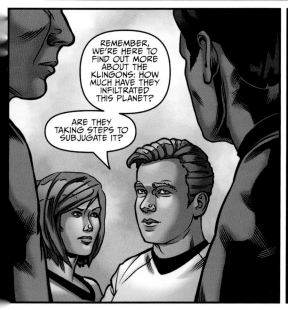

REMEMBER, WE'RE HERE TO FIND OUT MORE ABOUT THE KLINGONS: HOW MUCH HAVE THEY INFILTRATED THIS PLANET?

ARE THEY TAKING STEPS TO SUBJUGATE IT?

LOOK, FOOTPRINTS. AND NOT APE, EITHER— THOSE ARE HUMAN.

AND A HORSE, TOO.

THAT'S INTERESTING. I WOULDN'T HAVE EXPECTED THE HUMANS WE SAW EARLIER TO BE CAPABLE OF HORSEMANSHIP.

LET'S FOLLOW.

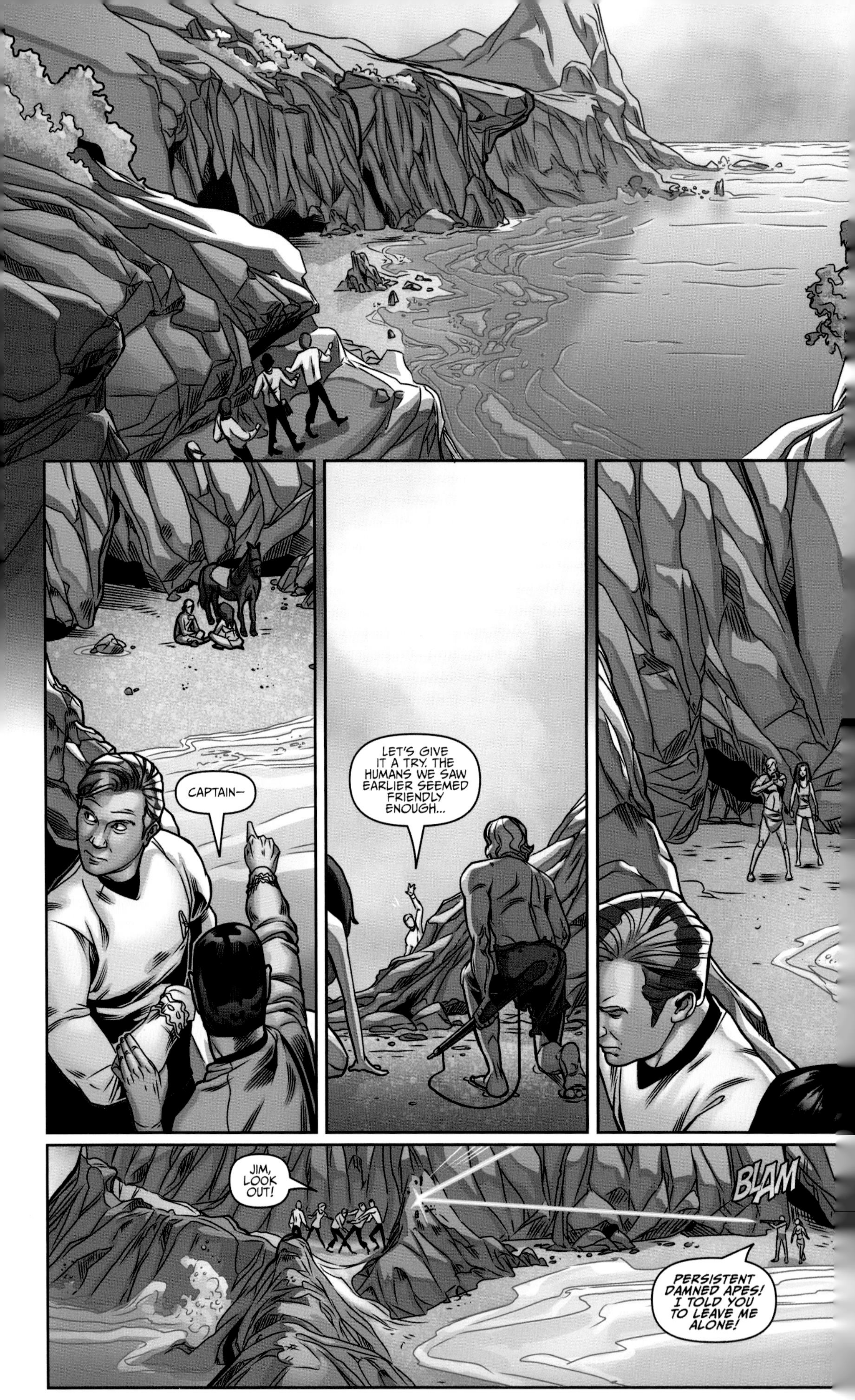
CAPTAIN—
LET'S GIVE IT A TRY. THE HUMANS WE SAW EARLIER SEEMED FRIENDLY ENOUGH...
JIM, LOOK OUT!
BLAM
PERSISTENT DAMNED APES! I TOLD YOU TO LEAVE ME ALONE!

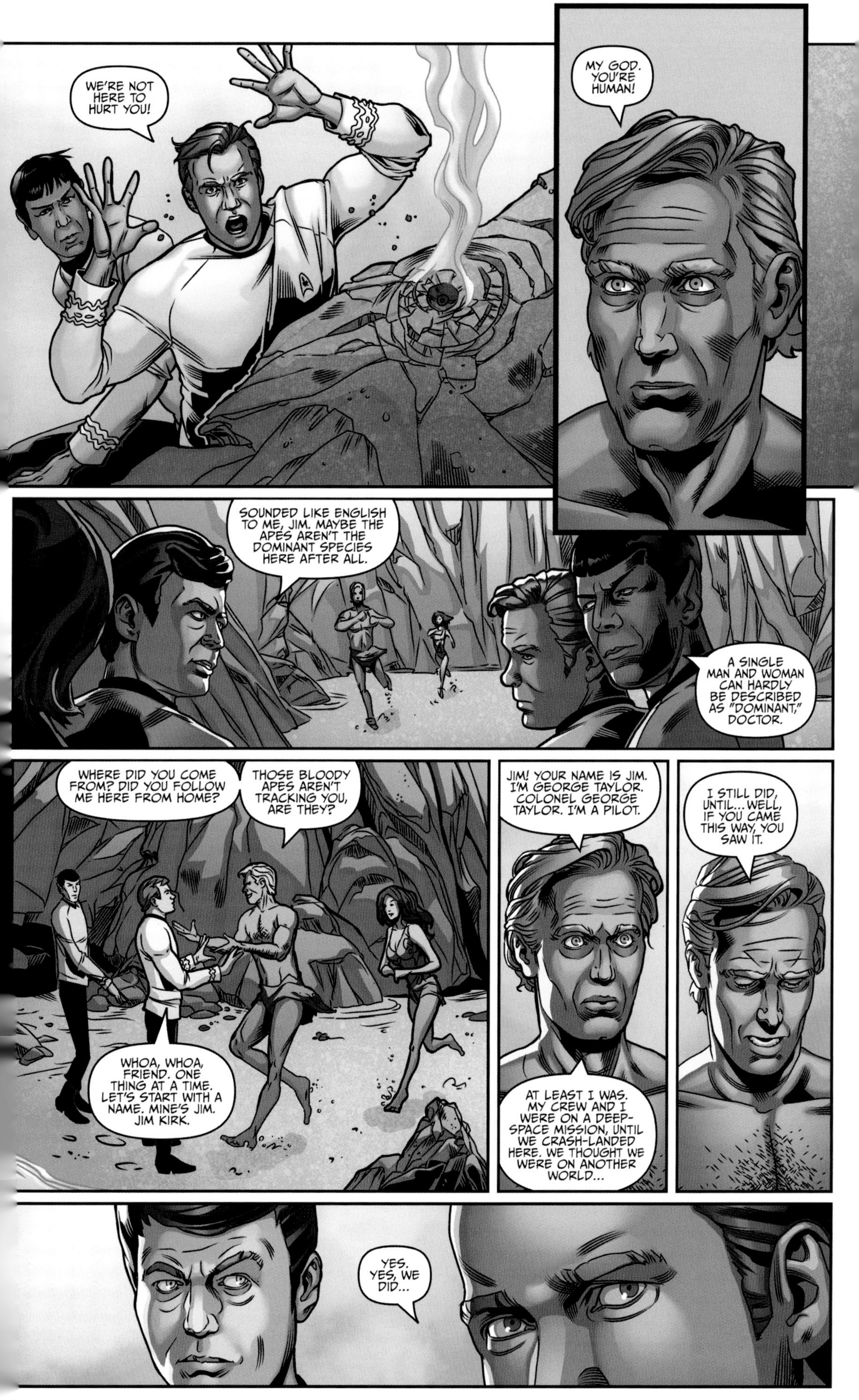
WE'RE NOT HERE TO HURT YOU!
MY GOD. YOU'RE HUMAN!
SOUNDED LIKE ENGLISH TO ME, JIM. MAYBE THE APES AREN'T THE DOMINANT SPECIES HERE AFTER ALL.
A SINGLE MAN AND WOMAN CAN HARDLY BE DESCRIBED AS "DOMINANT," DOCTOR.
WHERE DID YOU COME FROM? DID YOU FOLLOW ME HERE FROM HOME?
THOSE BLOODY APES AREN'T TRACKING YOU, ARE THEY?
WHOA, WHOA, FRIEND. ONE THING AT A TIME. LET'S START WITH A NAME. MINE'S JIM. JIM KIRK.
JIM! YOUR NAME IS JIM. I'M GEORGE TAYLOR. COLONEL GEORGE TAYLOR. I'M A PILOT.
AT LEAST I WAS. MY CREW AND I WERE ON A DEEP-SPACE MISSION, UNTIL WE CRASH-LANDED HERE. WE THOUGHT WE WERE ON ANOTHER WORLD...
I STILL DID, UNTIL... WELL, IF YOU CAME THIS WAY, YOU SAW IT.
YES. YES, WE DID...

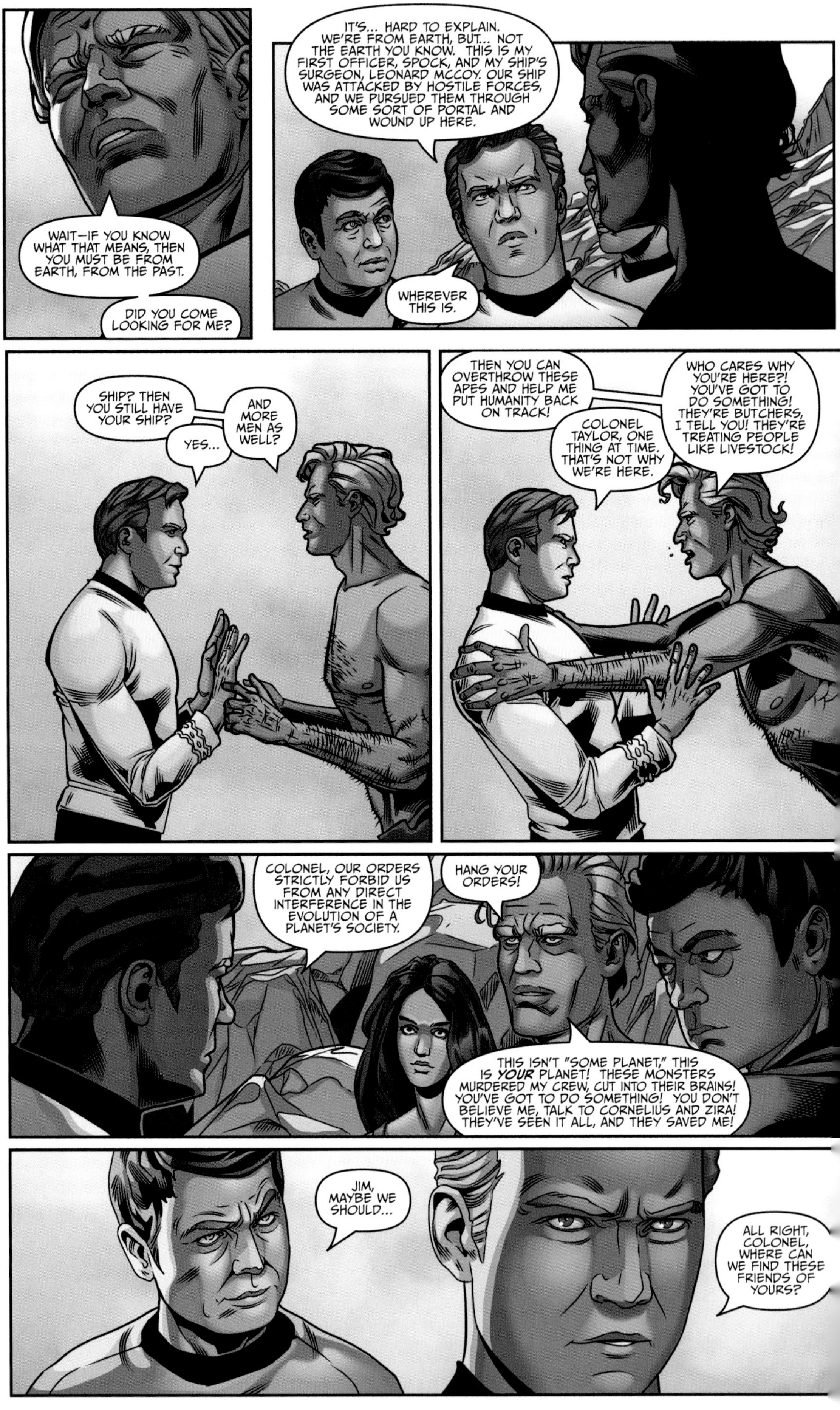
WAIT—IF YOU KNOW WHAT THAT MEANS, THEN YOU MUST BE FROM EARTH, FROM THE PAST.
DID YOU COME LOOKING FOR ME?
IT'S... HARD TO EXPLAIN. WE'RE FROM EARTH, BUT... NOT THE EARTH YOU KNOW. THIS IS MY FIRST OFFICER, SPOCK, AND MY SHIP'S SURGEON, LEONARD MCCOY. OUR SHIP WAS ATTACKED BY HOSTILE FORCES, AND WE PURSUED THEM THROUGH SOME SORT OF PORTAL AND WOUND UP HERE.
WHEREVER THIS IS.
SHIP? THEN YOU STILL HAVE YOUR SHIP?
YES...
AND MORE MEN AS WELL?
THEN YOU CAN OVERTHROW THESE APES AND HELP ME PUT HUMANITY BACK ON TRACK!
COLONEL TAYLOR, ONE THING AT TIME. THAT'S NOT WHY WE'RE HERE.
WHO CARES WHY YOU'RE HERE?! YOU'VE GOT TO DO SOMETHING! THEY'RE BUTCHERS, I TELL YOU! THEY'RE TREATING PEOPLE LIKE LIVESTOCK!
COLONEL, OUR ORDERS STRICTLY FORBID US FROM ANY DIRECT INTERFERENCE IN THE EVOLUTION OF A PLANET'S SOCIETY.
HANG YOUR ORDERS!
THIS ISN'T "SOME PLANET," THIS IS YOUR PLANET! THESE MONSTERS MURDERED MY CREW, CUT INTO THEIR BRAINS! YOU'VE GOT TO DO SOMETHING! YOU DON'T BELIEVE ME, TALK TO CORNELIUS AND ZIRA! THEY'VE SEEN IT ALL, AND THEY SAVED ME!
JIM, MAYBE WE SHOULD...
ALL RIGHT, COLONEL, WHERE CAN WE FIND THESE FRIENDS OF YOURS?

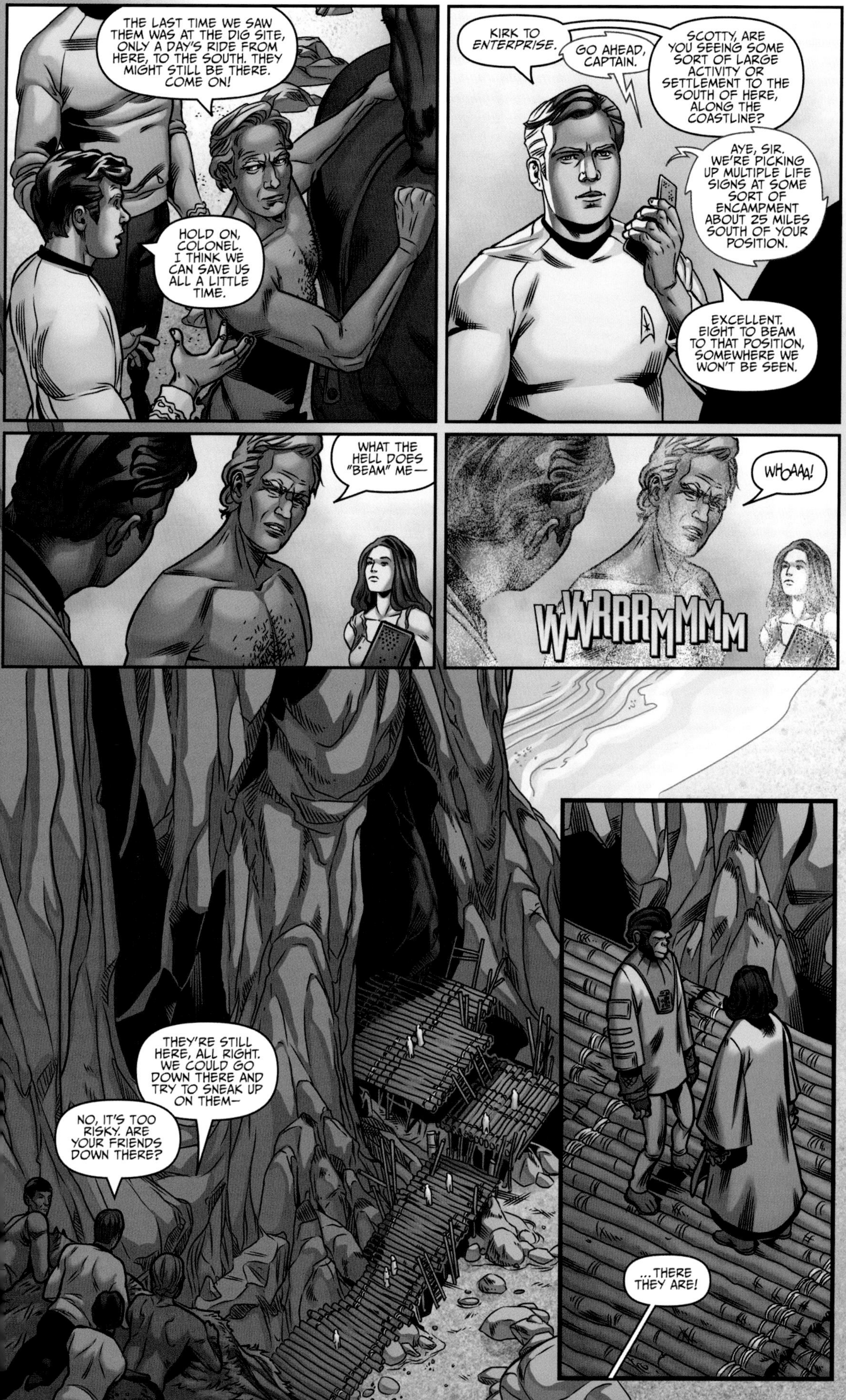
THE LAST TIME WE SAW THEM WAS AT THE DIG SITE, ONLY A DAY'S RIDE FROM HERE, TO THE SOUTH. THEY MIGHT STILL BE THERE. COME ON!
HOLD ON, COLONEL. I THINK WE CAN SAVE US ALL A LITTLE TIME.
KIRK TO ENTERPRISE.
GO AHEAD, CAPTAIN.
SCOTTY, ARE YOU SEEING SOME SORT OF LARGE ACTIVITY OR SETTLEMENT TO THE SOUTH OF HERE, ALONG THE COASTLINE?
AYE, SIR. WE'RE PICKING UP MULTIPLE LIFE SIGNS AT SOME SORT OF ENCAMPMENT ABOUT 25 MILES SOUTH OF YOUR POSITION.
EXCELLENT. EIGHT TO BEAM TO THAT POSITION, SOMEWHERE WE WON'T BE SEEN.
WHAT THE HELL DOES "BEAM" ME—
WHOAAA!
WWVRRRMMMM
THEY'RE STILL HERE, ALL RIGHT. WE COULD GO DOWN THERE AND TRY TO SNEAK UP ON THEM—
NO, IT'S TOO RISKY. ARE YOUR FRIENDS DOWN THERE?
...THERE THEY ARE!

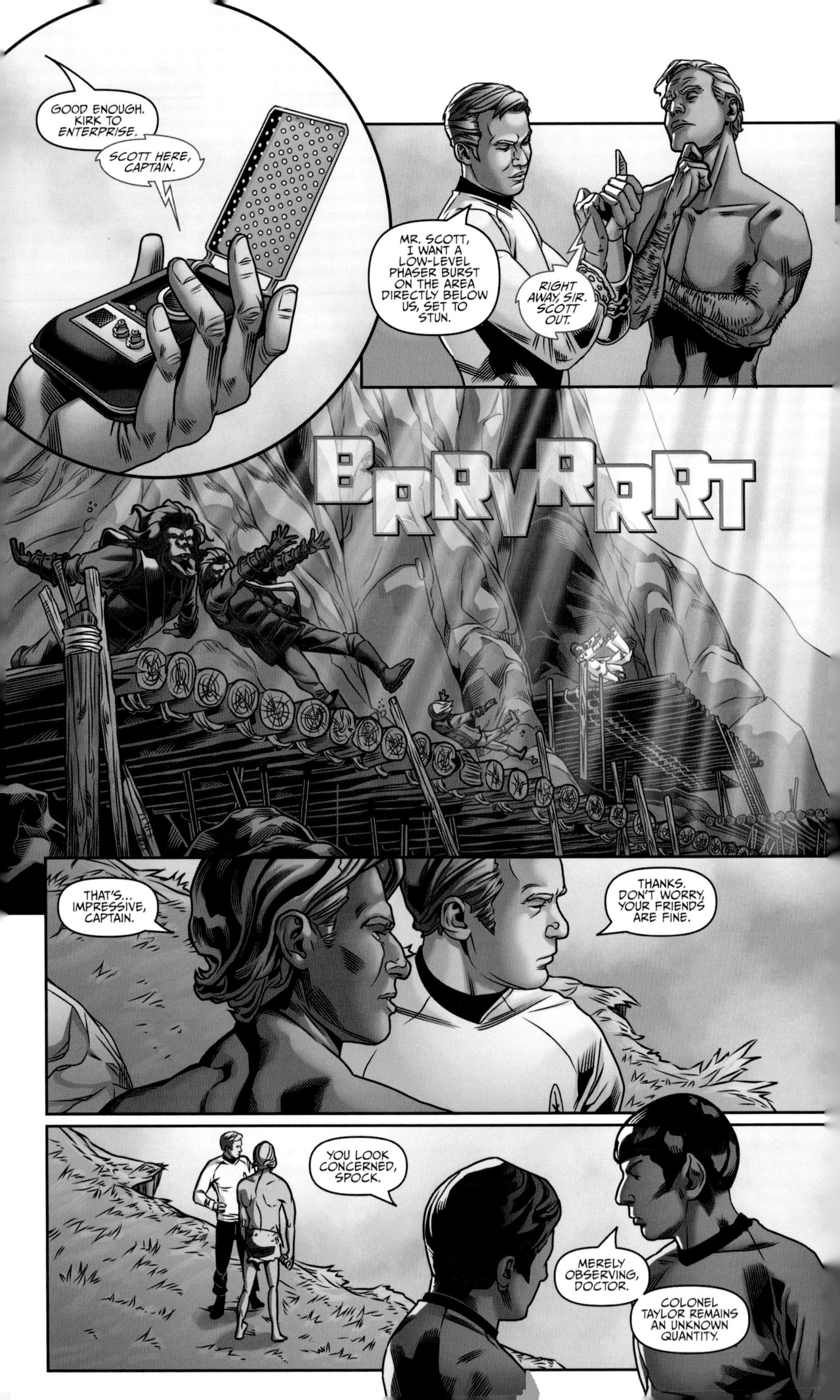
GOOD ENOUGH. KIRK TO ENTERPRISE.
SCOTT HERE, CAPTAIN.
MR. SCOTT, I WANT A LOW-LEVEL PHASER BURST ON THE AREA DIRECTLY BELOW US, SET TO STUN.
RIGHT AWAY, SIR. SCOTT OUT.
BRRVRRRT
THAT'S... IMPRESSIVE, CAPTAIN.
THANKS. DON'T WORRY, YOUR FRIENDS ARE FINE.
YOU LOOK CONCERNED, SPOCK.
MERELY OBSERVING, DOCTOR.
COLONEL TAYLOR REMAINS AN UNKNOWN QUANTITY.

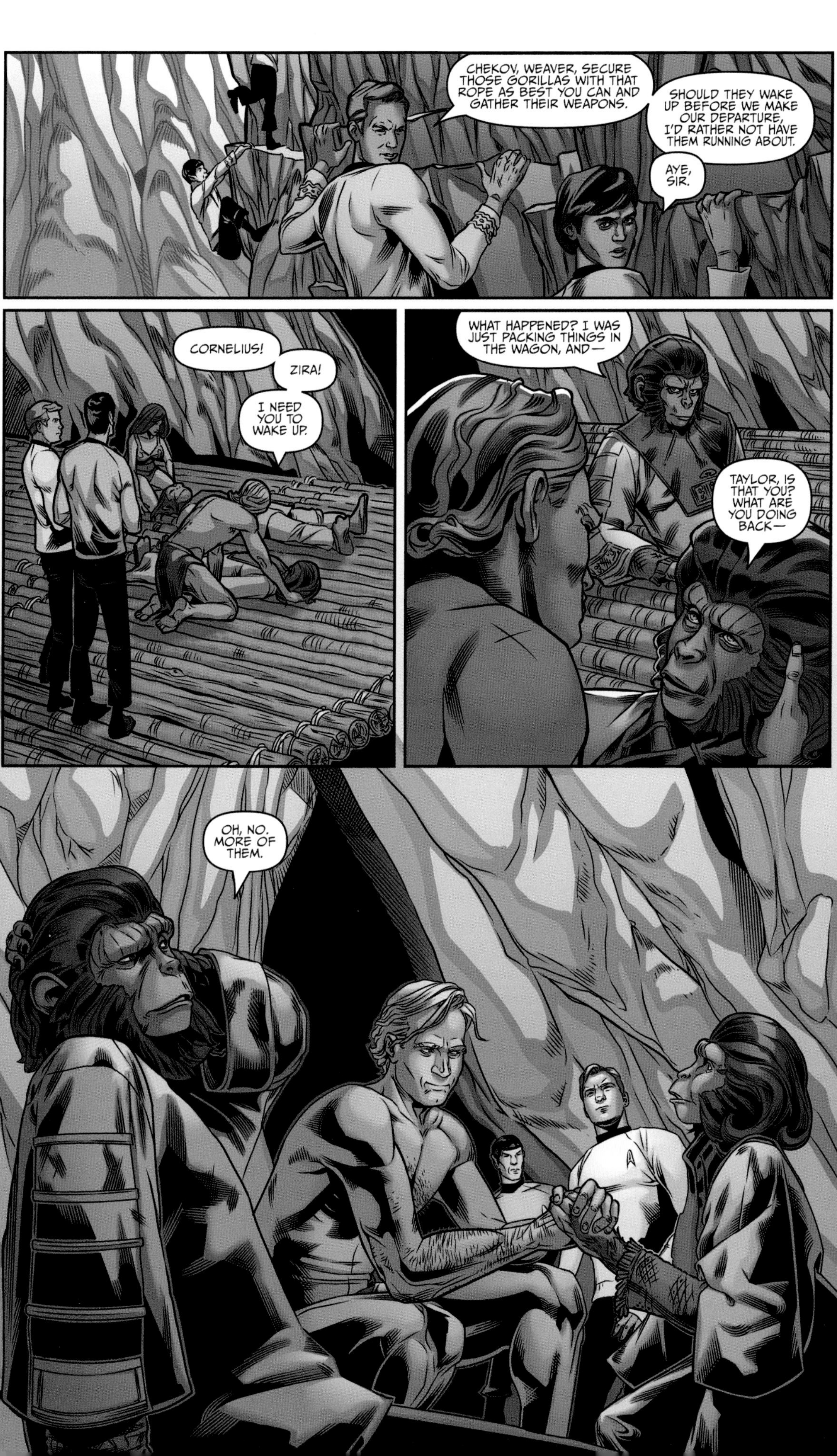
CHEKOV, WEAVER, SECURE THOSE GORILLAS WITH THAT ROPE AS BEST YOU CAN AND GATHER THEIR WEAPONS.
SHOULD THEY WAKE UP BEFORE WE MAKE OUR DEPARTURE, I'D RATHER NOT HAVE THEM RUNNING ABOUT.
AYE, SIR.
CORNELIUS!
ZIRA!
I NEED YOU TO WAKE UP.
WHAT HAPPENED? I WAS JUST PACKING THINGS IN THE WAGON, AND—
TAYLOR, IS THAT YOU? WHAT ARE YOU DOING BACK—
OH, NO. MORE OF THEM.

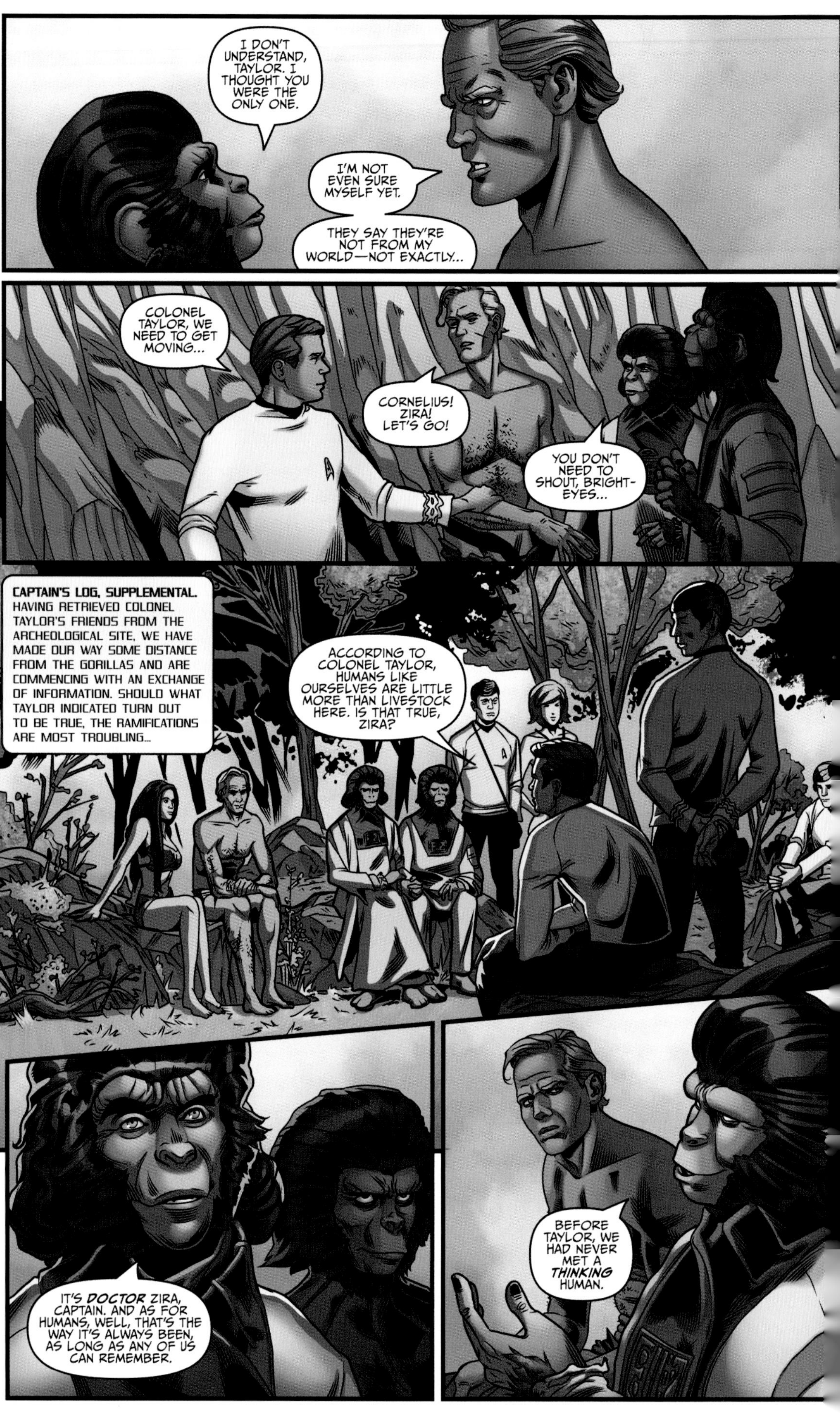
I DON'T UNDERSTAND, TAYLOR. I THOUGHT YOU WERE THE ONLY ONE.
I'M NOT EVEN SURE MYSELF YET.
THEY SAY THEY'RE NOT FROM MY WORLD—NOT EXACTLY...
COLONEL TAYLOR, WE NEED TO GET MOVING...
CORNELIUS! ZIRA! LET'S GO!
YOU DON'T NEED TO SHOUT, BRIGHT-EYES...
CAPTAIN'S LOG, SUPPLEMENTAL. HAVING RETRIEVED COLONEL TAYLOR'S FRIENDS FROM THE ARCHEOLOGICAL SITE, WE HAVE MADE OUR WAY SOME DISTANCE FROM THE GORILLAS AND ARE COMMENCING WITH AN EXCHANGE OF INFORMATION. SHOULD WHAT TAYLOR INDICATED TURN OUT TO BE TRUE, THE RAMIFICATIONS ARE MOST TROUBLING...
ACCORDING TO COLONEL TAYLOR, HUMANS LIKE OURSELVES ARE LITTLE MORE THAN LIVESTOCK HERE. IS THAT TRUE, ZIRA?
IT'S DOCTOR ZIRA, CAPTAIN. AND AS FOR HUMANS, WELL, THAT'S THE WAY IT'S ALWAYS BEEN, AS LONG AS ANY OF US CAN REMEMBER.
BEFORE TAYLOR, WE HAD NEVER MET A THINKING HUMAN.

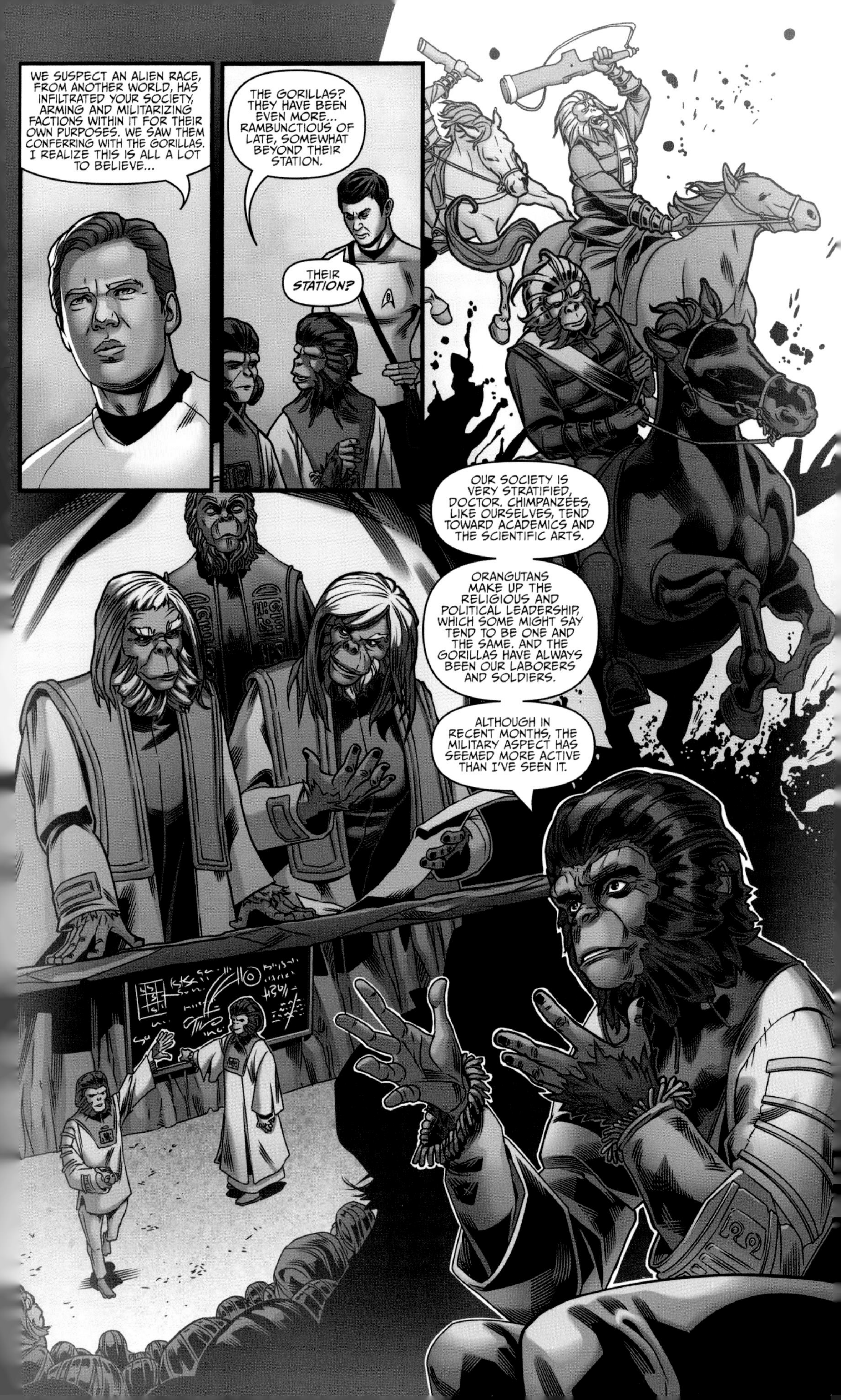

WE SUSPECT AN ALIEN RACE, FROM ANOTHER WORLD, HAS INFILTRATED YOUR SOCIETY, ARMING AND MILITARIZING FACTIONS WITHIN IT FOR THEIR OWN PURPOSES. WE SAW THEM CONFERRING WITH THE GORILLAS. I REALIZE THIS IS ALL A LOT TO BELIEVE...
THE GORILLAS? THEY HAVE BEEN EVEN MORE... RAMBUNCTIOUS OF LATE, SOMEWHAT BEYOND THEIR STATION.
THEIR *STATION?*
OUR SOCIETY IS VERY STRATIFIED, DOCTOR. CHIMPANZEES, LIKE OURSELVES, TEND TOWARD ACADEMICS AND THE SCIENTIFIC ARTS.
ORANGUTANS MAKE UP THE RELIGIOUS AND POLITICAL LEADERSHIP, WHICH SOME MIGHT SAY TEND TO BE ONE AND THE SAME. AND THE GORILLAS HAVE ALWAYS BEEN OUR LABORERS AND SOLDIERS.
ALTHOUGH IN RECENT MONTHS, THE MILITARY ASPECT HAS SEEMED MORE ACTIVE THAN I'VE SEEN IT.

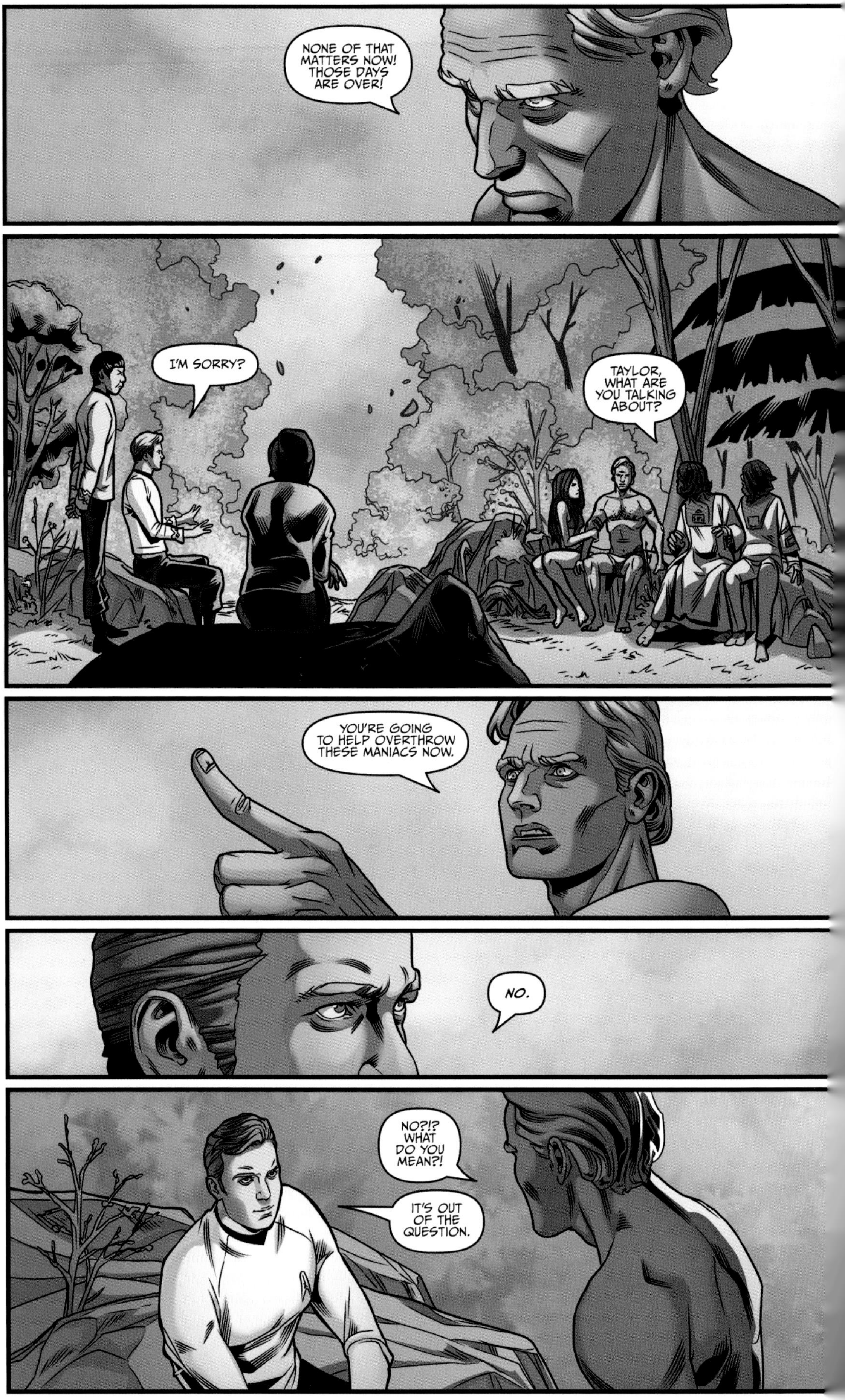
NONE OF THAT MATTERS NOW! THOSE DAYS ARE OVER!
I'M SORRY?
TAYLOR, WHAT ARE YOU TALKING ABOUT?
YOU'RE GOING TO HELP OVERTHROW THESE MANIACS NOW.
NO.
NO?!? WHAT DO YOU MEAN?!
IT'S OUT OF THE QUESTION.

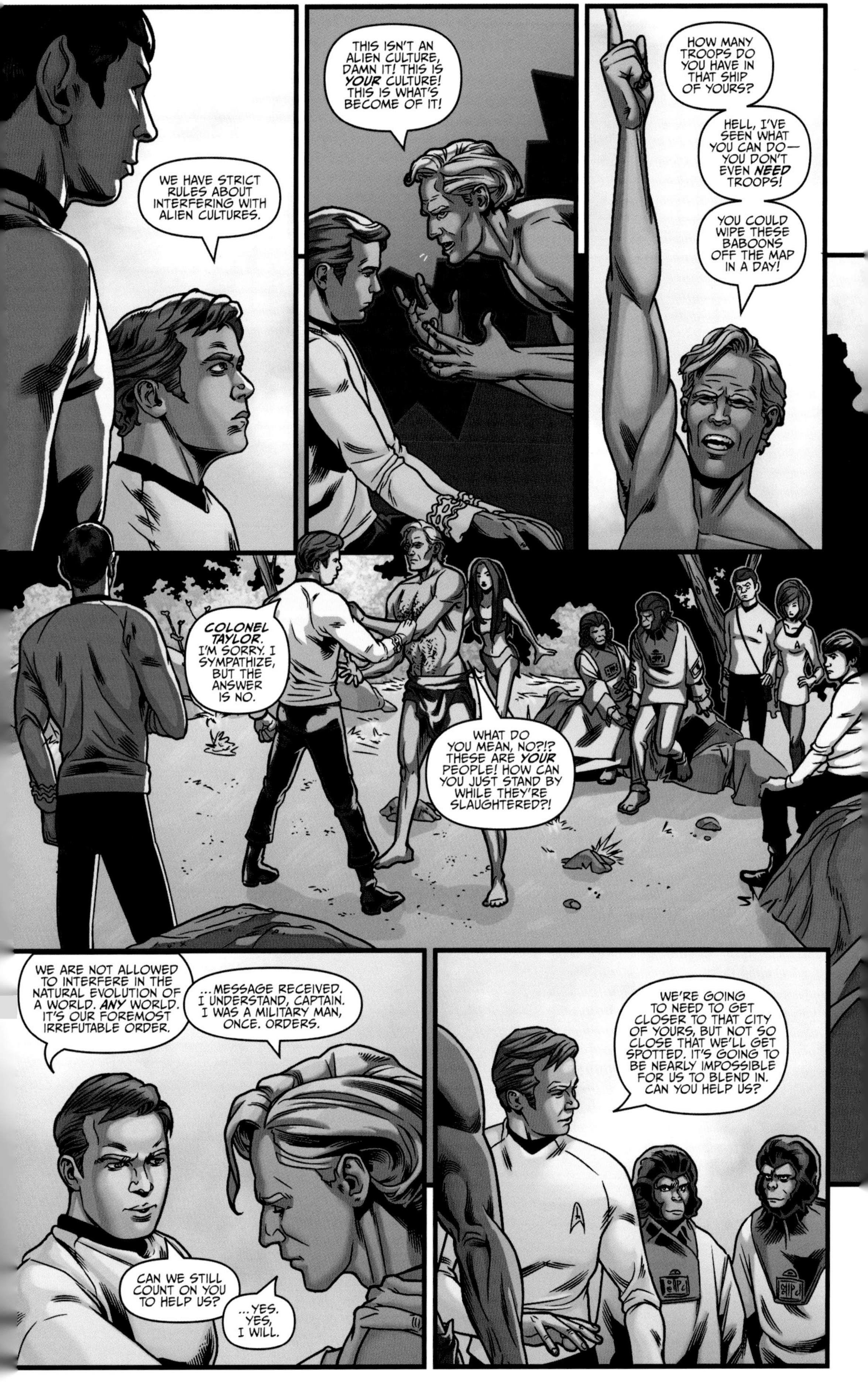
WE HAVE STRICT RULES ABOUT INTERFERING WITH ALIEN CULTURES.
THIS ISN'T AN ALIEN CULTURE, DAMN IT! THIS IS YOUR CULTURE! THIS IS WHAT'S BECOME OF IT!
HOW MANY TROOPS DO YOU HAVE IN THAT SHIP OF YOURS?
HELL, I'VE SEEN WHAT YOU CAN DO— YOU DON'T EVEN NEED TROOPS!
YOU COULD WIPE THESE BABOONS OFF THE MAP IN A DAY!
COLONEL TAYLOR. I'M SORRY. I SYMPATHIZE, BUT THE ANSWER IS NO.
WHAT DO YOU MEAN, NO?!? THESE ARE YOUR PEOPLE! HOW CAN YOU JUST STAND BY WHILE THEY'RE SLAUGHTERED?!
WE ARE NOT ALLOWED TO INTERFERE IN THE NATURAL EVOLUTION OF A WORLD. ANY WORLD. IT'S OUR FOREMOST IRREFUTABLE ORDER.
...MESSAGE RECEIVED. I UNDERSTAND, CAPTAIN. I WAS A MILITARY MAN, ONCE. ORDERS.
CAN WE STILL COUNT ON YOU TO HELP US?
...YES. YES, I WILL.
WE'RE GOING TO NEED TO GET CLOSER TO THAT CITY OF YOURS, BUT NOT SO CLOSE THAT WE'LL GET SPOTTED. IT'S GOING TO BE NEARLY IMPOSSIBLE FOR US TO BLEND IN. CAN YOU HELP US?

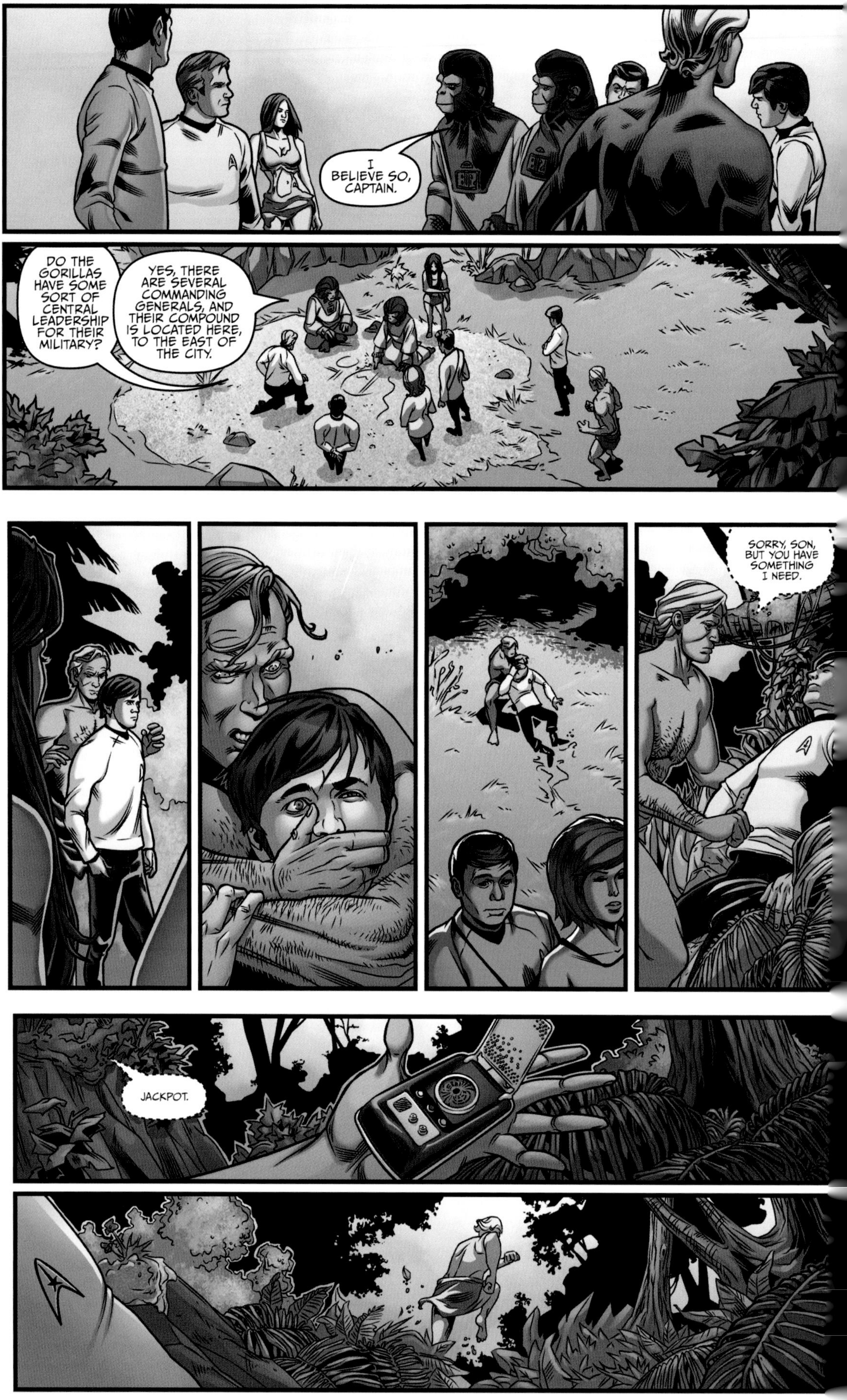
I BELIEVE SO, CAPTAIN.
DO THE GORILLAS HAVE SOME SORT OF CENTRAL LEADERSHIP FOR THEIR MILITARY?
YES, THERE ARE SEVERAL COMMANDING GENERALS, AND THEIR COMPOUND IS LOCATED HERE, TO THE EAST OF THE CITY.
SORRY, SON, BUT YOU HAVE SOMETHING I NEED.
JACKPOT.

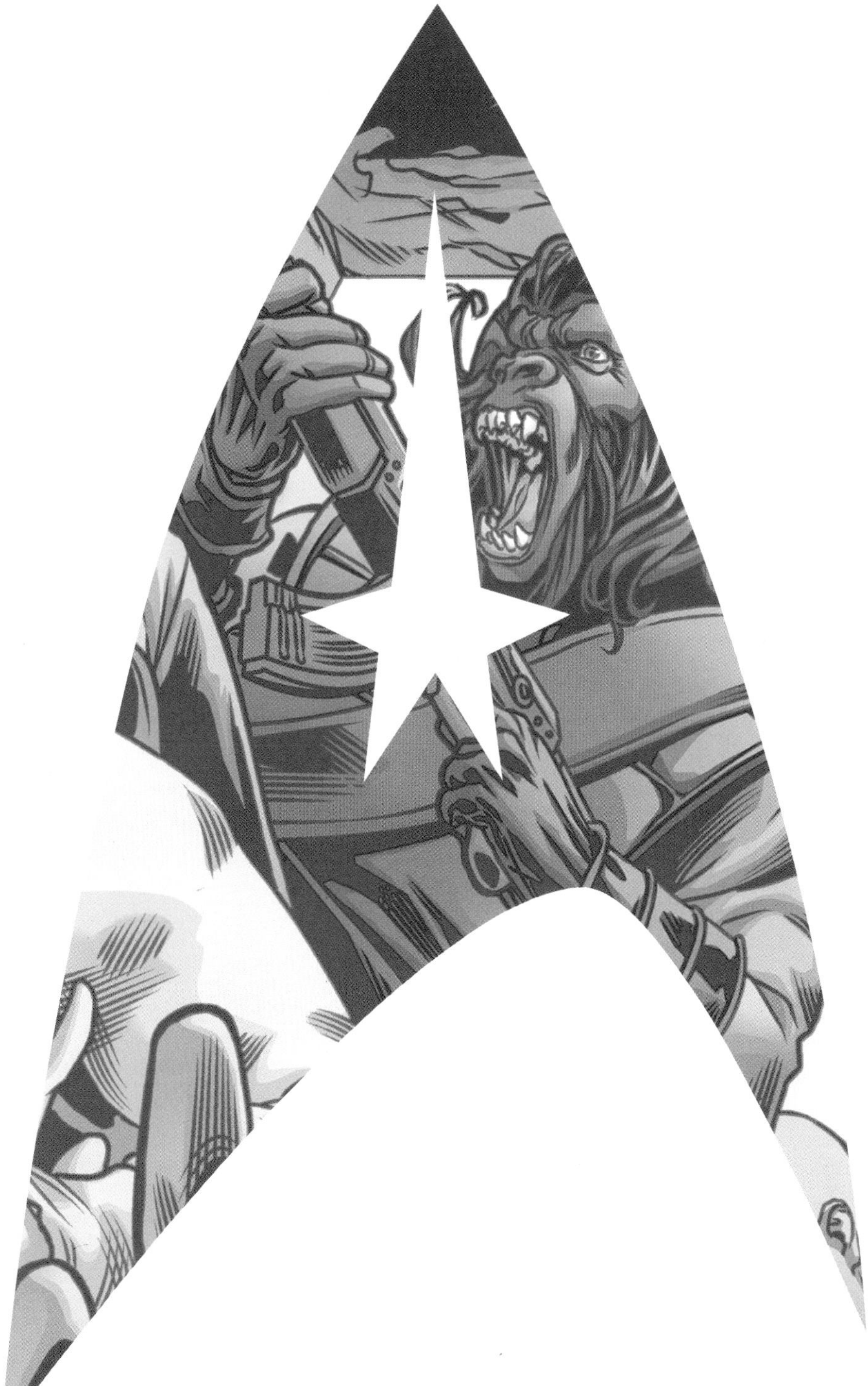

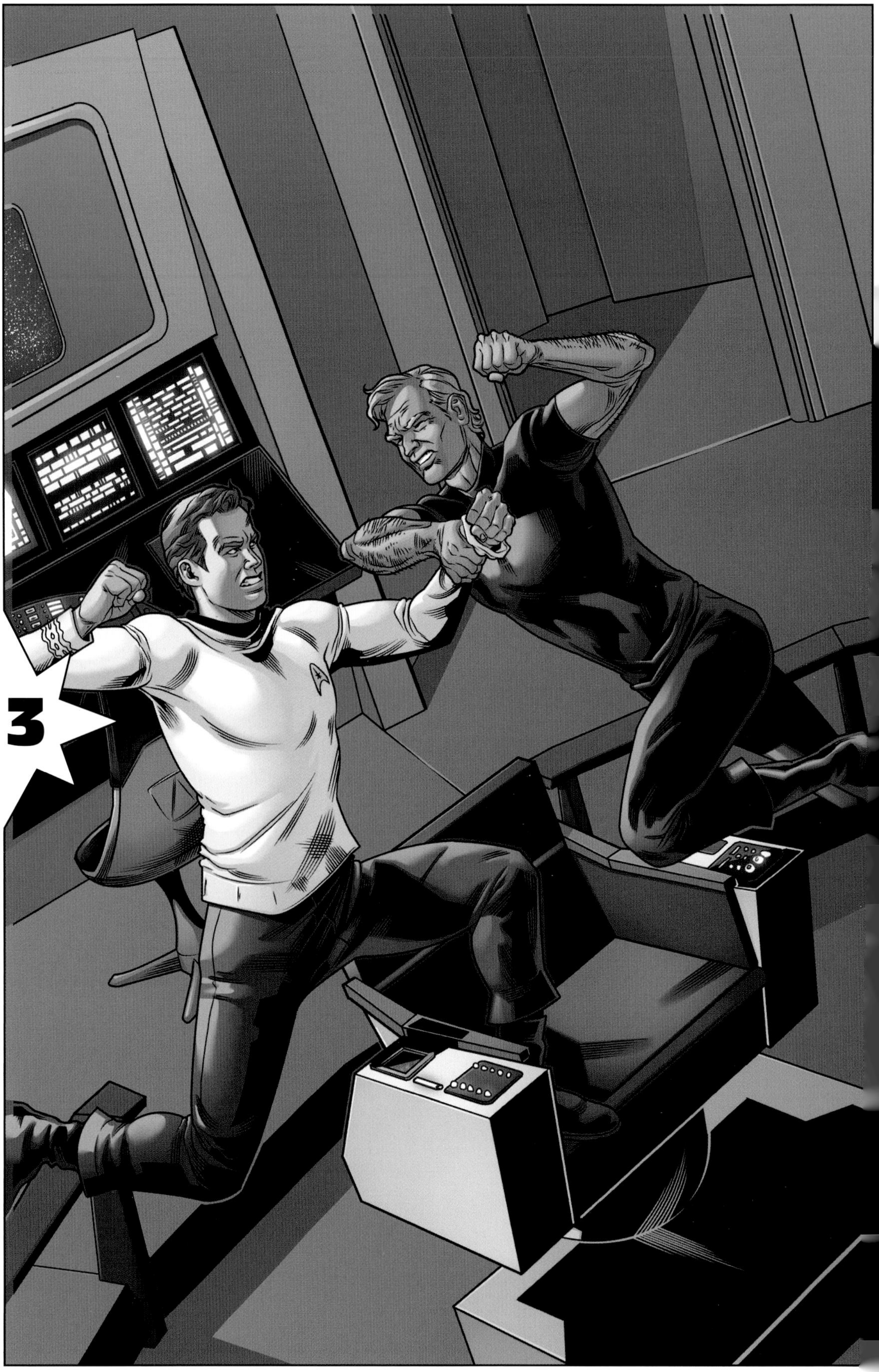
3

BY **RACHAEL STOTT** COLORS BY **CHARLIE KIRCHOFF**

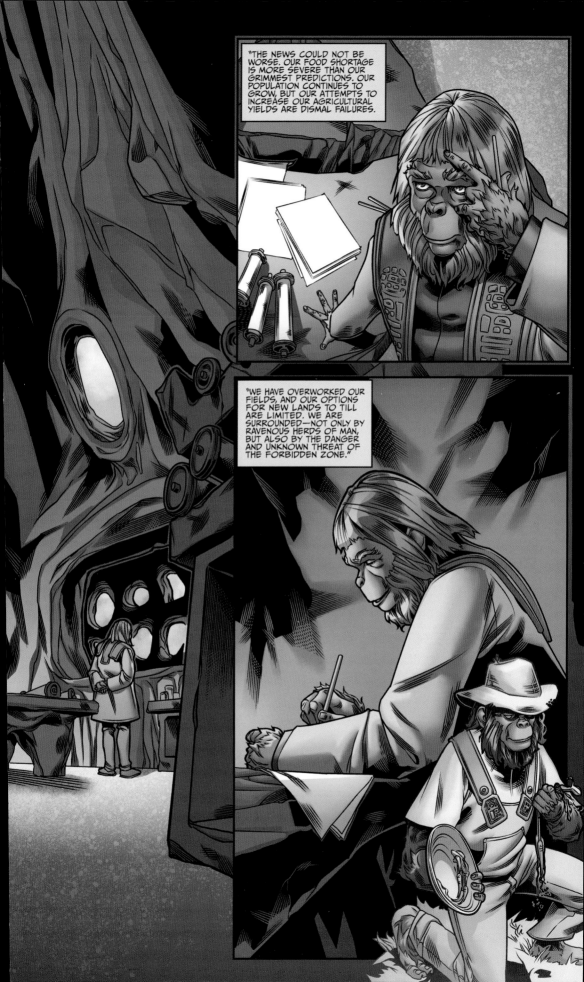

"THE NEWS COULD NOT BE WORSE. OUR FOOD SHORTAGE IS MORE SEVERE THAN OUR GRIMMEST PREDICTIONS. OUR POPULATION CONTINUES TO GROW, BUT OUR ATTEMPTS TO INCREASE OUR AGRICULTURAL YIELDS ARE DISMAL FAILURES."

"WE HAVE OVERWORKED OUR FIELDS, AND OUR OPTIONS FOR NEW LANDS TO TILL ARE LIMITED. WE ARE SURROUNDED—NOT ONLY BY RAVENOUS HERDS OF MAN, BUT ALSO BY THE DANGER AND UNKNOWN THREAT OF THE FORBIDDEN ZONE."

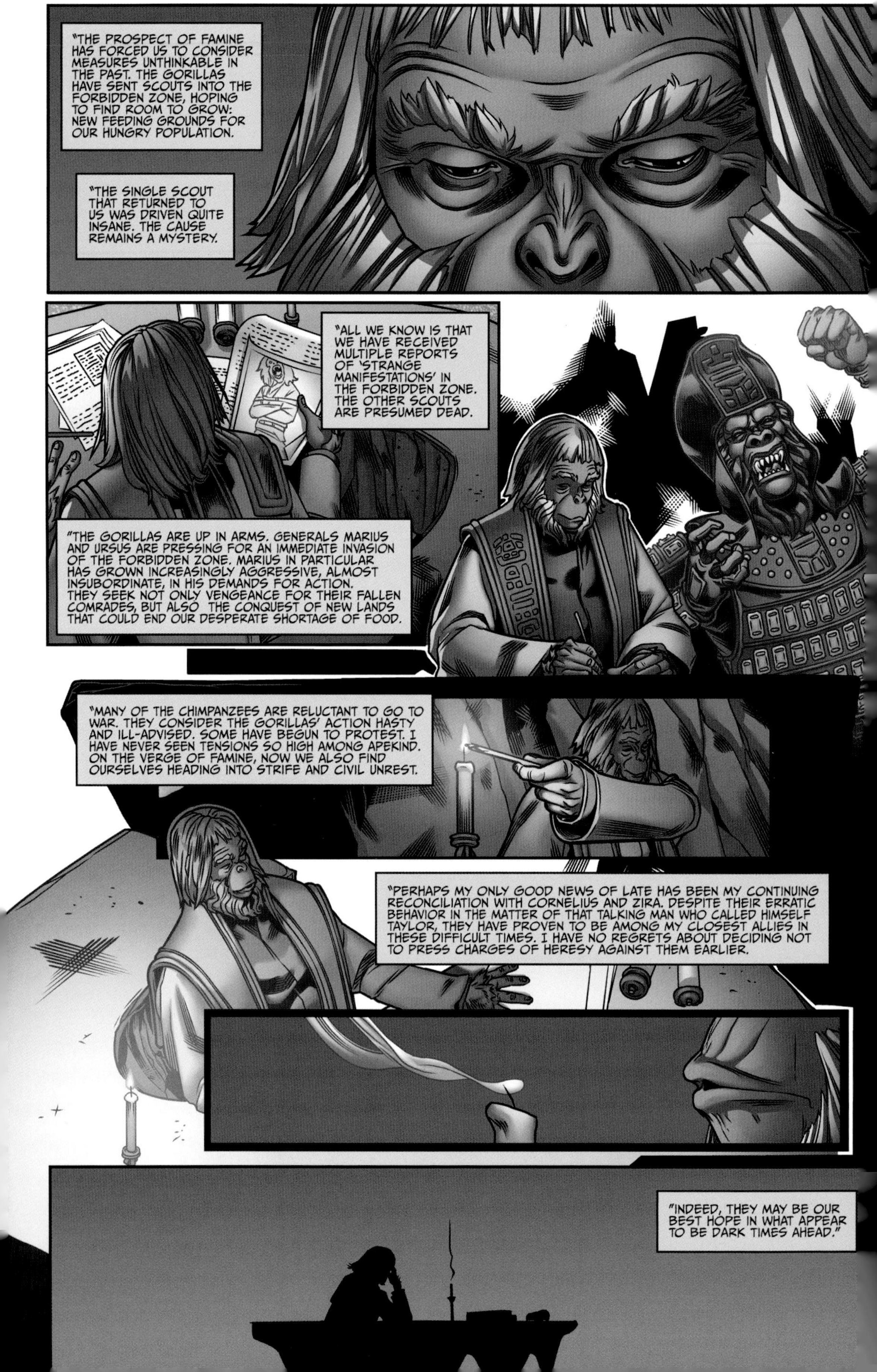
"THE PROSPECT OF FAMINE HAS FORCED US TO CONSIDER MEASURES UNTHINKABLE IN THE PAST. THE GORILLAS HAVE SENT SCOUTS INTO THE FORBIDDEN ZONE, HOPING TO FIND ROOM TO GROW: NEW FEEDING GROUNDS FOR OUR HUNGRY POPULATION.
"THE SINGLE SCOUT THAT RETURNED TO US WAS DRIVEN QUITE INSANE. THE CAUSE REMAINS A MYSTERY.
"ALL WE KNOW IS THAT WE HAVE RECEIVED MULTIPLE REPORTS OF 'STRANGE MANIFESTATIONS' IN THE FORBIDDEN ZONE. THE OTHER SCOUTS ARE PRESUMED DEAD.
"THE GORILLAS ARE UP IN ARMS. GENERALS MARIUS AND URSUS ARE PRESSING FOR AN IMMEDIATE INVASION OF THE FORBIDDEN ZONE. MARIUS IN PARTICULAR HAS GROWN INCREASINGLY AGGRESSIVE, ALMOST INSUBORDINATE, IN HIS DEMANDS FOR ACTION. THEY SEEK NOT ONLY VENGEANCE FOR THEIR FALLEN COMRADES, BUT ALSO THE CONQUEST OF NEW LANDS THAT COULD END OUR DESPERATE SHORTAGE OF FOOD.
"MANY OF THE CHIMPANZEES ARE RELUCTANT TO GO TO WAR. THEY CONSIDER THE GORILLAS' ACTION HASTY AND ILL-ADVISED. SOME HAVE BEGUN TO PROTEST. I HAVE NEVER SEEN TENSIONS SO HIGH AMONG APEKIND. ON THE VERGE OF FAMINE, NOW WE ALSO FIND OURSELVES HEADING INTO STRIFE AND CIVIL UNREST.
"PERHAPS MY ONLY GOOD NEWS OF LATE HAS BEEN MY CONTINUING RECONCILIATION WITH CORNELIUS AND ZIRA. DESPITE THEIR ERRATIC BEHAVIOR IN THE MATTER OF THAT TALKING MAN WHO CALLED HIMSELF TAYLOR, THEY HAVE PROVEN TO BE AMONG MY CLOSEST ALLIES IN THESE DIFFICULT TIMES. I HAVE NO REGRETS ABOUT DECIDING NOT TO PRESS CHARGES OF HERESY AGAINST THEM EARLIER.
"INDEED, THEY MAY BE OUR BEST HOPE IN WHAT APPEAR TO BE DARK TIMES AHEAD."

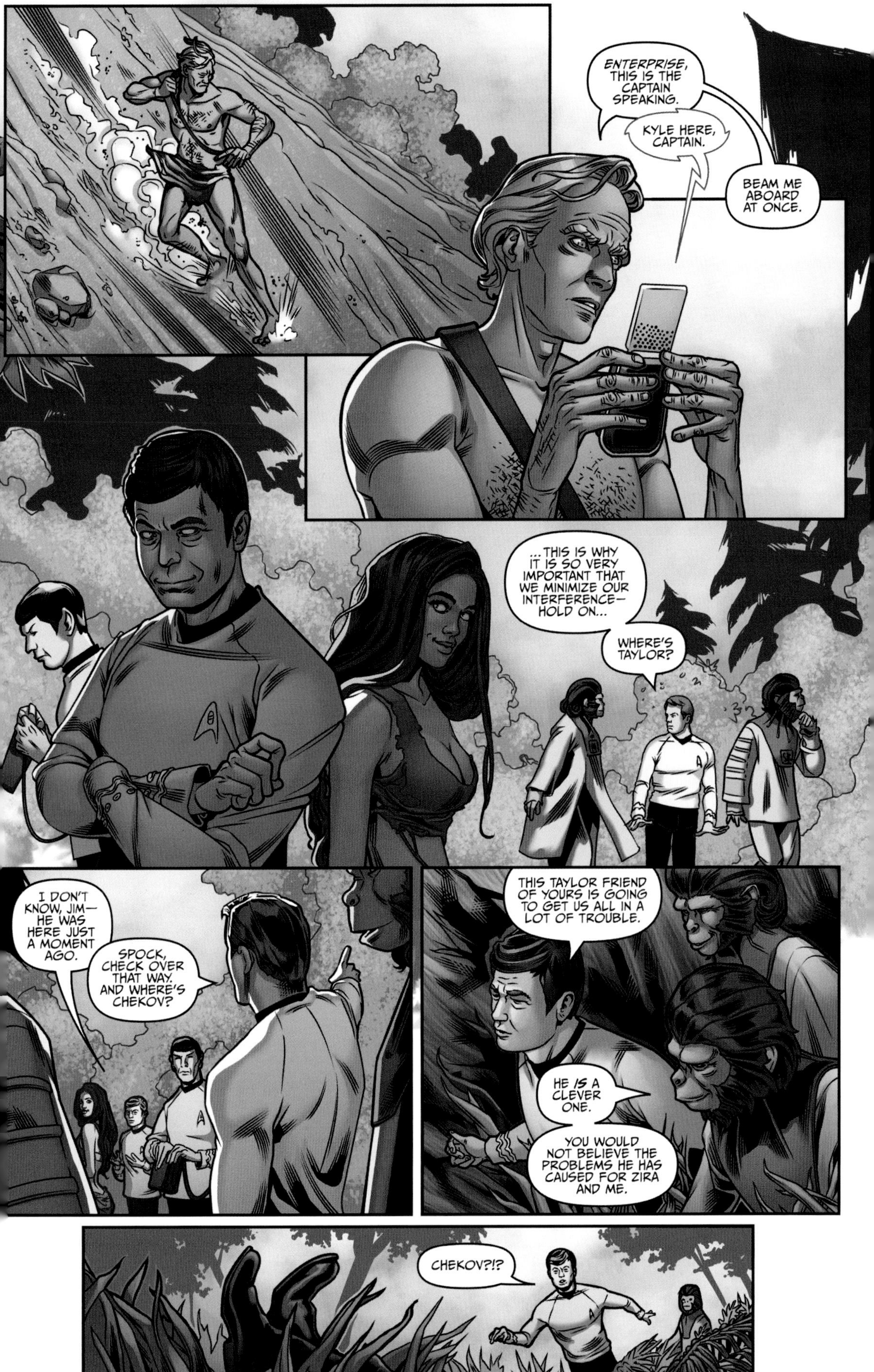
ENTERPRISE, THIS IS THE CAPTAIN SPEAKING.
KYLE HERE, CAPTAIN.
BEAM ME ABOARD AT ONCE.
...THIS IS WHY IT IS SO VERY IMPORTANT THAT WE MINIMIZE OUR INTERFERENCE—HOLD ON...
WHERE'S TAYLOR?
I DON'T KNOW, JIM—HE WAS HERE JUST A MOMENT AGO.
SPOCK, CHECK OVER THAT WAY. AND WHERE'S CHEKOV?
THIS TAYLOR FRIEND OF YOURS IS GOING TO GET US ALL IN A LOT OF TROUBLE.
HE IS A CLEVER ONE.
YOU WOULD NOT BELIEVE THE PROBLEMS HE HAS CAUSED FOR ZIRA AND ME.
CHEKOV?!?

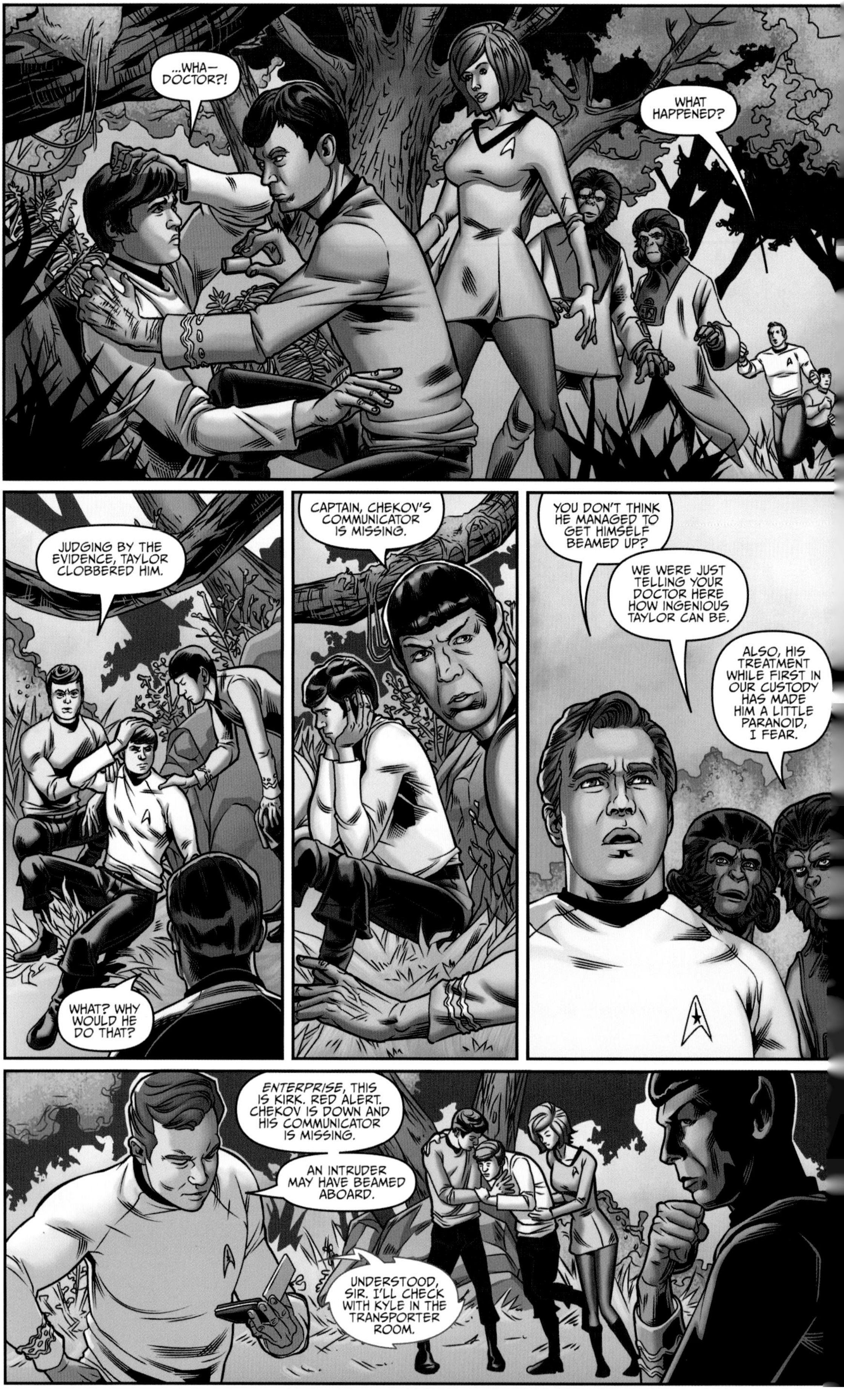
...WHA—
DOCTOR?!
WHAT HAPPENED?
JUDGING BY THE EVIDENCE, TAYLOR CLOBBERED HIM.
WHAT? WHY WOULD HE DO THAT?
CAPTAIN, CHEKOV'S COMMUNICATOR IS MISSING.
YOU DON'T THINK HE MANAGED TO GET HIMSELF BEAMED UP?
WE WERE JUST TELLING YOUR DOCTOR HERE HOW INGENIOUS TAYLOR CAN BE.
ALSO, HIS TREATMENT WHILE FIRST IN OUR CUSTODY HAS MADE HIM A LITTLE PARANOID, I FEAR.
ENTERPRISE, THIS IS KIRK. RED ALERT. CHEKOV IS DOWN AND HIS COMMUNICATOR IS MISSING.
AN INTRUDER MAY HAVE BEAMED ABOARD.
UNDERSTOOD, SIR. I'LL CHECK WITH KYLE IN THE TRANSPORTER ROOM.

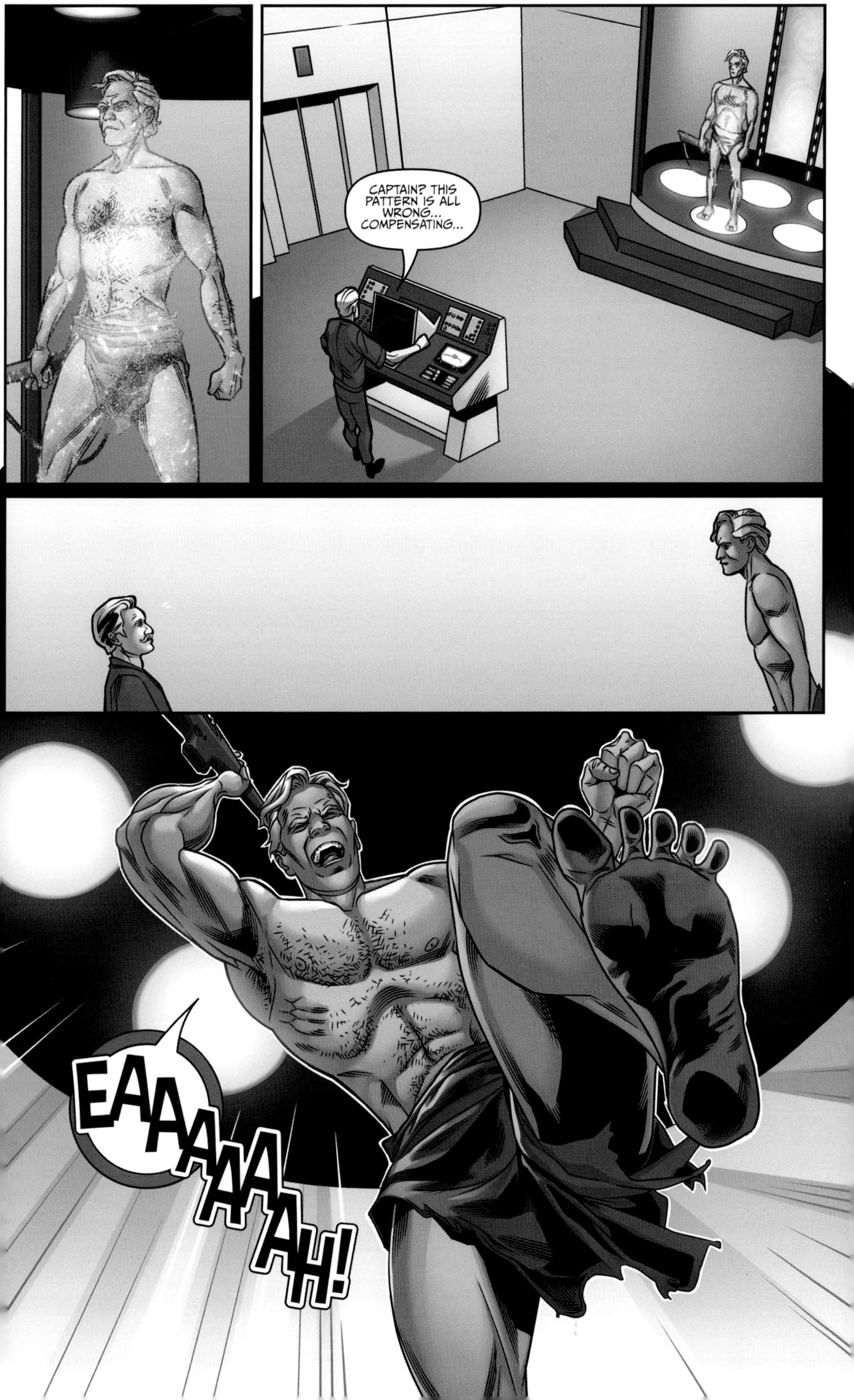
CAPTAIN? THIS PATTERN IS ALL WRONG... COMPENSATING...
EAAAAAAAH!

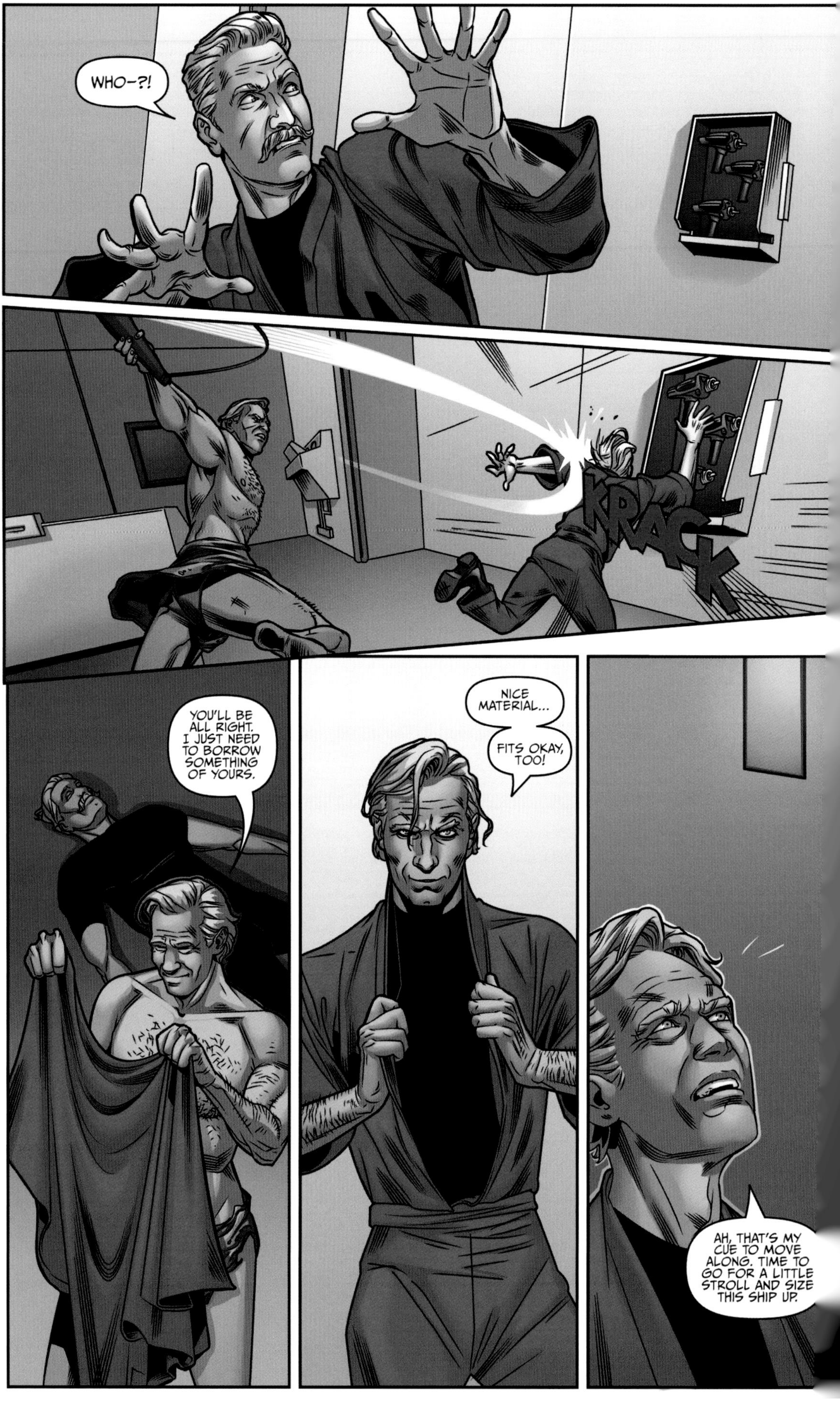
WHO-?!
KRACK
YOU'LL BE ALL RIGHT. I JUST NEED TO BORROW SOMETHING OF YOURS.
NICE MATERIAL...
FITS OKAY, TOO!
AH, THAT'S MY CUE TO MOVE ALONG. TIME TO GO FOR A LITTLE STROLL AND SIZE THIS SHIP UP.

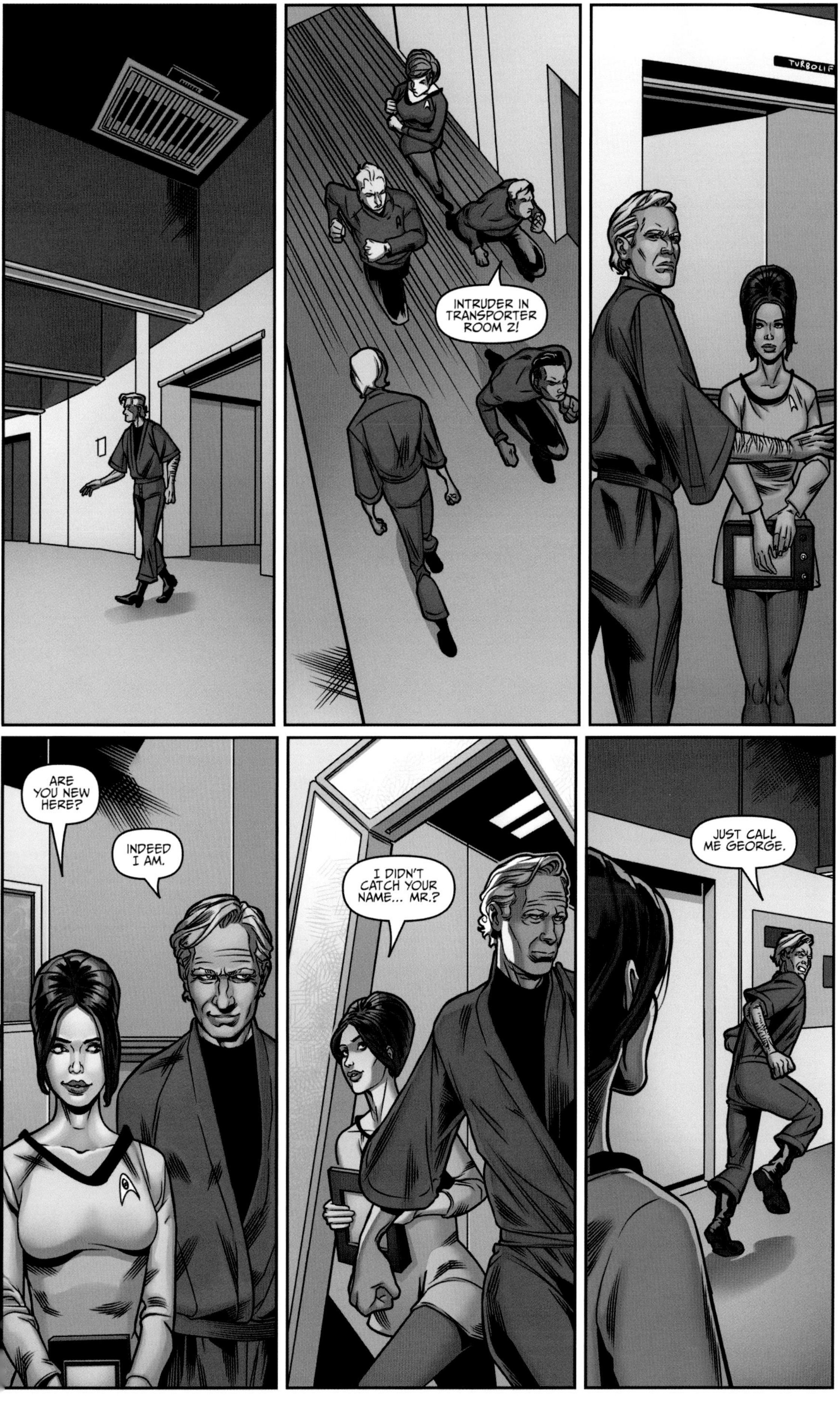
INTRUDER IN TRANSPORTER ROOM 2!
TURBOLIF
ARE YOU NEW HERE?
INDEED I AM.
I DIDN'T CATCH YOUR NAME... MR.?
JUST CALL ME GEORGE.

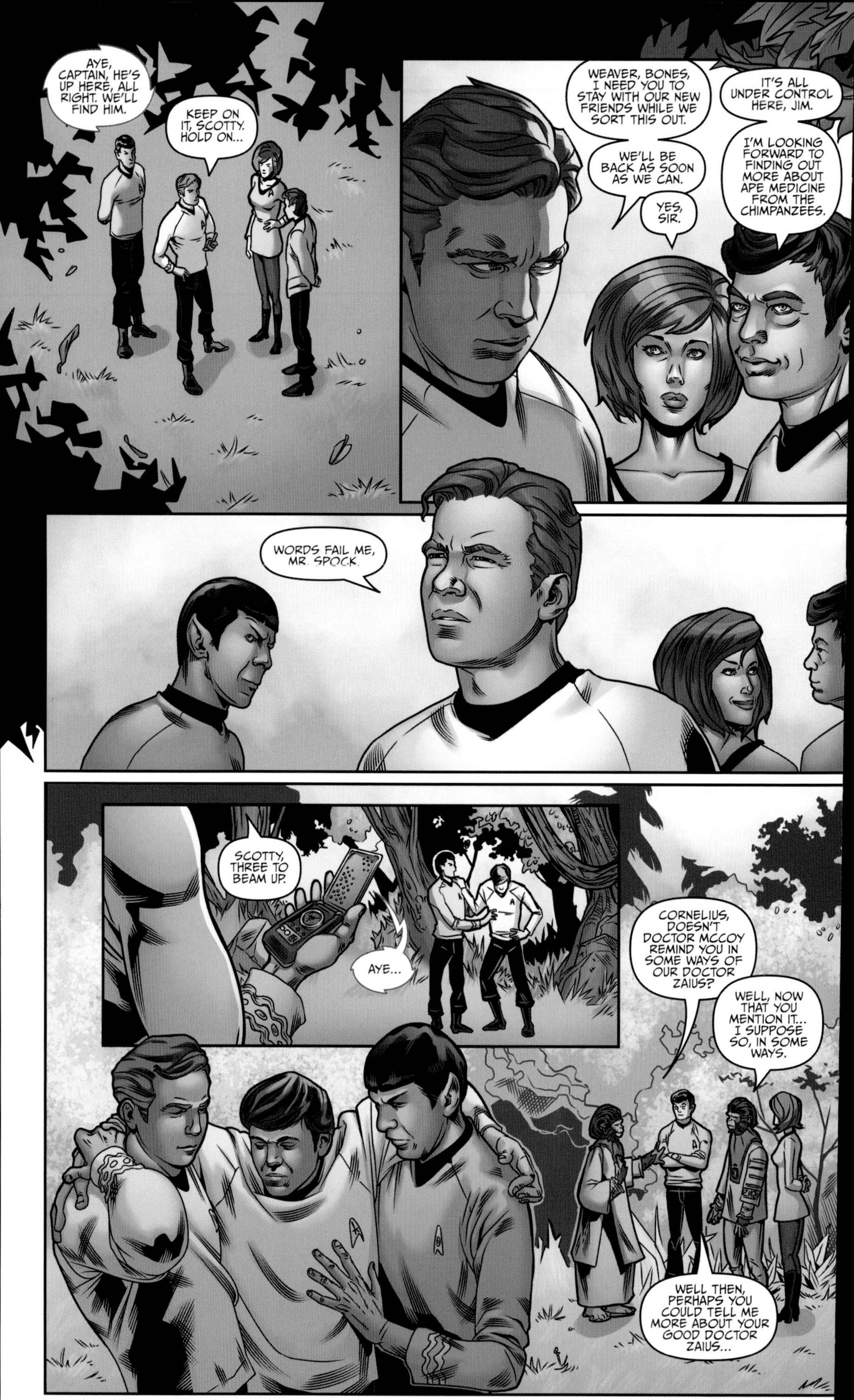
AYE, CAPTAIN, HE'S UP HERE, ALL RIGHT. WE'LL FIND HIM.
KEEP ON IT, SCOTTY. HOLD ON...
WEAVER, BONES, I NEED YOU TO STAY WITH OUR NEW FRIENDS WHILE WE SORT THIS OUT.
WE'LL BE BACK AS SOON AS WE CAN.
YES, SIR.
IT'S ALL UNDER CONTROL HERE, JIM.
I'M LOOKING FORWARD TO FINDING OUT MORE ABOUT APE MEDICINE FROM THE CHIMPANZEES.
WORDS FAIL ME, MR. SPOCK.
SCOTTY, THREE TO BEAM UP.
AYE...
CORNELIUS, DOESN'T DOCTOR MCCOY REMIND YOU IN SOME WAYS OF OUR DOCTOR ZAIUS?
WELL, NOW THAT YOU MENTION IT... I SUPPOSE SO, IN SOME WAYS.
WELL THEN, PERHAPS YOU COULD TELL ME MORE ABOUT YOUR GOOD DOCTOR ZAIUS...

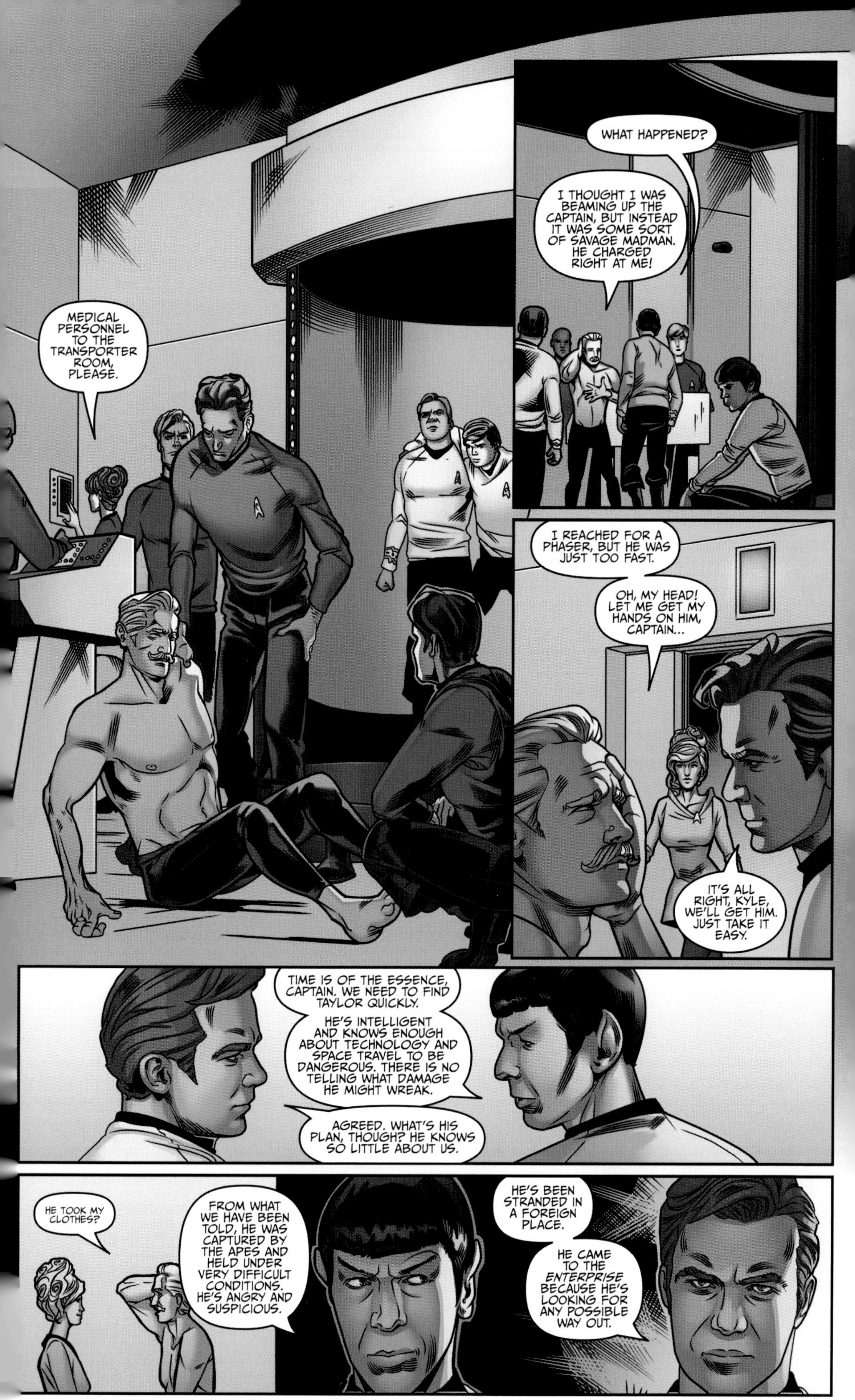

MEDICAL PERSONNEL TO THE TRANSPORTER ROOM, PLEASE.
WHAT HAPPENED?
I THOUGHT I WAS BEAMING UP THE CAPTAIN, BUT INSTEAD IT WAS SOME SORT OF SAVAGE MADMAN. HE CHARGED RIGHT AT ME!
I REACHED FOR A PHASER, BUT HE WAS JUST TOO FAST.
OH, MY HEAD! LET ME GET MY HANDS ON HIM, CAPTAIN...
IT'S ALL RIGHT, KYLE, WE'LL GET HIM. JUST TAKE IT EASY.
TIME IS OF THE ESSENCE, CAPTAIN. WE NEED TO FIND TAYLOR QUICKLY.
HE'S INTELLIGENT AND KNOWS ENOUGH ABOUT TECHNOLOGY AND SPACE TRAVEL TO BE DANGEROUS. THERE IS NO TELLING WHAT DAMAGE HE MIGHT WREAK.
AGREED. WHAT'S HIS PLAN, THOUGH? HE KNOWS SO LITTLE ABOUT US.
HE TOOK MY CLOTHES?
FROM WHAT WE HAVE BEEN TOLD, HE WAS CAPTURED BY THE APES AND HELD UNDER VERY DIFFICULT CONDITIONS. HE'S ANGRY AND SUSPICIOUS.
HE'S BEEN STRANDED IN A FOREIGN PLACE.
HE CAME TO THE *ENTERPRISE* BECAUSE HE'S LOOKING FOR ANY POSSIBLE WAY OUT.

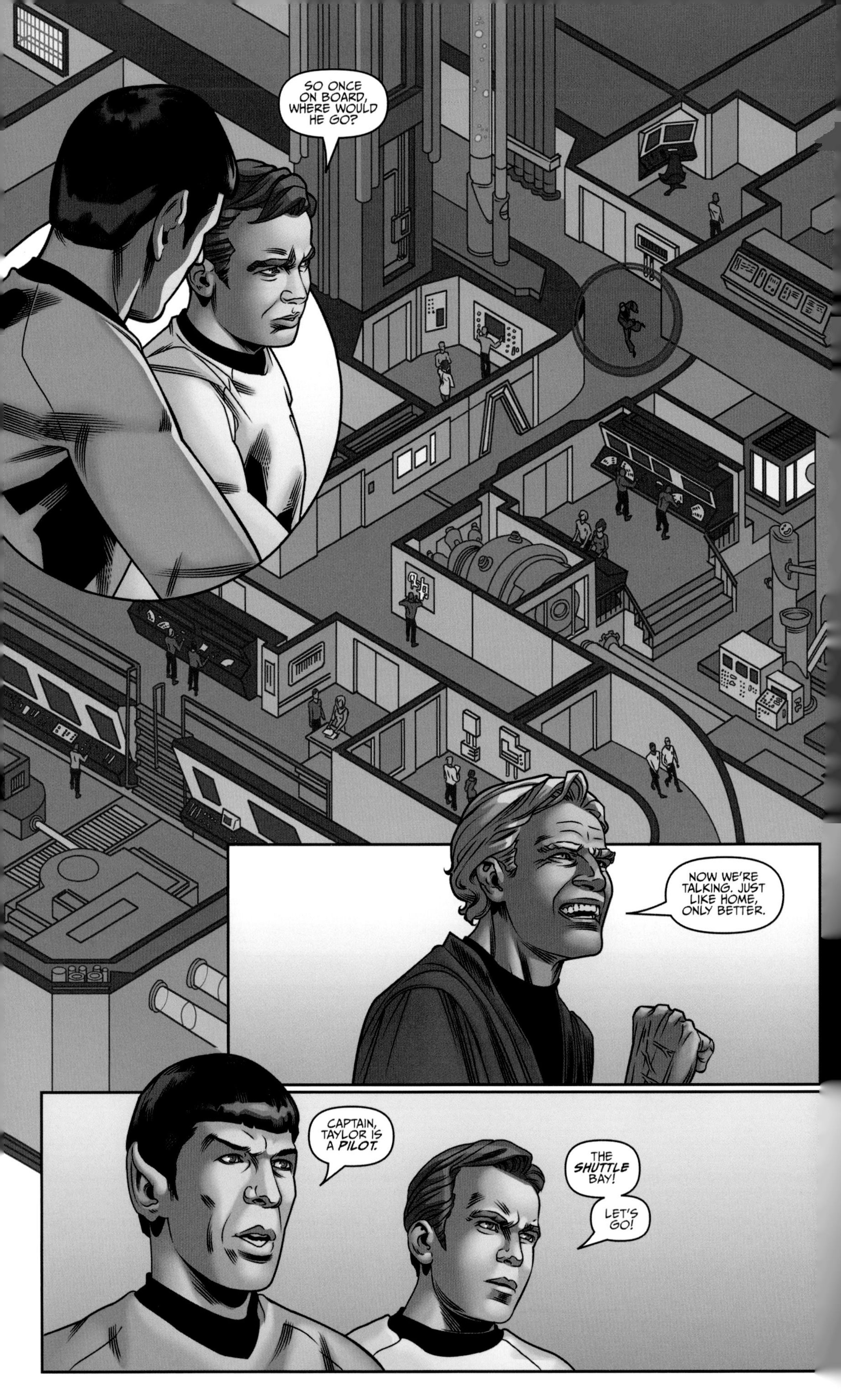
SO ONCE ON BOARD, WHERE WOULD HE GO?
NOW WE'RE TALKING. JUST LIKE HOME, ONLY BETTER.
CAPTAIN, TAYLOR IS A PILOT.
THE SHUTTLE BAY!
LET'S GO!

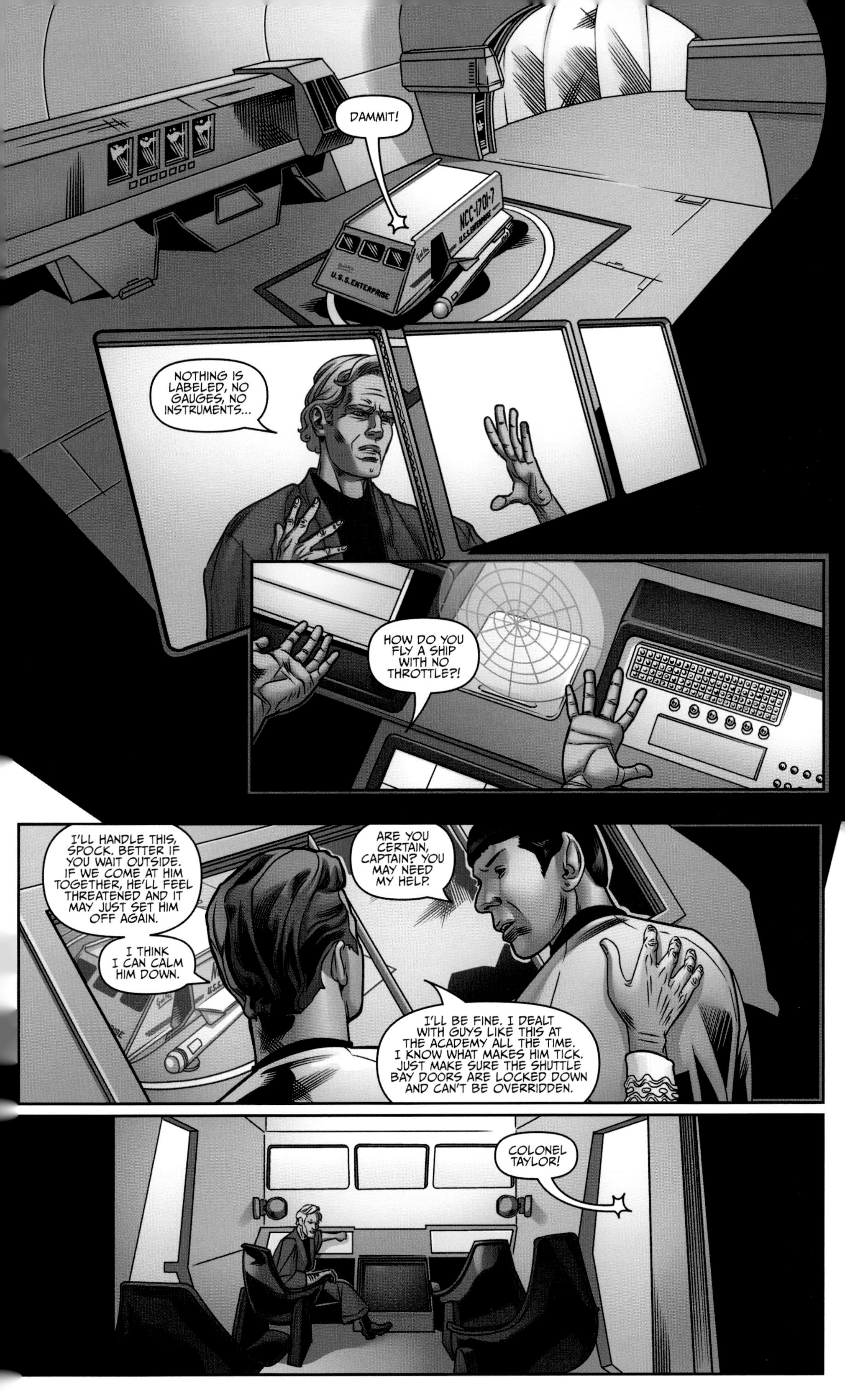
DAMMIT!
NCC-1701-7
U.S.S. ENTERPRISE
NOTHING IS LABELED, NO GAUGES, NO INSTRUMENTS...
HOW DO YOU FLY A SHIP WITH NO THROTTLE?!
I'LL HANDLE THIS, SPOCK. BETTER IF YOU WAIT OUTSIDE. IF WE COME AT HIM TOGETHER, HE'LL FEEL THREATENED AND IT MAY JUST SET HIM OFF AGAIN.
ARE YOU CERTAIN, CAPTAIN? YOU MAY NEED MY HELP.
I THINK I CAN CALM HIM DOWN.
I'LL BE FINE. I DEALT WITH GUYS LIKE THIS AT THE ACADEMY ALL THE TIME. I KNOW WHAT MAKES HIM TICK. JUST MAKE SURE THE SHUTTLE BAY DOORS ARE LOCKED DOWN AND CAN'T BE OVERRIDDEN.
COLONEL TAYLOR!

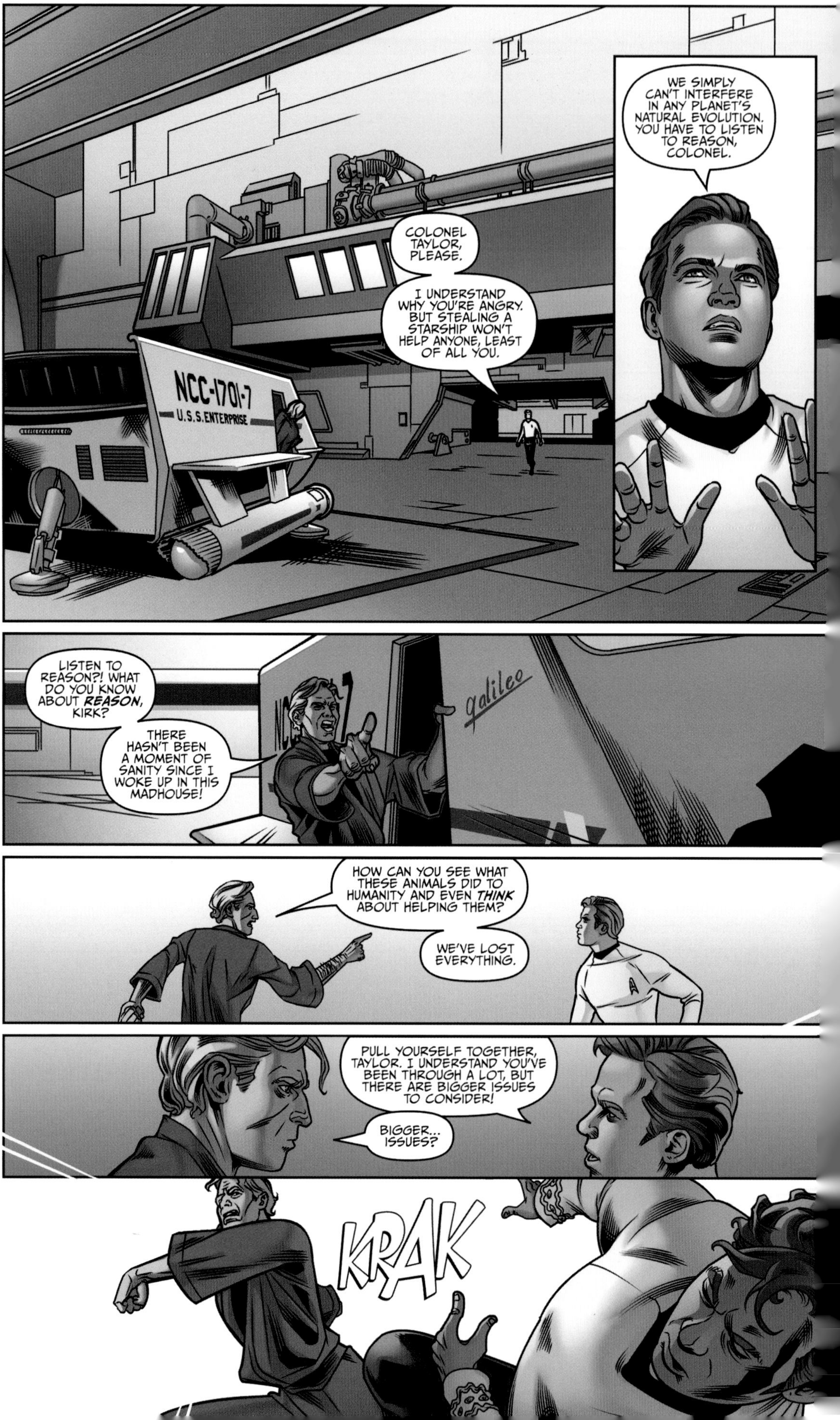

NCC-1701-7
U.S.S. ENTERPRISE
COLONEL TAYLOR, PLEASE.
I UNDERSTAND WHY YOU'RE ANGRY. BUT STEALING A STARSHIP WON'T HELP ANYONE, LEAST OF ALL YOU.
WE SIMPLY CAN'T INTERFERE IN ANY PLANET'S NATURAL EVOLUTION. YOU HAVE TO LISTEN TO REASON, COLONEL.
LISTEN TO REASON?! WHAT DO YOU KNOW ABOUT *REASON*, KIRK?
THERE HASN'T BEEN A MOMENT OF SANITY SINCE I WOKE UP IN THIS MADHOUSE!
galileo
HOW CAN YOU SEE WHAT THESE ANIMALS DID TO HUMANITY AND EVEN *THINK* ABOUT HELPING THEM?
WE'VE LOST EVERYTHING.
PULL YOURSELF TOGETHER, TAYLOR. I UNDERSTAND YOU'VE BEEN THROUGH A LOT, BUT THERE ARE BIGGER ISSUES TO CONSIDER!
BIGGER... ISSUES?
KRAK

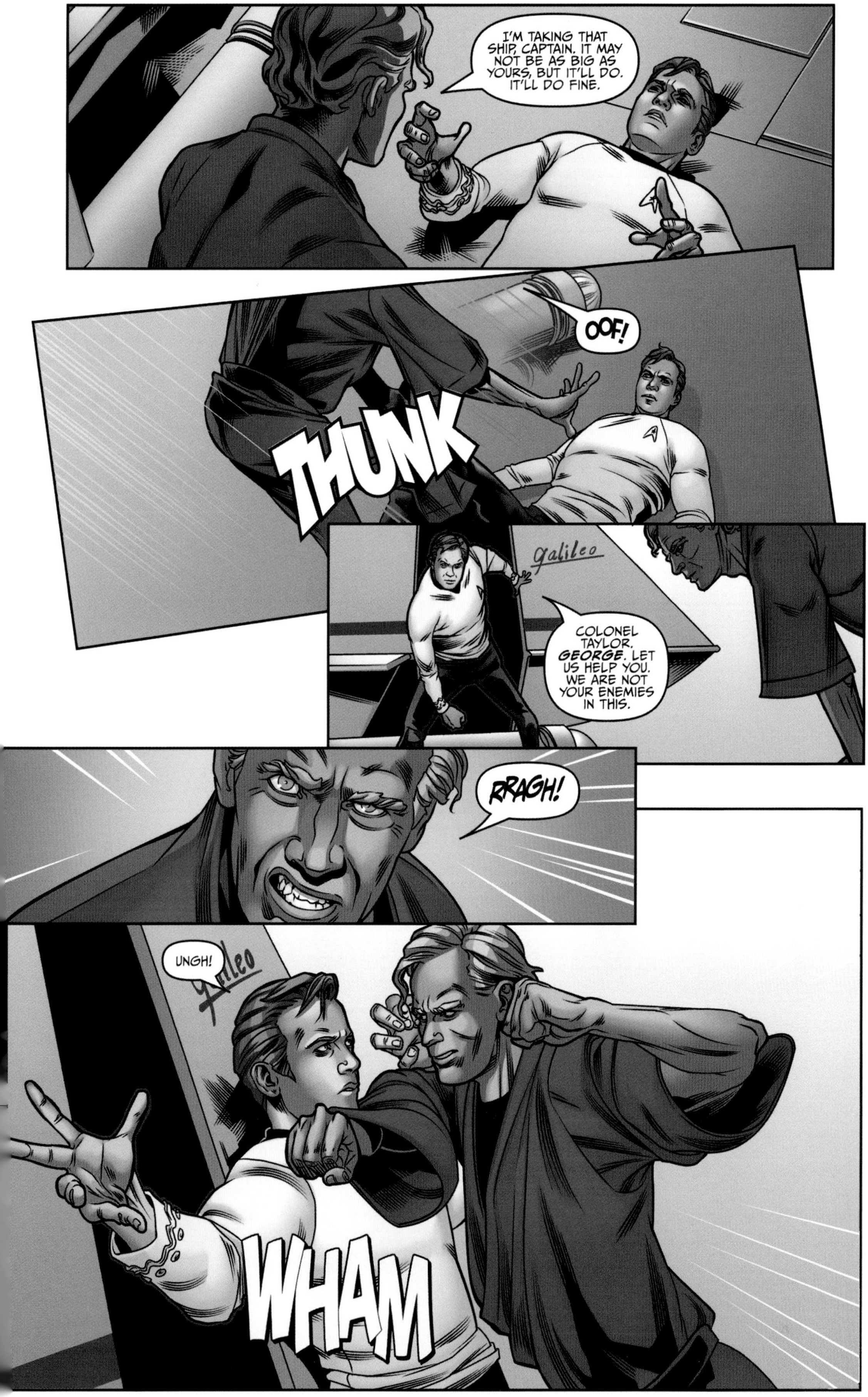

I'M TAKING THAT SHIP, CAPTAIN. IT MAY NOT BE AS BIG AS YOURS, BUT IT'LL DO. IT'LL DO FINE.
OOF!
THUNK
galileo
COLONEL TAYLOR. GEORGE. LET US HELP YOU. WE ARE NOT YOUR ENEMIES IN THIS.
RRAGH!
UNGH!
WHAM

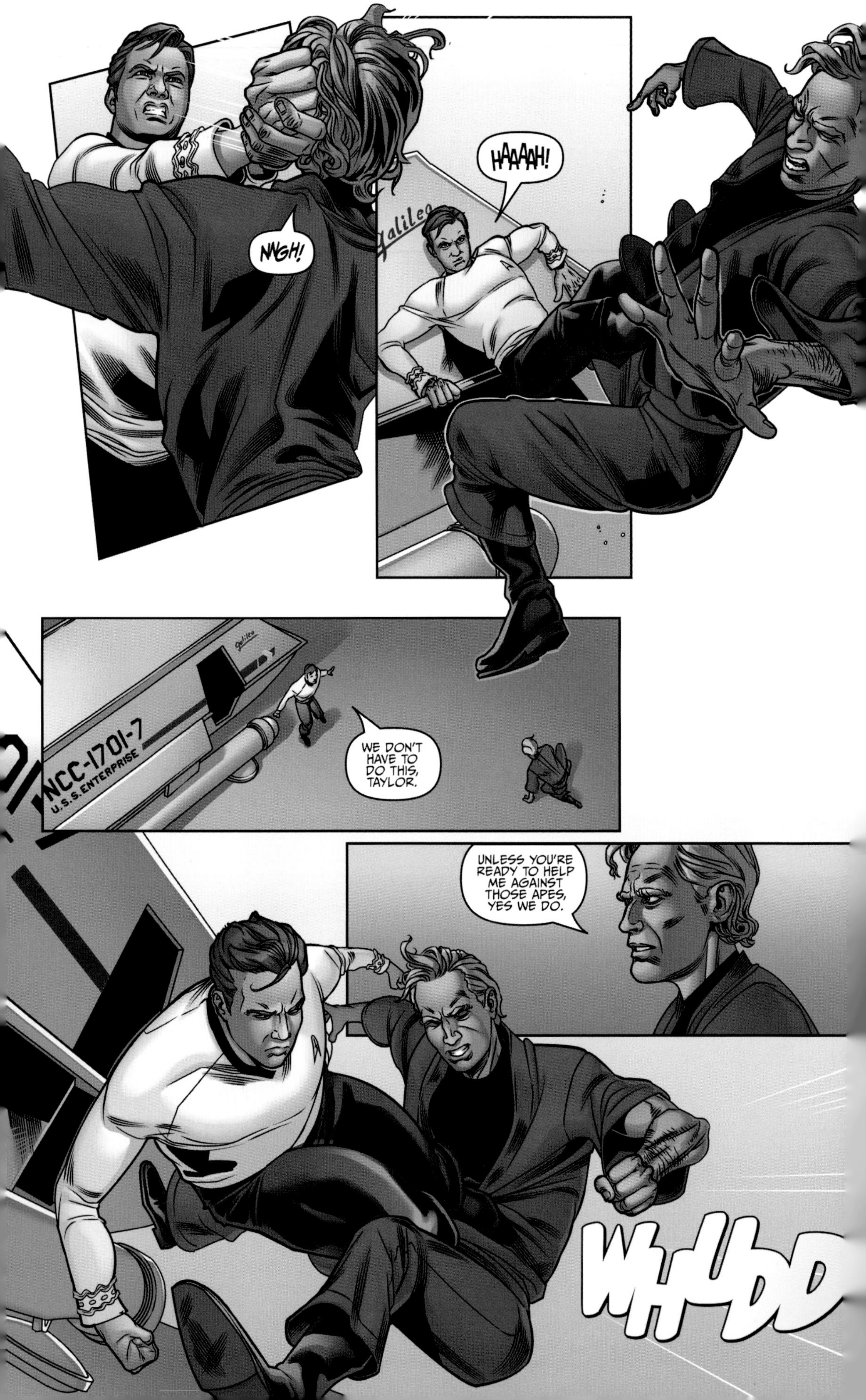
NNGH!
HAAAAH!
galileo
Galileo
NCC-1701-7
U.S.S. ENTERPRISE
WE DON'T HAVE TO DO THIS, TAYLOR.
UNLESS YOU'RE READY TO HELP ME AGAINST THOSE APES, YES WE DO.
WHUDD

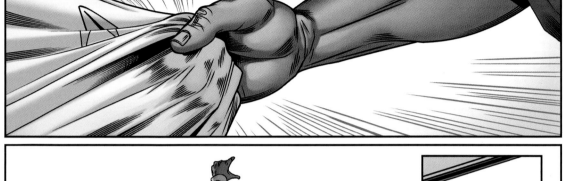

HAD...
ENOUGH...
CAPTAIN?

DAMN IT,
TAYLOR. THIS IS
POINTLESS.

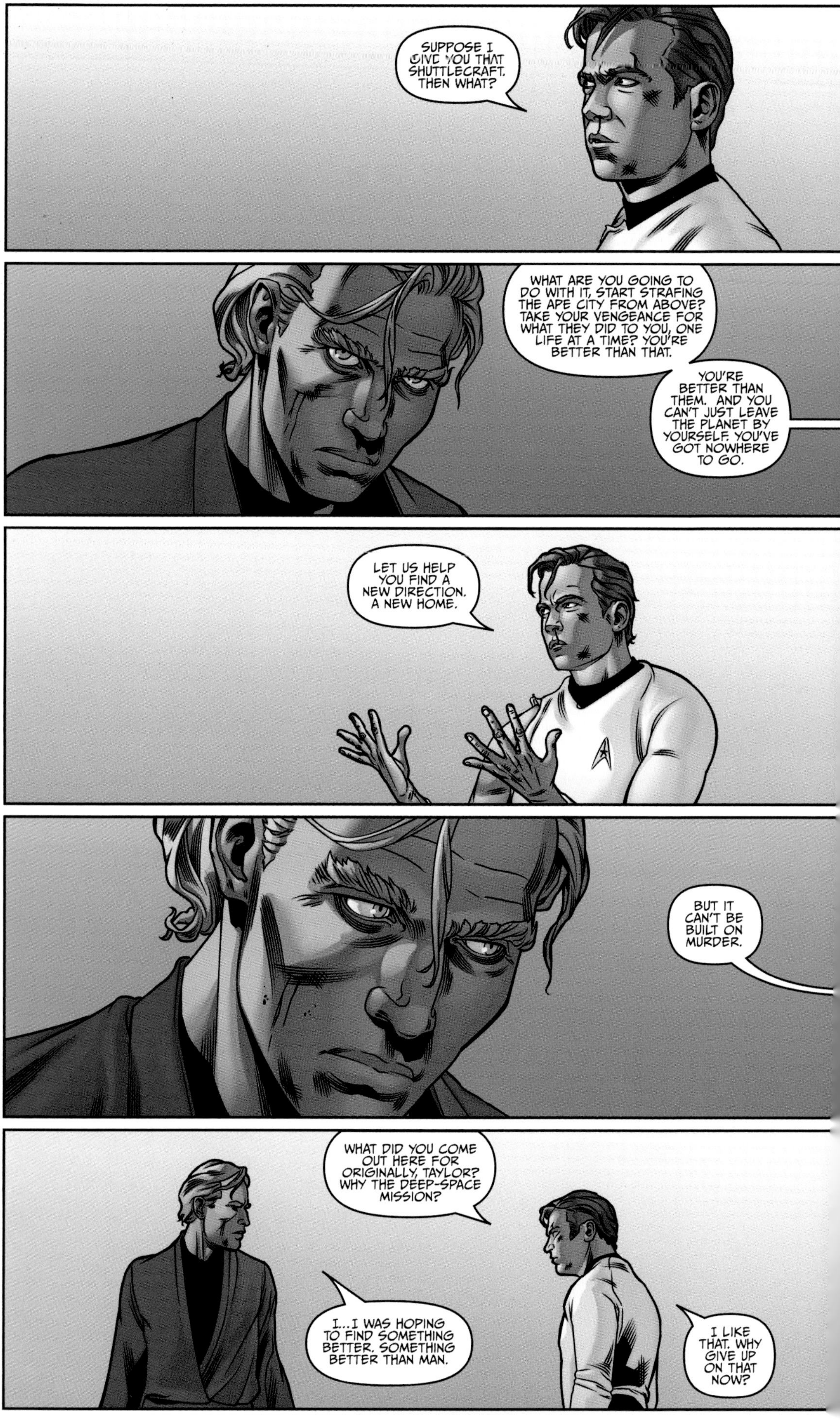
SUPPOSE I GIVE YOU THAT SHUTTLECRAFT. THEN WHAT?
WHAT ARE YOU GOING TO DO WITH IT, START STRAFING THE APE CITY FROM ABOVE? TAKE YOUR VENGEANCE FOR WHAT THEY DID TO YOU, ONE LIFE AT A TIME? YOU'RE BETTER THAN THAT.
YOU'RE BETTER THAN THEM. AND YOU CAN'T JUST LEAVE THE PLANET BY YOURSELF. YOU'VE GOT NOWHERE TO GO.
LET US HELP YOU FIND A NEW DIRECTION. A NEW HOME.
BUT IT CAN'T BE BUILT ON MURDER.
WHAT DID YOU COME OUT HERE FOR ORIGINALLY, TAYLOR? WHY THE DEEP-SPACE MISSION?
I...I WAS HOPING TO FIND SOMETHING BETTER. SOMETHING BETTER THAN MAN.
I LIKE THAT. WHY GIVE UP ON THAT NOW?

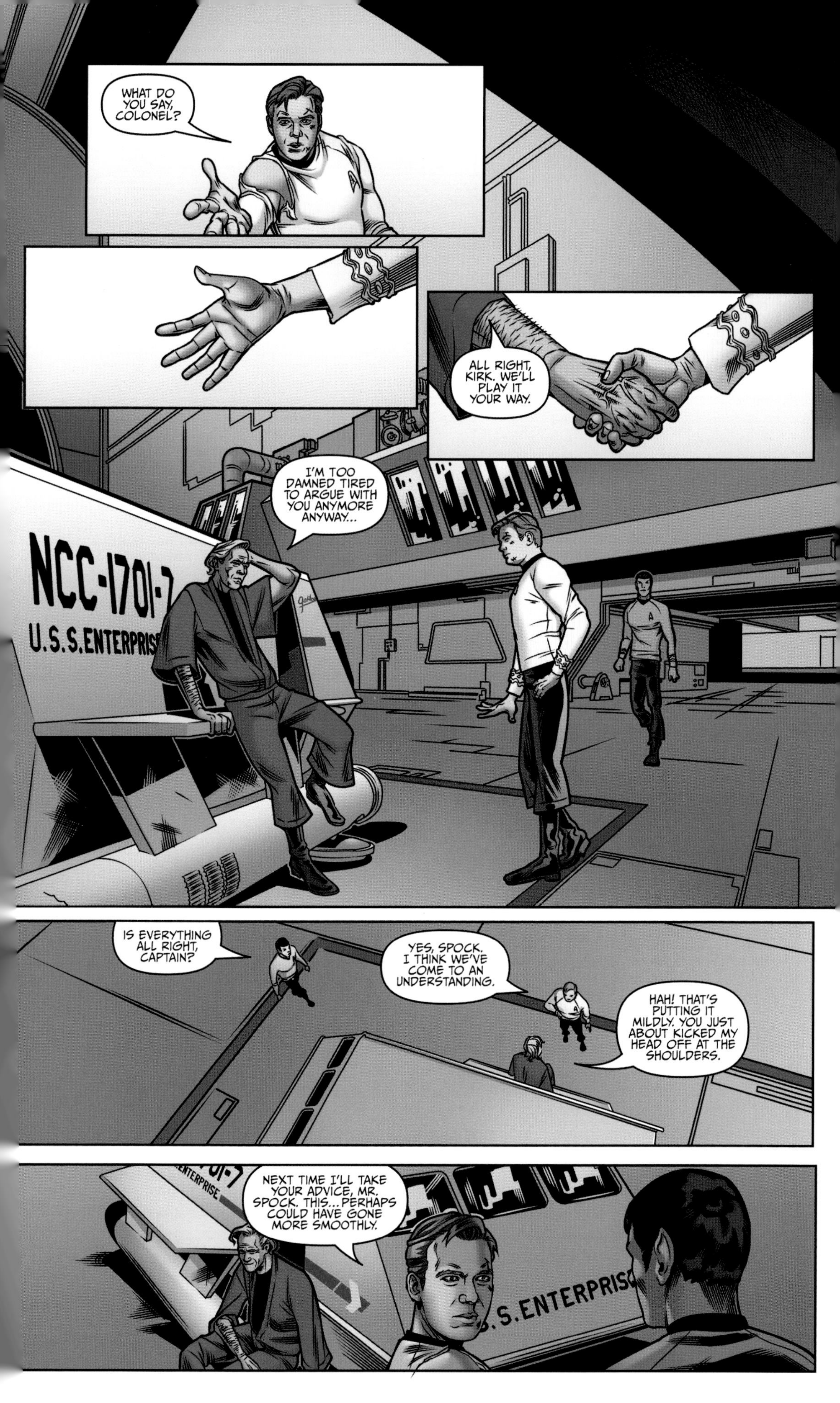

WHAT DO YOU SAY, COLONEL?
ALL RIGHT, KIRK. WE'LL PLAY IT YOUR WAY.
I'M TOO DAMNED TIRED TO ARGUE WITH YOU ANYMORE ANYWAY...
NCC-1701-7
U.S.S.ENTERPRISE
IS EVERYTHING ALL RIGHT, CAPTAIN?
YES, SPOCK. I THINK WE'VE COME TO AN UNDERSTANDING.
HAH! THAT'S PUTTING IT MILDLY. YOU JUST ABOUT KICKED MY HEAD OFF AT THE SHOULDERS.
NEXT TIME I'LL TAKE YOUR ADVICE, MR. SPOCK. THIS... PERHAPS COULD HAVE GONE MORE SMOOTHLY.

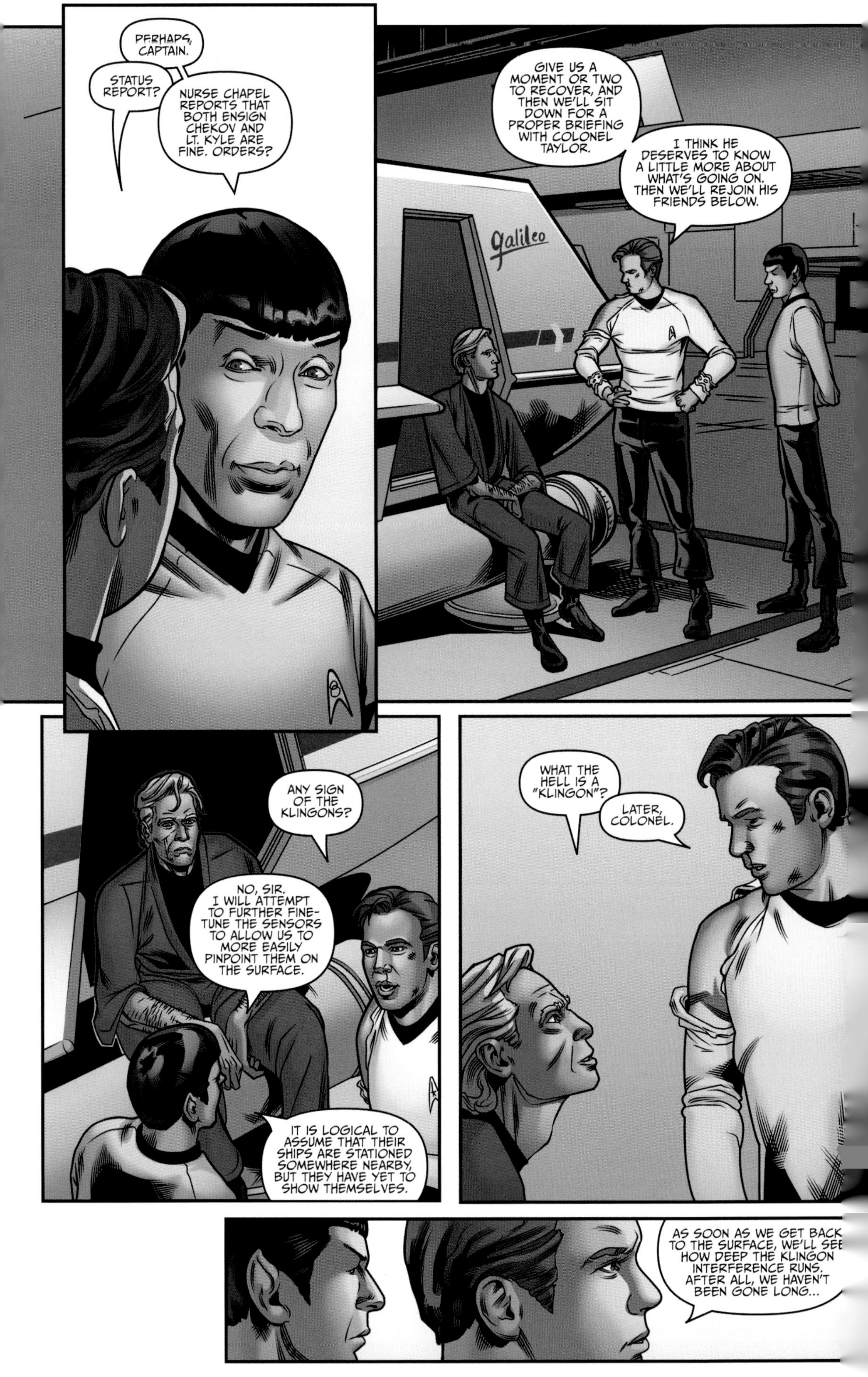

STATUS REPORT?
PERHAPS, CAPTAIN.
NURSE CHAPEL REPORTS THAT BOTH ENSIGN CHEKOV AND LT. KYLE ARE FINE. ORDERS?
GIVE US A MOMENT OR TWO TO RECOVER, AND THEN WE'LL SIT DOWN FOR A PROPER BRIEFING WITH COLONEL TAYLOR.
I THINK HE DESERVES TO KNOW A LITTLE MORE ABOUT WHAT'S GOING ON. THEN WE'LL REJOIN HIS FRIENDS BELOW.
Galileo
ANY SIGN OF THE KLINGONS?
NO, SIR. I WILL ATTEMPT TO FURTHER FINE-TUNE THE SENSORS TO ALLOW US TO MORE EASILY PINPOINT THEM ON THE SURFACE.
IT IS LOGICAL TO ASSUME THAT THEIR SHIPS ARE STATIONED SOMEWHERE NEARBY, BUT THEY HAVE YET TO SHOW THEMSELVES.
WHAT THE HELL IS A "KLINGON"?
LATER, COLONEL.
AS SOON AS WE GET BACK TO THE SURFACE, WE'LL SEE HOW DEEP THE KLINGON INTERFERENCE RUNS. AFTER ALL, WE HAVEN'T BEEN GONE LONG...

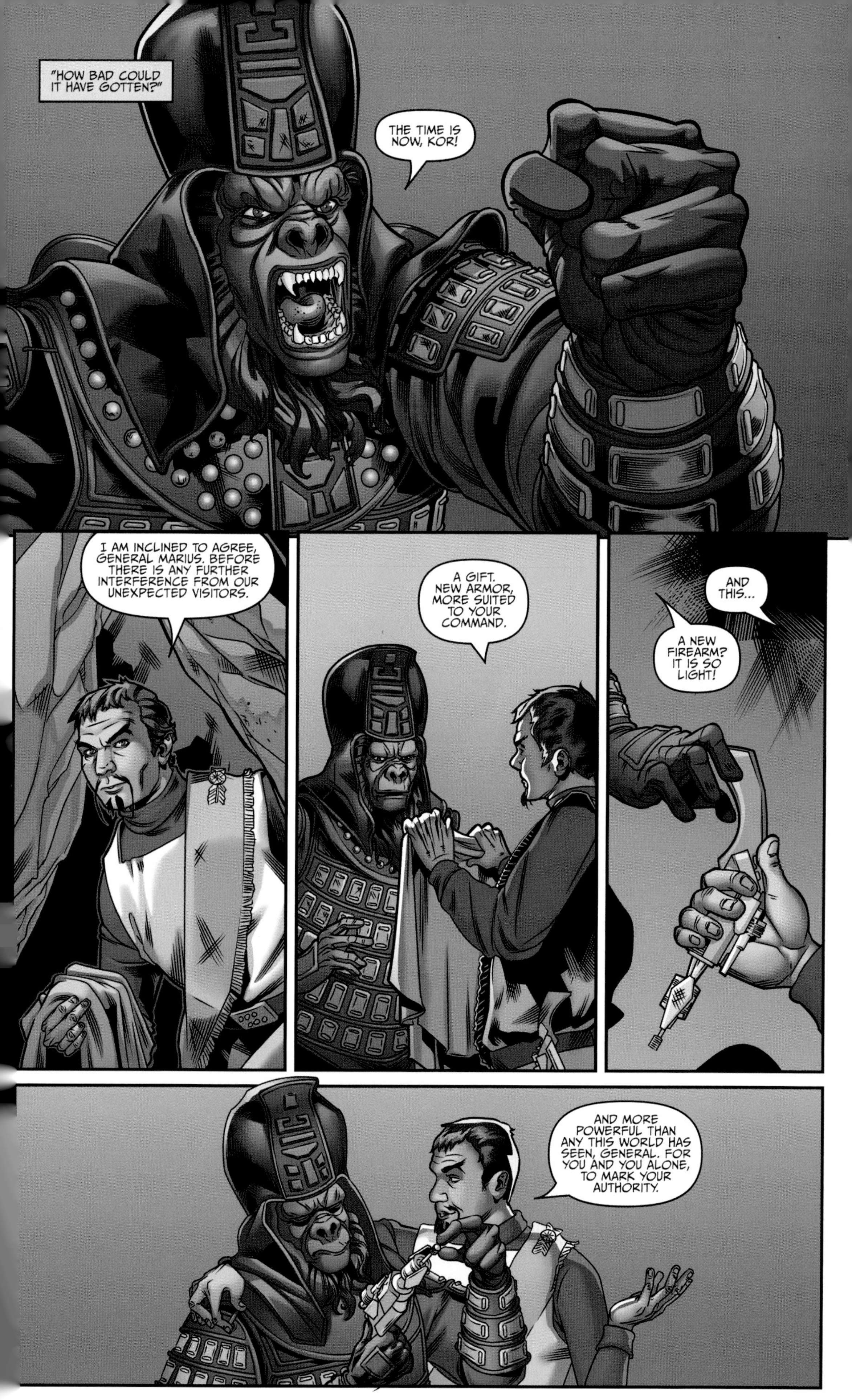
"HOW BAD COULD IT HAVE GOTTEN?"
THE TIME IS NOW, KOR!
I AM INCLINED TO AGREE, GENERAL MARIUS. BEFORE THERE IS ANY FURTHER INTERFERENCE FROM OUR UNEXPECTED VISITORS.
A GIFT. NEW ARMOR, MORE SUITED TO YOUR COMMAND.
AND THIS...
A NEW FIREARM? IT IS SO LIGHT!
AND MORE POWERFUL THAN ANY THIS WORLD HAS SEEN, GENERAL. FOR YOU AND YOU ALONE, TO MARK YOUR AUTHORITY.

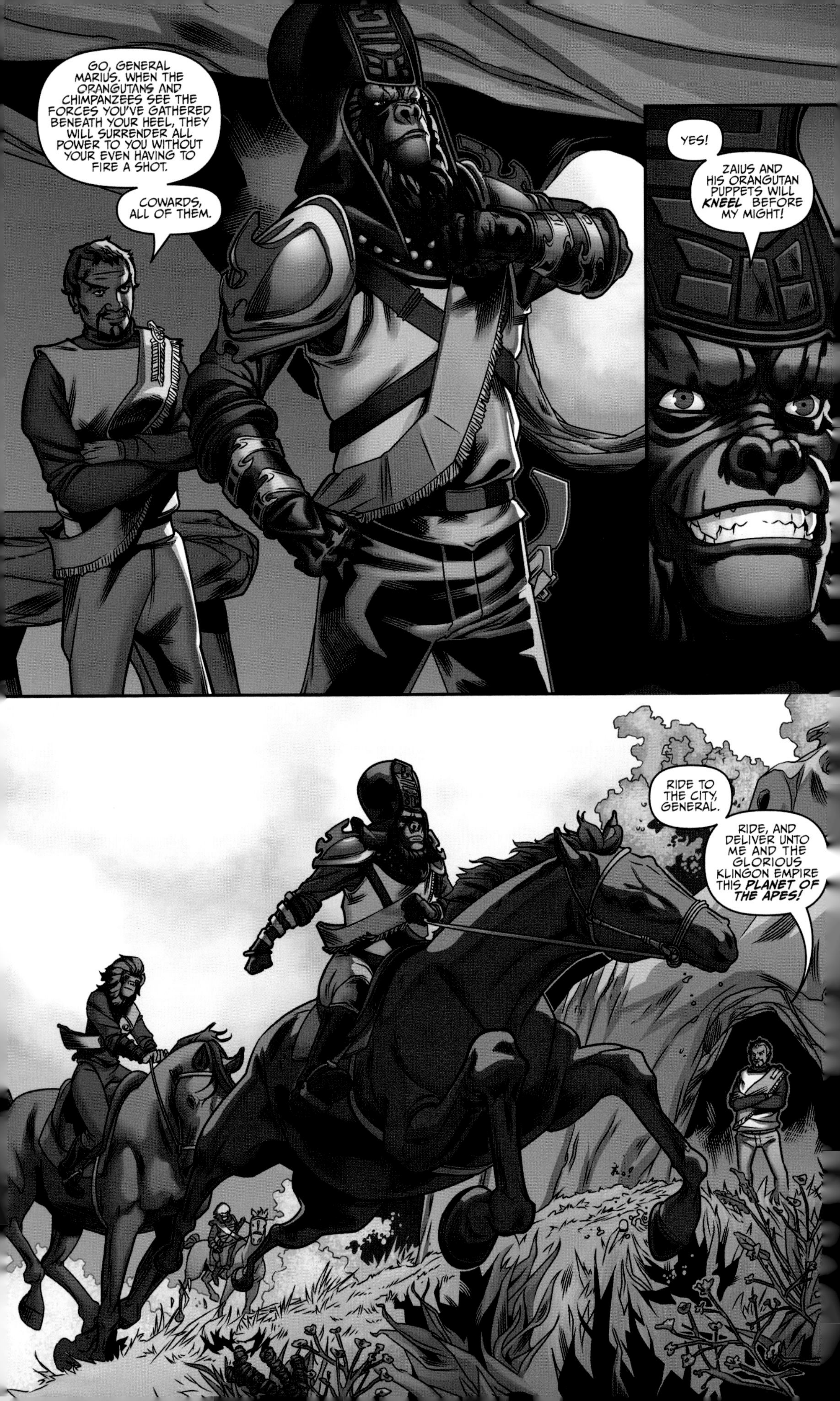
GO, GENERAL MARIUS. WHEN THE ORANGUTANS AND CHIMPANZEES SEE THE FORCES YOU'VE GATHERED BENEATH YOUR HEEL, THEY WILL SURRENDER ALL POWER TO YOU WITHOUT YOUR EVEN HAVING TO FIRE A SHOT.
COWARDS, ALL OF THEM.
YES!
ZAIUS AND HIS ORANGUTAN PUPPETS WILL **KNEEL** BEFORE MY MIGHT!
RIDE TO THE CITY, GENERAL.
RIDE, AND DELIVER UNTO ME AND THE GLORIOUS KLINGON EMPIRE THIS ***PLANET OF THE APES!***

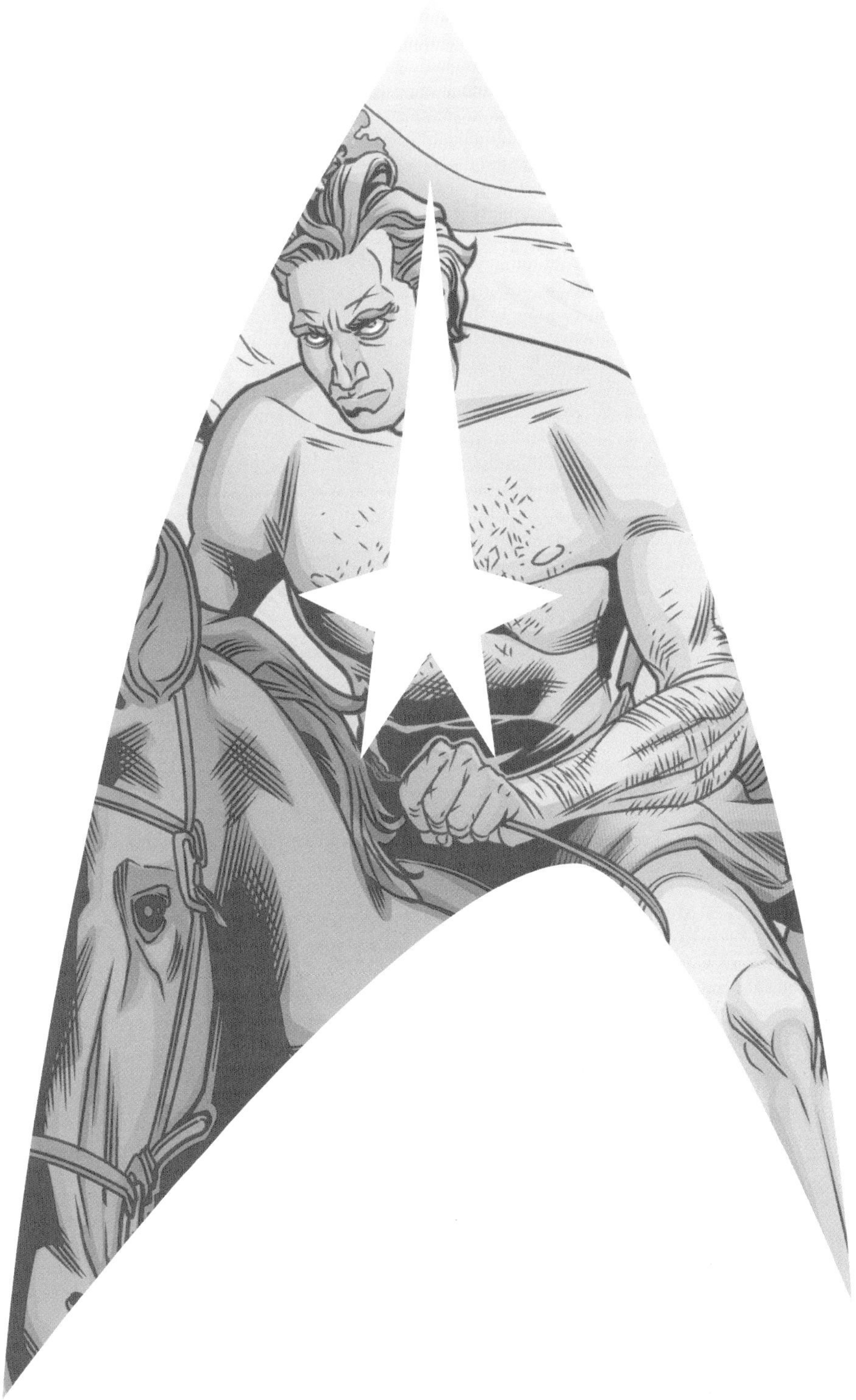

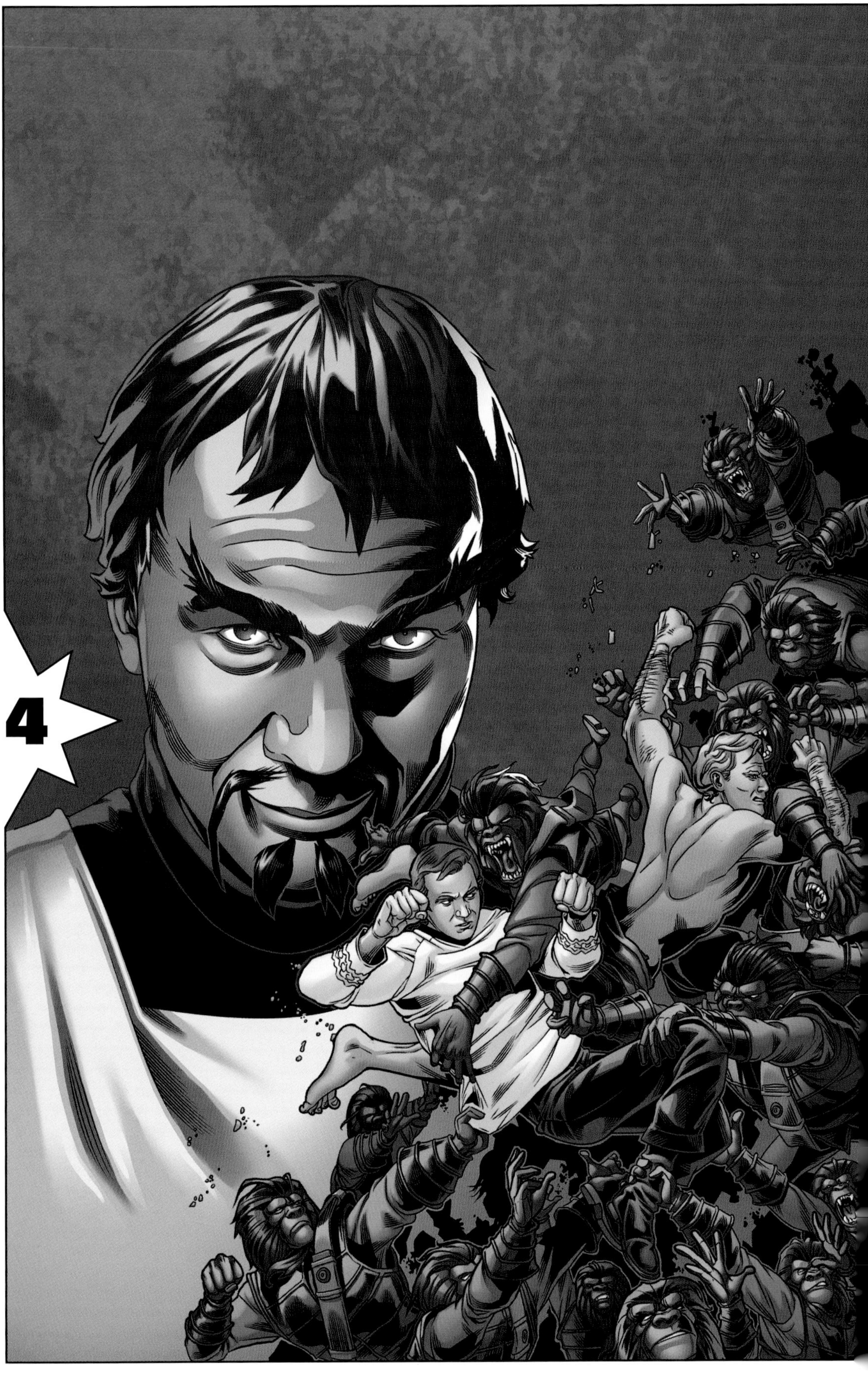
4

BY **RACHAEL STOTT** COLORS BY **CHARLIE KIRCHOFF**

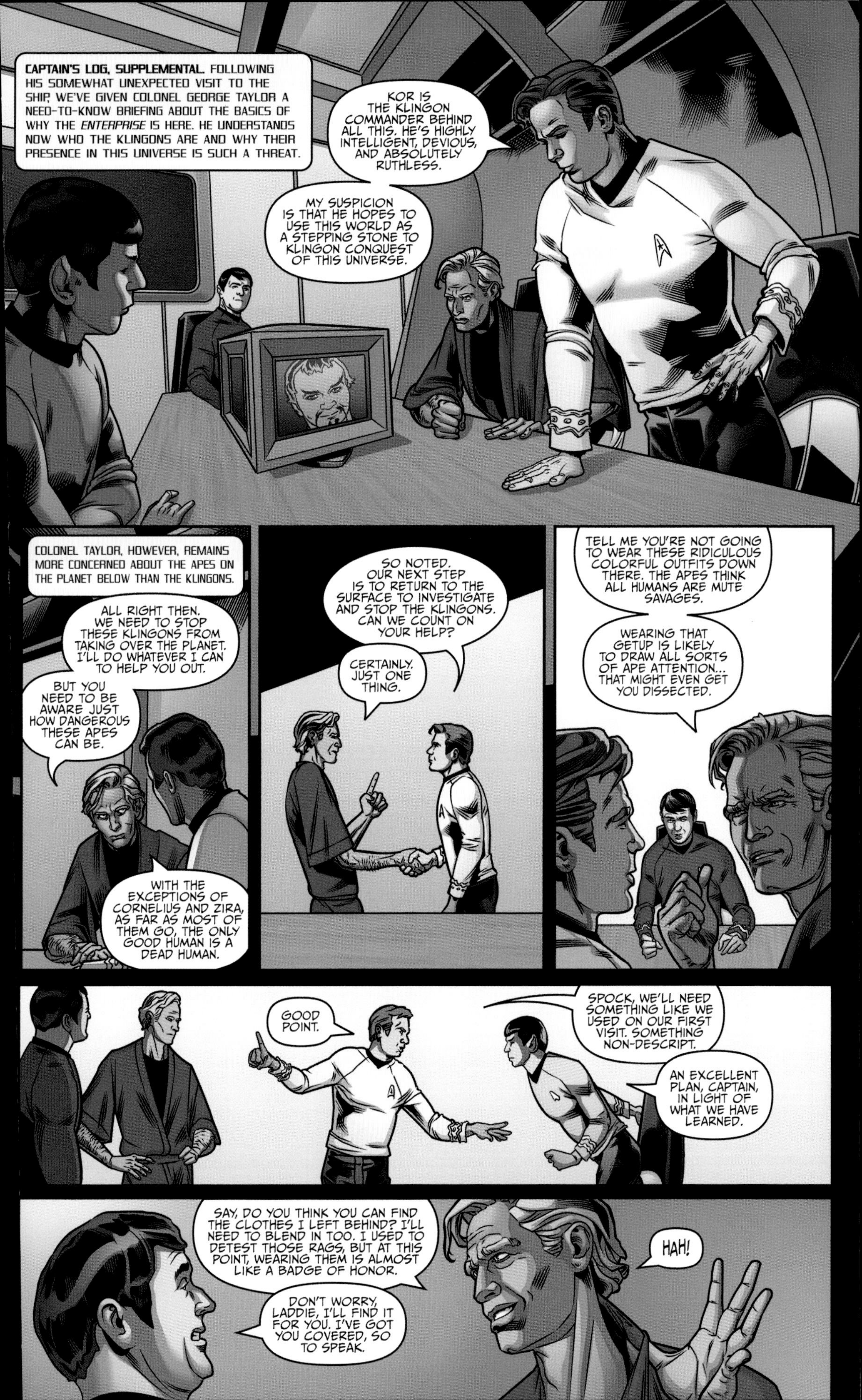
CAPTAIN'S LOG, SUPPLEMENTAL. FOLLOWING HIS SOMEWHAT UNEXPECTED VISIT TO THE SHIP, WE'VE GIVEN COLONEL GEORGE TAYLOR A NEED-TO-KNOW BRIEFING ABOUT THE BASICS OF WHY THE *ENTERPRISE* IS HERE. HE UNDERSTANDS NOW WHO THE KLINGONS ARE AND WHY THEIR PRESENCE IN THIS UNIVERSE IS SUCH A THREAT.
KOR IS THE KLINGON COMMANDER BEHIND ALL THIS. HE'S HIGHLY INTELLIGENT, DEVIOUS, AND ABSOLUTELY RUTHLESS.
MY SUSPICION IS THAT HE HOPES TO USE THIS WORLD AS A STEPPING STONE TO KLINGON CONQUEST OF THIS UNIVERSE.
COLONEL TAYLOR, HOWEVER, REMAINS MORE CONCERNED ABOUT THE APES ON THE PLANET BELOW THAN THE KLINGONS.
ALL RIGHT THEN. WE NEED TO STOP THESE KLINGONS FROM TAKING OVER THE PLANET. I'LL DO WHATEVER I CAN TO HELP YOU OUT.
BUT YOU NEED TO BE AWARE JUST HOW DANGEROUS THESE APES CAN BE.
WITH THE EXCEPTIONS OF CORNELIUS AND ZIRA, AS FAR AS MOST OF THEM GO, THE ONLY GOOD HUMAN IS A DEAD HUMAN.
SO NOTED. OUR NEXT STEP IS TO RETURN TO THE SURFACE TO INVESTIGATE AND STOP THE KLINGONS. CAN WE COUNT ON YOUR HELP?
CERTAINLY. JUST ONE THING.
TELL ME YOU'RE NOT GOING TO WEAR THESE RIDICULOUS COLORFUL OUTFITS DOWN THERE. THE APES THINK ALL HUMANS ARE MUTE SAVAGES.
WEARING THAT GETUP IS LIKELY TO DRAW ALL SORTS OF APE ATTENTION... THAT MIGHT EVEN GET YOU DISSECTED.
GOOD POINT.
SPOCK, WE'LL NEED SOMETHING LIKE WE USED ON OUR FIRST VISIT. SOMETHING NON-DESCRIPT.
AN EXCELLENT PLAN, CAPTAIN, IN LIGHT OF WHAT WE HAVE LEARNED.
SAY, DO YOU THINK YOU CAN FIND THE CLOTHES I LEFT BEHIND? I'LL NEED TO BLEND IN TOO. I USED TO DETEST THOSE RAGS, BUT AT THIS POINT, WEARING THEM IS ALMOST LIKE A BADGE OF HONOR.
DON'T WORRY, LADDIE, I'LL FIND IT FOR YOU. I'VE GOT YOU COVERED, SO TO SPEAK.
HAH!

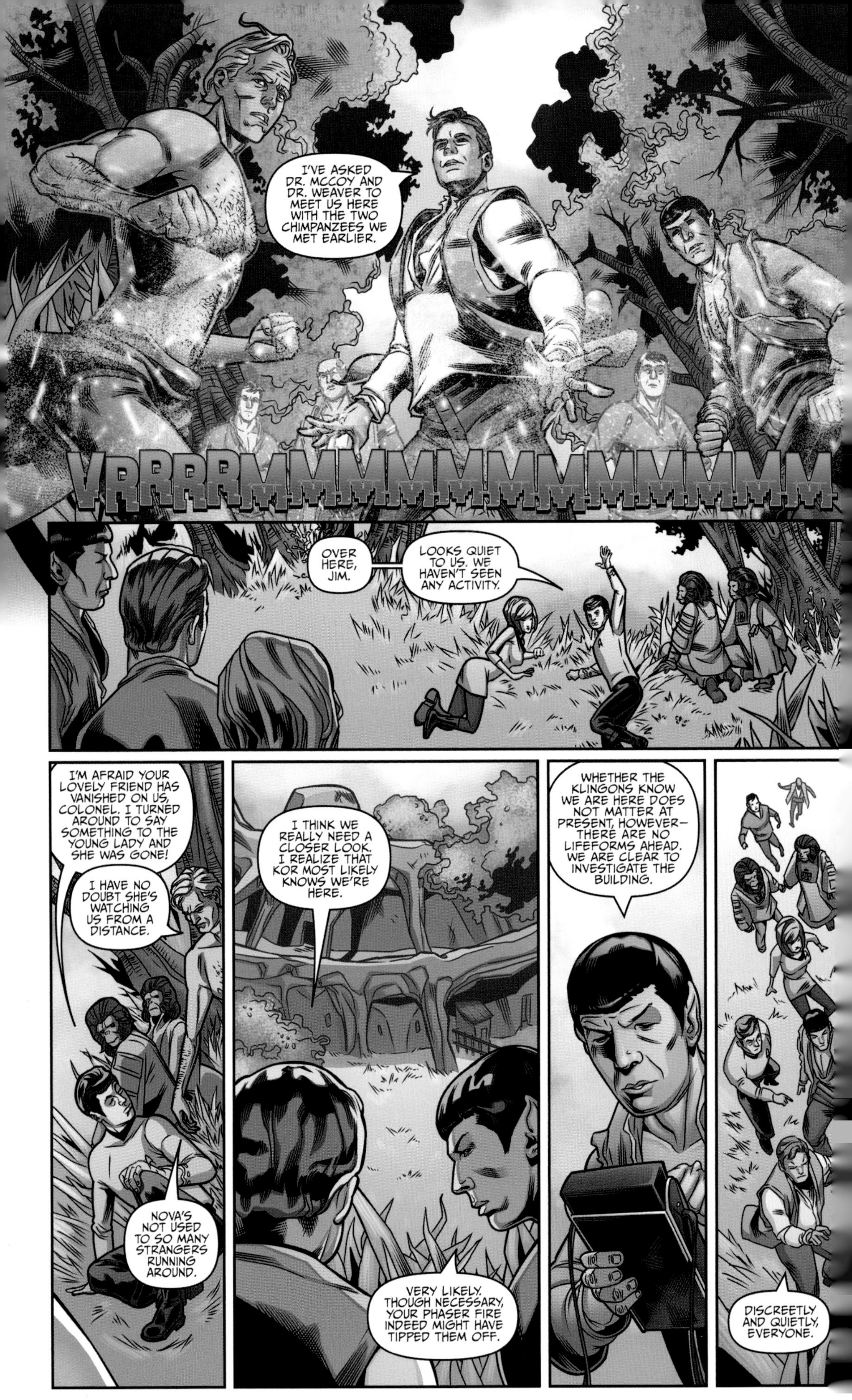
I'VE ASKED DR. MCCOY AND DR. WEAVER TO MEET US HERE WITH THE TWO CHIMPANZEES WE MET EARLIER.
VRRRRMMMMMMMMMMMMMMM
OVER HERE, JIM.
LOOKS QUIET TO US. WE HAVEN'T SEEN ANY ACTIVITY.
I'M AFRAID YOUR LOVELY FRIEND HAS VANISHED ON US, COLONEL. I TURNED AROUND TO SAY SOMETHING TO THE YOUNG LADY AND SHE WAS GONE!
I HAVE NO DOUBT SHE'S WATCHING US FROM A DISTANCE.
NOVA'S NOT USED TO SO MANY STRANGERS RUNNING AROUND.
I THINK WE REALLY NEED A CLOSER LOOK. I REALIZE THAT KOR MOST LIKELY KNOWS WE'RE HERE.
VERY LIKELY. THOUGH NECESSARY, YOUR PHASER FIRE INDEED MIGHT HAVE TIPPED THEM OFF.
WHETHER THE KLINGONS KNOW WE ARE HERE DOES NOT MATTER AT PRESENT, HOWEVER— THERE ARE NO LIFEFORMS AHEAD. WE ARE CLEAR TO INVESTIGATE THE BUILDING.
DISCREETLY AND QUIETLY, EVERYONE.

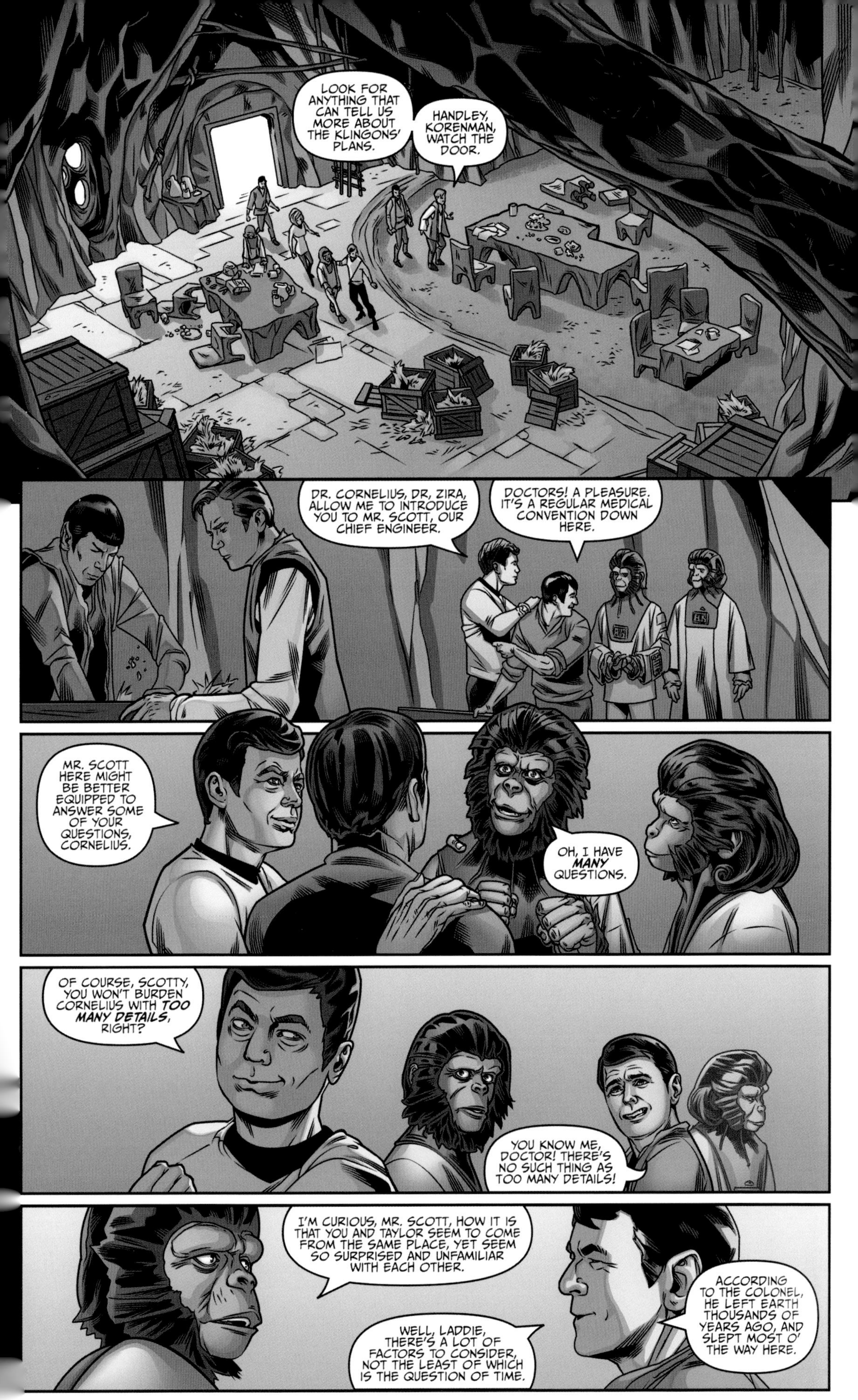
LOOK FOR ANYTHING THAT CAN TELL US MORE ABOUT THE KLINGONS' PLANS.
HANDLEY, KORENMAN, WATCH THE DOOR.
DR. CORNELIUS, DR, ZIRA, ALLOW ME TO INTRODUCE YOU TO MR. SCOTT, OUR CHIEF ENGINEER.
DOCTORS! A PLEASURE. IT'S A REGULAR MEDICAL CONVENTION DOWN HERE.
MR. SCOTT HERE MIGHT BE BETTER EQUIPPED TO ANSWER SOME OF YOUR QUESTIONS, CORNELIUS.
OH, I HAVE ***MANY*** QUESTIONS.
OF COURSE, SCOTTY, YOU WON'T BURDEN CORNELIUS WITH ***TOO MANY DETAILS***, RIGHT?
YOU KNOW ME, DOCTOR! THERE'S NO SUCH THING AS TOO MANY DETAILS!
I'M CURIOUS, MR. SCOTT, HOW IT IS THAT YOU AND TAYLOR SEEM TO COME FROM THE SAME PLACE, YET SEEM SO SURPRISED AND UNFAMILIAR WITH EACH OTHER.
WELL, LADDIE, THERE'S A LOT OF FACTORS TO CONSIDER, NOT THE LEAST OF WHICH IS THE QUESTION OF TIME.
ACCORDING TO THE COLONEL, HE LEFT EARTH THOUSANDS OF YEARS AGO, AND SLEPT MOST O' THE WAY HERE.

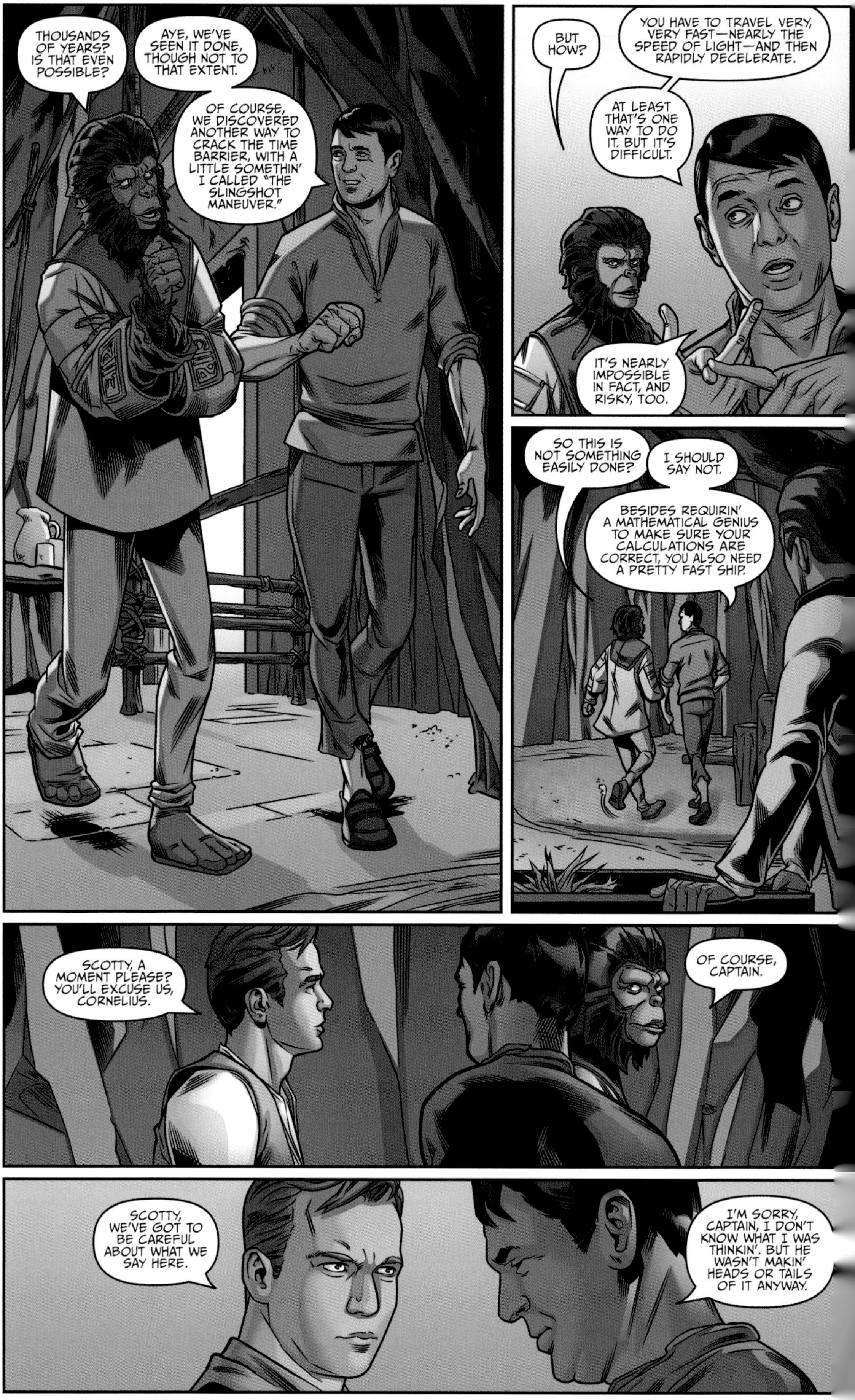
THOUSANDS OF YEARS? IS THAT EVEN POSSIBLE?
AYE, WE'VE SEEN IT DONE, THOUGH NOT TO THAT EXTENT.
OF COURSE, WE DISCOVERED ANOTHER WAY TO CRACK THE TIME BARRIER, WITH A LITTLE SOMETHIN' I CALLED "THE SLINGSHOT MANEUVER."
BUT HOW?
YOU HAVE TO TRAVEL VERY, VERY FAST—NEARLY THE SPEED OF LIGHT—AND THEN RAPIDLY DECELERATE.
AT LEAST THAT'S ONE WAY TO DO IT. BUT IT'S DIFFICULT.
IT'S NEARLY IMPOSSIBLE IN FACT, AND RISKY, TOO.
SO THIS IS NOT SOMETHING EASILY DONE?
I SHOULD SAY NOT.
BESIDES REQUIRIN' A MATHEMATICAL GENIUS TO MAKE SURE YOUR CALCULATIONS ARE CORRECT, YOU ALSO NEED A PRETTY FAST SHIP.
SCOTTY, A MOMENT PLEASE? YOU'LL EXCUSE US, CORNELIUS.
OF COURSE, CAPTAIN.
SCOTTY, WE'VE GOT TO BE CAREFUL ABOUT WHAT WE SAY HERE.
I'M SORRY, CAPTAIN, I DON'T KNOW WHAT I WAS THINKIN'. BUT HE WASN'T MAKIN' HEADS OR TAILS OF IT ANYWAY.

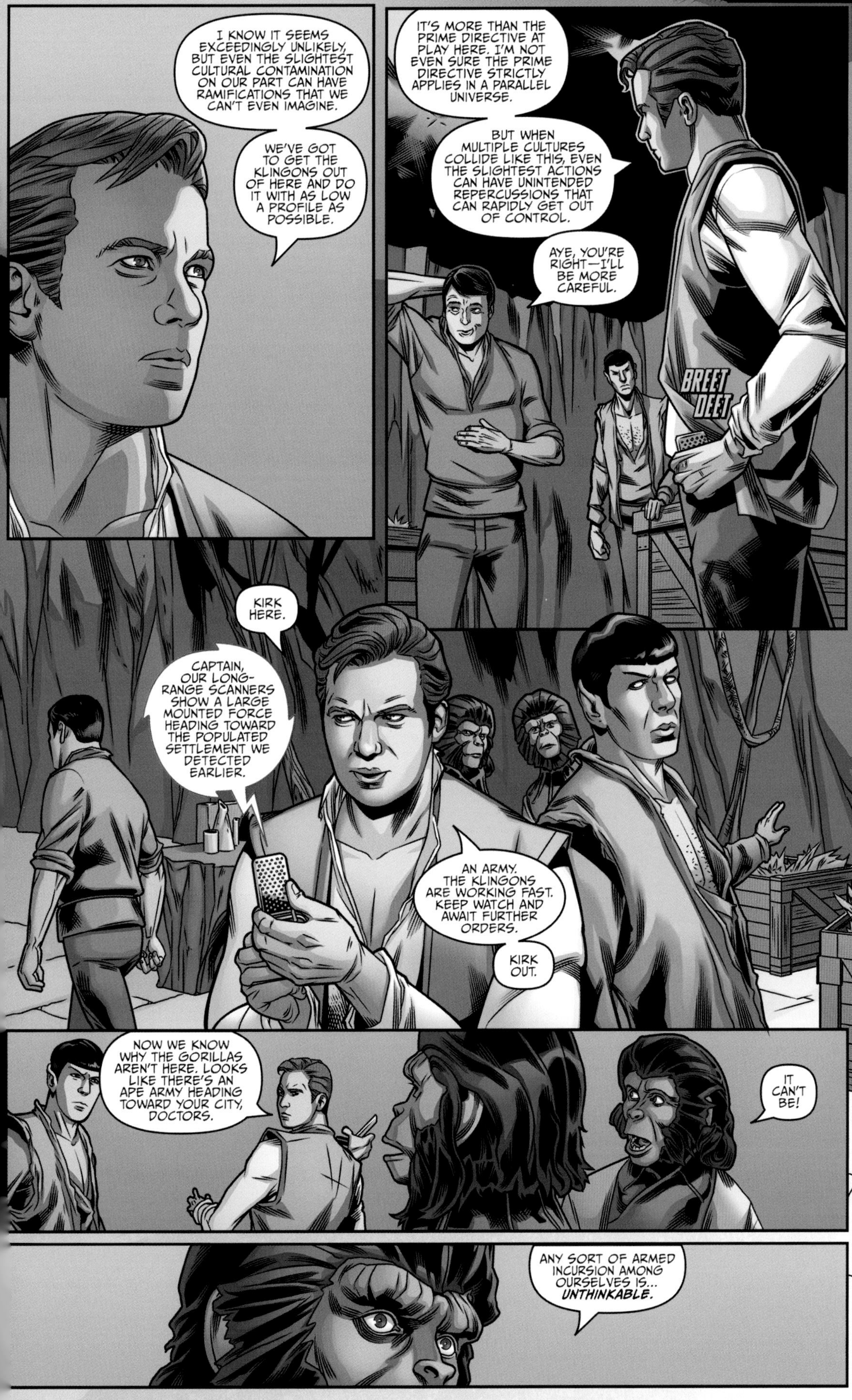
I KNOW IT SEEMS EXCEEDINGLY UNLIKELY, BUT EVEN THE SLIGHTEST CULTURAL CONTAMINATION ON OUR PART CAN HAVE RAMIFICATIONS THAT WE CAN'T EVEN IMAGINE.
WE'VE GOT TO GET THE KLINGONS OUT OF HERE AND DO IT WITH AS LOW A PROFILE AS POSSIBLE.
IT'S MORE THAN THE PRIME DIRECTIVE AT PLAY HERE. I'M NOT EVEN SURE THE PRIME DIRECTIVE STRICTLY APPLIES IN A PARALLEL UNIVERSE.
BUT WHEN MULTIPLE CULTURES COLLIDE LIKE THIS, EVEN THE SLIGHTEST ACTIONS CAN HAVE UNINTENDED REPERCUSSIONS THAT CAN RAPIDLY GET OUT OF CONTROL.
AYE, YOU'RE RIGHT—I'LL BE MORE CAREFUL.
BREET DEET
KIRK HERE.
CAPTAIN, OUR LONG-RANGE SCANNERS SHOW A LARGE MOUNTED FORCE HEADING TOWARD THE POPULATED SETTLEMENT WE DETECTED EARLIER.
AN ARMY. THE KLINGONS ARE WORKING FAST. KEEP WATCH AND AWAIT FURTHER ORDERS.
KIRK OUT.
NOW WE KNOW WHY THE GORILLAS AREN'T HERE. LOOKS LIKE THERE'S AN APE ARMY HEADING TOWARD YOUR CITY, DOCTORS.
IT CAN'T BE!
ANY SORT OF ARMED INCURSION AMONG OURSELVES IS... *UNTHINKABLE.*

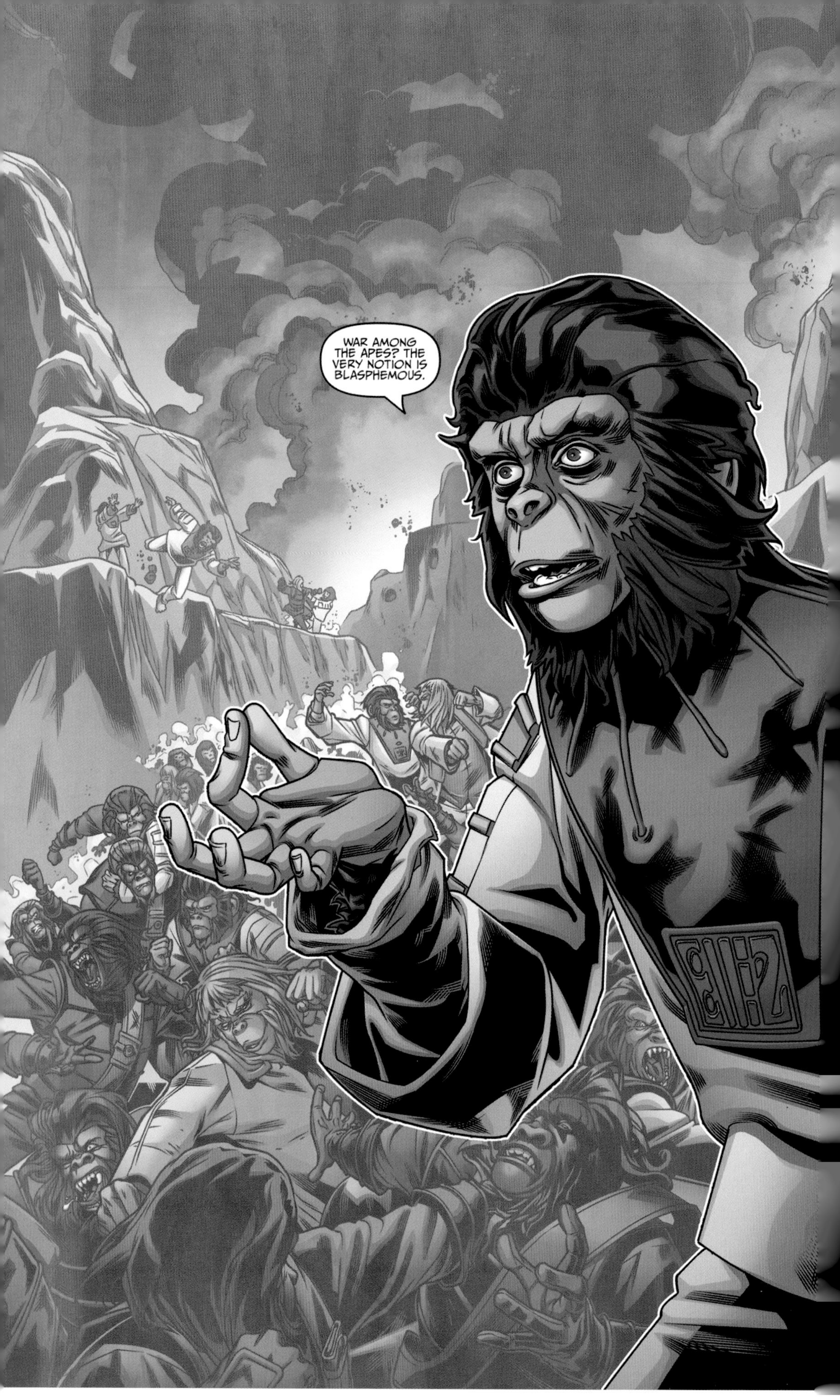
WAR AMONG THE APES? THE VERY NOTION IS BLASPHEMOUS.

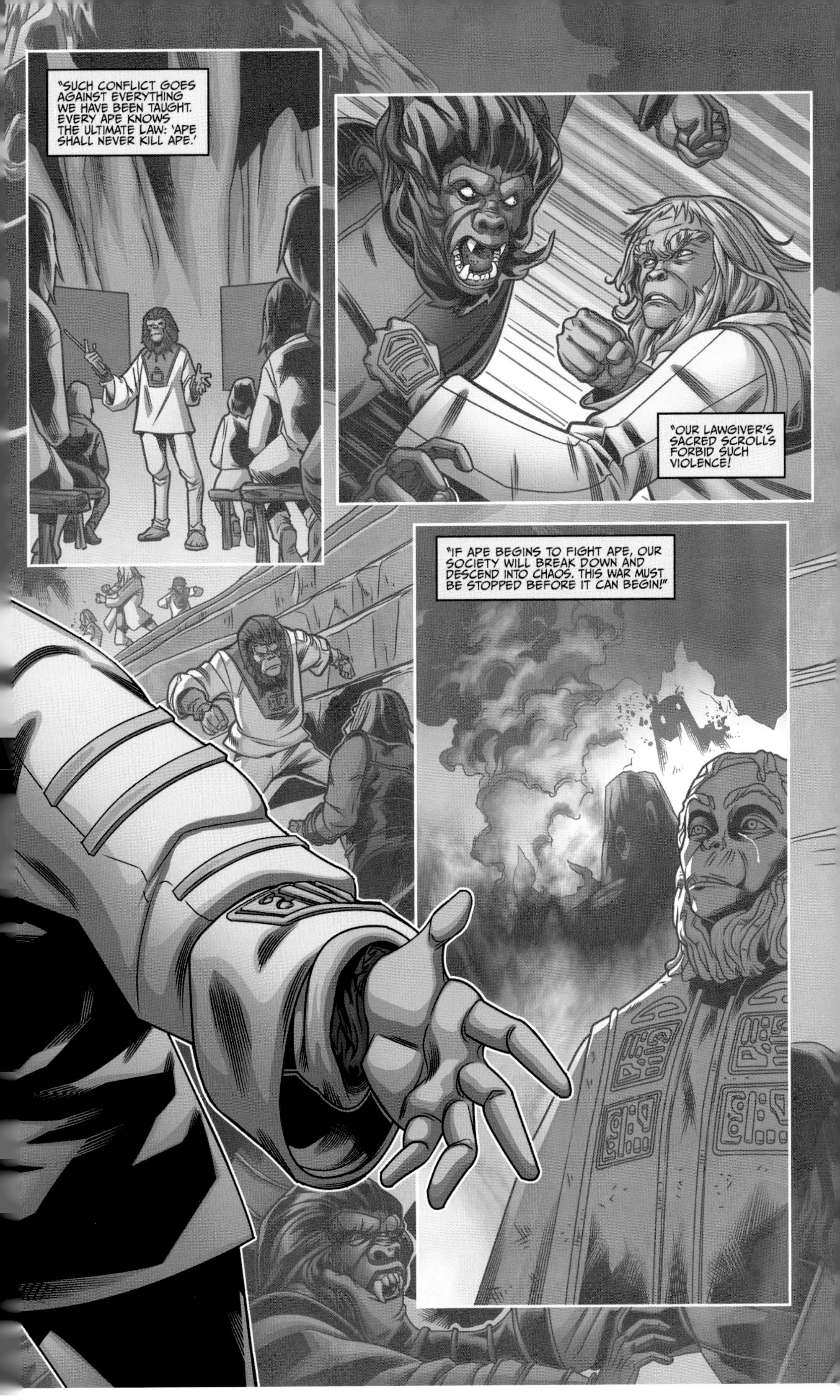
"SUCH CONFLICT GOES AGAINST EVERYTHING WE HAVE BEEN TAUGHT. EVERY APE KNOWS THE ULTIMATE LAW: 'APE SHALL NEVER KILL APE.'
"OUR LAWGIVER'S SACRED SCROLLS FORBID SUCH VIOLENCE!
"IF APE BEGINS TO FIGHT APE, OUR SOCIETY WILL BREAK DOWN AND DESCEND INTO CHAOS. THIS WAR MUST BE STOPPED BEFORE IT CAN BEGIN!"

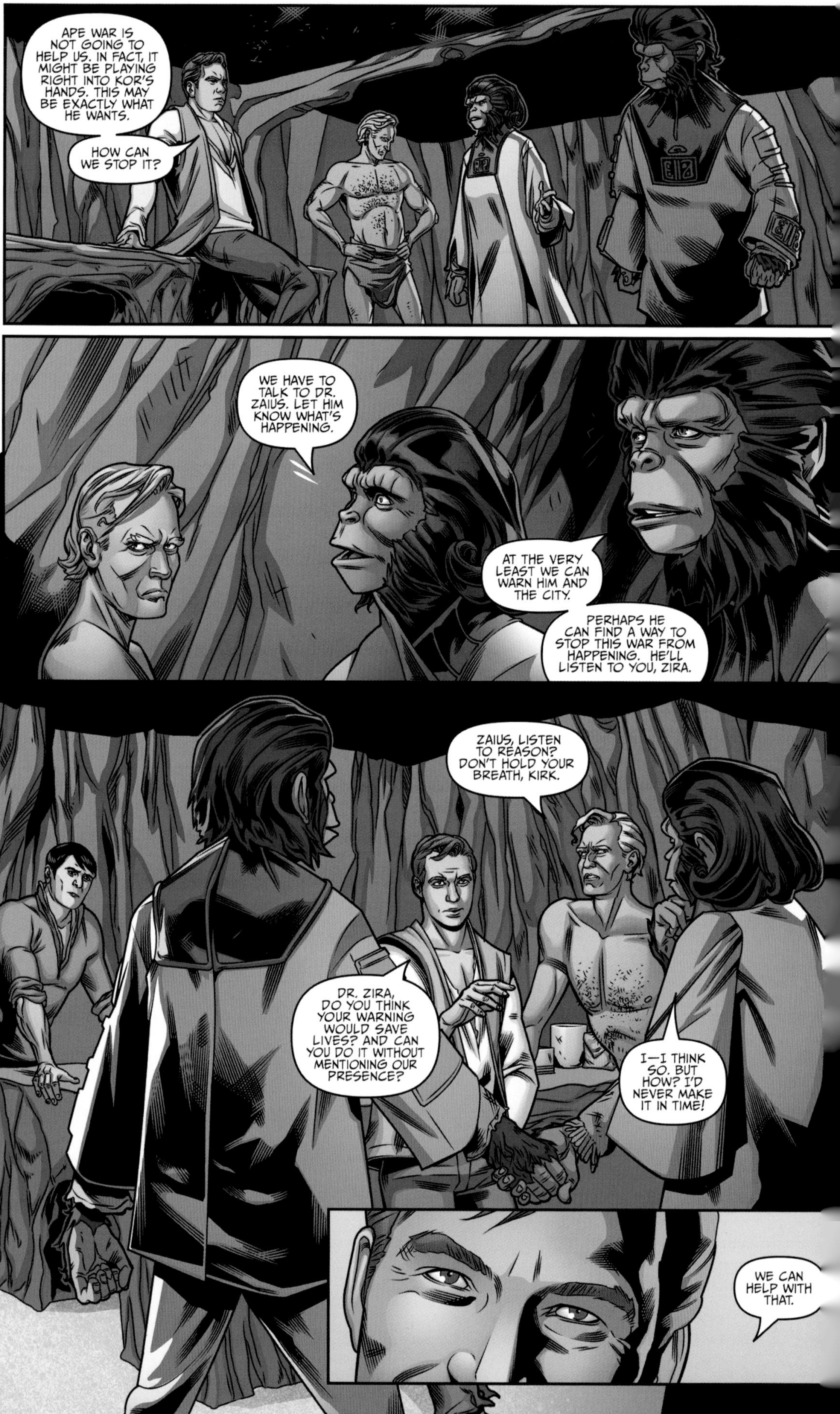
APE WAR IS NOT GOING TO HELP US. IN FACT, IT MIGHT BE PLAYING RIGHT INTO KOR'S HANDS. THIS MAY BE EXACTLY WHAT HE WANTS.
HOW CAN WE STOP IT?
WE HAVE TO TALK TO DR. ZAIUS. LET HIM KNOW WHAT'S HAPPENING.
AT THE VERY LEAST WE CAN WARN HIM AND THE CITY.
PERHAPS HE CAN FIND A WAY TO STOP THIS WAR FROM HAPPENING. HE'LL LISTEN TO YOU, ZIRA.
ZAIUS, LISTEN TO REASON? DON'T HOLD YOUR BREATH, KIRK.
DR. ZIRA, DO YOU THINK YOUR WARNING WOULD SAVE LIVES? AND CAN YOU DO IT WITHOUT MENTIONING OUR PRESENCE?
I—I THINK SO. BUT HOW? I'D NEVER MAKE IT IN TIME!
WE CAN HELP WITH THAT.

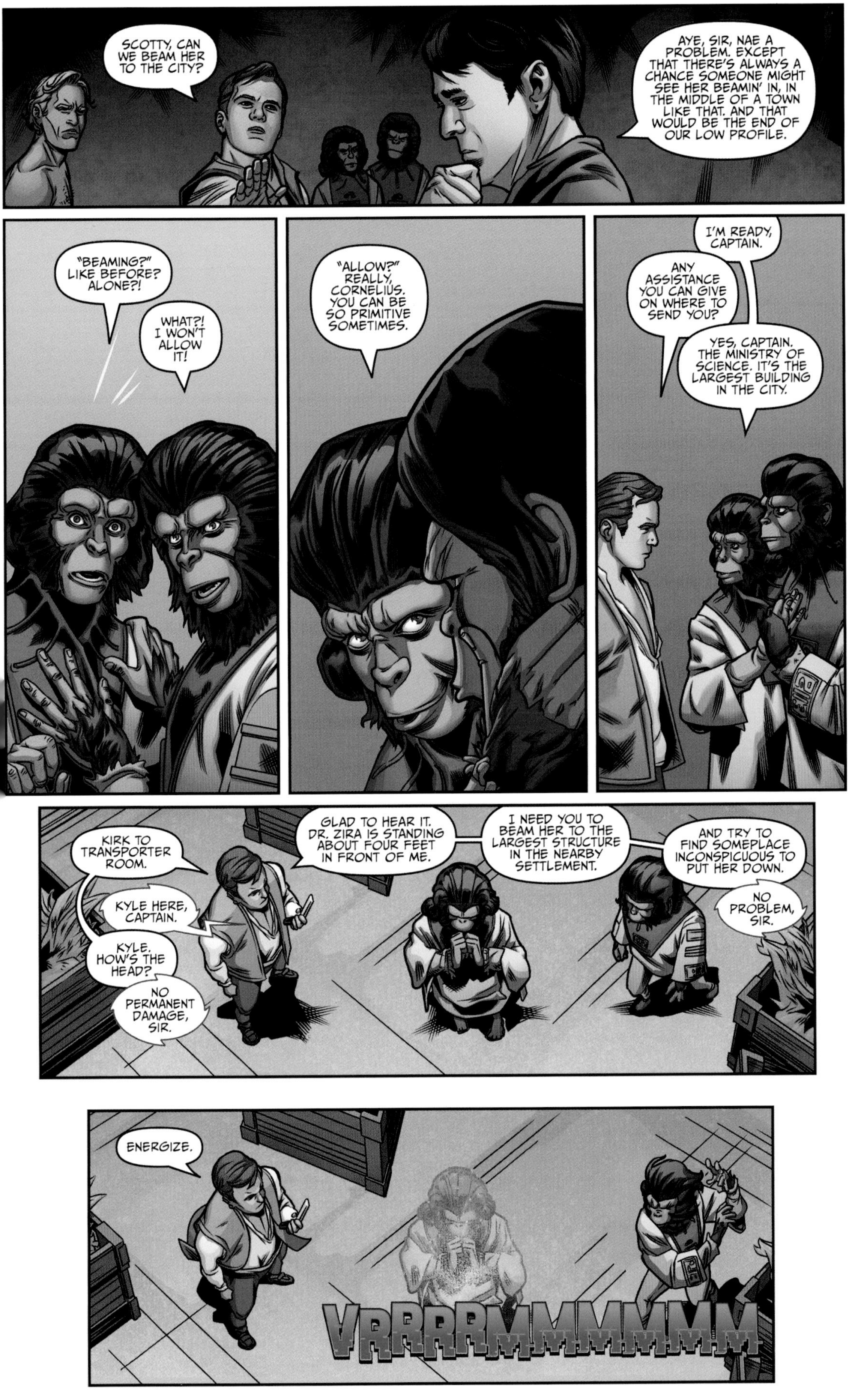
SCOTTY, CAN WE BEAM HER TO THE CITY?
AYE, SIR, NAE A PROBLEM. EXCEPT THAT THERE'S ALWAYS A CHANCE SOMEONE MIGHT SEE HER BEAMIN' IN, IN THE MIDDLE OF A TOWN LIKE THAT. AND THAT WOULD BE THE END OF OUR LOW PROFILE.
"BEAMING?" LIKE BEFORE? ALONE?!
WHAT?! I WON'T ALLOW IT!
"ALLOW?" REALLY, CORNELIUS. YOU CAN BE SO PRIMITIVE SOMETIMES.
I'M READY, CAPTAIN.
ANY ASSISTANCE YOU CAN GIVE ON WHERE TO SEND YOU?
YES, CAPTAIN. THE MINISTRY OF SCIENCE. IT'S THE LARGEST BUILDING IN THE CITY.
KIRK TO TRANSPORTER ROOM.
KYLE HERE, CAPTAIN.
KYLE. HOW'S THE HEAD?
NO PERMANENT DAMAGE, SIR.
GLAD TO HEAR IT. DR. ZIRA IS STANDING ABOUT FOUR FEET IN FRONT OF ME.
I NEED YOU TO BEAM HER TO THE LARGEST STRUCTURE IN THE NEARBY SETTLEMENT.
AND TRY TO FIND SOMEPLACE INCONSPICUOUS TO PUT HER DOWN.
NO PROBLEM, SIR.
ENERGIZE.
VRRRRMMMMMMM

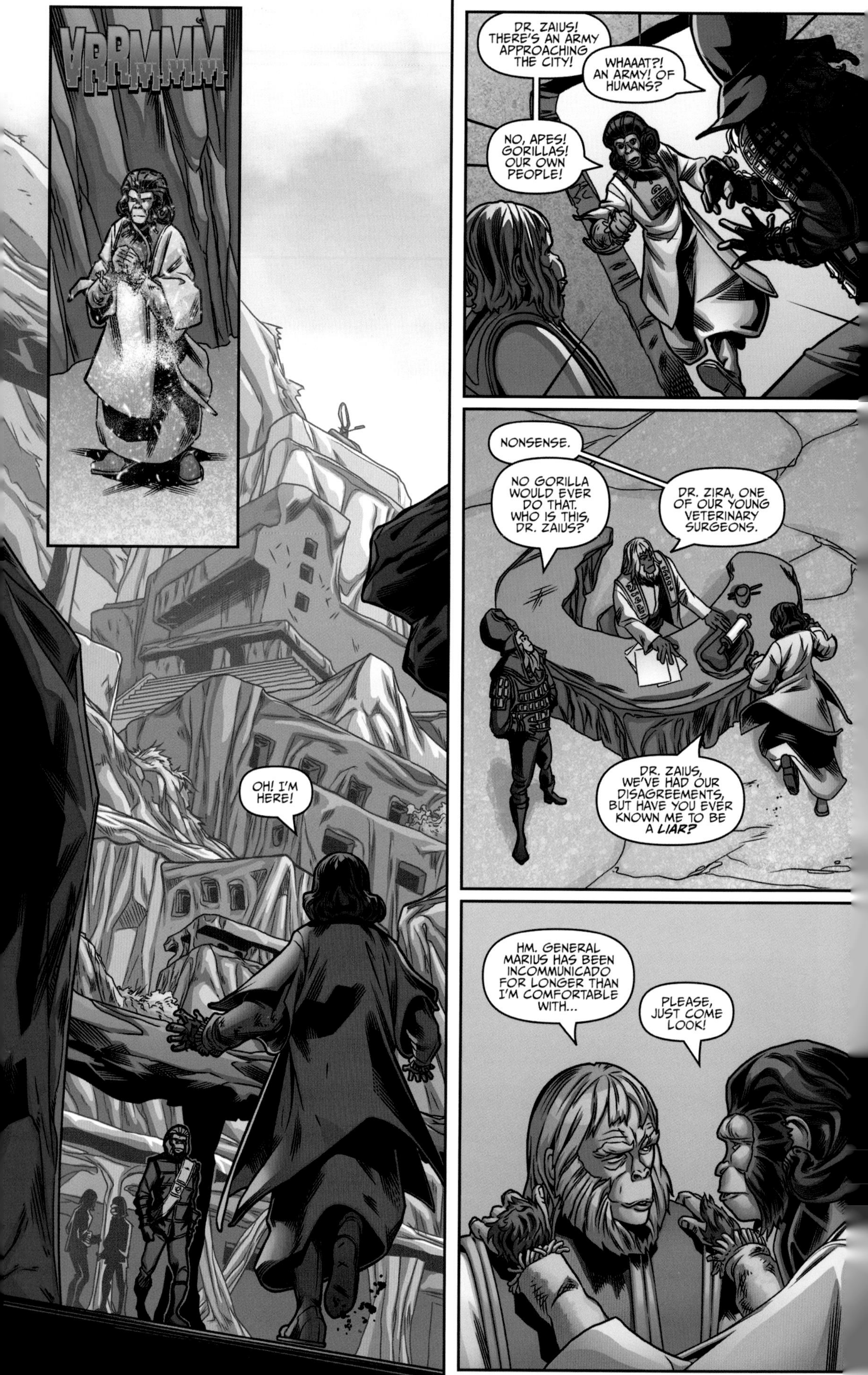
VRRMMM
OH! I'M HERE!
DR. ZAIUS! THERE'S AN ARMY APPROACHING THE CITY!
WHAAAT?! AN ARMY! OF HUMANS?
NO, APES! GORILLAS! OUR OWN PEOPLE!
NONSENSE.
NO GORILLA WOULD EVER DO THAT. WHO IS THIS, DR. ZAIUS?
DR. ZIRA, ONE OF OUR YOUNG VETERINARY SURGEONS.
DR. ZAIUS, WE'VE HAD OUR DISAGREEMENTS, BUT HAVE YOU EVER KNOWN ME TO BE A LIAR?
HM. GENERAL MARIUS HAS BEEN INCOMMUNICADO FOR LONGER THAN I'M COMFORTABLE WITH...
PLEASE, JUST COME LOOK!

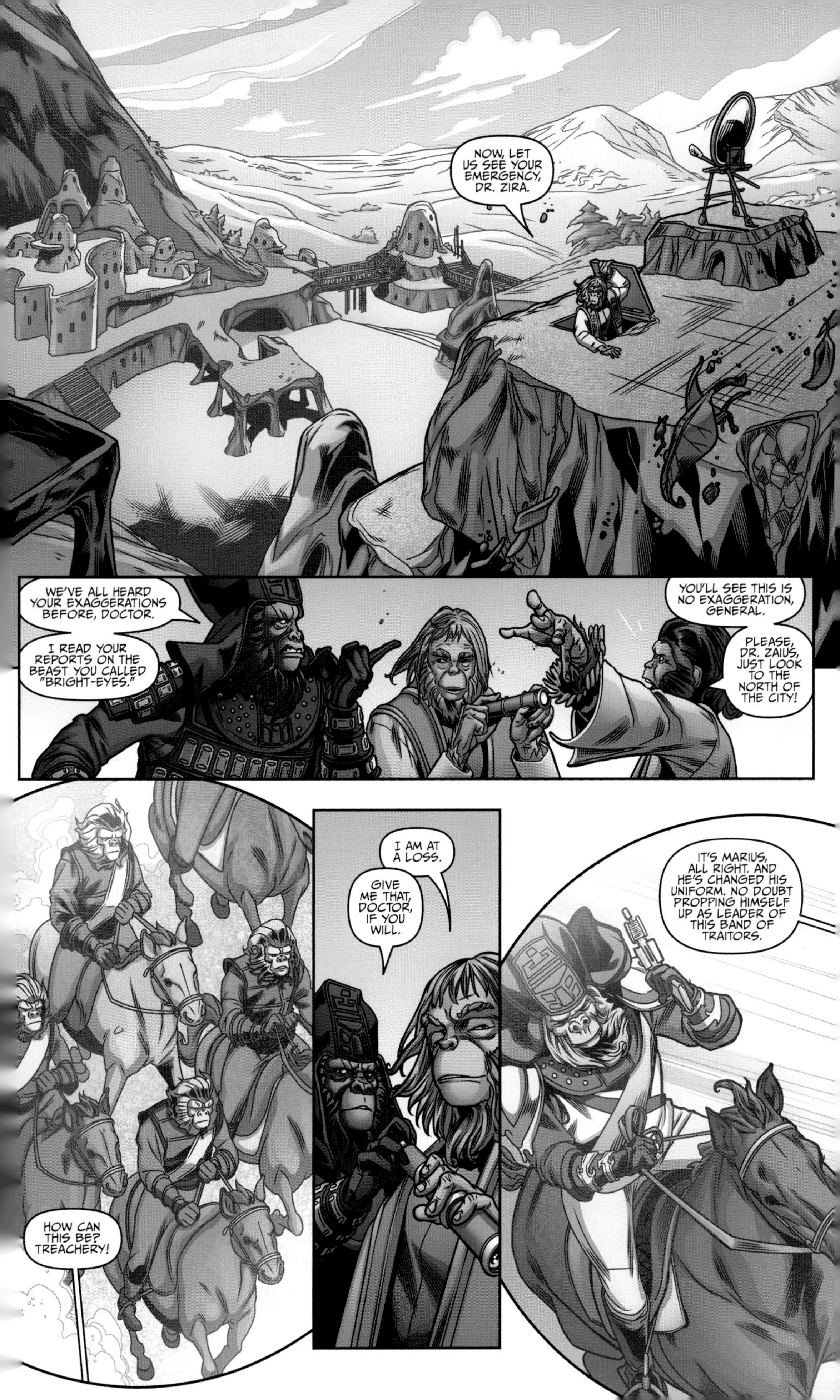
NOW, LET US SEE YOUR EMERGENCY, DR. ZIRA.
WE'VE ALL HEARD YOUR EXAGGERATIONS BEFORE, DOCTOR.
I READ YOUR REPORTS ON THE BEAST YOU CALLED "BRIGHT-EYES."
YOU'LL SEE THIS IS NO EXAGGERATION, GENERAL.
PLEASE, DR. ZAIUS, JUST LOOK TO THE NORTH OF THE CITY!
HOW CAN THIS BE? TREACHERY!
I AM AT A LOSS.
GIVE ME THAT, DOCTOR, IF YOU WILL.
IT'S MARIUS, ALL RIGHT. AND HE'S CHANGED HIS UNIFORM. NO DOUBT PROPPING HIMSELF UP AS LEADER OF THIS BAND OF TRAITORS.

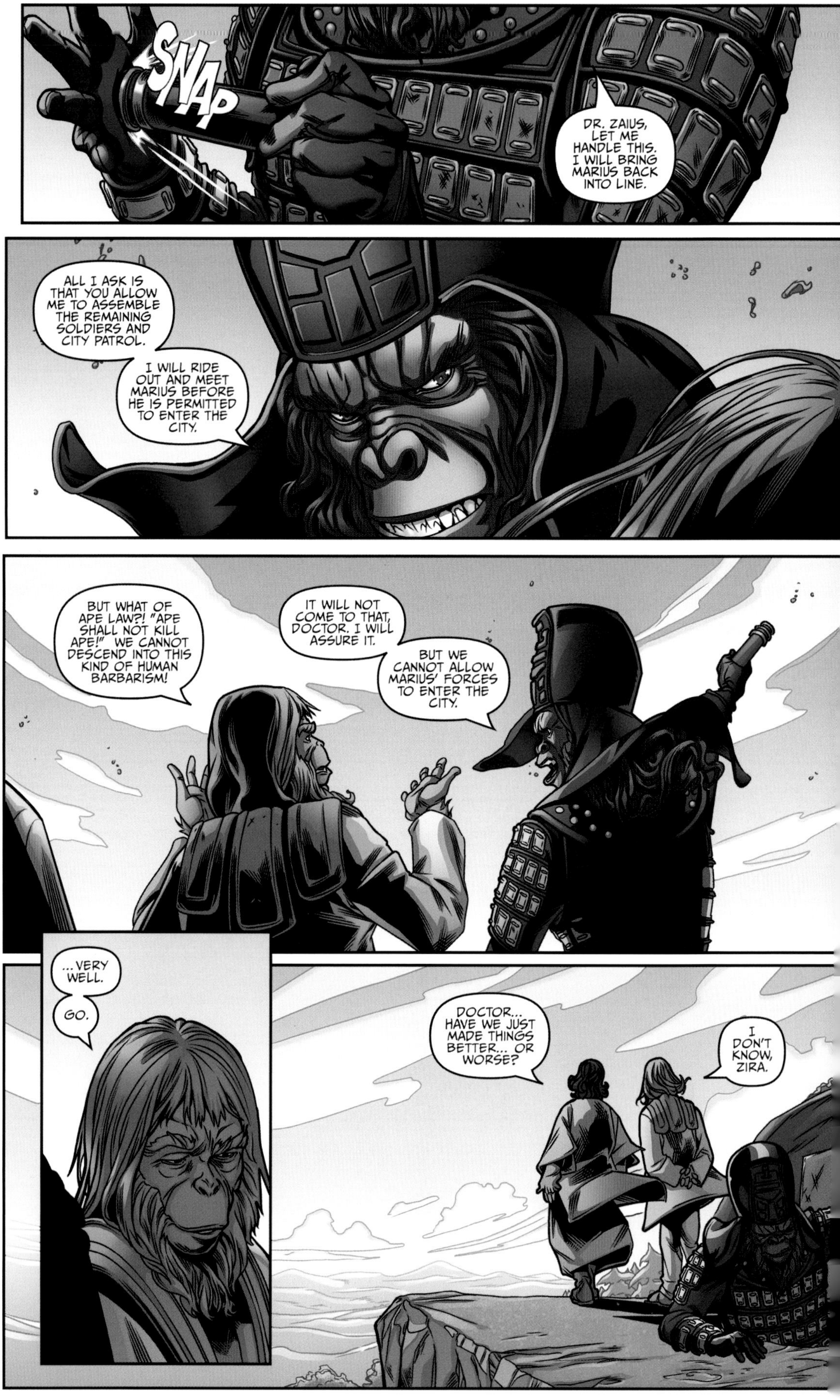
SNAP
DR. ZAIUS, LET ME HANDLE THIS. I WILL BRING MARIUS BACK INTO LINE.
ALL I ASK IS THAT YOU ALLOW ME TO ASSEMBLE THE REMAINING SOLDIERS AND CITY PATROL.
I WILL RIDE OUT AND MEET MARIUS BEFORE HE IS PERMITTED TO ENTER THE CITY.
BUT WHAT OF APE LAW?! "APE SHALL NOT KILL APE!" WE CANNOT DESCEND INTO THIS KIND OF HUMAN BARBARISM!
IT WILL NOT COME TO THAT, DOCTOR. I WILL ASSURE IT.
BUT WE CANNOT ALLOW MARIUS' FORCES TO ENTER THE CITY.
...VERY WELL.
GO.
DOCTOR... HAVE WE JUST MADE THINGS BETTER... OR WORSE?
I DON'T KNOW, ZIRA.

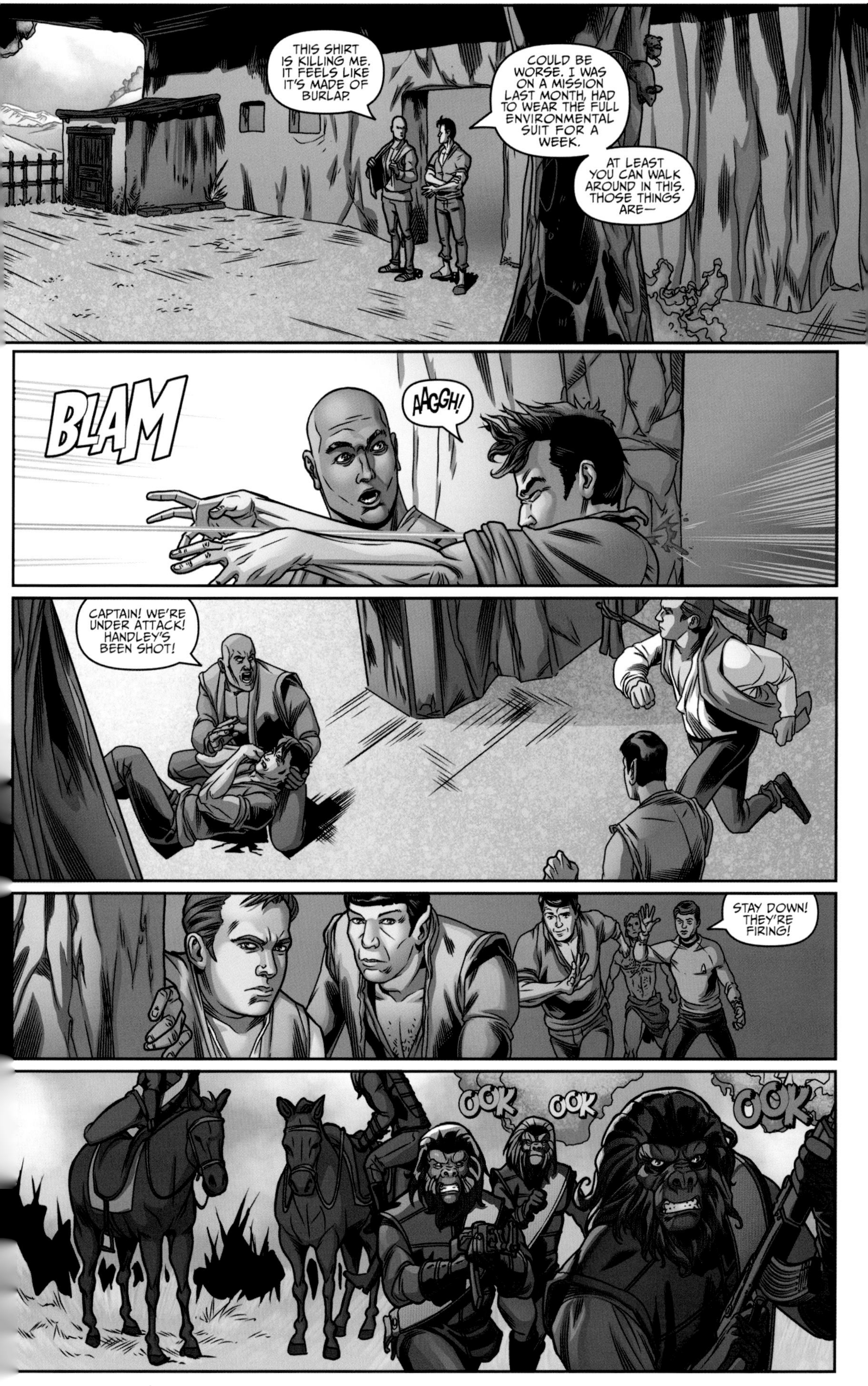
THIS SHIRT IS KILLING ME. IT FEELS LIKE IT'S MADE OF BURLAP.
COULD BE WORSE. I WAS ON A MISSION LAST MONTH, HAD TO WEAR THE FULL ENVIRONMENTAL SUIT FOR A WEEK.
AT LEAST YOU CAN WALK AROUND IN THIS. THOSE THINGS ARE—
BLAM
AAGGH!
CAPTAIN! WE'RE UNDER ATTACK! HANDLEY'S BEEN SHOT!
STAY DOWN! THEY'RE FIRING!
OOK
OOK
OOK

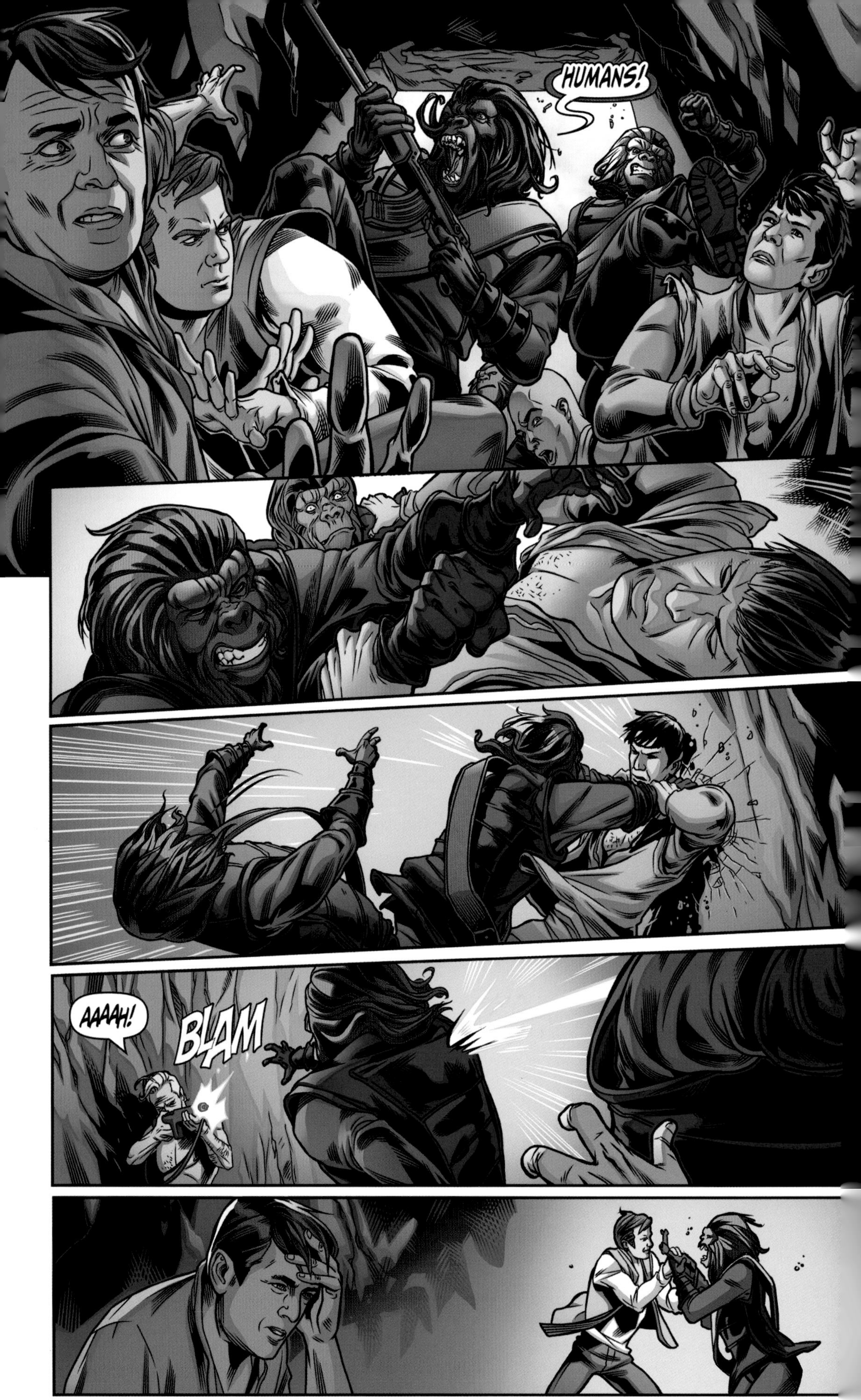
HUMANS!
AAAAH!
BLAM

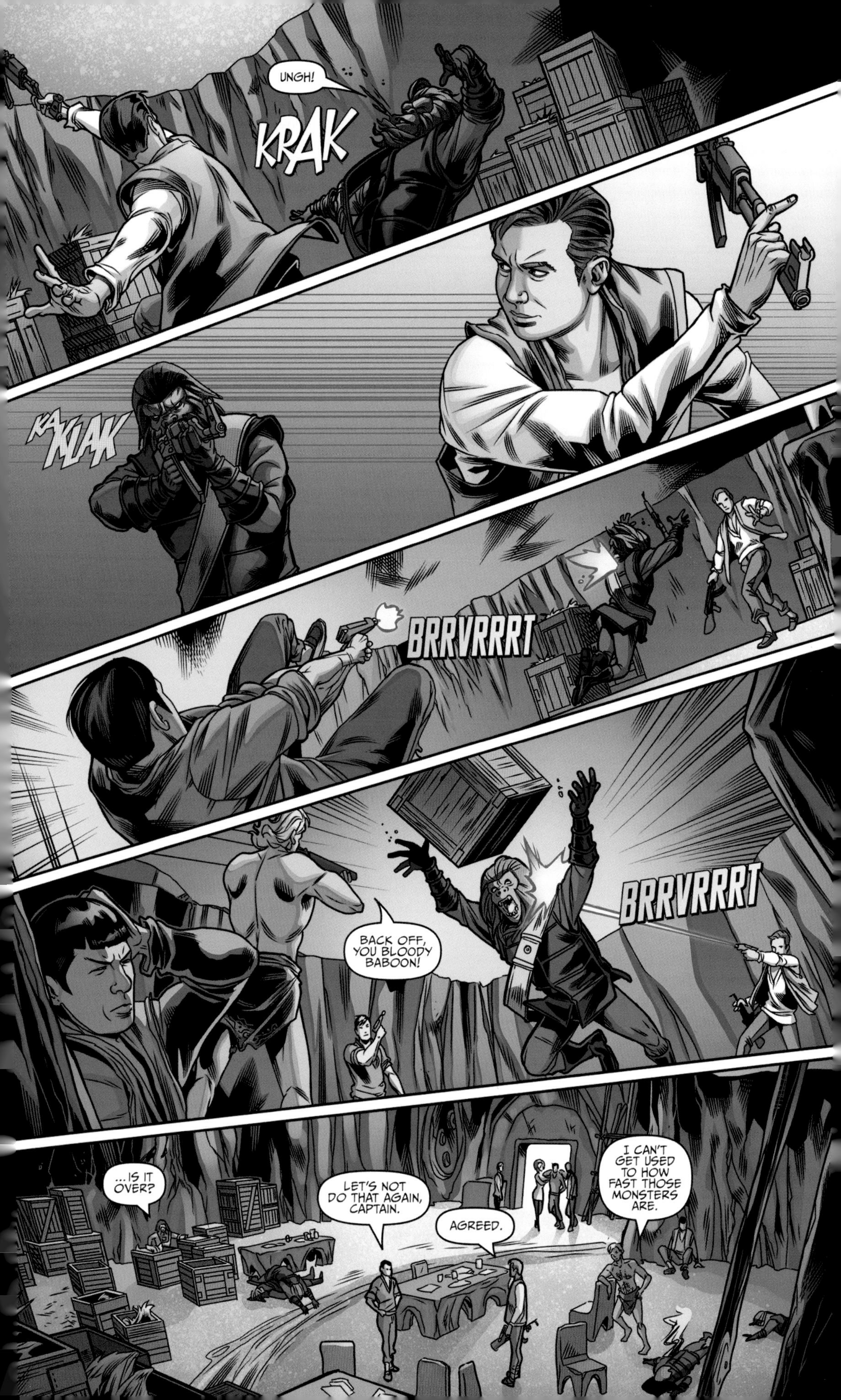
UNGH!
KRAK
KA KLAK
BRRVRRRT
BRRVRRRT
BACK OFF, YOU BLOODY BABOON!
...IS IT OVER?
LET'S NOT DO THAT AGAIN, CAPTAIN.
AGREED.
I CAN'T GET USED TO HOW FAST THOSE MONSTERS ARE.

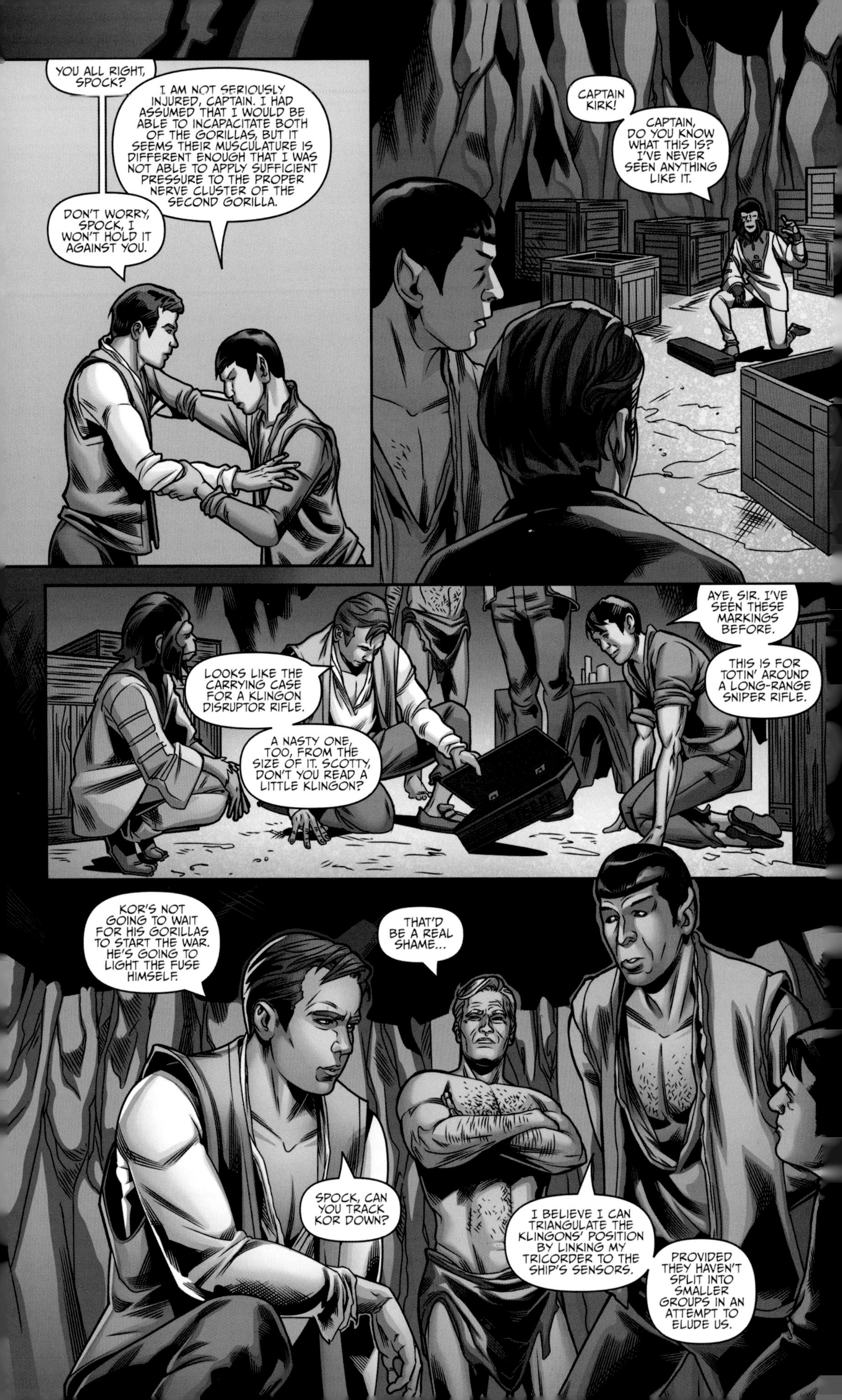

YOU ALL RIGHT, SPOCK?
I AM NOT SERIOUSLY INJURED, CAPTAIN. I HAD ASSUMED THAT I WOULD BE ABLE TO INCAPACITATE BOTH OF THE GORILLAS, BUT IT SEEMS THEIR MUSCULATURE IS DIFFERENT ENOUGH THAT I WAS NOT ABLE TO APPLY SUFFICIENT PRESSURE TO THE PROPER NERVE CLUSTER OF THE SECOND GORILLA.
DON'T WORRY, SPOCK, I WON'T HOLD IT AGAINST YOU.
CAPTAIN KIRK!
CAPTAIN, DO YOU KNOW WHAT THIS IS? I'VE NEVER SEEN ANYTHING LIKE IT.
LOOKS LIKE THE CARRYING CASE FOR A KLINGON DISRUPTOR RIFLE.
A NASTY ONE, TOO, FROM THE SIZE OF IT. SCOTTY, DON'T YOU READ A LITTLE KLINGON?
AYE, SIR. I'VE SEEN THESE MARKINGS BEFORE.
THIS IS FOR TOTIN' AROUND A LONG-RANGE SNIPER RIFLE.
KOR'S NOT GOING TO WAIT FOR HIS GORILLAS TO START THE WAR. HE'S GOING TO LIGHT THE FUSE HIMSELF.
THAT'D BE A REAL SHAME...
SPOCK, CAN YOU TRACK KOR DOWN?
I BELIEVE I CAN TRIANGULATE THE KLINGONS' POSITION BY LINKING MY TRICORDER TO THE SHIP'S SENSORS.
PROVIDED THEY HAVEN'T SPLIT INTO SMALLER GROUPS IN AN ATTEMPT TO ELUDE US.

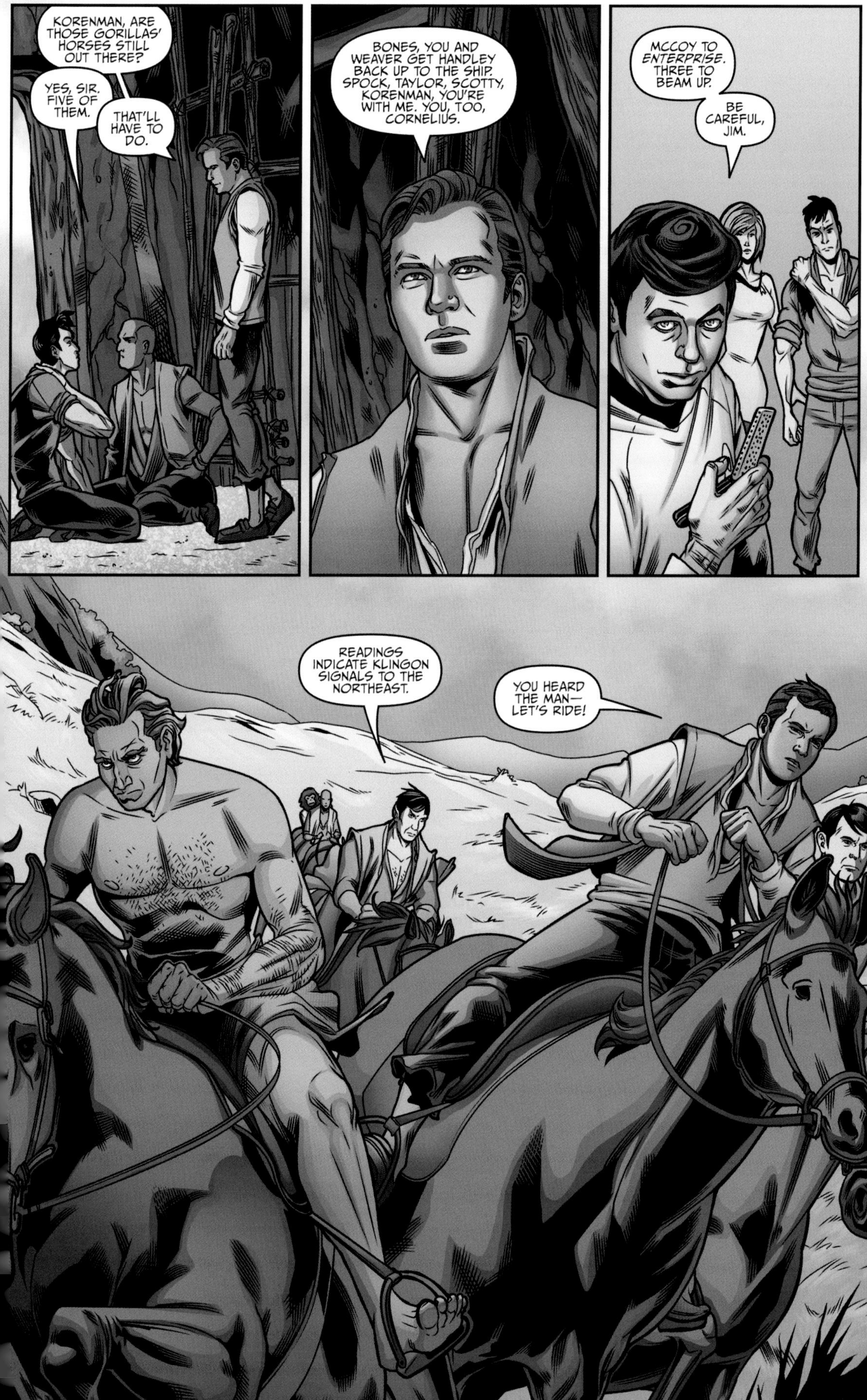
KORENMAN, ARE THOSE GORILLAS' HORSES STILL OUT THERE?
YES, SIR. FIVE OF THEM.
THAT'LL HAVE TO DO.
BONES, YOU AND WEAVER GET HANDLEY BACK UP TO THE SHIP. SPOCK, TAYLOR, SCOTTY, KORENMAN, YOU'RE WITH ME. YOU, TOO, CORNELIUS.
MCCOY TO *ENTERPRISE.* THREE TO BEAM UP.
BE CAREFUL, JIM.
READINGS INDICATE KLINGON SIGNALS TO THE NORTHEAST.
YOU HEARD THE MAN— LET'S RIDE!

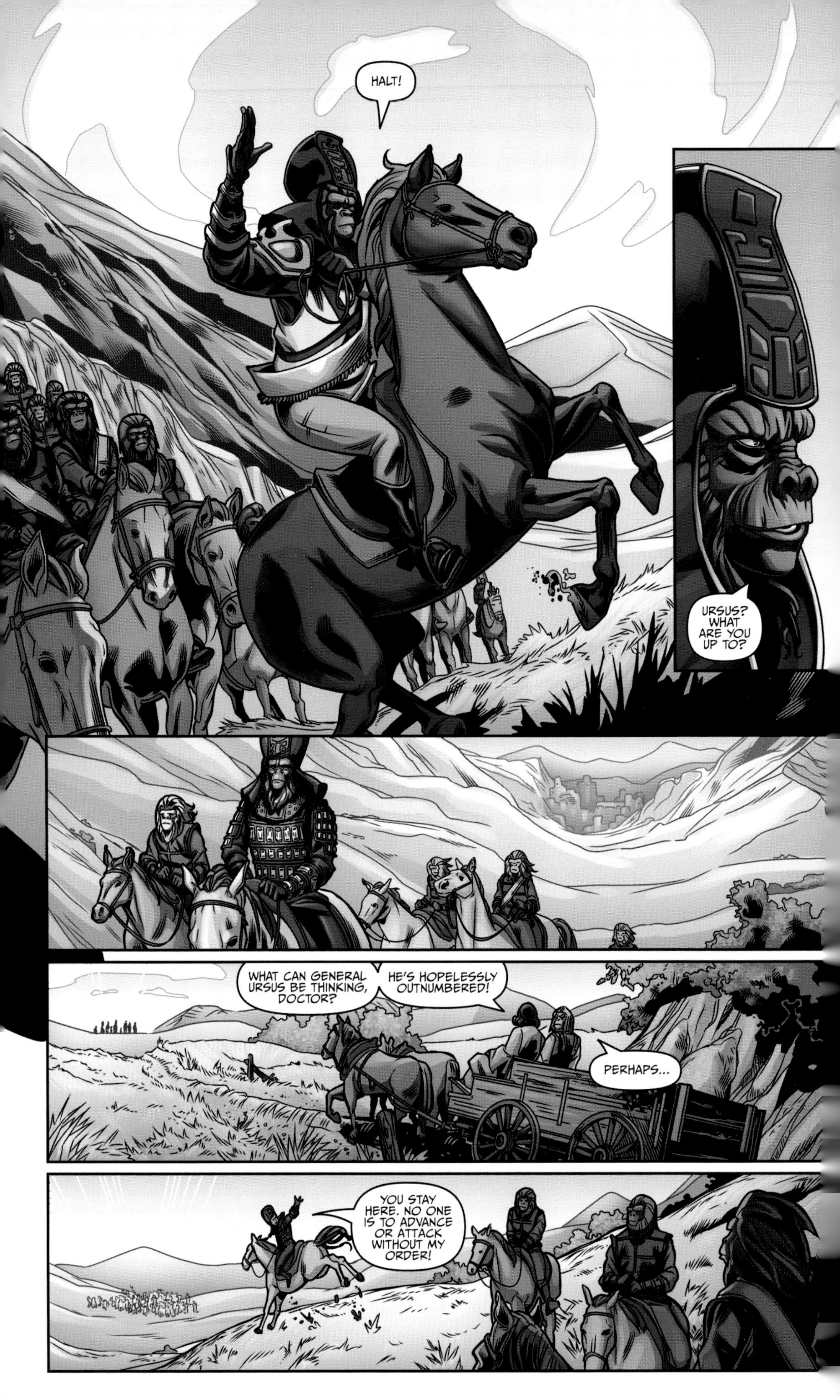
HALT!
URSUS? WHAT ARE YOU UP TO?
WHAT CAN GENERAL URSUS BE THINKING, DOCTOR?
HE'S HOPELESSLY OUTNUMBERED!
PERHAPS...
YOU STAY HERE. NO ONE IS TO ADVANCE OR ATTACK WITHOUT MY ORDER!

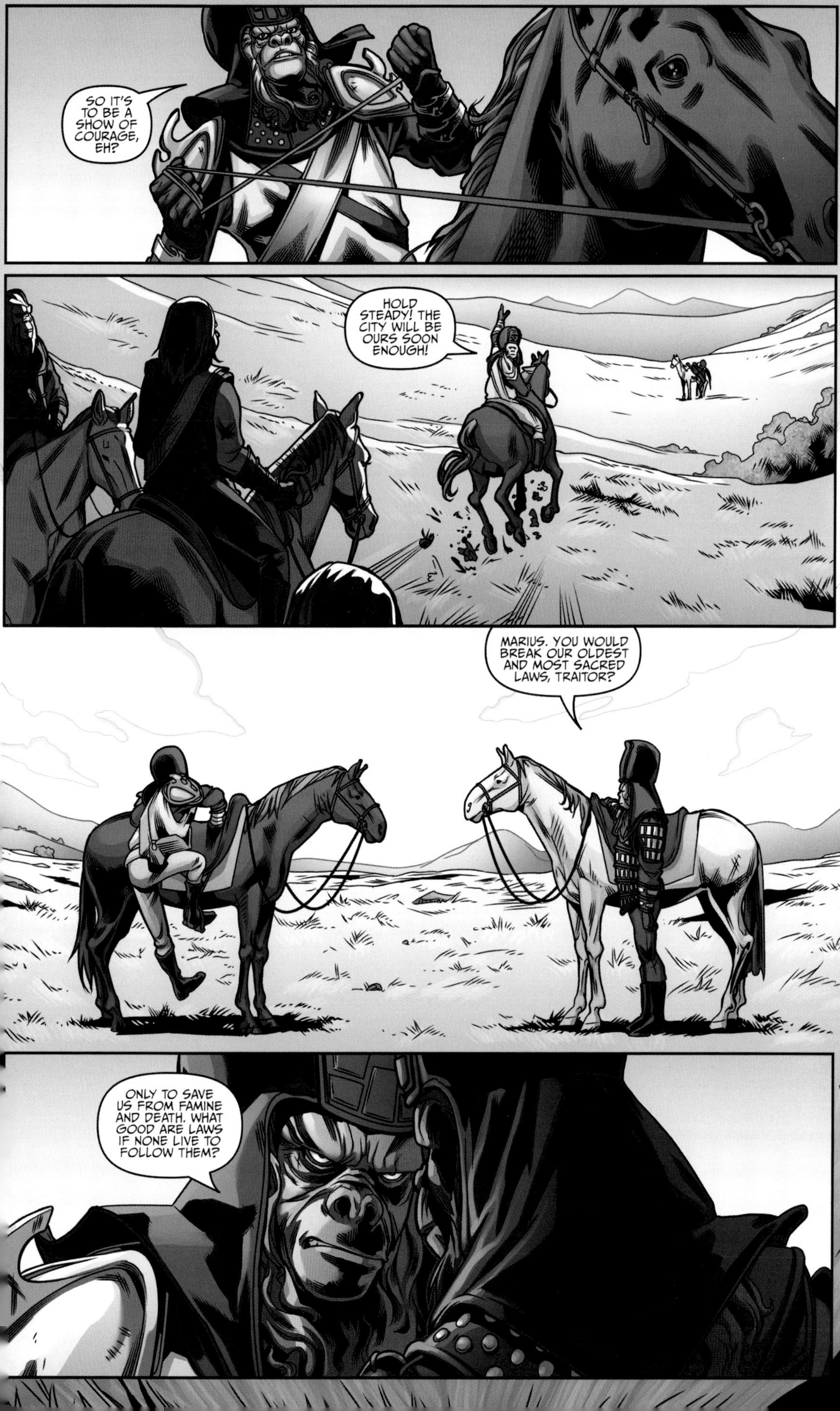
SO IT'S TO BE A SHOW OF COURAGE, EH?
HOLD STEADY! THE CITY WILL BE OURS SOON ENOUGH!
MARIUS. YOU WOULD BREAK OUR OLDEST AND MOST SACRED LAWS, TRAITOR?
ONLY TO SAVE US FROM FAMINE AND DEATH. WHAT GOOD ARE LAWS IF NONE LIVE TO FOLLOW THEM?

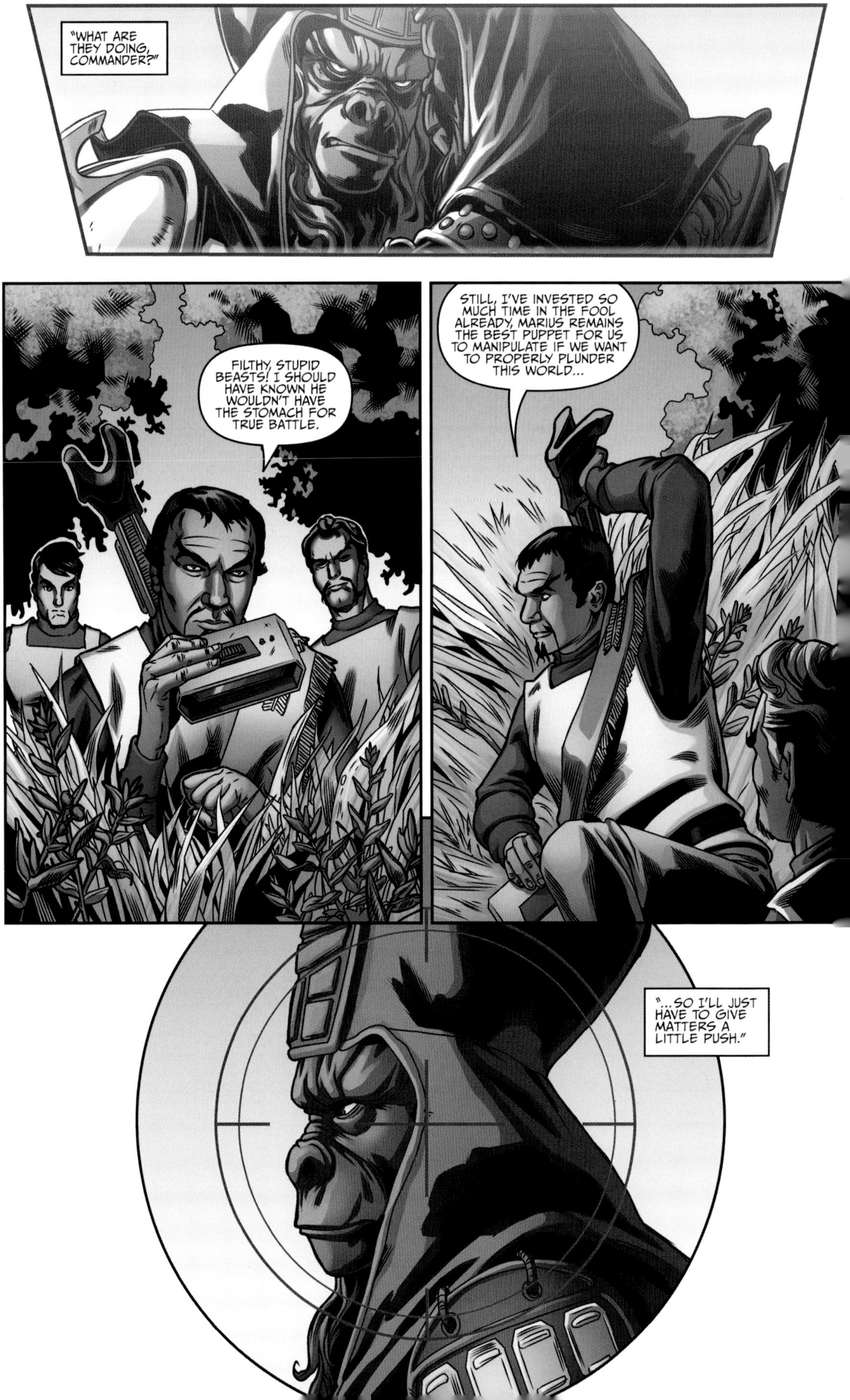
"WHAT ARE THEY DOING, COMMANDER?"
FILTHY, STUPID BEASTS! I SHOULD HAVE KNOWN HE WOULDN'T HAVE THE STOMACH FOR TRUE BATTLE.
STILL, I'VE INVESTED SO MUCH TIME IN THE FOOL ALREADY, MARIUS REMAINS THE BEST PUPPET FOR US TO MANIPULATE IF WE WANT TO PROPERLY PLUNDER THIS WORLD...
"...SO I'LL JUST HAVE TO GIVE MATTERS A LITTLE PUSH."

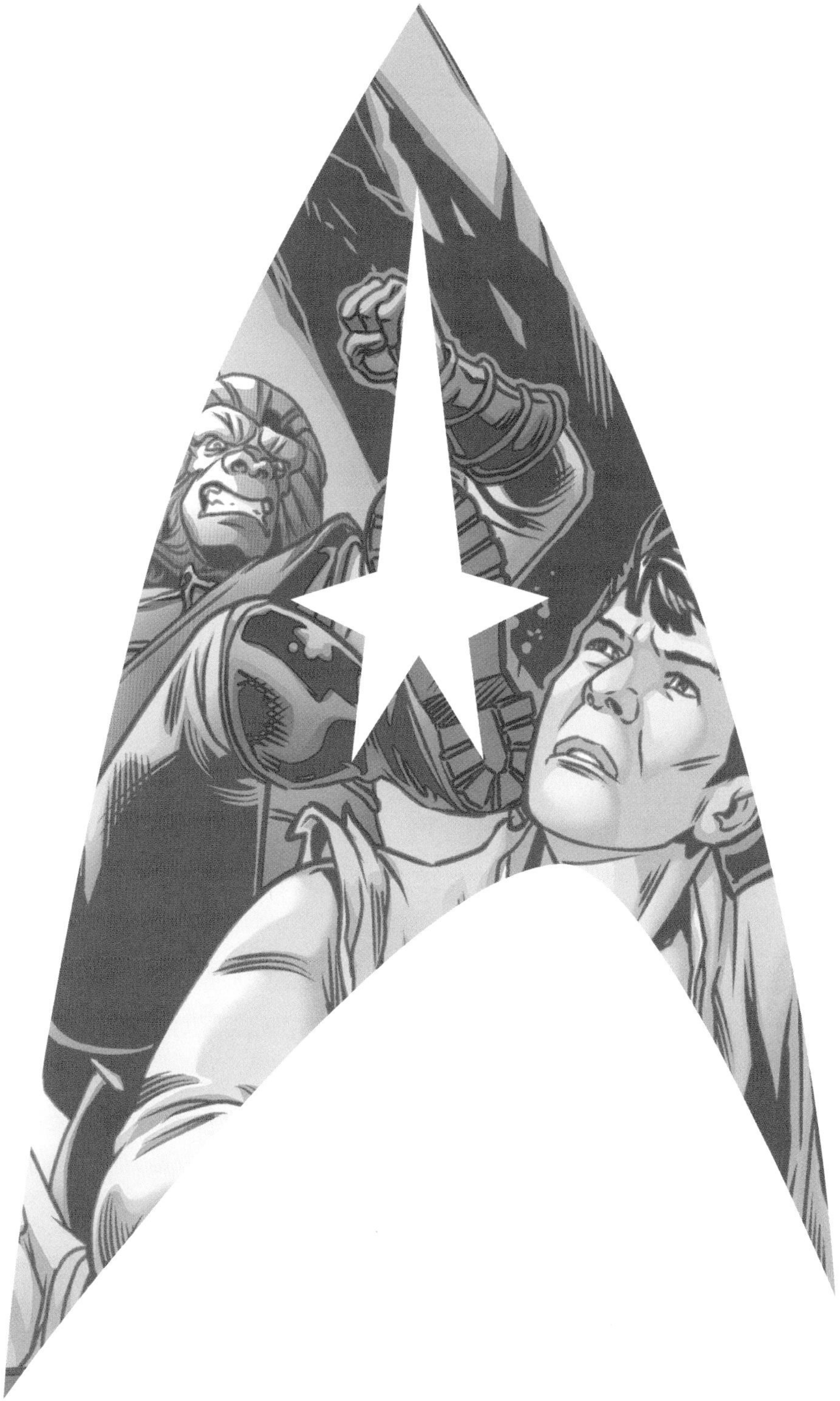

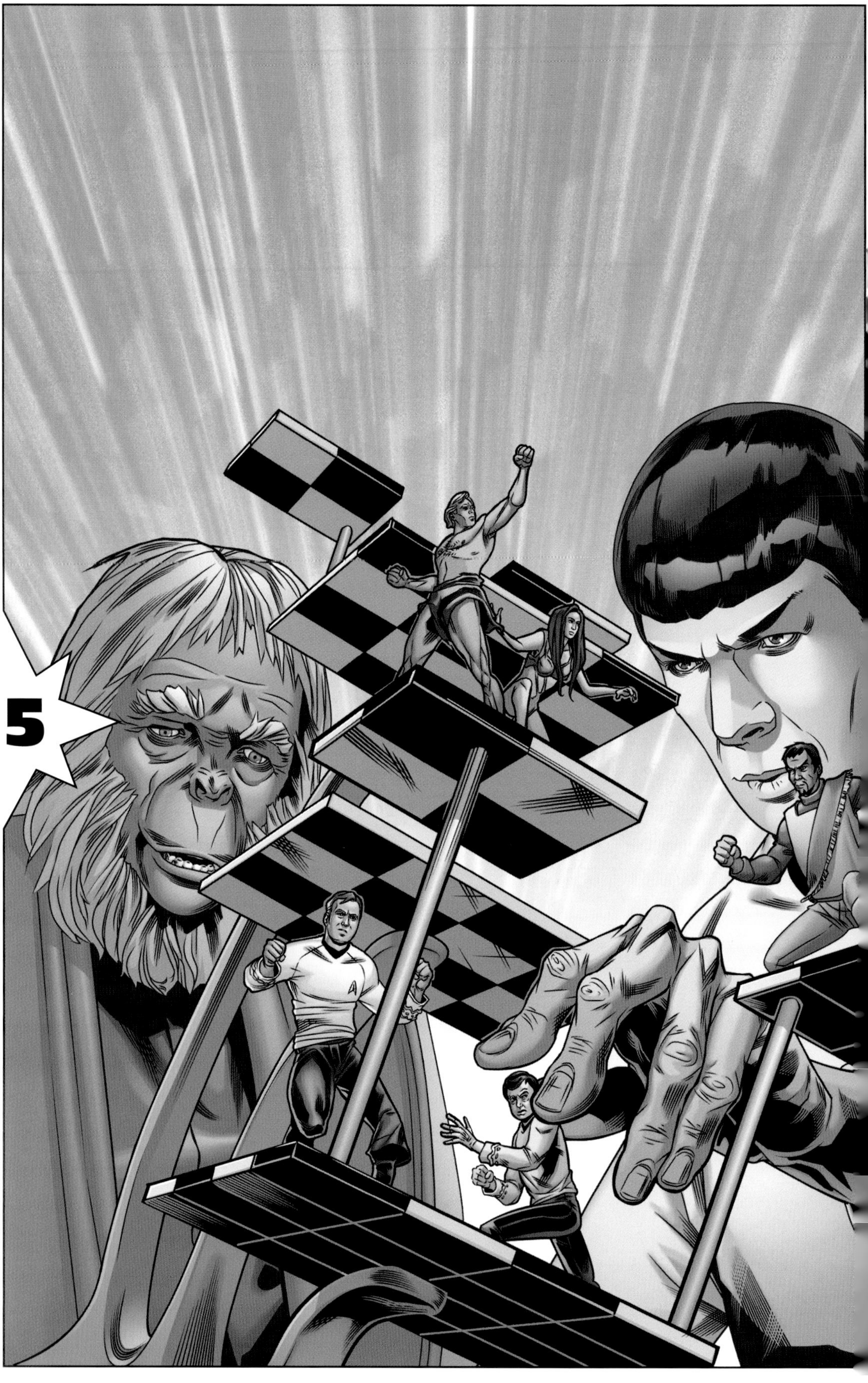
5

BY **RACHAEL STOTT** COLORS BY **CHARLIE KIRCHOFF**

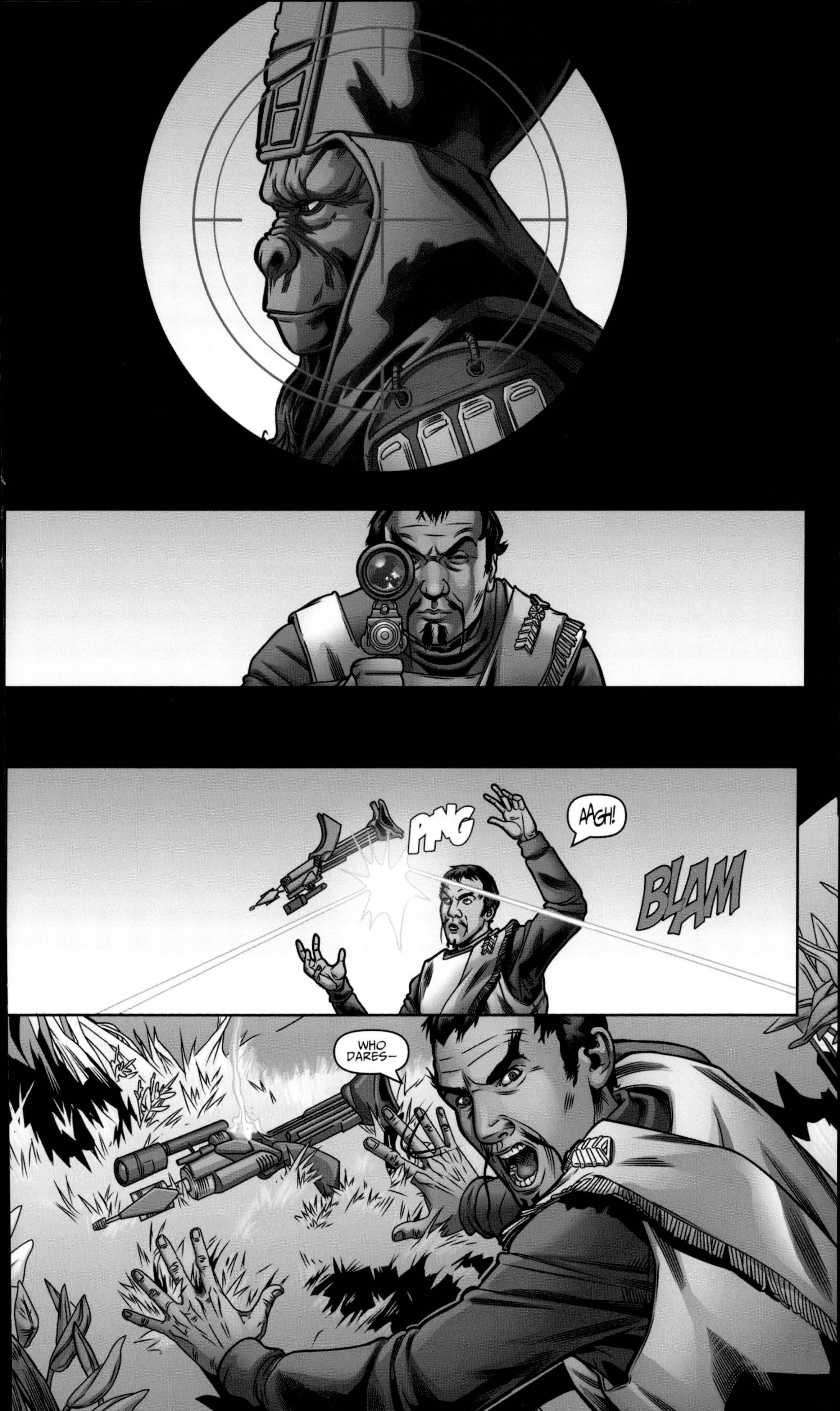
PING
AAGH!
BLAM
WHO DARES—

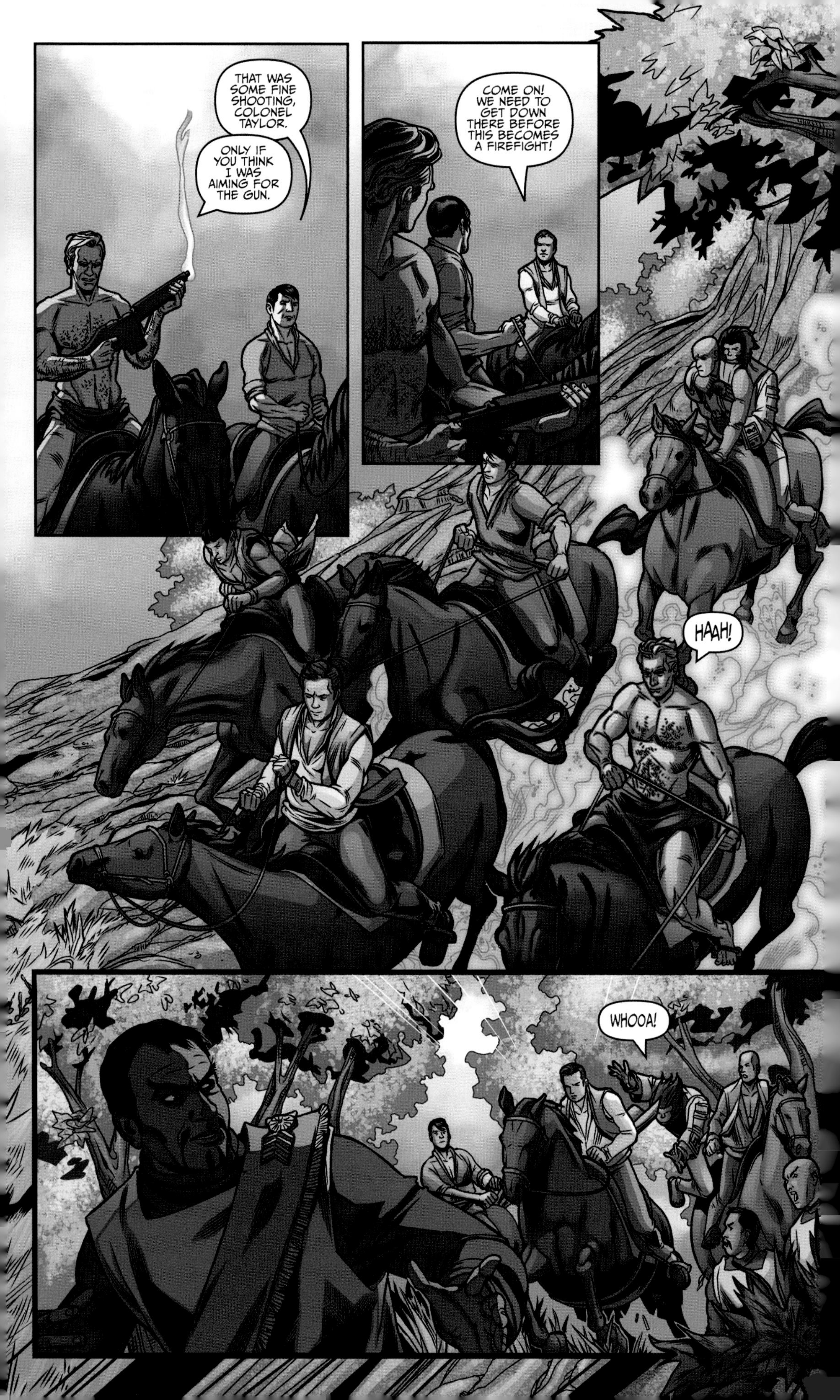
THAT WAS SOME FINE SHOOTING, COLONEL TAYLOR.
ONLY IF YOU THINK I WAS AIMING FOR THE GUN.
COME ON! WE NEED TO GET DOWN THERE BEFORE THIS BECOMES A FIREFIGHT!
HAAH!
WHOOA!

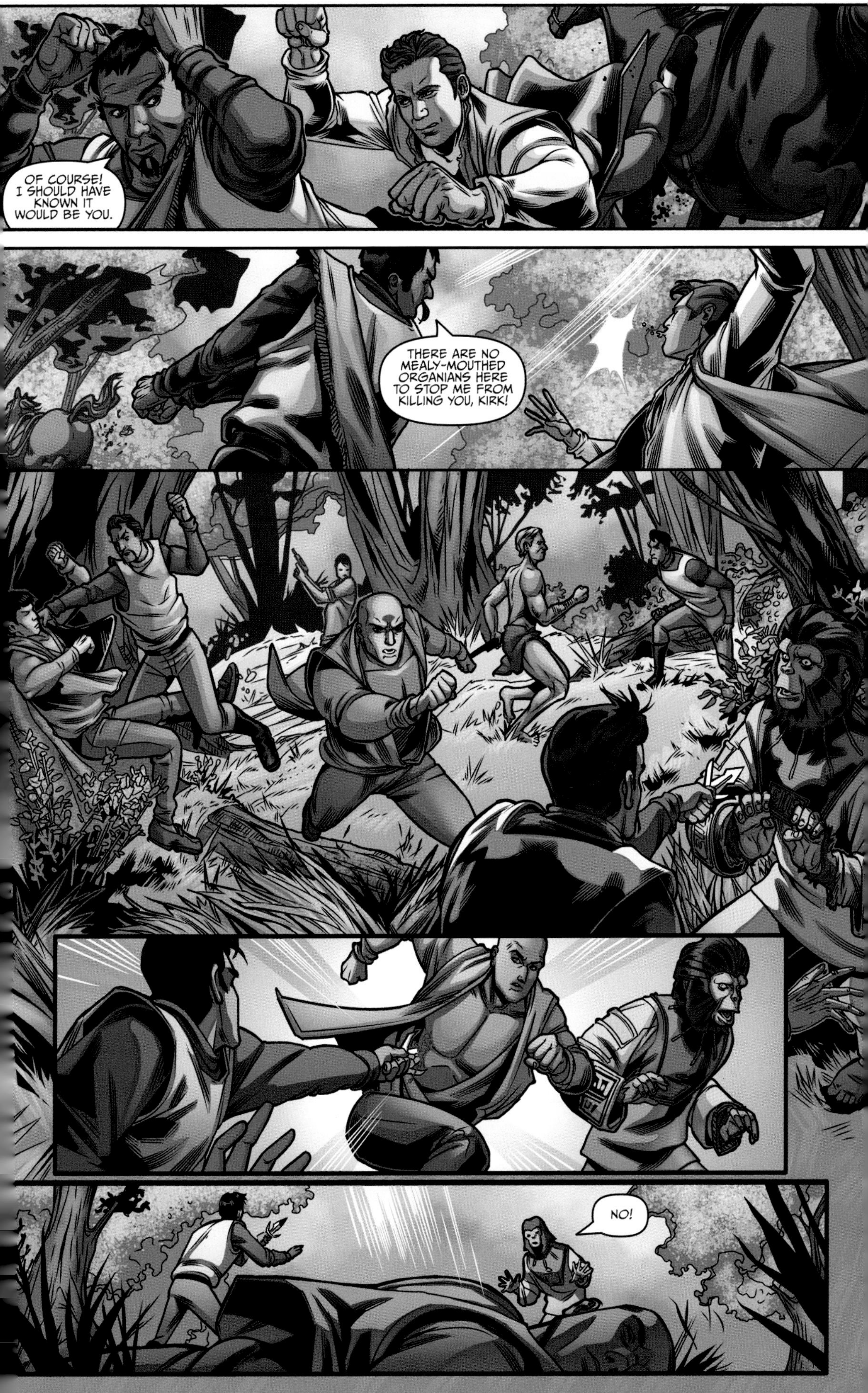
OF COURSE! I SHOULD HAVE KNOWN IT WOULD BE YOU.
THERE ARE NO MEALY-MOUTHED ORGANIANS HERE TO STOP ME FROM KILLING YOU, KIRK!
NO!

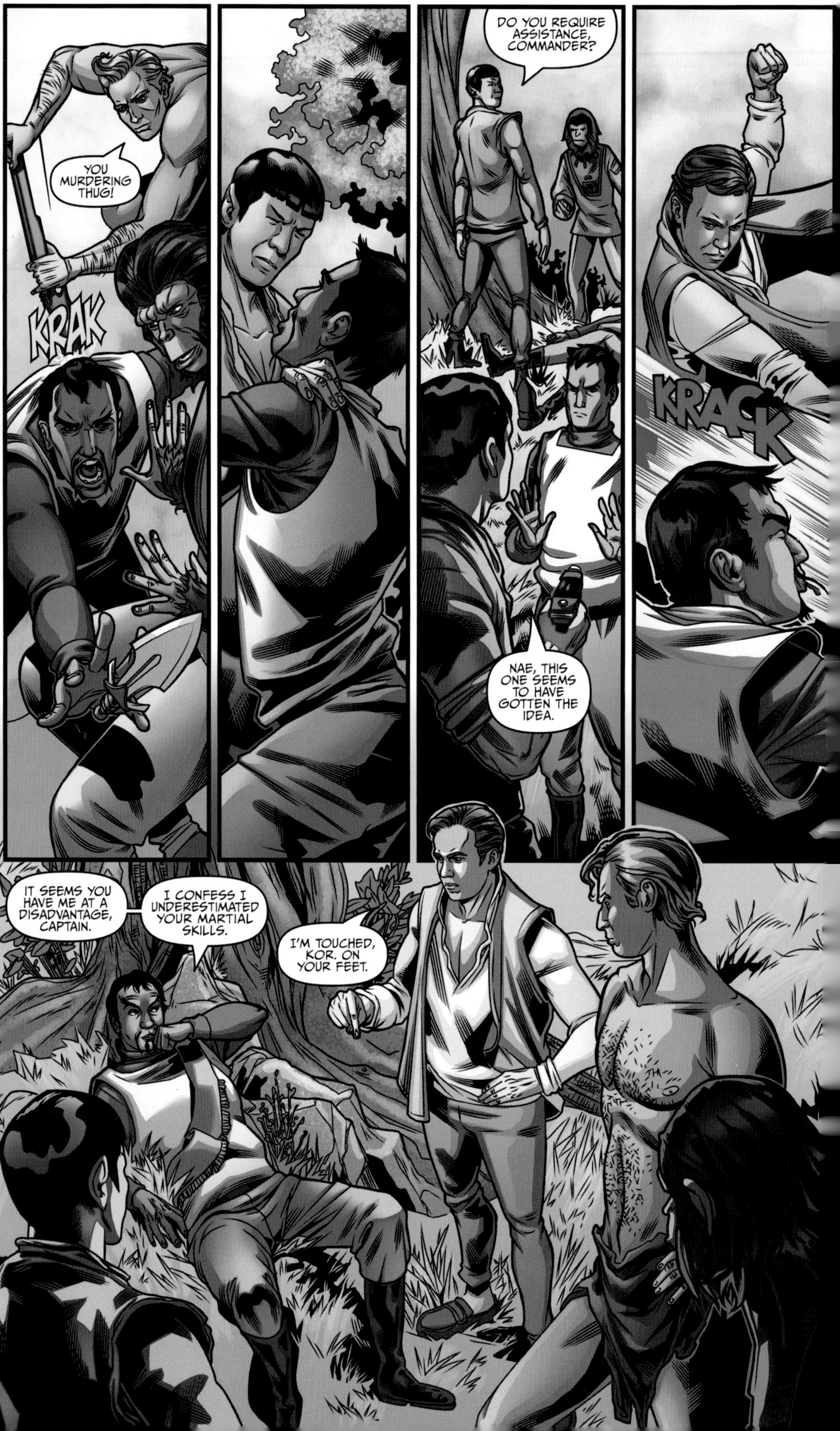
YOU MURDERING THUG!
KRAK
DO YOU REQUIRE ASSISTANCE, COMMANDER?
NAE, THIS ONE SEEMS TO HAVE GOTTEN THE IDEA.
KRACK
IT SEEMS YOU HAVE ME AT A DISADVANTAGE, CAPTAIN.
I CONFESS I UNDERESTIMATED YOUR MARTIAL SKILLS.
I'M TOUCHED, KOR. ON YOUR FEET.

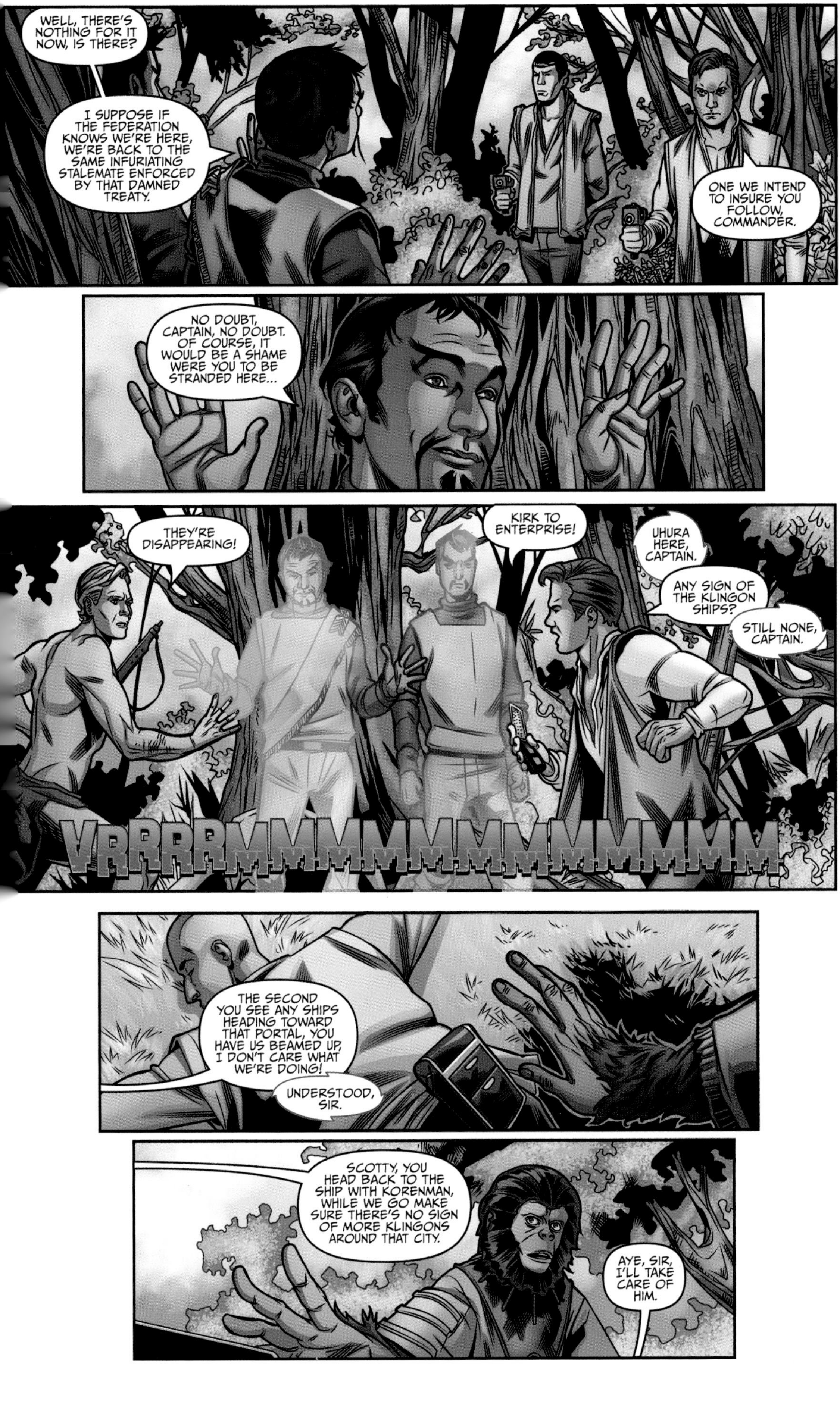
WELL, THERE'S NOTHING FOR IT NOW, IS THERE?
I SUPPOSE IF THE FEDERATION KNOWS WE'RE HERE, WE'RE BACK TO THE SAME INFURIATING STALEMATE ENFORCED BY THAT DAMNED TREATY.
ONE WE INTEND TO INSURE YOU FOLLOW, COMMANDER.
NO DOUBT, CAPTAIN, NO DOUBT. OF COURSE, IT WOULD BE A SHAME WERE YOU TO BE STRANDED HERE...
THEY'RE DISAPPEARING!
KIRK TO ENTERPRISE!
UHURA HERE, CAPTAIN.
ANY SIGN OF THE KLINGON SHIPS?
STILL NONE, CAPTAIN.
VRRRRMMMMMMMMMMMMMMMMM
THE SECOND YOU SEE ANY SHIPS HEADING TOWARD THAT PORTAL, YOU HAVE US BEAMED UP, I DON'T CARE WHAT WE'RE DOING!
UNDERSTOOD, SIR.
SCOTTY, YOU HEAD BACK TO THE SHIP WITH KORENMAN, WHILE WE GO MAKE SURE THERE'S NO SIGN OF MORE KLINGONS AROUND THAT CITY.
AYE, SIR, I'LL TAKE CARE OF HIM.

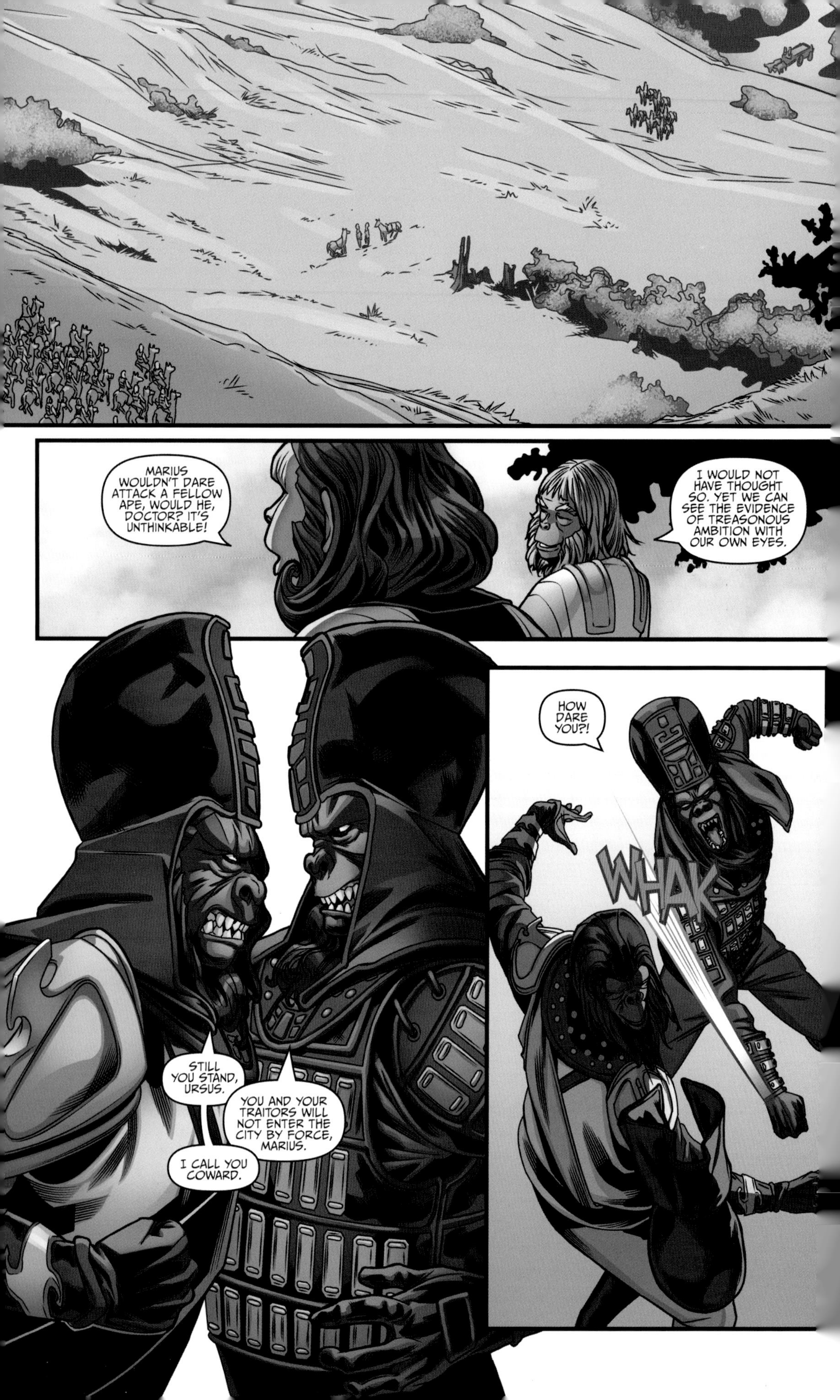
MARIUS WOULDN'T DARE ATTACK A FELLOW APE, WOULD HE, DOCTOR? IT'S UNTHINKABLE!
I WOULD NOT HAVE THOUGHT SO. YET WE CAN SEE THE EVIDENCE OF TREASONOUS AMBITION WITH OUR OWN EYES.
STILL YOU STAND, URSUS.
YOU AND YOUR TRAITORS WILL NOT ENTER THE CITY BY FORCE, MARIUS.
I CALL YOU COWARD.
HOW DARE YOU?!
WHAK

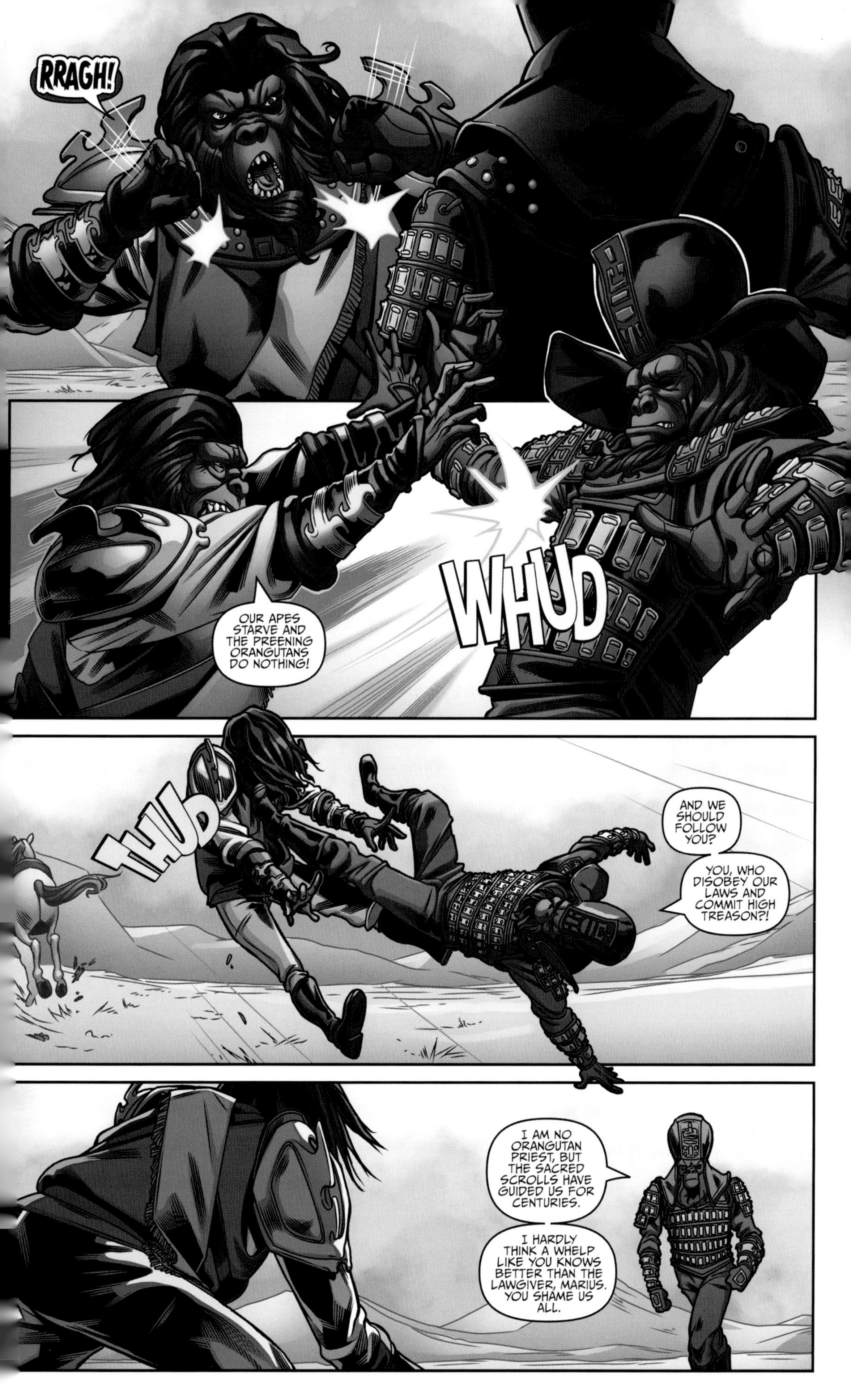
RRAGH!
OUR APES STARVE AND THE PREENING ORANGUTANS DO NOTHING!
WHUD
THUD
AND WE SHOULD FOLLOW YOU?
YOU, WHO DISOBEY OUR LAWS AND COMMIT HIGH TREASON?!
I AM NO ORANGUTAN PRIEST, BUT THE SACRED SCROLLS HAVE GUIDED US FOR CENTURIES.
I HARDLY THINK A WHELP LIKE YOU KNOWS BETTER THAN THE LAWGIVER, MARIUS. YOU SHAME US ALL.

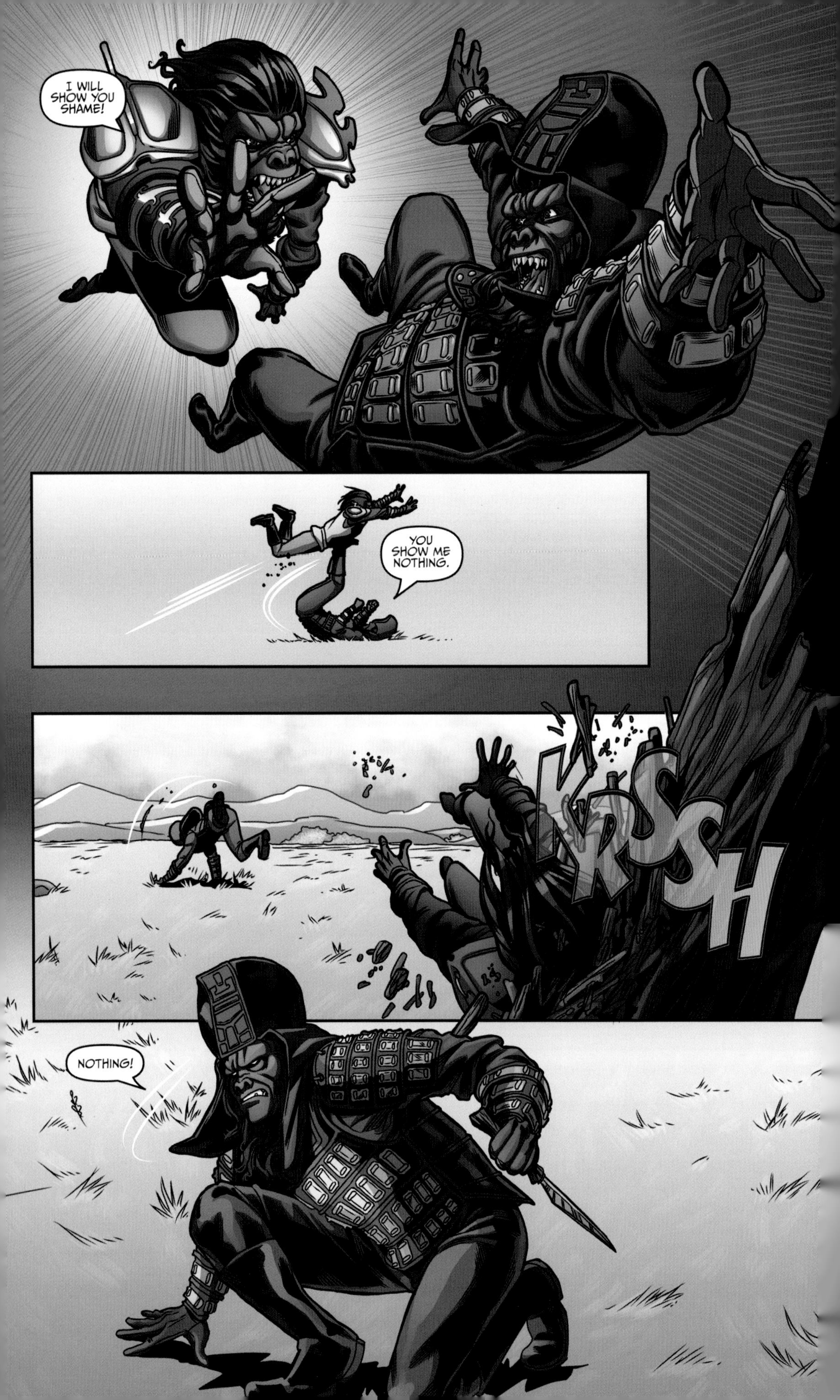
I WILL SHOW YOU SHAME!
YOU SHOW ME NOTHING.
KRSSH
NOTHING!

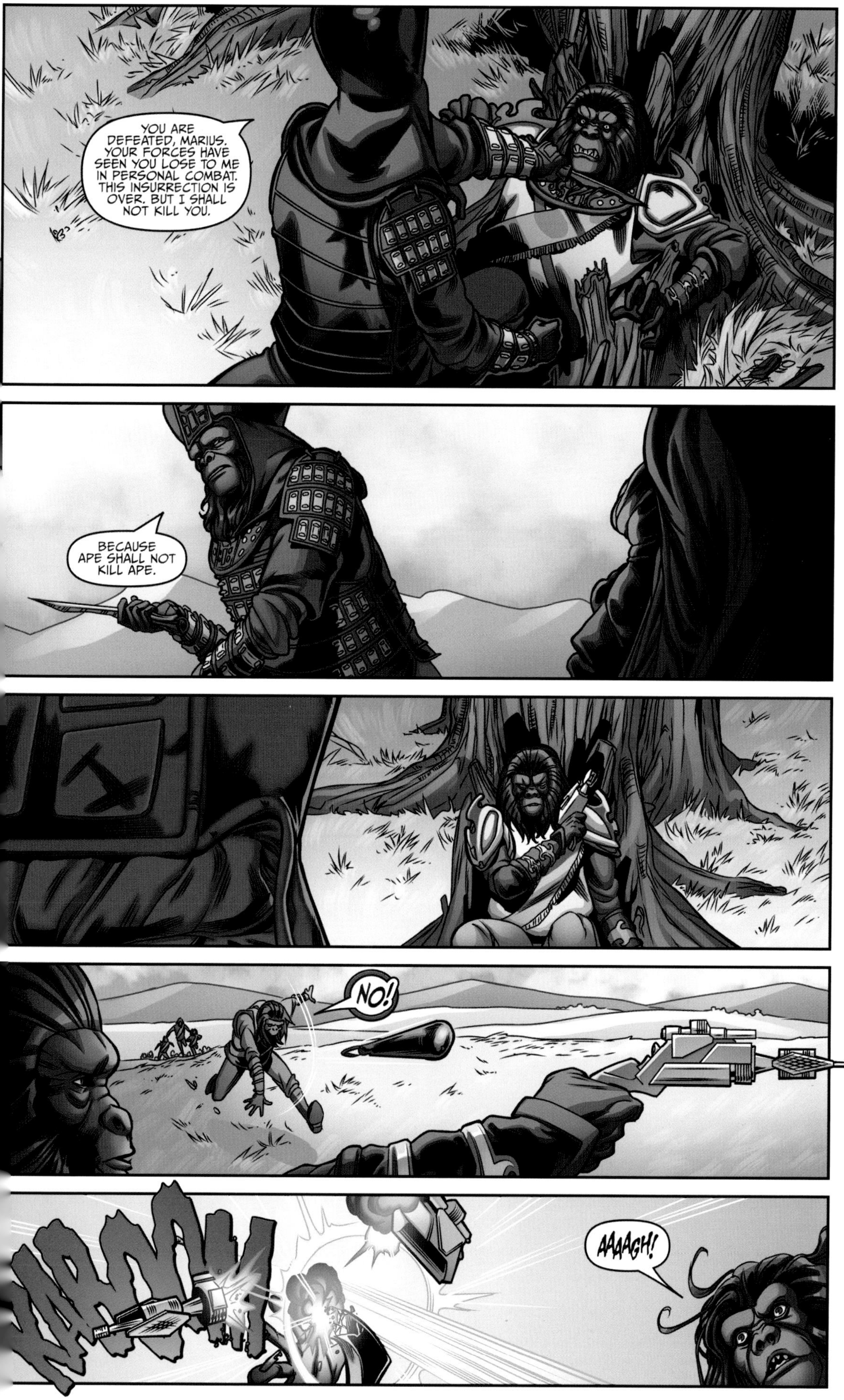
YOU ARE DEFEATED, MARIUS. YOUR FORCES HAVE SEEN YOU LOSE TO ME IN PERSONAL COMBAT. THIS INSURRECTION IS OVER. BUT I SHALL NOT KILL YOU.
BECAUSE APE SHALL NOT KILL APE.
NO!
AAAAGH!

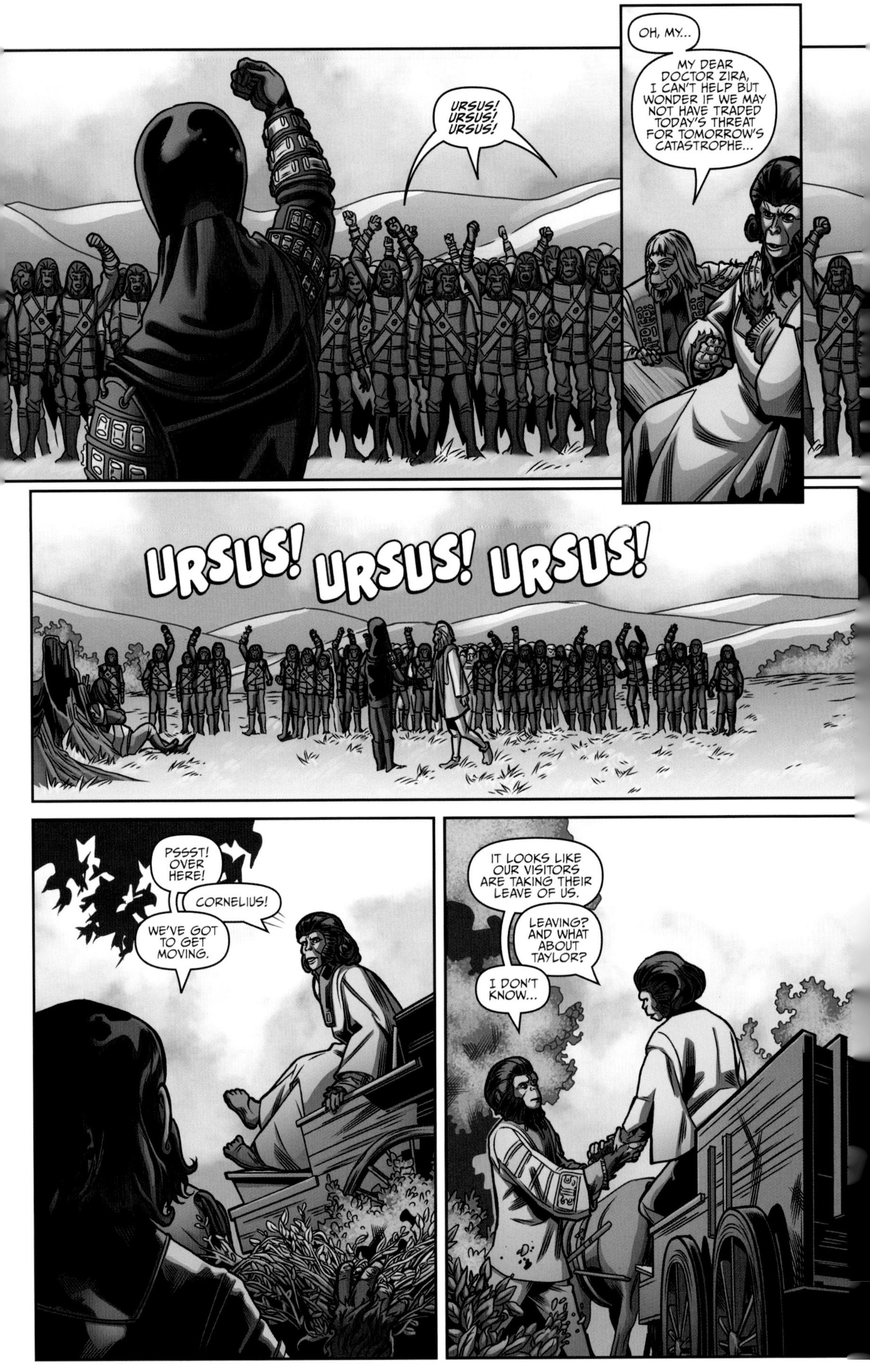
URSUS! URSUS! URSUS!
OH, MY...
MY DEAR DOCTOR ZIRA, I CAN'T HELP BUT WONDER IF WE MAY NOT HAVE TRADED TODAY'S THREAT FOR TOMORROW'S CATASTROPHE...
URSUS! URSUS! URSUS!
PSSST! OVER HERE!
CORNELIUS!
WE'VE GOT TO GET MOVING.
IT LOOKS LIKE OUR VISITORS ARE TAKING THEIR LEAVE OF US.
LEAVING? AND WHAT ABOUT TAYLOR?
I DON'T KNOW...

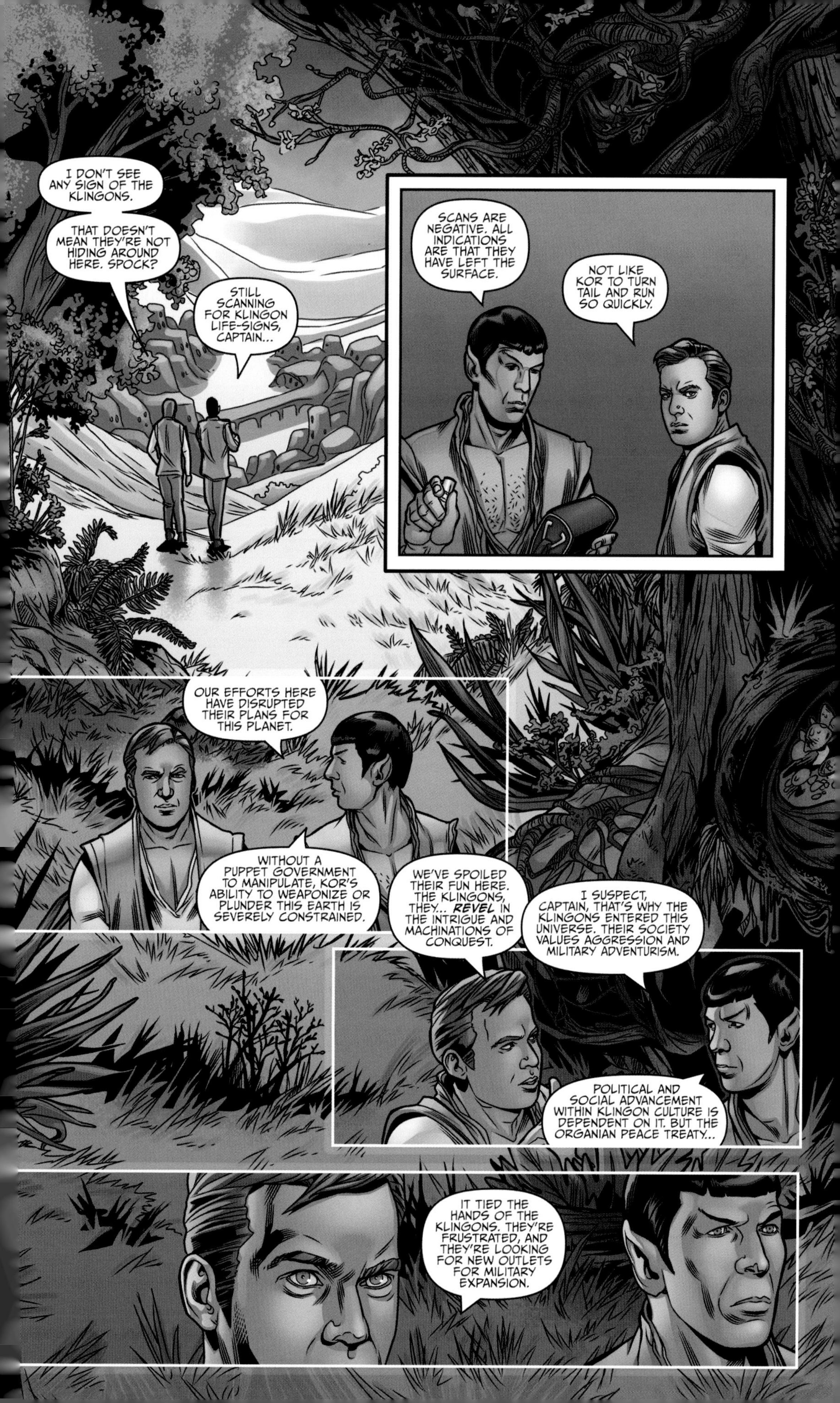
I DON'T SEE ANY SIGN OF THE KLINGONS.
THAT DOESN'T MEAN THEY'RE NOT HIDING AROUND HERE. SPOCK?
STILL SCANNING FOR KLINGON LIFE-SIGNS, CAPTAIN...
SCANS ARE NEGATIVE. ALL INDICATIONS ARE THAT THEY HAVE LEFT THE SURFACE.
NOT LIKE KOR TO TURN TAIL AND RUN SO QUICKLY.
OUR EFFORTS HERE HAVE DISRUPTED THEIR PLANS FOR THIS PLANET.
WITHOUT A PUPPET GOVERNMENT TO MANIPULATE, KOR'S ABILITY TO WEAPONIZE OR PLUNDER THIS EARTH IS SEVERELY CONSTRAINED.
WE'VE SPOILED THEIR FUN HERE. THE KLINGONS, THEY... REVEL IN THE INTRIGUE AND MACHINATIONS OF CONQUEST.
I SUSPECT, CAPTAIN, THAT'S WHY THE KLINGONS ENTERED THIS UNIVERSE. THEIR SOCIETY VALUES AGGRESSION AND MILITARY ADVENTURISM.
POLITICAL AND SOCIAL ADVANCEMENT WITHIN KLINGON CULTURE IS DEPENDENT ON IT. BUT THE ORGANIAN PEACE TREATY...
IT TIED THE HANDS OF THE KLINGONS. THEY'RE FRUSTRATED, AND THEY'RE LOOKING FOR NEW OUTLETS FOR MILITARY EXPANSION.

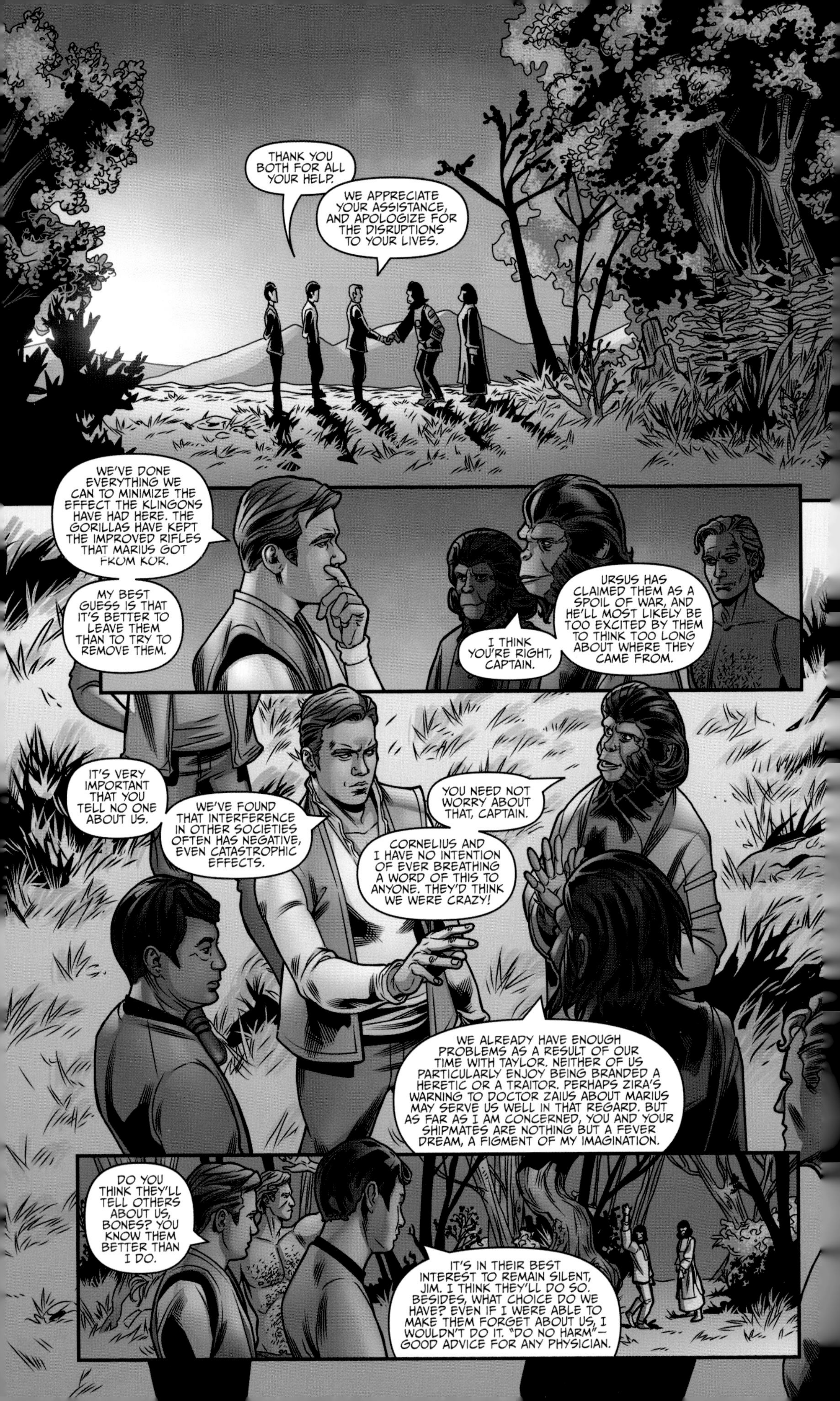
THANK YOU BOTH FOR ALL YOUR HELP.
WE APPRECIATE YOUR ASSISTANCE, AND APOLOGIZE FOR THE DISRUPTIONS TO YOUR LIVES.
WE'VE DONE EVERYTHING WE CAN TO MINIMIZE THE EFFECT THE KLINGONS HAVE HAD HERE. THE GORILLAS HAVE KEPT THE IMPROVED RIFLES THAT MARIUS GOT FROM KOR.
MY BEST GUESS IS THAT IT'S BETTER TO LEAVE THEM THAN TO TRY TO REMOVE THEM.
I THINK YOU'RE RIGHT, CAPTAIN.
URSUS HAS CLAIMED THEM AS A SPOIL OF WAR, AND HE'LL MOST LIKELY BE TOO EXCITED BY THEM TO THINK TOO LONG ABOUT WHERE THEY CAME FROM.
IT'S VERY IMPORTANT THAT YOU TELL NO ONE ABOUT US.
WE'VE FOUND THAT INTERFERENCE IN OTHER SOCIETIES OFTEN HAS NEGATIVE, EVEN CATASTROPHIC EFFECTS.
YOU NEED NOT WORRY ABOUT THAT, CAPTAIN.
CORNELIUS AND I HAVE NO INTENTION OF EVER BREATHING A WORD OF THIS TO ANYONE. THEY'D THINK WE WERE CRAZY!
WE ALREADY HAVE ENOUGH PROBLEMS AS A RESULT OF OUR TIME WITH TAYLOR. NEITHER OF US PARTICULARLY ENJOY BEING BRANDED A HERETIC OR A TRAITOR. PERHAPS ZIRA'S WARNING TO DOCTOR ZAIUS ABOUT MARIUS MAY SERVE US WELL IN THAT REGARD. BUT AS FAR AS I AM CONCERNED, YOU AND YOUR SHIPMATES ARE NOTHING BUT A FEVER DREAM, A FIGMENT OF MY IMAGINATION.
DO YOU THINK THEY'LL TELL OTHERS ABOUT US, BONES? YOU KNOW THEM BETTER THAN I DO.
IT'S IN THEIR BEST INTEREST TO REMAIN SILENT, JIM. I THINK THEY'LL DO SO. BESIDES, WHAT CHOICE DO WE HAVE? EVEN IF I WERE ABLE TO MAKE THEM FORGET ABOUT US, I WOULDN'T DO IT. "DO NO HARM"— GOOD ADVICE FOR ANY PHYSICIAN.

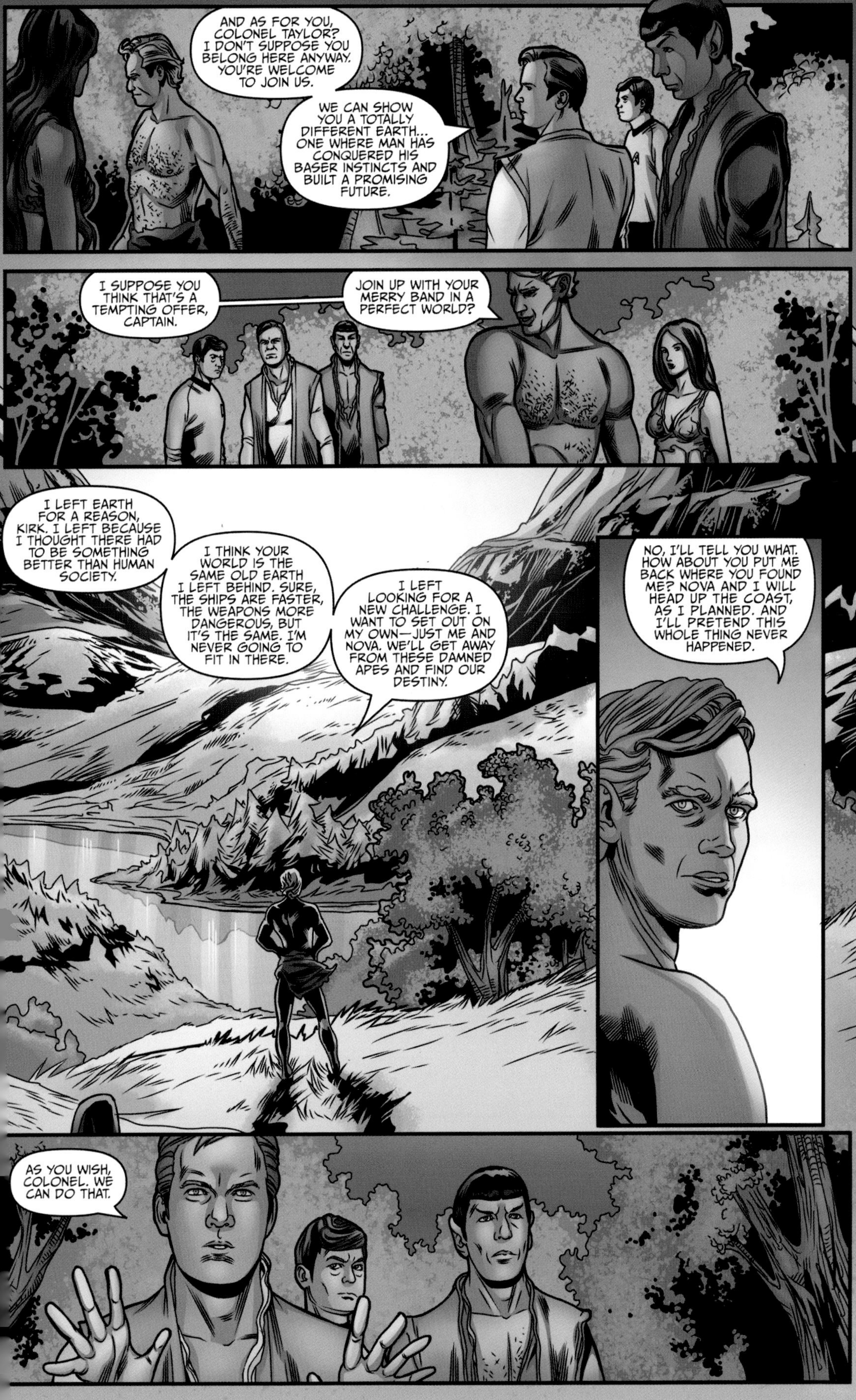
AND AS FOR YOU, COLONEL TAYLOR? I DON'T SUPPOSE YOU BELONG HERE ANYWAY. YOU'RE WELCOME TO JOIN US.
WE CAN SHOW YOU A TOTALLY DIFFERENT EARTH... ONE WHERE MAN HAS CONQUERED HIS BASER INSTINCTS AND BUILT A PROMISING FUTURE.
I SUPPOSE YOU THINK THAT'S A TEMPTING OFFER, CAPTAIN.
JOIN UP WITH YOUR MERRY BAND IN A PERFECT WORLD?
I LEFT EARTH FOR A REASON, KIRK. I LEFT BECAUSE I THOUGHT THERE HAD TO BE SOMETHING BETTER THAN HUMAN SOCIETY.
I THINK YOUR WORLD IS THE SAME OLD EARTH I LEFT BEHIND. SURE, THE SHIPS ARE FASTER, THE WEAPONS MORE DANGEROUS, BUT IT'S THE SAME. I'M NEVER GOING TO FIT IN THERE.
I LEFT LOOKING FOR A NEW CHALLENGE. I WANT TO SET OUT ON MY OWN—JUST ME AND NOVA. WE'LL GET AWAY FROM THESE DAMNED APES AND FIND OUR DESTINY.
NO, I'LL TELL YOU WHAT. HOW ABOUT YOU PUT ME BACK WHERE YOU FOUND ME? NOVA AND I WILL HEAD UP THE COAST, AS I PLANNED. AND I'LL PRETEND THIS WHOLE THING NEVER HAPPENED.
AS YOU WISH, COLONEL. WE CAN DO THAT.

VRRRRMMMMMMMMMMMMMMMMMMMMM

JIM, CAN WE LEAVE HIM SOME SUPPLIES? RATIONS AT LEAST?

NO, NO NEED FOR THAT, I'M GOING TO LIVE OFF THE LAND.

AFTER THE SHOCK OF SEEING THAT STATUE WORE OFF, I'D COME AROUND TO A CERTAIN PLAN, AND I INTEND TO FOLLOW UP ON THAT.

I WANT TO KNOW WHAT HAPPENED TO THIS PLACE. I HAVE NO LOVE FOR THOSE BLOODY BABOONS, BUT THAT DOESN'T MEAN THERE CAN'T BE A PLACE FOR ME HERE. MAYBE I'LL SEE WHAT I CAN DO TO TURN THINGS AROUND. IS MAN REALLY DOOMED TO EXTINCTION? THIS IS OUR DESTINY? I'M NOT SO SURE ANY MORE.

FOR BETTER OR WORSE, THIS IS MY HOME, CAPTAIN. I WON'T ABANDON IT.

BZZT BZZT

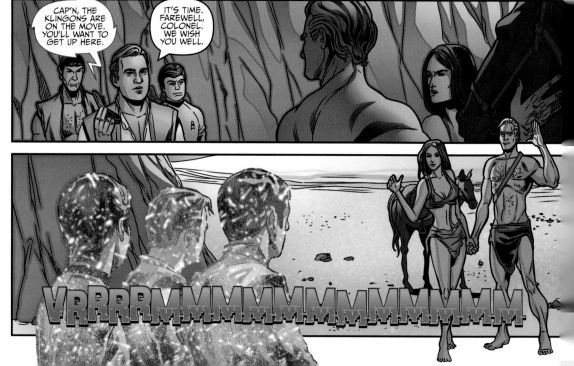

CAP'N, THE KLINGONS ARE ON THE MOVE. YOU'LL WANT TO GET UP HERE.

IT'S TIME. FAREWELL, COLONEL. WE WISH YOU WELL.

VRRRRMMMMMMMMMMMMMMMMMMMMM

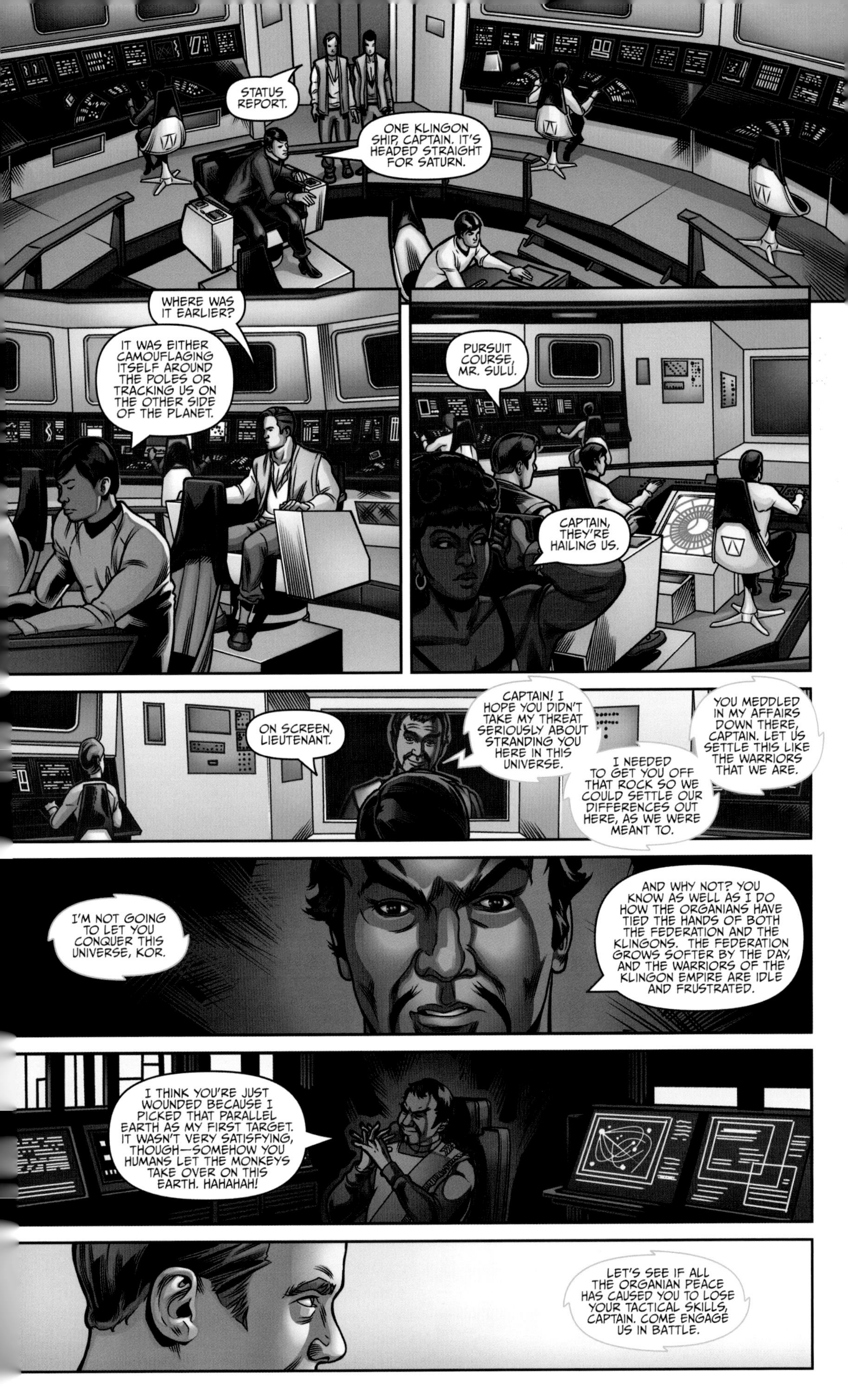
STATUS REPORT.
ONE KLINGON SHIP, CAPTAIN. IT'S HEADED STRAIGHT FOR SATURN.
WHERE WAS IT EARLIER?
IT WAS EITHER CAMOUFLAGING ITSELF AROUND THE POLES OR TRACKING US ON THE OTHER SIDE OF THE PLANET.
PURSUIT COURSE, MR. SULU.
CAPTAIN, THEY'RE HAILING US.
ON SCREEN, LIEUTENANT.
CAPTAIN! I HOPE YOU DIDN'T TAKE MY THREAT SERIOUSLY ABOUT STRANDING YOU HERE IN THIS UNIVERSE.
I NEEDED TO GET YOU OFF THAT ROCK SO WE COULD SETTLE OUR DIFFERENCES OUT HERE, AS WE WERE MEANT TO.
YOU MEDDLED IN MY AFFAIRS DOWN THERE, CAPTAIN. LET US SETTLE THIS LIKE THE WARRIORS THAT WE ARE.
I'M NOT GOING TO LET YOU CONQUER THIS UNIVERSE, KOR.
AND WHY NOT? YOU KNOW AS WELL AS I DO HOW THE ORGANIANS HAVE TIED THE HANDS OF BOTH THE FEDERATION AND THE KLINGONS. THE FEDERATION GROWS SOFTER BY THE DAY, AND THE WARRIORS OF THE KLINGON EMPIRE ARE IDLE AND FRUSTRATED.
I THINK YOU'RE JUST WOUNDED BECAUSE I PICKED THAT PARALLEL EARTH AS MY FIRST TARGET. IT WASN'T VERY SATISFYING, THOUGH—SOMEHOW YOU HUMANS LET THE MONKEYS TAKE OVER ON THIS EARTH. HAHAHAH!
LET'S SEE IF ALL THE ORGANIAN PEACE HAS CAUSED YOU TO LOSE YOUR TACTICAL SKILLS, CAPTAIN. COME ENGAGE US IN BATTLE.

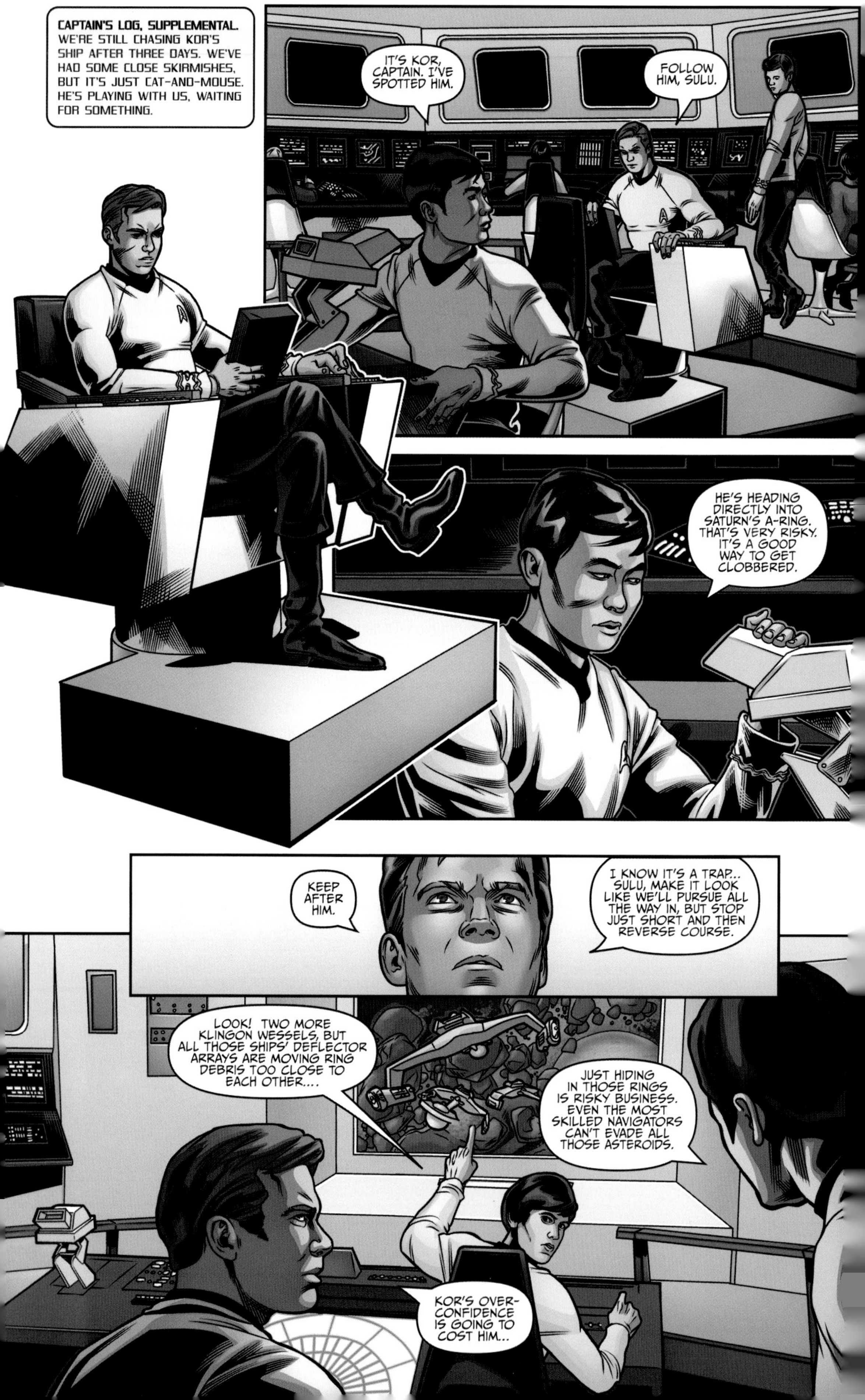
CAPTAIN'S LOG, SUPPLEMENTAL. WE'RE STILL CHASING KOR'S SHIP AFTER THREE DAYS. WE'VE HAD SOME CLOSE SKIRMISHES, BUT IT'S JUST CAT-AND-MOUSE. HE'S PLAYING WITH US, WAITING FOR SOMETHING.
IT'S KOR, CAPTAIN. I'VE SPOTTED HIM.
FOLLOW HIM, SULU.
HE'S HEADING DIRECTLY INTO SATURN'S A-RING. THAT'S VERY RISKY. IT'S A GOOD WAY TO GET CLOBBERED.
KEEP AFTER HIM.
I KNOW IT'S A TRAP... SULU, MAKE IT LOOK LIKE WE'LL PURSUE ALL THE WAY IN, BUT STOP JUST SHORT AND THEN REVERSE COURSE.
LOOK! TWO MORE KLINGON WESSELS, BUT ALL THOSE SHIPS' DEFLECTOR ARRAYS ARE MOVING RING DEBRIS TOO CLOSE TO EACH OTHER....
JUST HIDING IN THOSE RINGS IS RISKY BUSINESS. EVEN THE MOST SKILLED NAVIGATORS CAN'T EVADE ALL THOSE ASTEROIDS.
KOR'S OVER-CONFIDENCE IS GOING TO COST HIM...

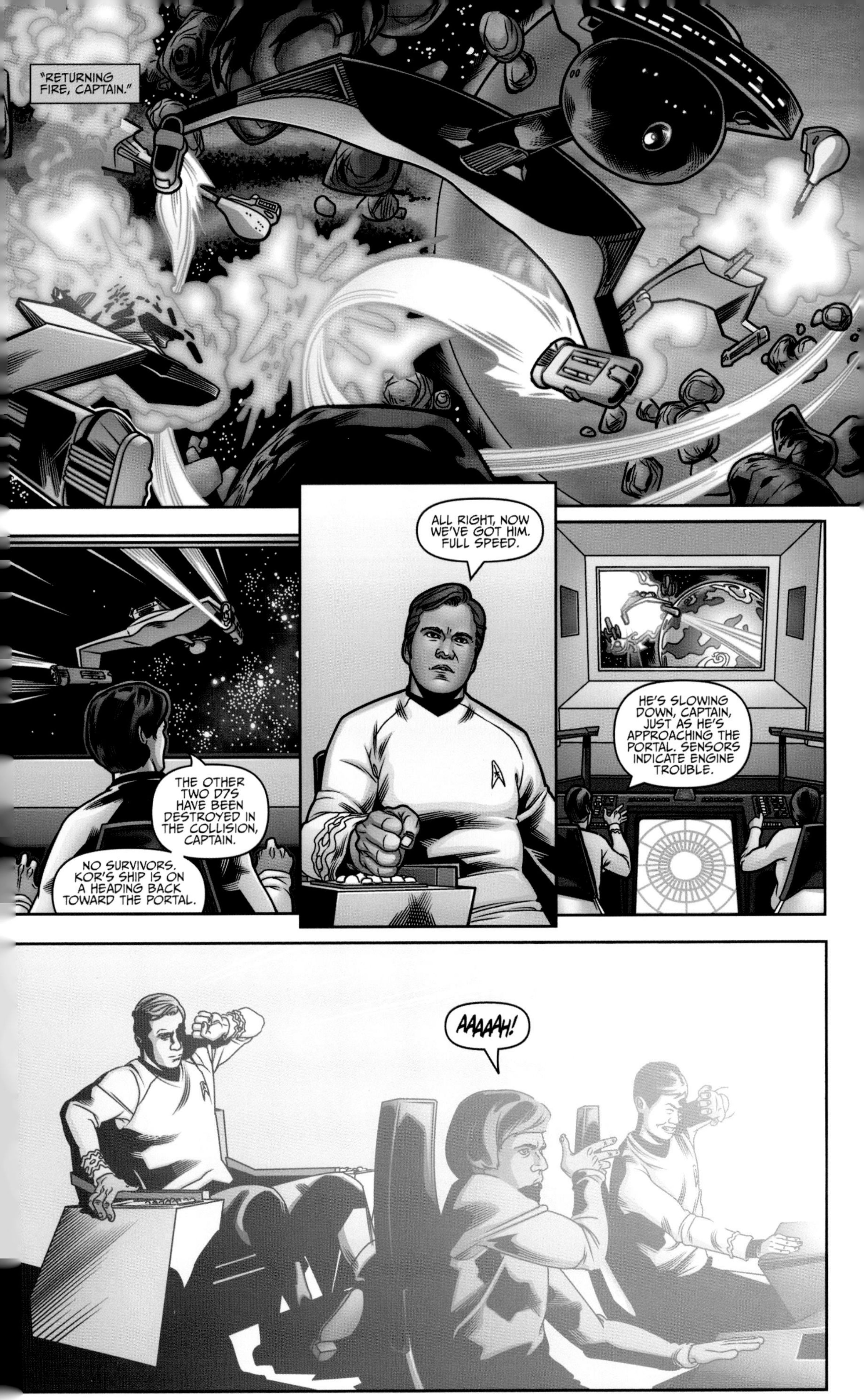
"RETURNING FIRE, CAPTAIN."
ALL RIGHT, NOW WE'VE GOT HIM. FULL SPEED.
THE OTHER TWO D7S HAVE BEEN DESTROYED IN THE COLLISION, CAPTAIN.
NO SURVIVORS. KOR'S SHIP IS ON A HEADING BACK TOWARD THE PORTAL.
HE'S SLOWING DOWN, CAPTAIN, JUST AS HE'S APPROACHING THE PORTAL. SENSORS INDICATE ENGINE TROUBLE.
AAAAAH!

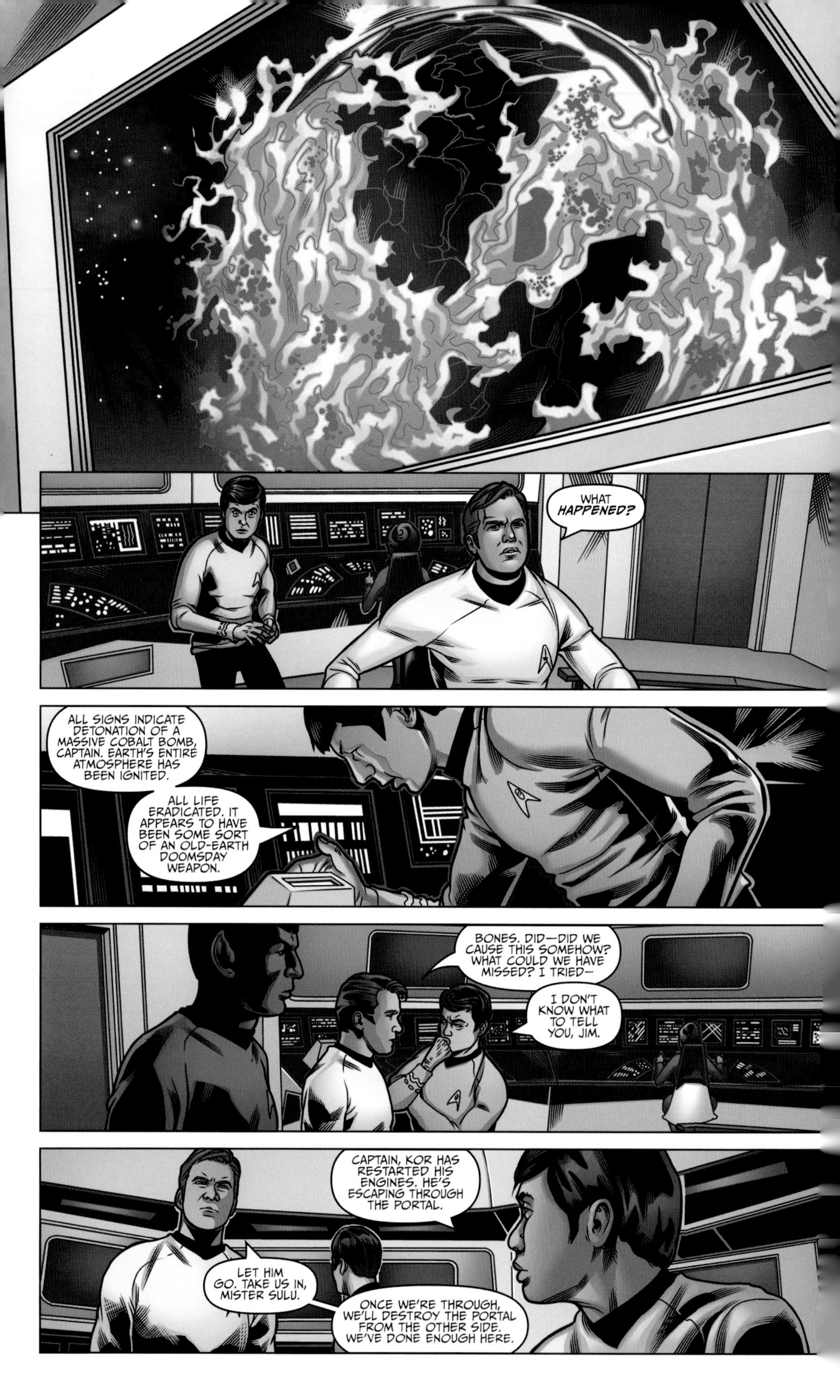
WHAT *HAPPENED?*
ALL SIGNS INDICATE DETONATION OF A MASSIVE COBALT BOMB, CAPTAIN. EARTH'S ENTIRE ATMOSPHERE HAS BEEN IGNITED.
ALL LIFE ERADICATED. IT APPEARS TO HAVE BEEN SOME SORT OF AN OLD-EARTH DOOMSDAY WEAPON.
BONES. DID—DID WE CAUSE THIS SOMEHOW? WHAT COULD WE HAVE MISSED? I TRIED—
I DON'T KNOW WHAT TO TELL YOU, JIM.
CAPTAIN, KOR HAS RESTARTED HIS ENGINES. HE'S ESCAPING THROUGH THE PORTAL.
LET HIM GO. TAKE US IN, MISTER SULU.
ONCE WE'RE THROUGH, WE'LL DESTROY THE PORTAL FROM THE OTHER SIDE. WE'VE DONE ENOUGH HERE.

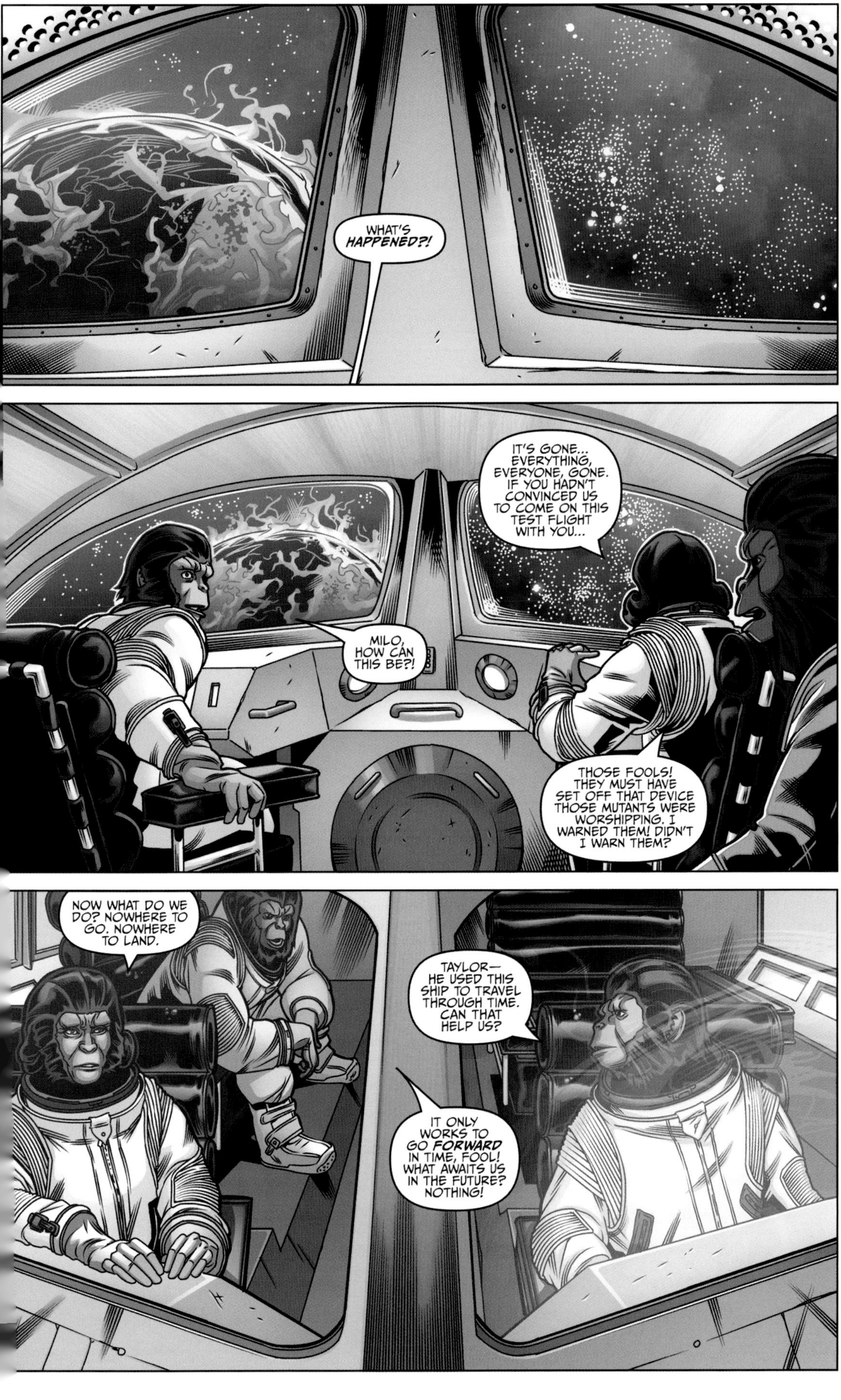
WHAT'S HAPPENED?!
IT'S GONE... EVERYTHING, EVERYONE, GONE. IF YOU HADN'T CONVINCED US TO COME ON THIS TEST FLIGHT WITH YOU...
MILO, HOW CAN THIS BE?!
THOSE FOOLS! THEY MUST HAVE SET OFF THAT DEVICE THOSE MUTANTS WERE WORSHIPPING. I WARNED THEM! DIDN'T I WARN THEM?
NOW WHAT DO WE DO? NOWHERE TO GO. NOWHERE TO LAND.
TAYLOR— HE USED THIS SHIP TO TRAVEL THROUGH TIME. CAN THAT HELP US?
IT ONLY WORKS TO GO FORWARD IN TIME, FOOL! WHAT AWAITS US IN THE FUTURE? NOTHING!

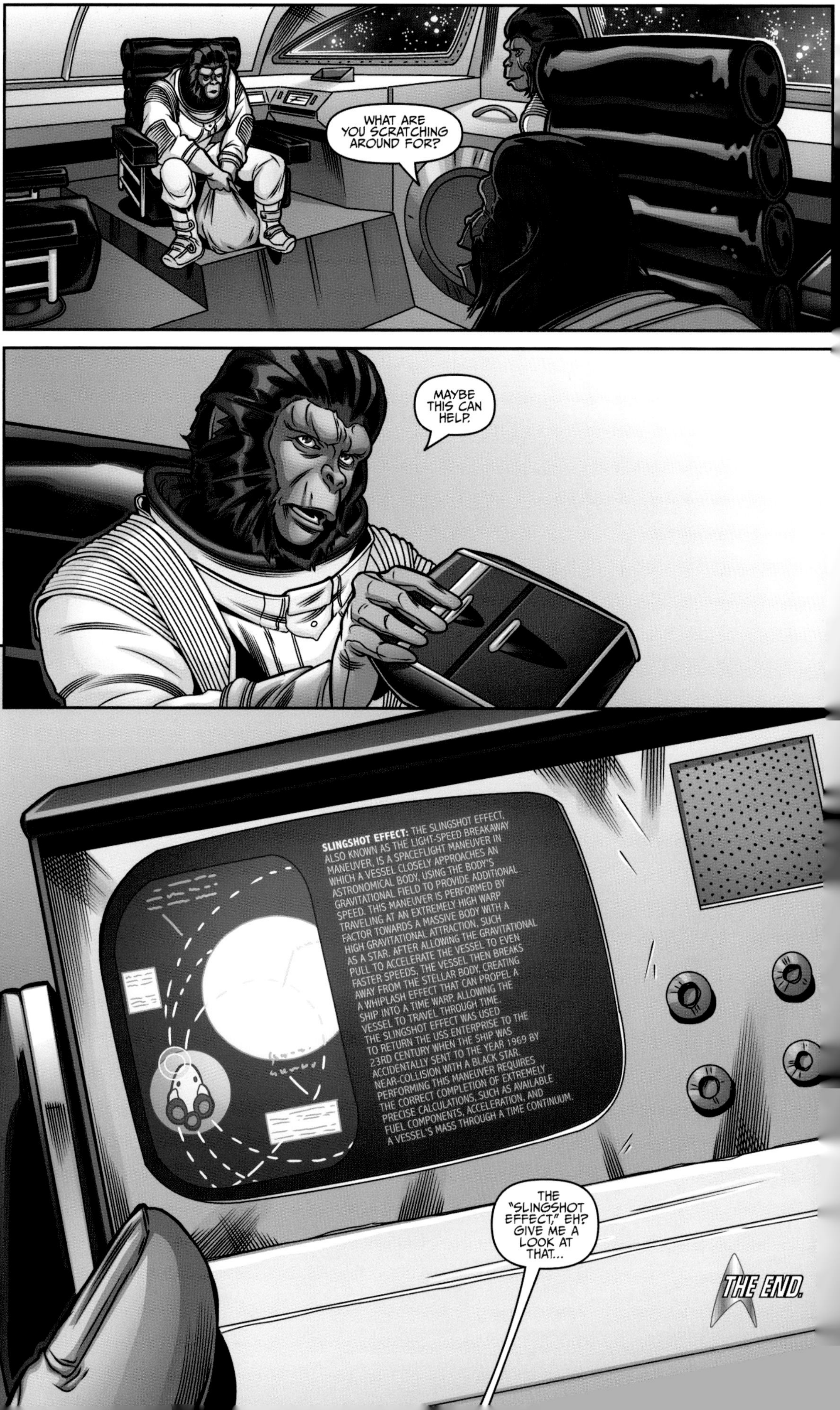
WHAT ARE YOU SCRATCHING AROUND FOR?
MAYBE THIS CAN HELP.
SLINGSHOT EFFECT: THE SLINGSHOT EFFECT, ALSO KNOWN AS THE LIGHT-SPEED BREAKAWAY MANEUVER, IS A SPACEFLIGHT MANEUVER IN WHICH A VESSEL CLOSELY APPROACHES AN ASTRONOMICAL BODY, USING THE BODY'S GRAVITATIONAL FIELD TO PROVIDE ADDITIONAL SPEED. THIS MANEUVER IS PERFORMED BY TRAVELING AT AN EXTREMELY HIGH WARP FACTOR TOWARDS A MASSIVE BODY WITH A HIGH GRAVITATIONAL ATTRACTION, SUCH AS A STAR. AFTER ALLOWING THE GRAVITATIONAL PULL TO ACCELERATE THE VESSEL TO EVEN FASTER SPEEDS, THE VESSEL THEN BREAKS AWAY FROM THE STELLAR BODY, CREATING A WHIPLASH EFFECT THAT CAN PROPEL A SHIP INTO A TIME WARP, ALLOWING THE VESSEL TO TRAVEL THROUGH TIME. THE SLINGSHOT EFFECT WAS USED TO RETURN THE USS ENTERPRISE TO THE 23RD CENTURY WHEN THE SHIP WAS ACCIDENTALLY SENT TO THE YEAR 1969 BY NEAR-COLLISION WITH A BLACK STAR. PERFORMING THIS MANEUVER REQUIRES THE CORRECT COMPLETION OF EXTREMELY PRECISE CALCULATIONS, SUCH AS AVAILABLE FUEL COMPONENTS, ACCELERATION, AND A VESSEL'S MASS THROUGH A TIME CONTINUUM.
THE "SLINGSHOT EFFECT," EH? GIVE ME A LOOK AT THAT...
THE END.

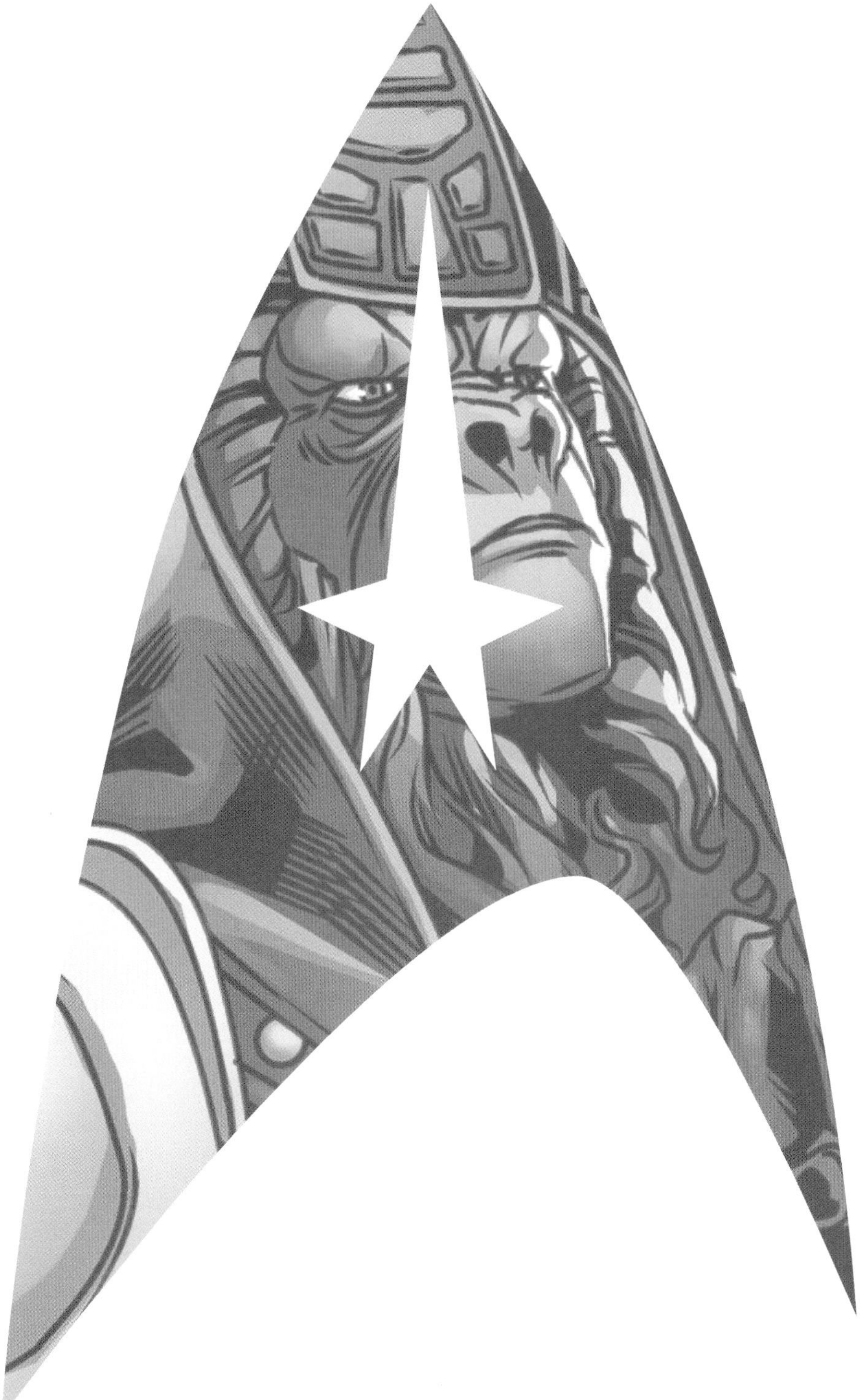

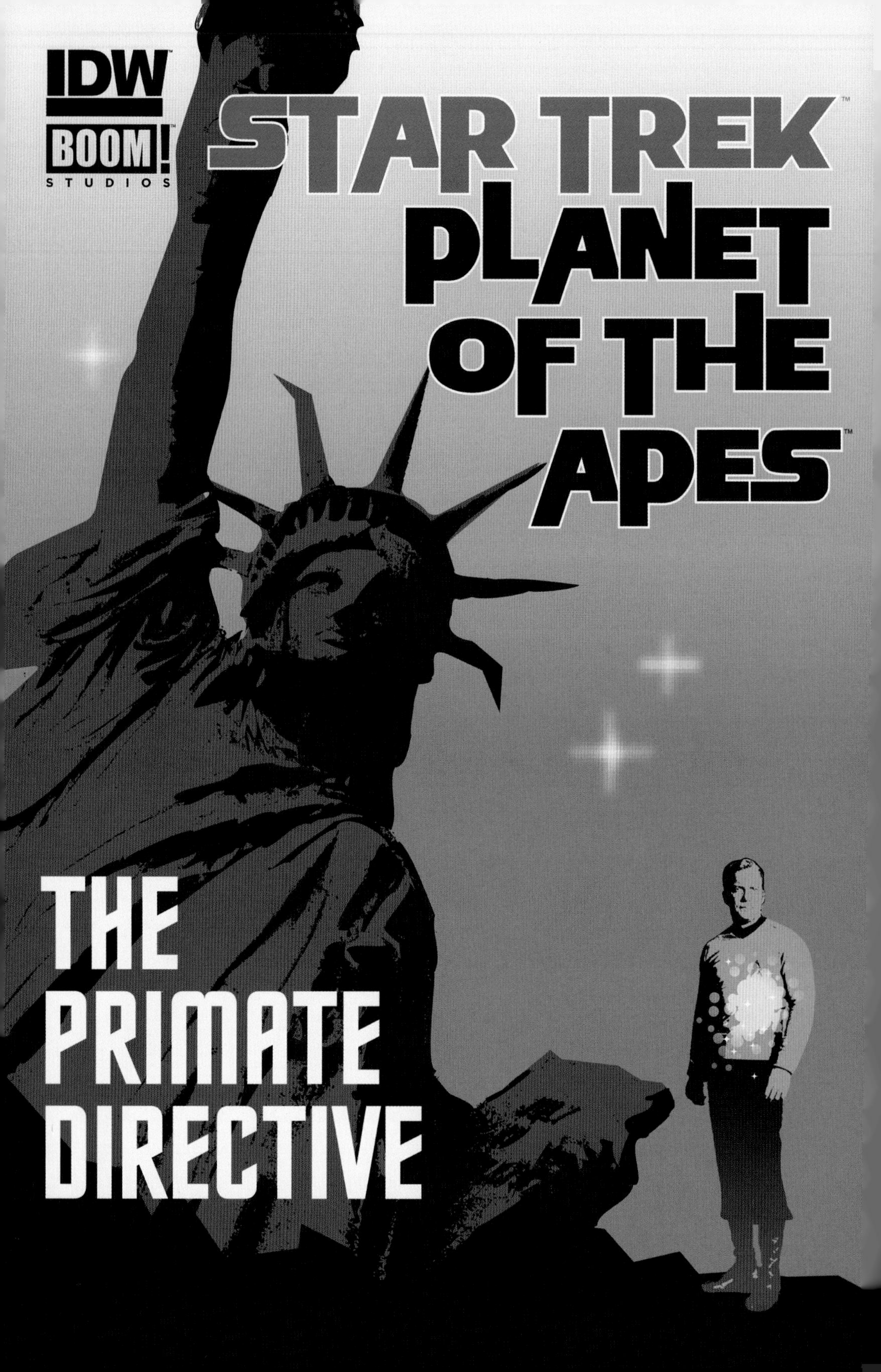
IDW
BOOM! STUDIOS
STAR TREK™
PLANET OF THE APES™
THE PRIMATE DIRECTIVE

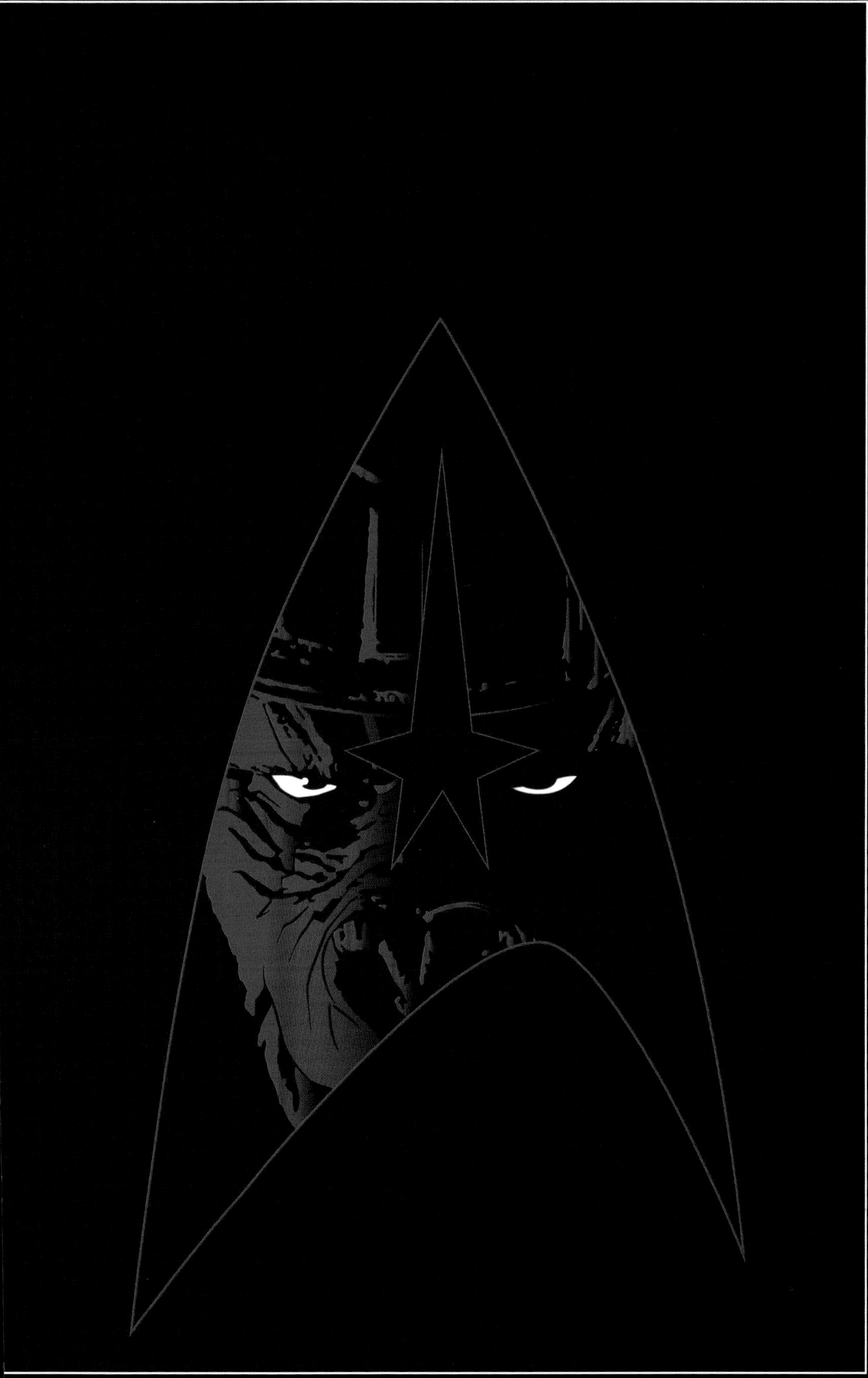

BY **JOHN MIDGLEY**

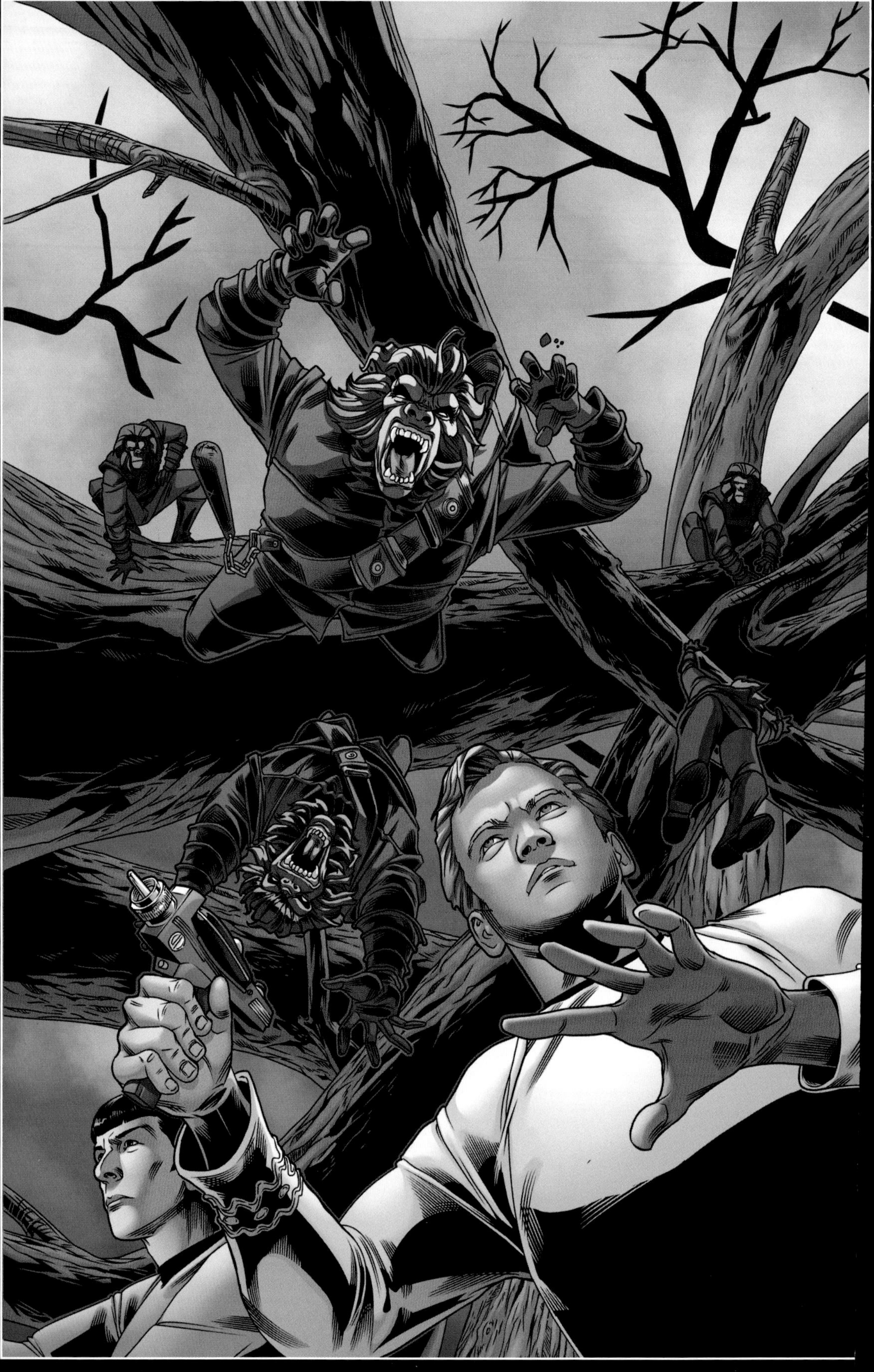

BY **RACHAEL STOTT** COLORS BY **CHARLIE KIRCHOFF**

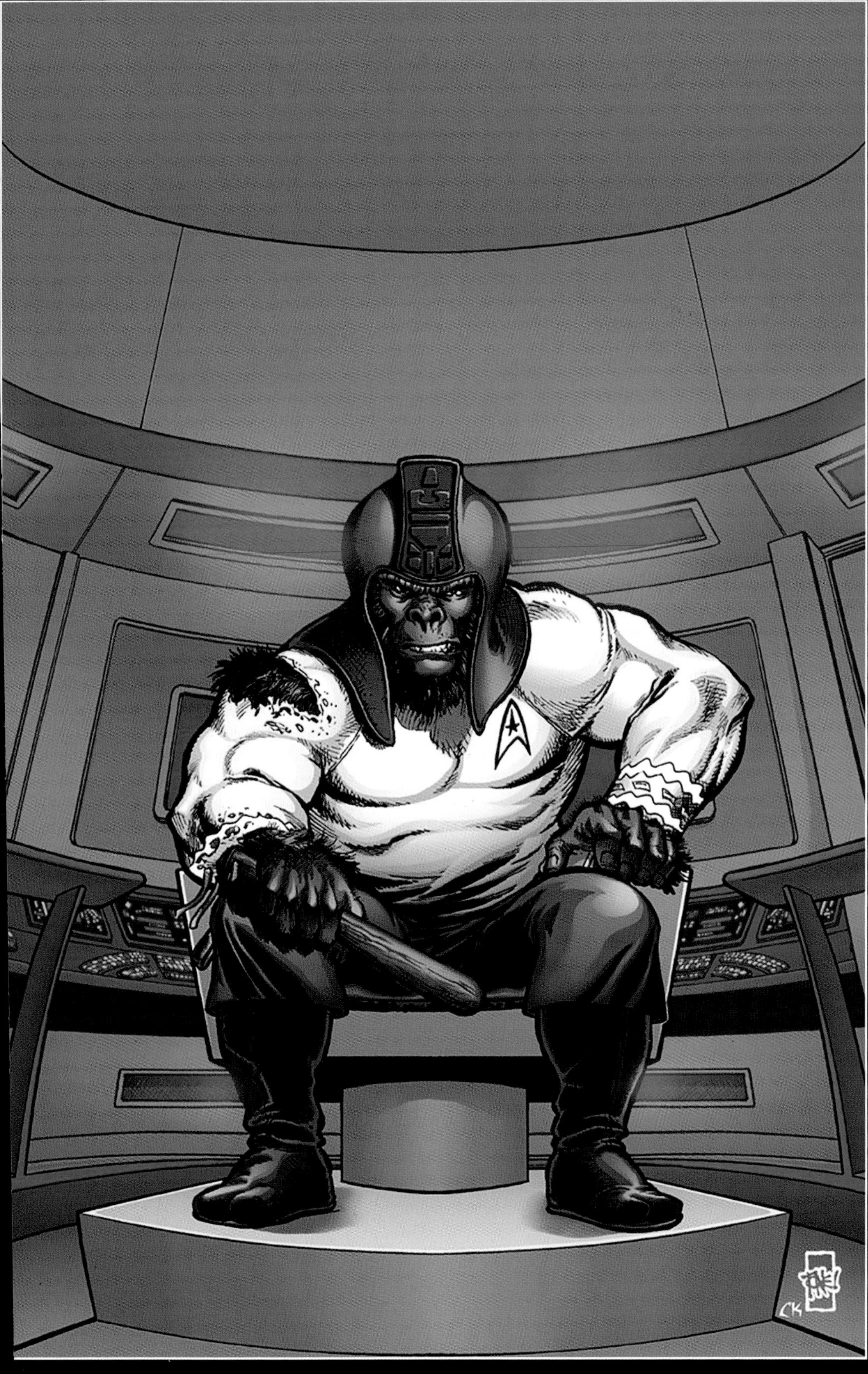

BY **TONE RODRIGUEZ** COLORS BY **CHARLIE KIRCHOFF**

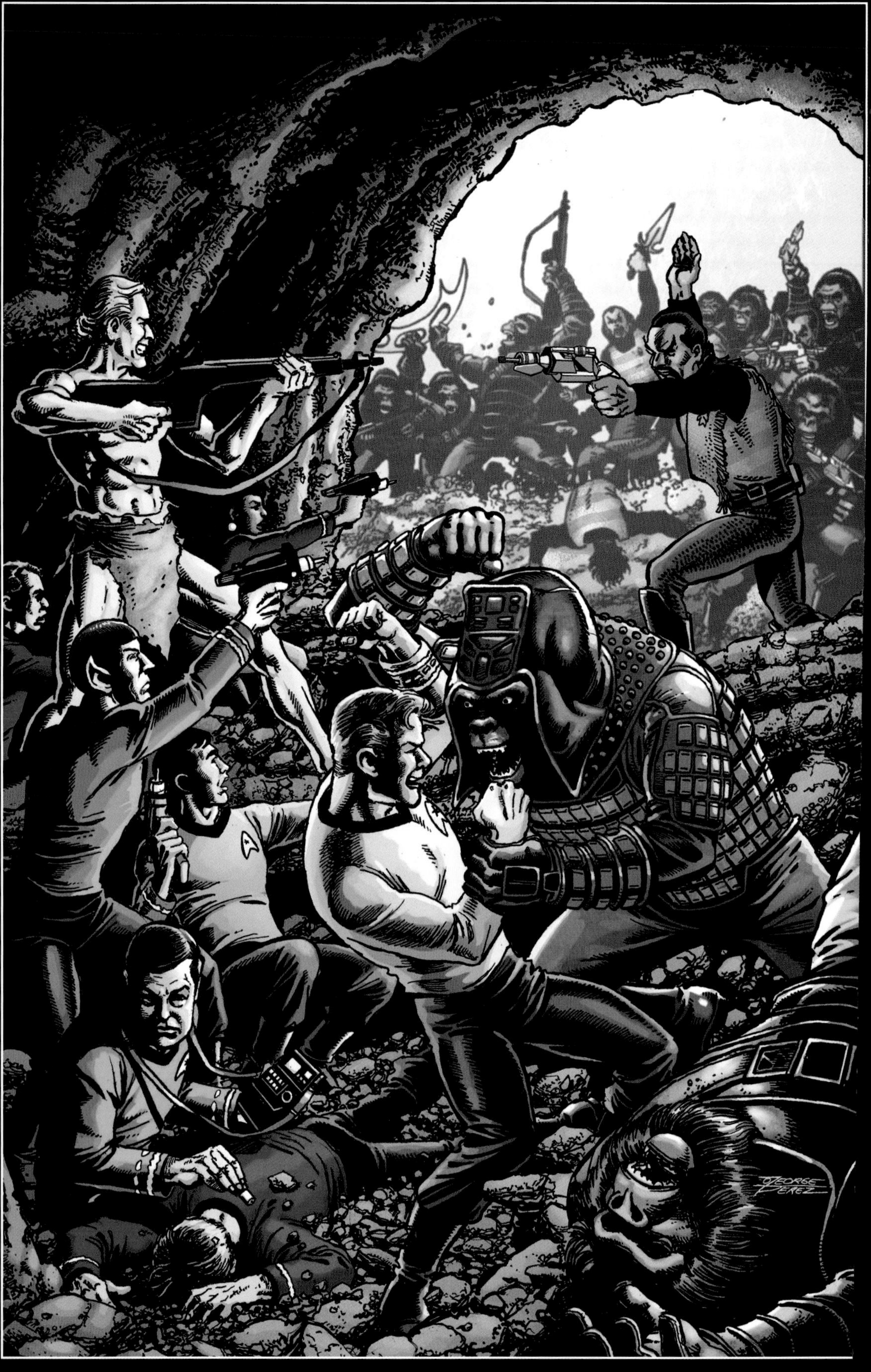
GEORGE PÉREZ

BY **GEORGE PÉREZ** COLORS BY **LEN O'GRADY**

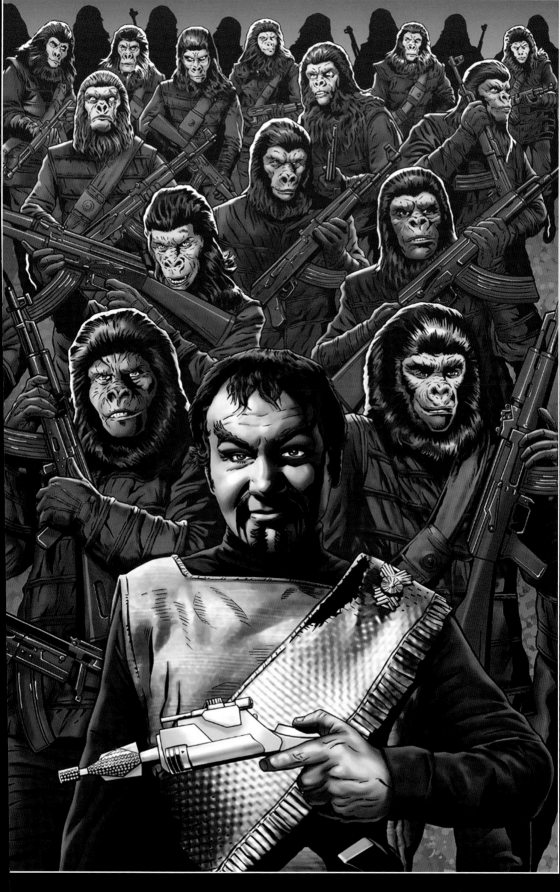

BY **JOE CORRONEY** COLORS BY **BRIAN MILLER**

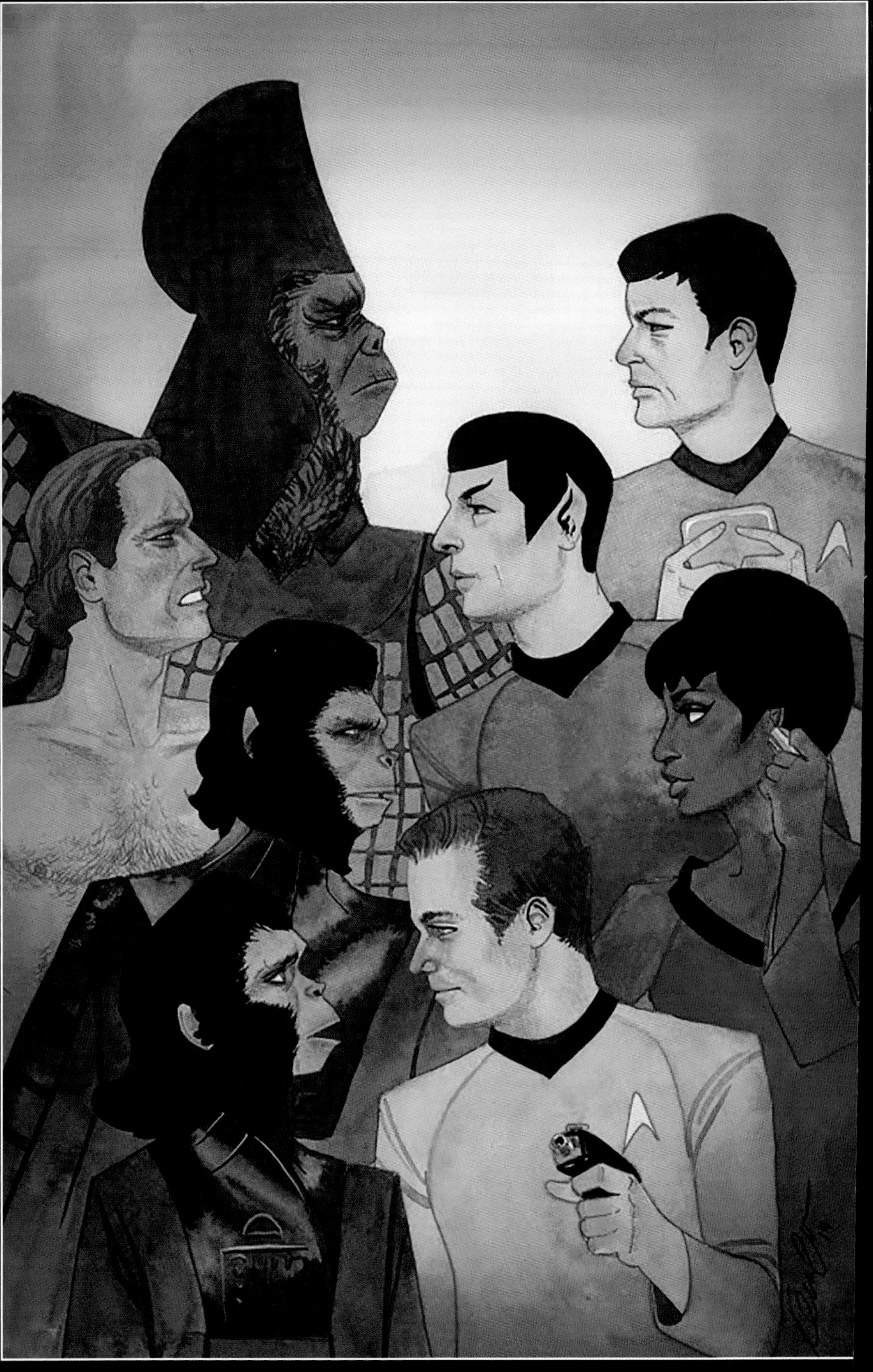

BY **KEVIN WADA**

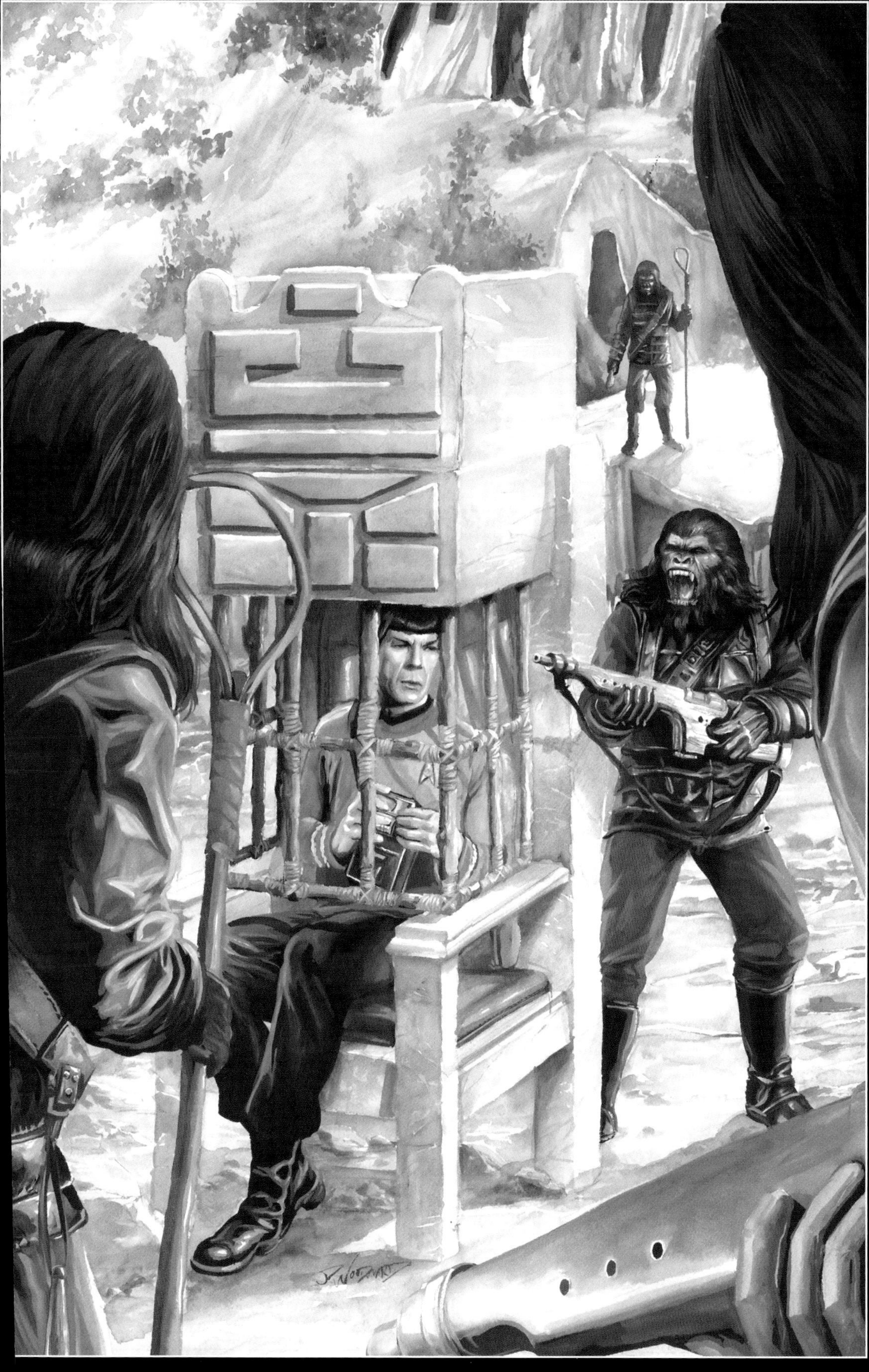

BY J.K. WOODWARD

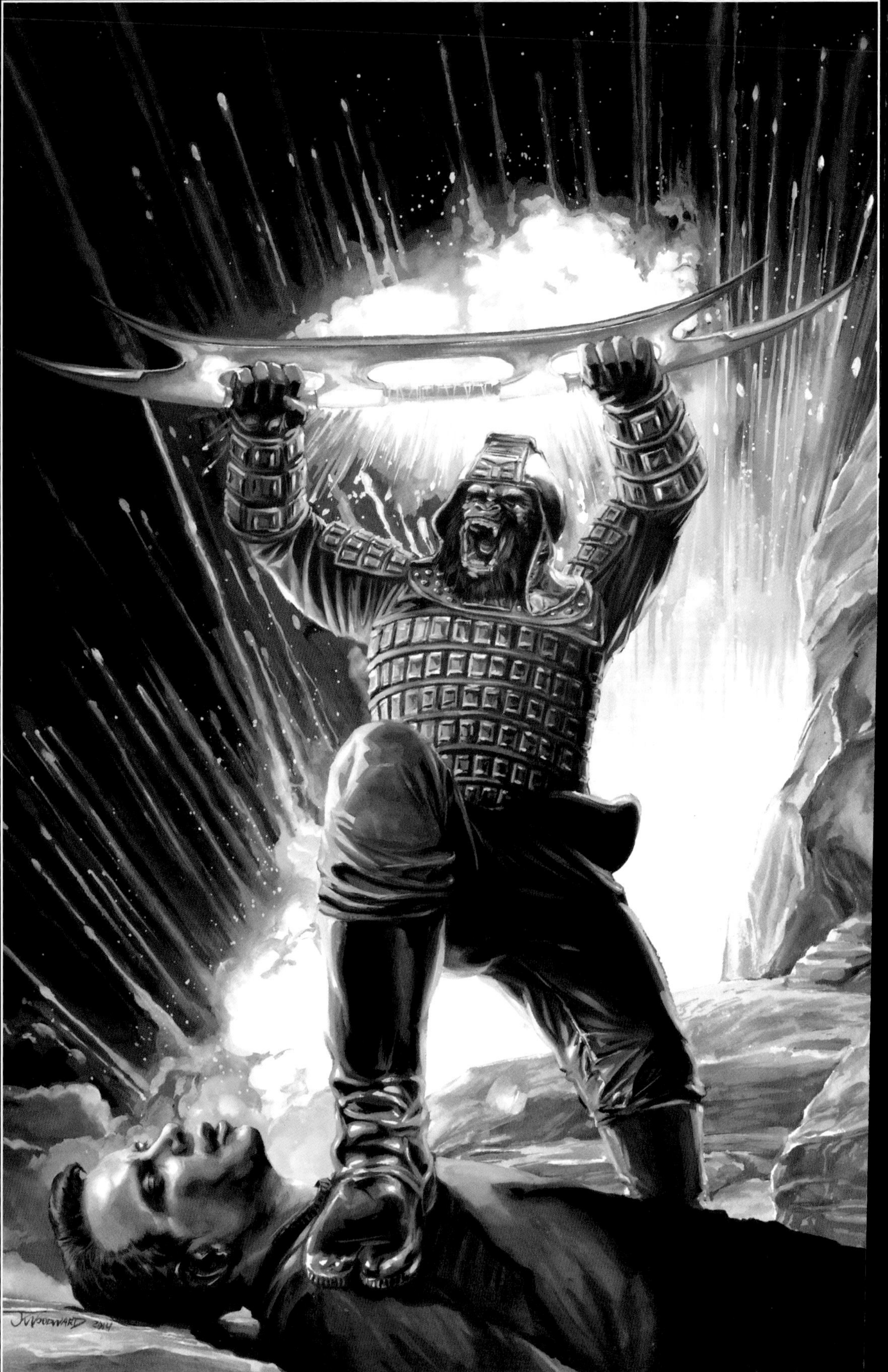
JKWOODWARD 2014

BY **J.K. WOODWARD**

THE MOTORCYCLE COP AND THE FRENCH DUDE

By Dana Gould

One began in the mind of an LAPD motorcycle cop, the other from the pen of a French dude. Two men from wildly different backgrounds, with wildly different temperaments, who both posed the question, "what if...?"

David Lynch, no slouch in the "what if?" department, once likened ideas to fish; you don't "have" an idea, you catch it. The really great ideas, I have found, are not the ones that you labor over, parse, whittle down and grind on. The great ones just show up in your brain fully formed, unannounced, demanding to be written up and tended to. They also usually start with the question, "what if?"

In the case of The Motorcycle Cop, it was, "What if there was a show like *Wagon Train*, but set in outer space?" *Wagon Train* was a popular television show in the late fifties, depicting the adventures of a group of settlers working their way across America during what I like to call "the cowboy times." The Motorcycle Cop's name was Gene Roddenberry.

For the mid-sixties, the idea of "*Wagon Train* in space" as a weekly TV show was more than a little implausible. It was, in fact, as they would say back then, "downright far out." Ironically, Gene Roddenberry, at that time, was about as un-far out as you could get.

World War II bomber pilot who flew close to a hundred missions and was awarded the Distinguished Flying Cross as a result, Gene returned from the war, took his creative ambitions and became... a pilot for Pan Am. But Roddenberry had a creative mind and wanted to become a writer. He moved to Hollywood and supported his family as an LAPD motorcycle cop. At nights and on weekends, he wrote and pondered and kept asking, "what if?"

After selling scripts to random television shows (mostly Westerns and police dramas, like *Highway Patrol* and *Have Gun Will Travel*), he scored his own series, a military drama called *The Lieutenant*, and soon after that, began shopping his "*Wagon Train* in space" idea to the networks. The only problem? No one wanted anything to do with it.

The tricky thing about making a TV show or movie is that it involves spending a lot of other people's money and, despite the fact that daring, risky stories are by far the most compelling to watch, they are exactly the kind that other people don't like spending their money on making. It's the old CATCH-22, which was a novel before it was a movie, which is something Roddenberry must have considered, since it costs the same amount of money to write about a flotilla of space ships as it does to write about a guy making a sandwich.

Which brings us to The French Dude: Pierre Boulle, who, like Roddenberry, also fought in World War II. Boulle was captured in Singapore and held for two years in a forced labor camp where, along with thousands of others, he was forced to work on the infamous "Railroad of Death." A terrible name for a railroad, it was so named because of the shocking number of conscripts who died in its creation.

After the war, Boulle wrote a novel based on his experience that became an international bestseller, *Bridge on the River Kwai*. Writing an international bestseller is like catching lightning in a bottle. There are precious authors who have pulled it off, and fewer still who've done it more than once. Boulle did it twice. Eleven years after *Bridge on the River Kwai*, Boulle asked a jaw-droppingly clever "what if?" What if mankind fell from its perch atop the evolutionary ladder and apes emerged to rule the planet?

It's easy to see how a former prisoner of war could develop so cynical a view of mankind's potential, and his novel, published in 1963 as *Monkey Planet*, drives the point home hard. Closer to *Gulliver's Travels* than science fiction, Boulle's story was essentially a satire.

It wasn't until the film version, produced five years later under the catchier title *Planet of the Apes*, that the gun-totin', horseback ridin', Charlton Heston chasin' world that we all know and love was introduced.

Just describing the world of the original Apes puts me in the mood to throw in the DVD again. The story is so original, so daring, so risky, and... guess what? You got it. No one wanted anything to do with it! Arthur P. Jacobs, the producer of the film version, got every door in Hollywood slammed in his face multiple times. But *Planet of the Apes*, like *Star Trek*, proved that you just can't keep a good idea down, and when it finally did prevail, and was subsequently loosed upon the public, its popularity spread like a panic.

Both *Star Trek* and *Apes* began with simple "what if?" questions posed by talented writers. Both were brought to life on film over the protestations of Hollywood money men, and both grew into globally successful franchises, still healthy and robust today. And now, lucky us, some new, ingenious writers have come along to ask another intriguing "what if?" In these pages, Scott and David Tipton pose the question "what if these two worlds collided?" The result, drawn by Rachael Stott and colored by Charlie Kirchoff, is insanely clever and entertaining, and poses yet another literary question: "Why didn't I think of that?"

Dana Gould is a writer and comedian living in Los Angeles, California. He has won two Emmy awards for his work as a writer and producer on The Simpsons. *His most recent comedy special is entitled* I Know It's Wrong, *and he can be heard monthly on his podcast,* The Dana Gould Hour.

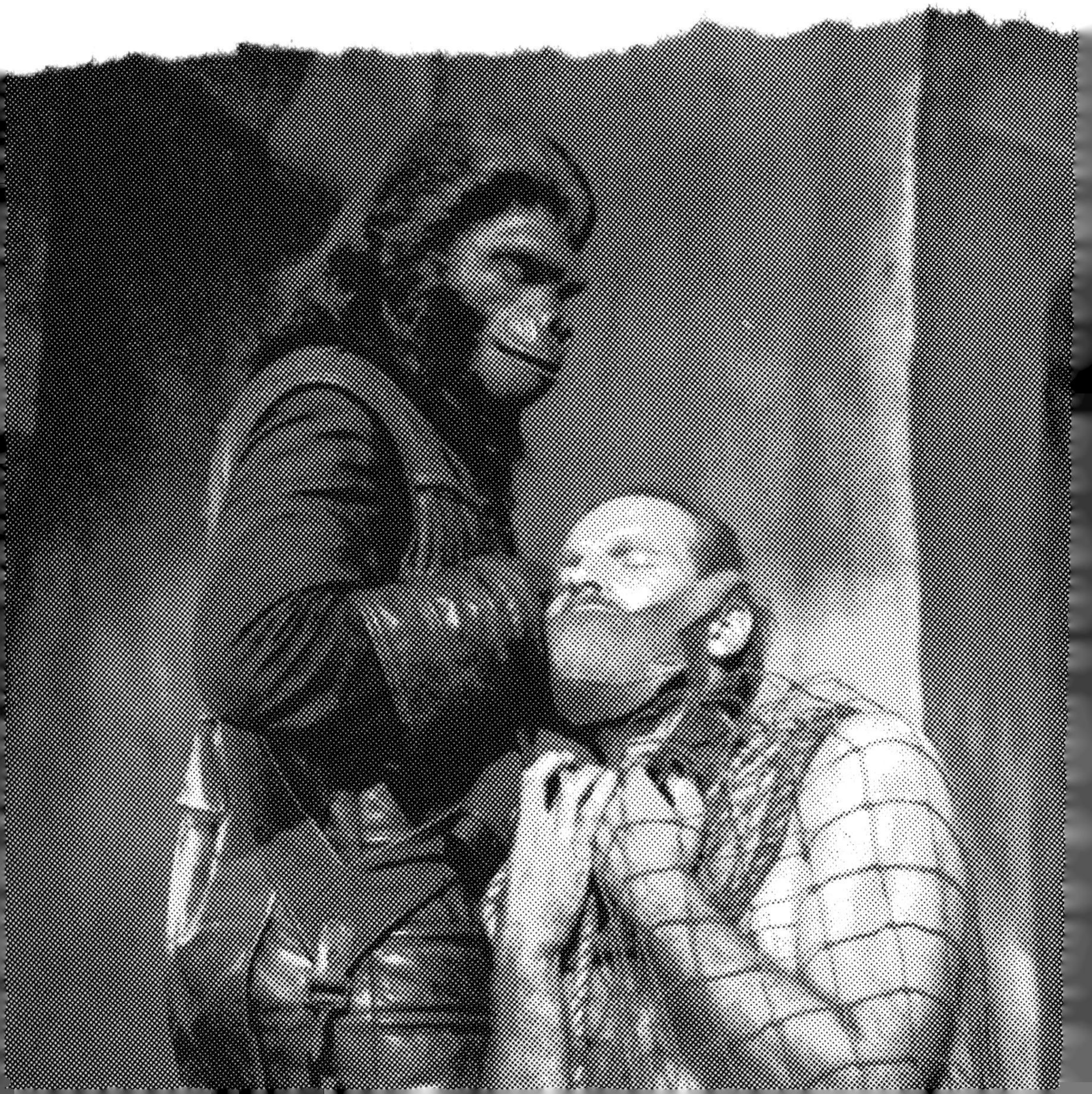

OPPOSITES ATTRACT

By Dana Gould

Sometimes, a person says something so concise and universal that it enters the lexicon and becomes "a wise old saying." Friedrich Nietzsche's "That which does not kill you makes you stronger," is an example. Or Confucius' "Choose a job you love and you will never have to work a day in your life." Into this hallowed lexicon, we must now add the prescient words of Paula Abdul, who, in her 1990 dance mega-hit, "Opposites Attract," uttered those timeless words, um, well, "opposites attract."

But it's true! Certainly more true than "That which does not kill you makes you stronger." Judging by those words, it's safe to assume that Nietzsche never met anyone who was almost, but not quite, crushed by a boulder.

Opposites attract. And what two franchises stand in starker opposition than *Star Trek* and *Planet of the Apes*. Although they both came out of the late sixties, it was *Apes* that encapsulated the sour, pessimistic outlook that had settled over the culture by the close of that watershed era. *Star Trek* hearkens back to a far, far brighter, more upbeat time. Namely, the early '60s.

In fact, the show's opening credits, describing space as "the final frontier," slyly parrot President Kennedy's view of the decade that lie ahead, saying in his 1960 acceptance speech, "We stand today on the edge of a new frontier – the frontier of the 1960s."

A brave young leader, boldly taking a merry band of explorers into uncharted territory. Despite being created after its leader's life was so unceremoniously snuffed out on a curvy street in Dallas, *Star Trek* could have been called the Kennedy Administration In Space.

Apes? Not so much. Unlike Captain James T. Kirk, who views space as a place "to boldly go where no man has gone before," *Apes'* Colonel George Taylor stares into the vast expanse, and can only bemoan, "it squashes a man's ego. I feel lonely."

Kirk ventured into space "to explore strange new worlds. Seek out new life and new civilizations."

In his own words, Taylor left to satisfy a nagging, personal curiosity. "Somewhere in the universe, there has to be something better than man. Has to be."

Lastly, whereas Capt. Kirk personifies the clear-headed, sharp-eyed, can-do spirit of the post-World War II generation, Taylor is the personification of the melancholy frustrations of the Vietnam era. Let's just say it. Taylor's a jerk. In fact, the first twenty minutes of the original *Apes* is given over to his endless brow-beating of his fellow astronaut Landon. Never mind that Taylor is Landon's superior officer, and as such probably shouldn't be picking fights with his subordinates, but additionally, as commander of the mission, isn't Taylor responsible for crew morale? Perhaps constantly reminding them that their loved ones are all dead and forgotten isn't the best way to keep their spirits up? It would be as if Sulu alerted Captain Kirk that Klingon warships had surrounded the *Enterprise*, and Kirk just slumped forward in his chair and muttered, "We deserve to die. Especially you."

Let's not even get into Taylor's appraisal of Lt. Stewart, the only female crewmember on the mission. Or, as he so inelegantly describes her, "the most precious cargo we brought along. She was to be the new Eve. With our hot and eager help, of course."

Really? Was that the plan? Did she know about this? Why do I get the feeling Operation: New Eve was something they were going to spring on her once they landed. I bet she thought she was the geologist.

Nowhere are the sunny and rainy viewpoints of these two series spelled out more clearly than in the endings of the first three films of each franchise. *Star Trek: The Motion Picture*, which unfurled onto screens in December of 1979, told the story of V'ger (spoiler alert!) an old Earth Voyager satellite that had travelled the universe, accumulating so much knowledge it gained sentience and, in its journey to complete its mission, threatened the Earth's very existence. Kirk and crew dispatched it handily, ditching the new guy and the bald chick along the way, and the film concluded with the words "The Human Adventure Is Just Beginning." How's that for optimism? Even the ending isn't the end.

Star Trek II: The Wrath of Khan brought back to the series elements from the televised run that were missing the first time out: color, action, humor, fun, and a story. *Star Trek II* is a ripping good yarn, well told. At the film's exciting conclusion, we learn that everything comes at a price, as the beloved Mr. Spock sacrifices his own life to save the ship. Yes, Spock is dead.

Until he isn't!

The film ends with the virtual assurance that, no, some kind of space thing happened, and he's not quite as dead as we thought. Talk about optimistic! And *Star Trek III* went on to prove it, putting the assurance of his survival in the very title: *The Search For Spock*. But alas, that film came with its own set of sacrifices, and in *Star Trek III*, the *Enterprise* itself bit the big one. Yes, the Starship *Enterprise* went down in flames and was destroyed.

Until it wasn't!

Kirk, No-Longer-Dead Spock and company head home to Starfleet HQ, but are forced into the time-travelling detour to present-day Earth that became known as Star Trek IV. But at that movie's conclusion, once they finally arrive back home, they are greeted by... a brand-new, rebuilt, not-destroyed, replica *Enterprise*!

The original *Planet of the Apes*, released in February of 1968, quite rightly blew people's minds, not the least of which because of its ending, which would go down as one of the great shockaroos in cinema history. Charlton Heston, Moses himself, one of cinema's larger-than-life heroic figures, slumps in the sand, shattered and defeated, before the (spoiler alert!) broken remains of the Statue of Liberty. Turns out he was on Earth the whole time. No music swells on the soundtrack. The screen just fades silently to black as the credits crawl slowly over the mournful sound of the waning surf. Mankind blew it. Literally. We suck. The End. See you later.

But people wanted more, understandably, and so we got 1970's *Beneath the Planet of the Apes*. A film that is, for my dollar, one of the bleakest, weirdest, darkest major studio movies of all time. Shot in 1969, the year after the assassinations of Robert Kennedy and Martin Luther King, at the height of the Vietnam War, *Beneath the Planet of the Apes* is very much a product of its time, and as such, concludes with what might be the single most depressing ending of any movie in history. Quite simply, the world ends and everyone dies. Th-th-th-that's all folks! Charlton Heston, shot in the chest, literally holding his heart in his hand, staggers up and falls onto the controls of a thermonuclear weapon that incinerates the planet and everyone on it. Thanks for coming and don't forget to validate!

It's a far cry indeed from the "no-character-you-care-about-will-stay-dead-for-long" world of *Star Trek*. In fact, one imagines the studio honchos looking at the still-boffo grosses from *Beneath* and asking, "could anything be a bigger bummer?"

"I dunno," one suit must have ventured, "maybe we could murder a baby."

"You're on!"

Which brings us to the third film in the series, 1971's somewhat goofy *Escape From the Planet of the Apes*. Taking a page from an old movie serial, we learn that not everyone died in the previous film. Our favorite characters somehow managed to make it back to present-day Earth, where they are to live out a tongue-in-cheek role reversal of the original film. The film plays as a charming romantic comedy of sorts, until the very end, when things go south in a big way. A nasty German scientist chases down the renegade chimps and fills them full of holes. Including their baby. Especially their baby. In a nice medium shot. BLAM! BLAM! BLAM! As it turns out, the apes pulled a switcheroo insuring another sequel, but make no mistake, the film ends with a baby chimp getting shot to death, and its mother then drops its corpse into the oily waters of San Pedro Harbor before crawling off to die on her dead husband's chest.

Under the credits, we hear the 1965 Lesley Gore hit, "Sunshine, Lollipops and Roses."

I'm kidding. There's just more silence.

And yet, as drastically different as these films are in tone, they are all soooo incredibly compelling. So eternally watchable. They not only worked like gangbusters, but they each set up their respective franchises on such a sturdy foundation that they're both still chugging along half a century later.

Maybe they need each other. Paul McCartney's sunny optimism always worked best in counterpoint to John Lennon's acerbic cynicism. The dark fantasy of *The Empire Strikes Back* seemed all the more enthralling after the **bright, shiny,** cinematic apple that was *Star Wars*. Maybe, as is evidenced by the book you're holding now in your damn dirty paws, these two were always meant to be together.

Paula Abdul said it best. Opposites attract.

A GOOD, FIVE-CENT TIME MACHINE

By Dana Gould

I recently got an email from a company that produces specialty action figures (sorry ladies, I'm taken). This particular company was announcing the release of their newest creation, a MEGO-style likeness of Boris Karloff from *The Raven*. We live in truly wondrous times, at least in terms of collectibles. They really do make everything nowadays. As an experiment, I recently entered "*Star Trek*, Cyrano Jones, action figure" into Google's search field and got almost eight hundred results.

That said, unlike a good many *Star Trek* or *Planet of the Apes* fans, I do not have a massive collection of memorabilia foaming up off every shelf in my home. To repeat, I do not. Oh, don't get me wrong, I have stuff, but I like to keep things specific. I collect memorabilia for one reason and one reason only: time travel.

A little over a decade ago, my wife and I were shopping for a house. We had been married a couple years and it had become The Time: when young couples start planning for a tiny roommate, the kind that is always making a mess, staying up all night, won't chip in financially and doesn't think to apologize for throwing up on you. Yes, we were planning on renting a room to Lindsay Lohan. But she was in jail at the time, so we decided to have a baby instead.

We drove around Los Angeles wanting only the perfect house at the perfect price in the perfect neighborhood. And we found it! Not a week into our search we stumbled upon a beautiful, two-story ranch with enough bedrooms for several little you-know-whos located in a beautiful, woodsy neighborhood. And the house was right in our price range, provided we could expand our price range by several hundred thousand unattainable dollars!

We were standing in the dining room thinking of banks we could rob when the realtor said, "This house used to belong to a famous actor, that guy Roddy McDowall."

I was glad I was not chewing gum because I didn't want to die in Roddy McDowall's house choking on Hubba-Bubba. My wife's head rotated around like an owl spotting a field mouse and one terrifying mortgage loan later we owned Roddy McDowall's house. It was surely the most expensive piece of *Planet of the Apes* memorabilia in existence, and I, a card-carrying *Apes* nut, owned it.

It's an awesome house. Unlike Roddy's residency, when movie stars and other beautiful people came to drink Chardonnay by the pool and ogle the rose bushes that Elizabeth Taylor planted, the house is now full of kids, toys, Razor scooters, skateboards, bikes, dogs, cats, fish and a rabbit that long ago escaped its hutch but can still be seen darting out from under the playhouse on sunny afternoons. As a conversation piece, my house is hard to beat. As a piece of *Apes* memorabilia, it comes up flat as a cheap tire, because it does not fulfill the primary function of all good memorabilia: it does not transport me through time.

Time travel is the key element to the original *Apes* film franchise, and to some of the very best *Star Trek* stories. No, I don't mean the whale movie, I mean "City on the Edge of Forever," "Assignment: Earth," First Contact, etc.

If I could travel to any place, in any time, I'd like to visit Los Angeles in the summer of 1967. Seriously. I can hear you now, "Hey rube! What about the French Revolution? Or maybe preventing World War II?"

Nope. Not going down that wormhole. Why not go back to that fateful night at Ford's Theater, and stop John Wilkes-Booth on his way to the balcony.... dressed in a Gorn suit! That'd spice up the history books. No, I'm keeping things light and simple. I'm only going to look. No interference. I have a Prime Directive too, you know.

If you were in Los Angeles during the summer of 1967, you could, all on the same day, see the original *Planet of the Apes* being filmed on the Twentieth Century Fox lot, along with *Lost in Space*, *Voyage to the Bottom of the Sea* and... BOFF! POW! Adam West's Batman TV series. All on the same day! Not only that, but a thirty-minute drive east to Desilu Studios would put you right smack-dab on the *Star Trek* set.

After Kirk and company wrapped for the day, you could cruise north on Gower for a few blocks and hang a left onto the fabulous Sunset Strip, where The Doors were the house band at the Whiskey A-Go-Go. Los Angeles in the summer of 1967 was a hip, happening place, and I sincerely want to go there, be there, see it, feel it. I want to have been a part of it.

But that will probably never happen. Let me ask you this: if someone in the future did invent a time machine, wouldn't they have already come back to brag about it? The closest we can come to time travel is to possess an item from that time that will transport us back *emotionally*. Enter Marcel Proust who, in his novel *Remembrance of Things Past*, introduced the theory that became known as the Proustian Flashback. In the novel, the hero is eating a piece of cake, and its taste, so evocative of the cake from his childhood, triggers a sudden flood of memory: bright, clear and brimming with detail.

Life is full of Proustian Flashbacks. The opening theme music of *It's The Great Pumpkin, Charlie Brown* brings the smell and feel and sound of crumpled, autumn leaves so clearly to my mind that I might as well be jumping into a pile of them. If I hear the opening "Pling-Pla-Pling-Pling" of Alexander Courage's original *Star Trek* theme, I need only close my eyes and I'm back in the freezing blackness of a Massachusetts winter night, sprinting home from pick-up hockey on "the pond" to rendezvous with the *Enterprise* crew from 6:00 to 7:00 p.m. on Channel 56.

I know this because I own both of these soundtracks, and when I want to travel back in time, I need only hit the play button.

In the film *Somewhere in Time*, Christopher Reeve comes to possess a locket belonging to a woman from the previous century, and by staring at it long enough, is able to hypnotize himself back in time to be at her side. This is memorabilia at its best, and if anyone has a locket that can send me back to the set of *The Avengers* TV series on the day Diana Rigg wore that black leather catsuit, you may write to me care of the publisher.

Sadly, I don't own anything that can send me back to L.A. in the Summer of Love, but I do have a cardboard box that can shoot me back to Massachusetts in 1968. I do. And it works every time.

In 1968, I was four years old, living in a small mill town in New England called Hopedale, Massachusetts. The Sixties, as people think of them, did not touch Hopedale, Massachusetts. In 1968, Hopedale was pretty much like Mayberry on *The Andy Griffith Show*, only with colder winters and flatter accents.

One afternoon, in the early summer of 1968, I went to the drugstore with my older brother. Hopedale Drug was a small pharmacy with an adjacent luncheonette and candy counter (I told you, it really was like Mayberry), and on this particular day, I recall quite vividly glancing up to a top shelf and seeing an ape. A chimpanzee, to be precise, peering out at me from the side of a bright, yellow box. Next to it, in red letters, were the words *Planet of the Apes*.

What of the Huh? Well, I liked monkeys, and whatever it was in that box, I wanted it. And I would get it, in time. I say "in time" because my brother was not about to buy me anything that I wanted, if only for the reason that I wanted it. But by the end of the long, hot summer, I owned a great, big stack of Topps' *Planet of the Apes* bubble-gum cards. At four years old, concepts like doubles and complete sets were over my head, but, bound with several thick, beige, rubber bands, I had a big, battered stack of "greenbacks," as they came to be known, and I clutched them to my chest as if they were the One Ring itself.

Until I lost them. Or, more likely, my brother filched them and used them as BB gun targets. And as I grew older, I assumed I would never again lay my eyes on those magical images: the strangely muted color, the orange, paisley-shaped title box on each card, the images themselves, from a movie I had not even seen yet, but one that already held me in its thrall.

Then, one fateful day in the curiously inverted year of 1986, I went to a yard sale, where three of them lay scattered on a card table alongside a bunch of other stuff that had me wondering if I was actually at a yard sale or if some people just

decided to put their garbage out on a table instead of into the can if only to see what would happen. But there they were, cardboard diamonds in the discarded rough.

I took one look and, WHOOSH, I could instantly see it all. There was Hopedale Drug with its long, Formica lunch counter and its tantalizing wall of slanted, candy-laden shelves. My old backyard with that big, smooth rock behind the doghouse, my dog's reeky, old blanket hanging out the doorway like his tongue lolled out his mouth. I could see my old living-room couch, with its itchy, wool cushions and chipped, wooden, wagon-wheel arms. Every spot I had ever sat and stared and wondered and daydreamed while thumbing through that big, square, rubber-banded stack came flooding back to me.

A couple years later, I was attending a collector's show, which is where sophisticates like myself went to complete our collection of mint-condition *Famous Monsters* magazines in the pre-eBay days, when I passed by a dealer with a table full of bubble-gum cards. As always, I searched through them hoping to purloin one or two more stray *Apes* cards when, PLOP, I happened upon a complete set, mint and pristine, in a clear plastic case, no less.

"These *Apes* cards? Are they the originals?"

"Yeah, all fifty-five. Full set."

I don't recall the price, but it wasn't important. Those cards left that table when I did, and as thrilled as I was to once again feel my hand around that familiar-feeling little green-backed stack of wonder, I had yet to find the box. The display box. The flimsy, cardboard rectangle bearing a photo of a chimpanzee that peered out at me from the top shelf of the Hopedale Drug candy counter in 1968. My unending search had yielded other treasures. I eventually came to own not only a complete set of cards, but also an untorn wrapper and even a complete unopened pack (half century-old gum!), but the display box, my cardboard Moby Dick, was ever on the horizon, never in my net.

Until eBay, and then, as the Great Man sang, "Wham-bam, Thank you, ma'am." And when it showed up in my mailbox, it did not disappoint.

As I said, physical time travel will, in all likelihood, remain impossible. To begin with, where's the money in it? I'm sure we have more resources dedicated to creating zero-calorie cheesecake than we do to temporal shift manipulation. But psychological time travel is ready and available around the clock. All you need is that one, collectible little object to send you back. Call it your Rosebud, a talisman from the past, from the time when something first cut through the din and rang your imagination's bell so hard it's still echoing in your head. It's a lot safer than jumping through a wormhole, and a lot cheaper than buying a house.

CHAMBERS, JOHN CHAMBERS

y Dana Gould

---

tar Trek and Planet of the Apes. A TV show and a movie. lmed simultaneously in the same city. Both slammed head- ng into popular culture, leaving their marks on the national syche and creating franchises that still flourish four de- ades hence.

uthor's note: I knew, if I wrote enough of these essays, I ould eventually get to use the word "hence." And I just did. oom!)

s far as individuals who contributed to both projects, ere is only one name that stands out. A quiet, unassuming entleman, universally praised and fiercely beloved, without hom the Star Trek we know would not be the Star Trek we ow, and without whom Planet of the Apes might not exist all. I am speaking, of course, about John Chambers.

ho?

ohn Chambers. The man who created Spock's ears, an en- re planet of apes and who revolutionized the makeup in- ustry in the process. Oh, yeah, and the whole time, he was orking undercover for the CIA.

ue.

hambers, John Chambers.

an interview in 1978, Charlton Heston said, "Taylor reflects own views of mankind. I have infinite faith and admiration r the extraordinary individual man – the Gandhi, the Mi- elangelo, the Shakespeare – but very low expectations for an as a species."

anks, Chuck. Anyway, while it may be too much to compare hn Chambers to Gandhi or Shakespeare, he was indisput- ly an extraordinary individual.

hambers was born in Chicago, Illinois, and started his ca- er designing, of all things, jewelry and carpets. You know, at job. He served in the army during World War II as a den- l technician, which, everyone knows, is the next natural ep after jewelry-making carpet design. It wasn't until after e war that his particular genius began to find an outlet.

hambers worked at the U.S. Army Veterans' Hospital in nes, Illinois, designing prosthetic limbs for wounded sol- ers. His abilities soon led him to sculpting and designing re- acement eyes and even reconstructive facial prosthetics.

1953, Chambers wrote a letter to NBC Television in Bur-

bank, California, explaining his areas of expertise and sug- gesting that, quite possibly, his talents could be useful to the network in its live, televised dramas. The network, quite wise- ly, bit, and summoned Chambers west. He never looked back.

Chambers' abilities as sculptor and designer but also as an engineer and chemist revolutionized creative makeup de- sign. Chambers did not just sculpt a fake nose, he designed it to be worn the same way a prosthetic nose would be. His pieces weren't masks so much as extensions of human mus- culature. A fake nose by John Chambers didn't just look real, it also twitched when yours did. This is also because, as a chemist, he was able to design and manufacture more light- weight, porous forms of foam rubber, unlike any used before.

For obvious reasons, Chambers quickly became one of the most in-demand makeup artists in Hollywood, leaving NBC for a more prestigious position at Universal Studios. Over time, Chambers would come to design iconic makeups for The Outer Limits, The Munsters, and scores of other shows.

In 1964, impressed with his work on The Outer Limits, Gene Roddenberry contacted Chambers for his NBC pilot Star Trek. Not long after, a young Leonard Nimoy paid a visit to Chambers' garage workshop in sunny Encino, California, where the Wizard of Illinois fashioned the first of many, many, many, pairs of pointy Vulcan ears. Possibly, the most famous pair of ears this side of Dumbo.

This accomplishment alone would guarantee a person some degree of show-biz immortality, but to Chambers, it's little more than a footnote. The peaks of his career still lie ahead, and one of them, by far the most fantastic, would be kept a secret almost until his death.

At some point in the late 1960s, Chambers came to the at- tention of a CIA agent named Tony Mendez. Mendez believed, correctly, that Chambers' ability to create believable facial prosthetics would be helpful disguises to agents in the field. Soon after, Chambers began creating "Identity Transforma- tion Kits" for the CIA. He was under orders to tell no one.

The kits were used extensively and with great success. In one instance, Mendez recently told Wired magazine, Cham- bers made it possible for an African-American CIA agent and an Asian diplomat to move freely about the city of Commu- nist Laos disguised as two Caucasians. The two men, work- ing from life masks Chambers made of actors Rex Harrison and Victor Mature, passed easily among the population, al- beit as dead ringers for Rex Harrison and Victor Mature.

But that triumph was a government secret. His next Hollywood job would win him an Oscar, and make him as close to a household name as a makeup artist could be.

In 1966, a script with the provocative title *Planet of the Apes* began circulating through the production departments at 20th Century Fox. The studio's main concern was that, despite the involvement of super-serious, silver-screen big shot Charlton Heston, audiences would laugh at the concept of talking apes, and the film would be an unintended disaster. A makeup test was shot with Heston as astronaut "Thomas" and *film noir* baddie Edward G. Robinson as Dr. Zaius. The makeup, by Fox's Ben Nye, Sr., was primitive, reminiscent of Bert Lahr's Cowardly Lion from *The Wizard of Oz*. But no one laughed, and the film was greenlit.

Nye must have thought, "be careful what you wish for." He and Fox's make-up head Dan Striepeke knew that what passed muster for an eight-minute test scene would not carry 200 apes over a two-hour film. With only four months to go before cameras started rolling (unbelievable, but true), there was only one man to call.

But they almost called the wrong one.

In 1963, Universal Pictures made a film called *The List of Adrian Messenger*, a crime thriller with a clever gimmick; the film boasted several big-name stars, completely hidden under elaborate makeup. Tony Curtis, Kirk Douglas, Frank Sinatra and Robert Mitchum were all in the film, unbilled and unrecognizable until the ending's big reveal.

Nye and Striepeke felt that the sophisticated appliance work in *Messenger* was just what the doctor ordered for their *Apes* headache, and, assuming that work to have been done by Universal's Bud Westmore (it was, after all, a Universal picture), set about contacting him. It was Tom Burman, at the time an apprentice in the Fox shop, who literally overheard the discussion and, swallowing hard, interrupted his bosses by saying, "Excuse me, but John Chambers did most of that work."

And the rest, as they say, is history. And foam rubber. And wigs. And horses. And leather vests. And weird music. And the guy who played Moses dressed up like Tarzan running around what looks like a half-melted version of Fred Flintstone's Bedrock. (*"One day, maybe Bright Eyes will win the fight / Then that cat will stay out for the night…"*)

It's hard to fully appreciate what an impossible task *Apes* must have been for Chambers, and the terrifyingly short time he had to pull it off. He not only designed the apes' unique look (they don't really look like apes, after all, but no one seemed to notice), he also invented a new form of foam rubber, porous enough to allow the actors to actually sweat through their ape appliances. He hired a veritable squadron of nearly a hundred makeup artists, trained in special ape makeup classes that he taught, working in shifts, quite literally, around the clock. If you needed a makeup artist in Los Angeles during the summer of 1967, you were out of luck. Everyone in town was working for John Chambers.

He won a special Oscar for his efforts, and was later given a star on Hollywood Boulevard's Walk of Fame. He worked constantly up to his retirement, although nothing ever came close to the profile of his work on *Apes*.

Nothing, that is, that the public could know about. But his most amazing achievement, surpassing his work on *Apes* in terms of the sheer audacity of the project, still lie ahead, and would remain a secret for decades.

CUT TO: the real world. In 1979, Iranian revolutionaries, backed by Muslim cleric the Ayatollah Khomeini, overthrew the U.S.-backed government of the Shah of Iran, taking fifty-two American embassy workers hostage. They remained imprisoned for 444 excruciating days, a sobering reminder of the limits of America's power, and a shattering deathblow to the presidency of Jimmy Carter.

What was not known publicly at that time was that six Americans escaped the embassy raid and were hiding in the residence of the Canadian ambassador. Enter CIA agent Tony Mendez, charged with getting the six "secret hostages" out of the country.

Mendez hit upon the ingenious idea of staging a fake movie production, purportedly to be shot in the Middle East. He and his team would pose as Canadians on a location scout and afterwards, sneak the half-dozen Americans out of Iran by having them pose as members of the crew. He contacted his man in Hollywood, father of the CIA's Identity Transformation Kit, John Chambers.

Together, Mendez, Chambers and fellow makeup artist Robert Sidell created the fictitious Studio Six Productions (named so for the six hostages). They had a real fake script, opened a real fake production office, staged a real fake table read, and took out real fake ads in the real *Hollywood Reporter* and *Variety*. All as part of the CIA's ruse.

The story, declassified in 1997, only four years before Chambers' passing in 2001, is the subject of the Ben Affleck film *Argo*, in which John Goodman plays Chambers to great and reportedly freakishly accurate effect.

John Chambers. A man without whom it is doubtful the *Argo* operation could have been pulled off. A man without whom Spock would have no ears. A man without whom the *Planet of the Apes* would have no apes.

John Chambers. A man even Taylor could love.

HAPPY TRAILS

By Dana Gould

"He's not dead, so long as we remember him."
- Dr. Leonard McCoy
STAR TREK II: THE WRATH OF KHAN

All good things must come to an end. Or must they? In the worlds of *Star Trek* and *Planet of the Apes*, endings have a funny way of being not so final. More often than not, they're just the thing that happens before the next beginning.

Often. Not always.

Star Trek ended, for the first time, in 1968, when rumors spread that, in response to the show's less than stellar ratings, NBC was planning on cancelling the series at the end of its second season. This led to a now-famous letter writing campaign helmed by *Trek* superfan Bjo Trimble. The next thing you know, NBC executive suites on both coasts were inundated with pleas to keep the show on the air. Inundated. Most of these letters came from university students, professionals and upwardly-mobile young adults. In other words, an advertiser's wet dream. So successful was the campaign that NBC went to the extraordinary length of announcing *Star Trek*'s third season on the air. In other words, "Please stop writing us letters."

The story of the letter writing campaign has been told so many times, it's easy to overlook the story, if not behind it, then underneath it. It's not that the letters saved the show, it's that *people wrote the letters*. *I Dream of Jeannie* had many more viewers than *Star Trek* did, but not as many of them would have written a letter to save it. *I Dream of Jeannie* was a show a lot of people liked. *Star Trek* was a show a smaller number of people really loved.

It's a wonderful feeling when you stumble across something, an author, a band or a TV show that speaks to you. This is especially true during adolescence, when anyone worth a damn feels like an isolated freak anyway. To find something, anything, that makes you think, "Yeah, you get me," is truly priceless. *Star Trek* was one of those shows. The kind of show you could hang out alone in your room with.

It's important to appreciate just how difficult a thing that is for a TV show to achieve. Authors and musicians have a direct line to their readers and listeners. An author sits alone and writes a book, the reader sits alone and reads it. It's a very intimate, one-to-one relationship. Television shows are, by the nature of their physical production, huge bureaucracies. Television shows are created by committee and then run through a never-ending series of gauntlets where, it seems, anyone with an opinion is allowed to impose it upon and thereby influence the final product. Get-ting anything worthwhile through that system is difficult to say the least. Getting something that actually speaks to people, that resonates with something deep inside, is practically impossible.

There are shows that have done it. *The Twilight Zone* did it. *Twin Peaks* did it. But nobody did it like *Star Trek*. Nobody before and nobody since.

And so, in 1968, the fans wrote letters, and NBC spared *Star Trek* the executioner's blade and announced season 3. Or, as it came to be known, The Last Season, for in a move so devoid of logic it would be alarming if it hadn't occurred in the chronically illogical and irrational world of network television, NBC took *Star Trek*, the darling of the 18-34 year-old, disposable-income possessing, upwardly mobile, young professionals, and moved it to the one time slot on their schedule that would guarantee that none of them would be home to watch it: Friday nights at 10:00 PM.

And lo, it came to be that on June 3, 1969, NBC aired, "The Turnabout Intruder," the final first-run episode of *Star Trek*, and then the show was gone.

Well, you know...

Battle for the Planet of the Apes, on the other hand, was released in 1973 and advertised as the end of the *Apes* films. In fact, "The Final Chapter In The Incredible Apes Saga," was the tagline on the poster. This was it, kids. Get your s*#! together.

Of the five original *Apes* films, *Battle* is, um, definitely one of them.

But I have a strange love for it, not only because, lumbering through the film's final "showdown of the civilizations," is a bunch of radioactive mutants on a school bus. It's not just that, but for me, that's a huge part of it.

Battle was another one of those things that, along with Kirk and the crew of the *Enterprise*, really spoke to me as a kid. *Battle* was, along with 1971's *Escape*, one of the two original *Apes* films I saw in their original theatrical run (my parents hid the PG-rated *Conquest* from my young peepers). The novelization of *Battle*, by "The Trouble With Tribbles" scribe David Gerrold, was the first "chapter book" I ever bought for myself. I still have, and cherish, the actual copy. I recall that, thanks to that book, I was one of the only nine year-old kid in Hopedale, Massachusetts who knew what the word "cadre" meant, and I took every opportunity to put it to use. ("I'd like a cadre of powdered, mini-donuts, please.")

For that alone, I owe *Battle* a solid. And did I mention the school bus full of mutants? Well, you can't mention it enough as far as I'm concerned.

But after *Battle*, *Apes*, like *Star Trek*, was over. But it did not stay over. Ninety-nine times out of a hundred when things end, they stay ended. What is it about these two series that will not stay down?

Not everyone liked them, but the people who did, loved them.

Star Trek returned in syndicated re-runs in 1970 and, now on nightly at 6:00 PM, instead of just Fridays at 10:00, people discovered it. People like, well, me. We saw it, realized that it got us, that it got us the way that we got it, and we held each other to our bosoms and never let go. *Trek* eventually returned as a movie, then a series of movies, then as another TV series, then *another* TV series, then the new TV series became its own movie series, then *another* TV series, and now a new movie series functioning as an alternate timeline remake of the original series. Not everybody likes them, but an ever-growing, smaller amount of people, really love them. An Associated Press article in 1972 on *Trek*'s syndication success called *Star Trek*, "the show that won't die."

Apes came back almost immediately as a TV series, then an animated series, then, eventually, a remake. Then, a prequel of sorts, the "wow-this-is-great," *Rise of the Planet of the Apes*, and then the prequel's sequel, the "wow-this-is-also-great," *Dawn of the Planet of the Apes*, which is, in fact, nothing if not a plucky remake of *Battle*. So yes, the prequel's sequel is a remake, but they did leave out the school bus full of mutants. You can't have everything.

But movies are movies and people are people, and they're governed by very different laws. Recently, the world learned of the sad passing of Leonard Nimoy. Because *StarTrek* was one of those shows that spoke right to you, and because Spock, specifically, was the character that isolated adolescents related to the most, Mr. Nimoy's passing, even in his eighties, shook many people very deeply. I heard from friends, more often than not, "This is affecting me more than I thought it would."

A feeling I shared. The world expressed its sadness and sympathies, but the sentiment that summed it up the best for me came from, of all places, Instagram. "Mortons_salt_zombiegirl" posted the Vulcan salute, and said, simply, "You were awesome and you made my childhood brighter. Happy trails."

I could not have said it better myself. *Planet Of The Apes*, *Star Trek*, Leonard Nimoy, James Doohan, DeForest Kelley, Roddy McDowall, Kim Hunter, Charlton Heston, Rod Serling, etc. etc. et al. You were awesome and you made my childhood brighter. Happy trails.

LEONARD NIMOY
1931–2015

Investigating rumors of Klingon expansionism, Captain Kirk and the crew of the *U.S.S. Enterprise* discover a mysterious transdimensional portal being used by the Klingons. Following the Klingons through the portal, the *Enterprise* crew is surprised to find themselves orbiting a far-future parallel Earth, one where the Federation apparently never existed. Upon beaming down to the planet, Kirk and Spock find a familiar face! ***Star Trek*** and ***Planet of the Apes*** crossover in "The Primate Directive" written by **SCOTT TIPTON** and **DAVID TIPTON** with art by **RACHAEL STOTT**.

"Need more!"
— *Comics: The Gathering*

"Carries a cadence very similar to so many episodes of Gene Roddenberry's most famous creation and quickly welcomes the reader in."
— *Comic Book Resources*

"A very fun, interesting, and well-done crossover."
— *Geeks of Doom*

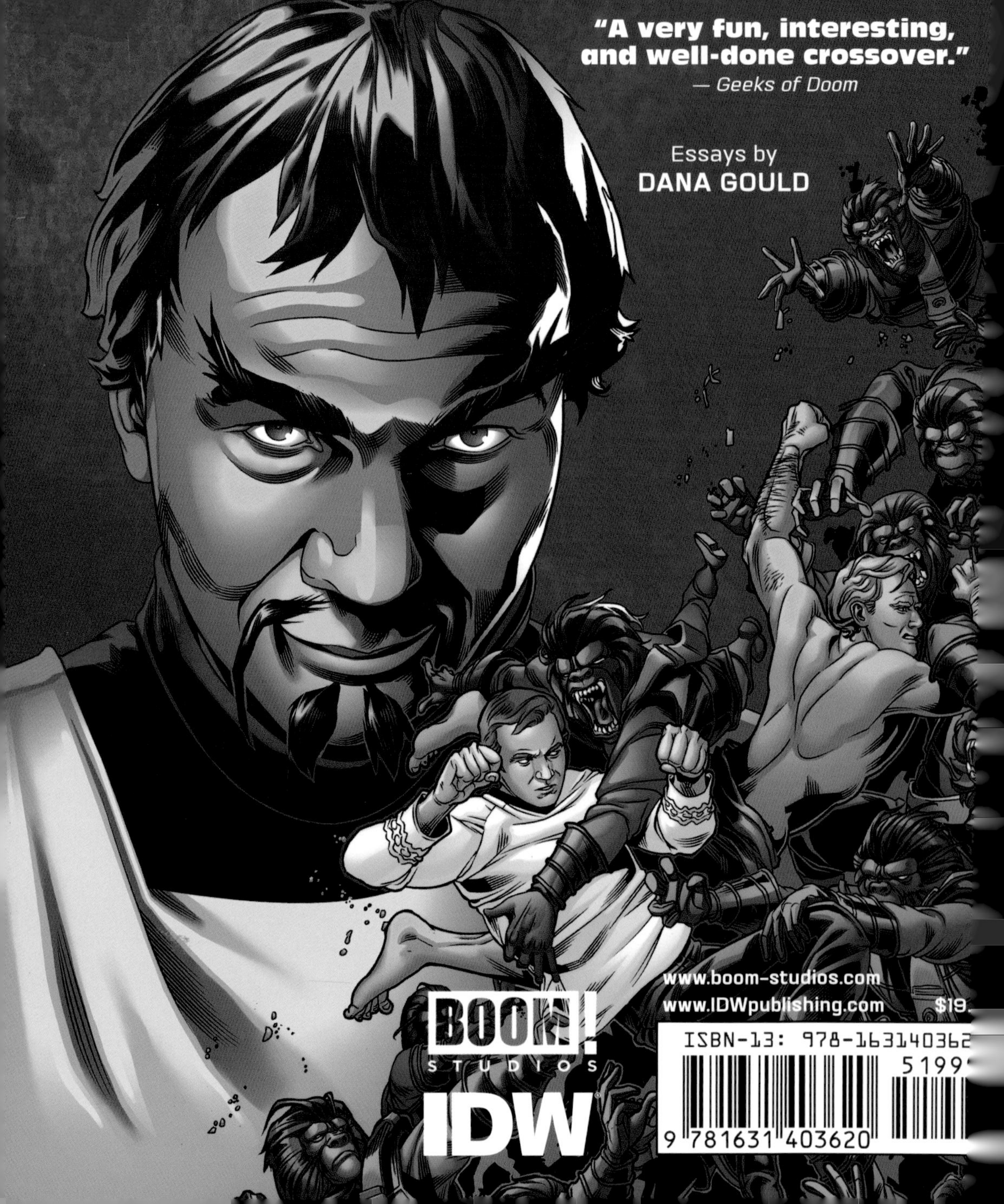

Essays by
DANA GOULD

www.boom-studios.com
www.IDWpublishing.com
$19.

BOOM! STUDIOS
IDW

ISBN-13: 978-1631403620
5199
9 781631 403620

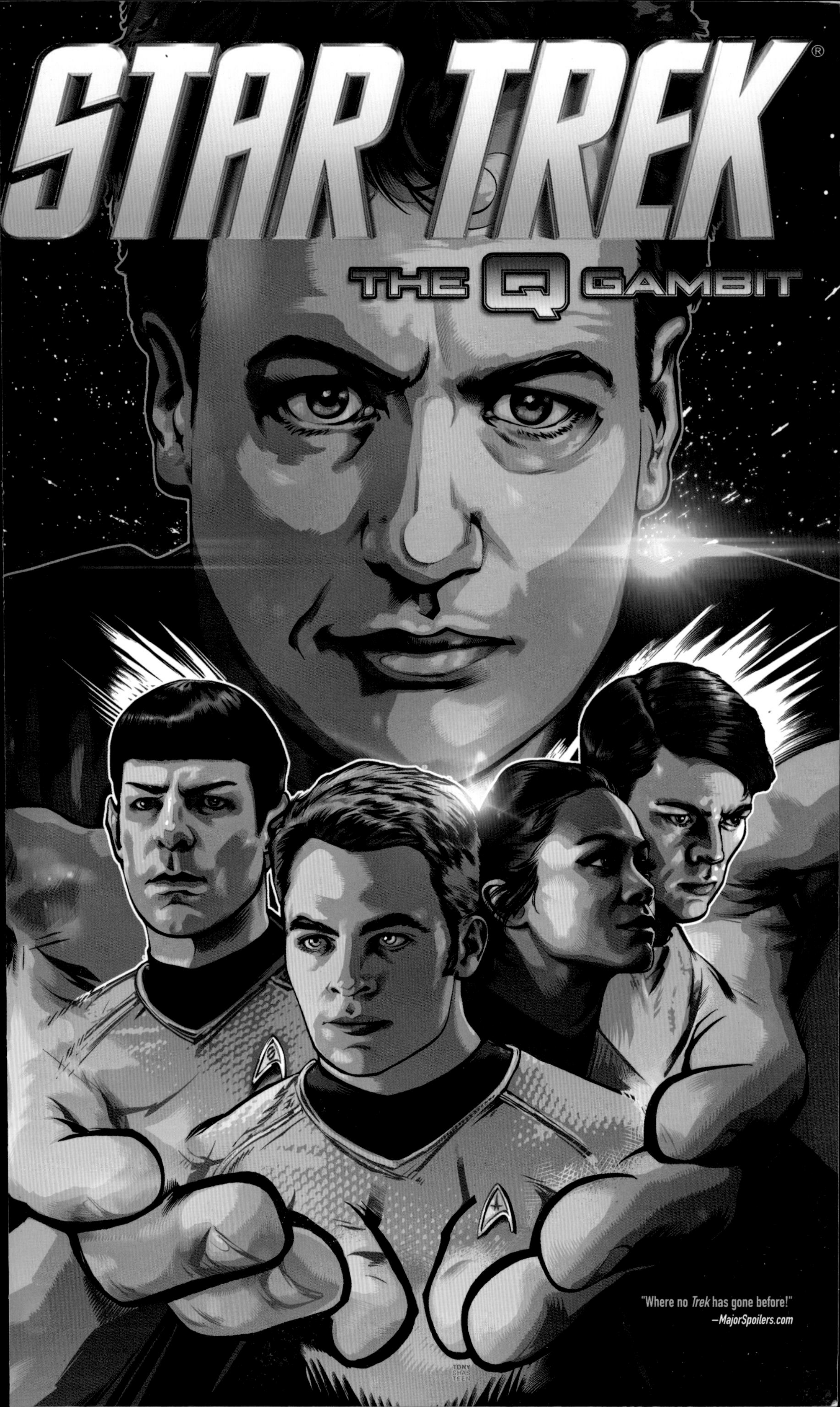
STAR TREK®
THE Q GAMBIT
"Where no *Trek* has gone before!"
—MajorSpoilers.com
TONY SHASTEEN

STAR TREK®

VOLUME 9

Story Consultant:
ROBERTO ORCI

Cover by
TONY SHASTEEN

Collection Edits by
JUSTIN EISINGER and ALONZO SIMON

Collection Design by
CLAUDIA CHONG

Star Trek created by Gene Roddenberry.
Special thanks to Risa Kessler and John Van Citters of CBS Consumer Products for their invaluable assistance.

ISBN: 978-1-63140-276-0

18 17 16 15   1 2 3 4

Ted Adams, CEO & Publisher
Greg Goldstein, President & COO
Robbie Robbins, EVP/Sr. Graphic Artist
Chris Ryall, Chief Creative Officer/Editor-in-Chief
Matthew Ruzicka, CPA, Chief Financial Officer
Alan Payne, VP of Sales
Dirk Wood, VP of Marketing
Lorelei Bunjes, VP of Digital Services
Jeff Webber, VP of Digital Publishing & Business Development

www.IDWPUBLISHING.com
IDW founded by Ted Adams, Alex Garner, Kris Oprisko, and Robbie Robbins

Facebook: facebook.com/idwpublishing
Twitter: @idwpublishing
YouTube: youtube.com/idwpublishing
Instagram: instagram.com/idwpublishing
deviantART: idwpublishing.deviantart.com
Pinterest: pinterest.com/idwpublishing/idw-staff-faves

Originally published as STAR TREK issues #35–40.